THE SILVER THREAD

Book Four
THE CHRONICLES OF THE GOLDEN FRONTIER

THE SILVER THREAD

GILBERT MORRIS

and

J. LANDON FERGUSON

CROSSWAY BOOKS • WHEATON, ILLINOIS
A DIVISION OF GOOD NEWS PUBLISHERS

mor

The Silver Thread

Copyright © 2000 by Gilbert Morris and J. Landon Ferguson.

Published by Crossway Books
   A division of Good News Publishers
   1300 Crescent Street
   Wheaton, Illinois 60187

Cover illustration: Tony Meers
Cover design: Cindy Kiple

First printing, 2000

Printed in the United States of America

Library of Congress Cataloging-in-Publication Data
Morris, Gilbert.
   The silver thread / Gilbert Morris and J. Landon Ferguson.
      p.   cm.
   (The chronicles of the golden frontier ; bk. 4)
   ISBN 1-58134-212-8 (alk. paper)
      1. Brothers and sisters—Fiction. I. Ferguson, J. Landon, 1952– II. Title.
PS3563.O8742 S56 2000
813'.54—dc21   00-009402
                                                                      CIP

15	14	13	12	11	10	09	08	07	06	05	04	03	02	01	00
15	14	13	12	11	10	9	8	7	6	5	4	3	2	1	

God has blessed me
with three wonderful and beautiful daughters—
Rachelle, Amy, and Jamey.
This is for them.

J. Landon Ferguson

CONTENTS

PART ONE

THE
SEARCH

CHAPTER

~ 1 ~

Vanished

A bby DeSpain, now in her mid-twenties, had disappeared without leaving a hint of where she'd gone. She'd left her room neat and tidy, leaving none of her belongings and clothes behind.

After discovering her absence, Grant DeSpain returned to the office and stood tall against the front window, staring out into the busy street where heavy clouds tumbled in a free mountain wind and skimmed the rooftops of the taller buildings. His stone-like face was etched with worry for his missing sister. Twenty-six, he was tall and stout, his shoulders and arms big and muscular; yet his face revealed a gentle inner man. The wide-set green eyes were those of a thinker. The high cheekbones, square jaw, and wavy auburn hair set him apart in a crowd, which explained why women's eyes often secretly followed him.

"She won't make it out there," Grant complained to the window pane in disgust.

A heavy smell of ink and machine oil and his mother's sweet perfume lingered in the thin air. The Leadville newspaper-like office was that of *Western Magazine*, a well-established periodical that had been the idea of Jason and Jennifer Stone, Grant's stepfather and mother. After striking a rich gold vein some years earlier, Jason and Jennifer had suffered the consequences of instant wealth mixed with foolhardiness and soon found themselves impoverished. Through great effort and resilient faith, they made a successful venture of a bakery and saved enough to get back to the business they truly loved—writing and reporting stories to the public.

By 1890 *Western Magazine* was a successful enterprise, not as a newspaper but rather as a monthly report of exclusive news and stories of interest. Much of the sales came from back east, where the magazine was shipped by mail to curious readers interested in the developments and scandals of the western boomtowns of Colorado.

"What do you mean she won't make it? What do you know about Abby's being gone?" Jennifer questioned as she approached her son.

Turning, Grant looked down into the loving green eyes of his mother, eyes the same color as his. Her face still held the beauty of youth, her features fine and clear, her mouth and lips expressive. The only clue to her age of forty-three was the few sparkling streaks of silver in her lengthy auburn hair.

"Mother," Grant said softly, placing his large hands on her small shoulders, "I think Abby ran away. She's been threatening to do just that since she was a small girl, and I think she's followed Billy Rogers, chasing dreams that will never come true. I'm afraid she'll get herself into some trouble she can't get out of."

Fretting, Jennifer DeSpain Stone turned her pretty eyes to the floor, thinking of the daughter she knew so well. She couldn't help but feel partially responsible for Abby's unhappiness. It had all started in what seemed like yesterday and at the same time so terribly long ago. At a young age Jennifer had set out from New Orleans to make a new life in the western frontier where the discovery of gold and silver brought people by the thousands. Because of previous experience in the newspaper business, she felt nothing could be more important than publishing the stories found in the rambunctious boomtowns. She and her children had first traveled to Virginia City, Nevada, home of the Comstock Lode, and there she made a go of running a newspaper. She also met Jason there and became acquainted with a true love that took many years to blossom.

Then they moved to Black Hawk and Central City, Colorado, where she suffered the great despair of a misleading romance and severe poverty. After that came the tragedy of being lost in the great wealth that a gold mine had so generously poured forth. Business led the family to Leadville, where the wealth disappeared as fast as it had come, though the story had a happy ending. She had managed to salvage a great faith in God and had her loving husband, Jason, at her side.

But through it all, Abby was a different story. The innocent and pretty little girl grew up in the middle of the wild and crazy ways of boomtown life. She had seen it all—poverty and great wealth; and she was perpetually obsessed with hopes of having such wealth. It had been Jennifer's intentions to raise her children with a strong faith in God, to prepare them for life armed with a strong knowledge of the Holy Scriptures. But she didn't feel she had succeeded.

"I feel like this is all my fault," Jennifer said with despair. "I should have been a better mother." Her large green eyes swelled with tears as she recalled the past.

"Nonsense!" Jason Stone said firmly as he came to his feet and left his desk. "Abby is a grown woman, and she makes her own decisions."

Jason was a man of determined faith and a confidence that all things happen for a reason, a purpose that brings glory and honor to God, a lesson he had learned through many trials over a period of long years. He had come a long way, from alcoholic to editor of a magazine and author of three fictional novels based on the true history of the western boomtowns. Now he had the look of success at an age of forty-five, wearing a gray vest over a white dress shirt and dark tie, tailored gray pants, his matching coat and bowler hanging proudly on a coat rack beside his desk. His blond hair had dulled over the years with graying sideburns, but his slate-blue eyes still held the intensity of stern conviction. At 5'10" his angular build remained, his shoulders wide and his posture straight, his confidence reassuring.

"You can't blame yourself, Jennifer," Jason continued as he came closer. His convincing eyes met Grant's briefly. "She has a mind of her own, a life of her own. We've done as much as we can; now she has to find her own way."

"Yes, I suppose so," Jennifer agreed reluctantly, trying not to be a typical mother who always pictures her daughter as a child.

Grant turned away, both angry and worried about Abby. He was determined to find out what could be done.

~

Abby had never shut God out of her life. However, she blamed God for her misfortunes and made no bones about being angry with Him when anyone confronted her about it.

The seething anger in young Abby was first born when she blamed God for the death of her biological father, Drake DeSpain. When she later turned seventeen and the family struck it rich, her anger quickly disappeared as she enjoyed the opulent life of the nouveau riche of Denver and Leadville. She no longer held any animosity toward God, for she figured He'd redeemed Himself for her earlier misfortunes. But then the family lost their wealth and struggled to regain their footing in a town where they were the subject of whispered criticisms.

The bakery had proved to be a small gold mine in itself, for the miners had a sweet tooth for the fluffy delights Jennifer had learned to bake in New Orleans. Once enough capital had been saved, Jason and Jennifer began publishing their magazine in order to return to their love of chronicling the frontier, putting life and pictures into words for others to breathe and feel. Because her parents were reluctant to sell a business as profitable as the bakery, Abby took it over and did quite well, serving coffee and pastries to the miners, whose hungry eyes followed Abby's every move, eager to help her in any way they could.

At the age of twenty-five, Abby was beautiful, her hair long and brown and wavy around an oval face, her bright blue eyes mysterious and alluring, all of which accented her taunting and captive brilliant smile. Quick-witted and playful, she attracted a crowd of regulars at the bakery, where the men sat at small tables gulping black coffee and eating sugared donuts while flirting happily with Abby.

"So how many does that make, Abby?" a grizzly, old, gray-headed miner inquired one morning as he winked at his conspiring friends sitting at a table with him.

"How many does what make, Old Frazier?" Abby teased defensively.

"Well," the man started, rolling his red eyes upward as if he were recalling a picture in his mind, "last night I seen your old flame crying his eyes out in his beer and telling his sad story to anyone who'd lend an ear. Looks like another broken heart, and what I was a-wonderin'—well, how many hearts does that make you done broke?" He smiled.

"None," answered Abby quickly. "You can't break a man's heart if he doesn't have one!" She smiled back.

Old Frazier banged the table with his fist as he held his woolly head back and hee-hawed. The others laughed as well. It was hard to pull one over on Abby, as Old Frazier had just proved.

Many of the single men in Leadville wished they could win Abby's hand, but most feared her, knowing that toying with her affections was like playing with fire and that they would eventually get burned. Her flirtatious ways were bold and daring, but there was a line, and any man who dared cross it would open himself to embarrassment and humiliation by Abby's whip-like tongue.

But unknown to most, Abby harbored a shadow that she kept well hidden behind the curtain of sharp wit and clever humor. When she was alone, the curtain would lift, and out came the vague and dark emotions of resentfulness and a desire for vengeance, especially against God, who had dealt her an unfair life and had taken away everything she dearly loved. First her father, a man she remembered as loving and perfect and who had died a horrible death when she was only a small child. Then, after a rough childhood and times of severe poverty, God finally gave her a life of great wealth and comfort, only to take it away. Now in her routine at the bakery and coffee shop she fenced verbally with the best, using words as swords, often resulting in idiotic humor that helped everyone forget the real world and its problems.

But the frolicking Abby of the morning bakery turned into a predator at night, her beauty and piercing eyes the weapons of a skilled huntress. She attended social affairs and the theater, clubs and restaurants, having no use for any fool who wasted time with drunken talk at a saloon. The man she hoped to capture had to be young, handsome, rich, smart, and above all would cater to her, granting her every wish. Many a man had tried to fill the bill, and all had failed, until the appearance of the lighthearted and carefree Billy Rogers.

Her meeting Billy Rogers had been a fluke, Abby thought at first, a simple meeting that amused her temporarily but would quickly become a distant memory. But that's not what happened.

One evening the play at Horace Tabor's theater had been delightful, and the crowd was in a jovial mood as they departed through the elaborate lobby. Late-night Leadville was as busy as any other time of the day, and the restaurants and bars expected a burst of business following the play. Abby was escorted by Theodore Fryer, a tall young man with curly hair who worked with his father's silver mining company and expected someday to inherit a fortune. But Abby, knowing he was a bit on the lazy side, gave him no serious thought and certainly wouldn't wait for an inheritance. But she would accept an invitation to a play and dinner afterward.

Theodore clutched her hand tightly as he led Abby through the crowd pouring out of the opera house into the dark but busy street, where flickering gas lights showed the way. At the edge of the board-walk they stopped at the street sloppy with mud and animal drop-pings. A few wide boards were stretched here and there so the well-dressed could keep their feet more or less clean. Before Abby attempted the crossing, the crowd pushed against her, forcing her to take a step into the mire, into which she sank up to her ankle. Theodore still held her hand awkwardly and tried to pull her back without stepping into the muck himself, but he couldn't manage it.

"Let loose of my hand, you baboon!" Abby shouted in a quick fit of temper.

Regaining her balance, she tried to pull her foot out of the mud, but the shoe remained, one of an expensive pair of shoes she had recently purchased. And in trying to keep her balance, she again stepped into the muck with her bare foot. Theodore tried to stretch a leg from the boardwalk to a board so he could lean over to offer a hand, but he was unwilling to step in the slop. The scene had become hopelessly embarrassing for both Abby and Theodore.

"Look out!" a young man ordered as he pushed his way past Theodore and stepped right into the messy street with Abby. He lifted her in his strong arms, holding her free of the dark muck below, then stooped to pluck her shoe from the hole it was buried in. Sloshing back onto the boardwalk, he slowly set her back on her feet.

Taking a deep breath, the young gentleman whispered in her ear, "A pretty lady like you doesn't deserve to be slippin' in the mud." He grinned, then gave her the dripping shoe, his dark brown eyes and smiling face only inches away.

Theodore observed the scene awkwardly, embarrassed he hadn't taken such bold action. Unable to find the right words he simply gawked, his palms held up in a gesture suggesting he didn't know what to do.

"I'm Billy Rogers," the dark-haired young man said cheerfully, his eyes a twinkling reflection of the nearby gaslight.

Abby still felt frustrated, her feet muddy and stinking as she held the sloppy shoe away from her to keep from soiling her blue and white dress. Then it dawned on her what had just happened. In the middle of a difficult situation, there had been a pleasurable moment. In the darkness of the night chill she could still feel the warmth of the young man who had gathered her up, the bulging of the young muscles in his arms and his solid chest.

Appraising him further she could see that he was very handsome, probably in his late twenties with dark, almost black eyes and black hair with a slight wave. His nose was straight and eyebrows black, lifted in expectation of a response from her. His mouth seemed to hold a continuous, almost mischievous smile. His tuxedo was sleek and dark and fit him impeccably. Unfortunately, his feet and slacks were covered with mud.

"My name is Abby," she finally said, "and this," she gestured with the muddy shoe, "is Theodore."

Billy knew immediately that Abby and Theodore's relationship was nothing serious. So he hardly acknowledged Theodore, who stood there like a bewildered buffalo.

"Is there anything else I can do? Perhaps offer you two a ride home? I have a horse and buggy."

"I have a buggy too," Theodore grunted.

Abby turned to Theodore hastily. "Well, go get it then! You don't think I can go to dinner like this, do you?"

Theodore moped off with a long face, his shoulders hunched over.

Glancing back at Billy, Abby could see slight amusement in his expression. "I'm glad *you* think it's funny!" she snapped.

"Funny? I was thinking this meeting was more like a blessing," Billy said gingerly. "Where do you live, Abby? I'd like to see you again."

"You might say I *live* in a bakery," Abby replied in a smart-alecky tone, implying that her long hours were like a prison sentence.

"The one at the end of Chestnut Street?"

"That's the one," Abby answered, softening.

Billy was evidently a happy-go-lucky kind of guy who didn't get discouraged easily. He hadn't removed his eyes from Abby once since rescuing her, and her eyes involuntarily returned the stare.

"Well, here comes Theodore," Abby said as if she were stepping into the mud again. She felt a slight relief at being able to say or do something besides just sit there and stare at Billy like a dumbfounded mule.

The perfect gentleman, Billy helped Abby into the buggy before Theodore had a chance to do so. "Good night, Abby," he said happily, waving as they pulled away.

Abby gave a slight wave back without realizing there was an invitation in her blue eyes.

~

As days passed and Billy didn't show up at the bakery, Abby felt disappointed but kept hoping he would drop by. As her memory of his face began to blur, she desperately tried to recall his exact features but couldn't. She assumed her feelings would pass and that would be that.

Meanwhile, Billy was deliberately taking his time in hopes that would increase his chances of winning over such a beautiful young woman. He figured he would wait just long enough to make her think about him more than she would like to, long enough to convince herself he was something special, but not so long enough that she would forget their chance meeting. As usual, his plan was successful.

Busy with a tray of pastries, Abby had all but given up on Billy Rogers. The morning had been busy right up to the noon hour, and since the crowd had dwindled she was taking time to bake more delicacies. The bell over the front door jingled, and she set the tray down and went to tend to the new customer. To her surprise, it was Billy, dapper in his fine suit and smiling cheerfully. She quickly wiped her flour-coated hands on her apron and smoothed her hair.

"You look lovely in flour," Billy teased.

"Oh, well . . ." Abby said, subconsciously brushing at her laced apron. "The pastries aren't any good unless I get in it all the way up to my elbows."

Billy liked a woman with a ready wit and a sense of humor. "How's the coffee? You didn't take a bath in it, did you?"

"No," Abby scorned playfully. "Would you like some?"

"Sure. You have time to join me?"

Glancing toward the back, Abby could see that the two older women who helped her were busy with the daily routine and could take care of things for a short while. Untying her apron, she poured two cups, then came around the counter and placed them on a small table. Taking a seat, she watched Billy as he sat down. He was carrying a sack and gently set it on the table.

"So this is what you do," he observed, the fragrance of sweet baked goods and coffee filling the air. Checkered red-and-white cloths covered the tables, and matching curtains hung over the tall, thin windows.

"It's not easy," Abby suggested. "I'm up at 4 in the morning, and I generally don't get out of here until 5 in the afternoon."

Billy was impressed. Abby was a woman with energy and spunk. "I take it you made it home all right the other night."

Abby nodded as a smile crossed her lips. "Yes, and then I took a hot bath. I had to throw my shoes away."

Having anticipated this, Billy couldn't hide the smile on his face as he pushed the sack toward her. "I brought you something."

Surprised, Abby took the sack and peered into it, then removed an oblong box. Opening it, she was delighted to see an expensive pair of black leather shoes with high lace-up tops and tall heels.

"What's this for?" Abby remarked. She noticed that the size was correct.

Billy felt proud that he'd correctly guessed her shoe size. "Try them on!" he insisted. "Here, let me help you."

Before Abby knew what was happening, Billy was on his knees with her foot in his hand, unlacing her old shoe. Removing her shoe, he gently massaged her foot. He slipped the new shoe onto her foot and carefully laced it up. There seemed to be something intimate in his touch, and Abby sat motionless.

After Billy had the new pair laced up, he stood and took Abby's hand to help her to her feet. "So, what do you think?"

Temporarily overcome, Abby gathered herself and took a few steps. The soft leather felt good on her ankles, and the shoes were snug and comfortable. "They fit just right," Abby said, astonished. "How'd you know what size to get?"

"A lucky guess. I've always been lucky," Billy boasted. "They look lovely on you. Maybe you could wear them tonight—to the theater and dinner? How about it?"

The sudden offer caught Abby off guard. After days of wondering if Billy would ever show up, she'd begun to doubt herself and to question what she'd done wrong the night of the encounter, what she would do differently if she had a chance to do it over again. "I'd love to," she answered enthusiastically

∾

Each day Abby woke up with a spirit of excitement and anticipation greater than any she'd ever experienced before. All she could think about was Billy and his cool and clever wit, his dark and mysterious eyes, his solid physique and exceptional ability to persuade people into liking him. No doubt about it, he was the kind of man who would rise to the top, and Abby wanted to be beside him all the way and so live life to the fullest.

It appeared his business was that of managing money through many adventures and investments, something many men with money did. And yet when Jason questioned him in the office when Abby brought him by to introduce him, the young man's answers were vague. However, Billy was so good with words that he was still convincing.

Grant hadn't been inquisitive when he met Billy but just sat quietly and let Billy do all the talking while he formed his own judgment. It didn't take Grant long to do so either.

"He's very good," Grant told his mother one morning at the office.

"I don't know about that," Jason inserted. "I didn't get the idea he was good at all."

"You two shouldn't be so critical," Jennifer defended, standing up for Abby more than for Billy. "I've never seen Abby like this before—I think she's in love."

"Heaven forbid," Grant grumbled.

"What do you mean he's good?" Jason asked curiously.

"I mean he's good at what he does, better than most."

"I couldn't get a straight answer out of him as to what he does," Jason said as he rolled his white cotton sleeves up to the elbows, getting ready for the day's work.

"He's a confidence man," Grant went on. "At least that's what *I* think. He knows all the right things to say and do to get people to see things his way and to talk them out of their money, or women out of—"

"Grant," Jennifer interrupted, "be careful how you talk about others! Besides, it sounds to me like you're describing the average politician. Maybe Billy will end up in politics."

"Or in jail," Jason conceded.

"Yeah, there's a fine line," Grant commented.

"Give it a chance," Jennifer demanded. "I'll tolerate no preformed judgments, and if either one of you hurt Abby over this, you'll have me to deal with!"

Grant and Jason gave each other a knowing look; they would have to lay off for a while, at least until they had proof to confirm their suspicions. They both knew better than to be on Jennifer's wrong side.

It was after a brief and happy-go-lucky romance that Abby and Billy Rogers disappeared. Both had been known to recently be wearing a wide grin as if they knew something nobody else knew. A week before Abby vanished, Billy had disappeared himself, but Abby would say nothing about his whereabouts but just kept showing that mysterious smile she'd been wearing for weeks.

~

Another conversation at *Western Magazine* about Abby's disappearance was mostly grim. "I think she and Billy eloped," Jennifer blurted out.

Grant protested, "She better not have!"

"Do I detect an older brother who's playing watchdog over his younger sister?" Jennifer questioned.

"No. I just don't approve of the fellow, that's all."

"And who would you approve of?" Jennifer continued.

Grant shrugged. "I don't have a good feeling about this—that's all."

Jennifer nodded knowingly. "But you have to admit, we've never seen Abby so happy as she's been since she met Billy."

Jason began to speak but thought better of it.

"I just don't like what's happened," Grant said, more to himself than to anyone else.

"So what are you going to do about it?" Jennifer asked, trying to lift her discouraged son's spirits.

"I don't know yet," Grant replied solemnly. "But I have to do something."

Dissension

For days Grant moped around, at times regretting that Abby had failed to confide in him, at other times finding himself angry at her stubborn streak and naiveté. It was unsettling to have absolutely no idea of her whereabouts or her well-being. Was she thinking about family and home, people she had never been apart from in her entire life?

What would lead her to leave behind life as she knows it and take on a completely unsure future? Grant wondered as he sat on a wooden stoop outside the front door of his rented room. The day had grown dark, and the street was filled with the smells of the evening—wood smoke and hot grease and frying food. It was time for the bars and dance halls to become even noisier. The sounds of a piano competed with the noises of horses and wagons. The mills maintained their constant drumming in the far-off distance, only briefly interrupted by the irritated voices of angry people somewhere nearby.

Leadville had grown considerably in sophistication and technology since the day Grant had first arrived. Now in 1890 it was a well-established and organized city with law enforcement and bureaucrats, natural gas and some electricity. Just behind Denver in population, Leadville was a sprawling complex dependent on silver mining and the industries that supplemented the mines—stores, theaters and hotels, railroads and banks. No longer was Leadville the dangerous and rowdy boomtown of years before when a man had to carry a cocked pistol on the streets in the evening.

Grant had enjoyed a good life. He had his loved ones and friends and plenty of work to challenge his mind and develop strong muscles. Abby had been his closest friend, and they had often shared their inner feelings, always being there for each other to listen and to offer comforting advice. He couldn't understand why she'd leave without even talking to him.

Grant's rented room had an entrance off a wide alley, which he now gazed at as he sat at the bottom of the stairs right outside the door, tossing around ideas in his head. He rubbed a shallow rut in the weathered gray wooden step with his boot heel. Two older men carried on an intense conversation as they shuffled down the alley in their worn britches and overcoats. But when they saw Grant sitting silently, they grew quiet until they were almost out of sight, then continued their talk. The evenings were getting cooler, a sign that fall was coming to the high country, even if it was only early September. Grant realized that if he was going to try to find his sister, he'd have to do it soon, before the wrath of winter blew in like a runaway train.

⁓

Frustrated by his dilemma, the next day Grant strolled along the cold and windy streets of Leadville with his hands shoved deep in his pockets. He had some ideas, but he wasn't sure where to start. Heavy clouds rolled overhead like smoke bellowing from factory smokestacks. Throwing a stiff shoulder into the wind, he pressed onward, dust and dirt swirling at his feet.

He stopped first at a place called Isabella's, a white building garnished on the outside with curly scrolls of pink wood trim and a sign that advertised *Women's House of Beauty*. Grant knew Abby went there frequently to have her hair fixed, as she put it. Probably very few men had crossed this threshold, and he felt uneasy, unsure of what was inside, and not at all confident of how he would approach the women there.

Fortunately on the other side of the windowed door Grant found a reception area or waiting room, where frilly curtains covered doors behind which were the secrets to making women beautiful. The aromas of various beauty products combined to fill the room like steam in a steam bath.

"May I help you, sir?" an aggravated, buxom, red-haired woman asked.

Grant glanced around nervously. A few women in the waiting room hid behind newspapers as he glanced back at the woman who had addressed him. Though older, she was wearing a red, revealing outfit, making her look like the type of women Grant would be ashamed to be seen with in public. Her face tensed, making her lips pucker and her dark eyes squint between the long black lashes.

"Could be," Grant answered sheepishly. "A friend of mine has come here fairly regularly—had her hair done or something, you know?" Grant swirled a finger in the air around his head in a kind of sign language. "Her name was Abby, and I need to find her."

The woman looked at Grant, her impatience clearly evident, assuming he was in search of the beautiful Abby for romantic reasons.

"We don't give out information about our customers," she snapped sharply and glared at him, daring him to pursue the matter any further.

His hands tight in his pockets, Grant swung around on the heel of one boot, looked behind him, then turned back to the woman. "She's missing and—well, she's my sister, and I'm afraid she might be in danger."

The red-haired woman lifted an eyebrow in interest. Studying Grant intensely, sizing him up like a package of meat at the market, she uttered, "Are you really her brother?"

"Yes. I'm Grant DeSpain."

Her expression relaxed as she took on a more human quality. "I'm Isabella. To answer your question, yes, Abby is a regular customer, and I might add she's one of the prettiest ladies in Leadville. Of course we can take some of the credit—we bring the best out in a woman. As far as finding Abby, you should talk to Mendy Wheeler. She's one of Mendy's regulars." The woman batted her eyes as if she were swatting her lashes at something, then offered, "I'll go see if she can speak with you." She disappeared swiftly behind a velvet curtain.

In a few moments a small, young woman appeared, her hair long and blonde and flowing in waves like corn silk in the morning dew. She had bangs and a simple, easygoing charm. Big, round blue eyes addressed Grant with a bit of worry, her face smooth and expressionless. She held her hands clasped under her chin almost as if she were praying, then lowered them slowly while she studied the young man before her. "You're Grant?" she asked in a whisper.

To Grant, Mendy looked like she was a farm girl from the Midwest, pretty and honestly bashful, though her eyes were alive and full of hope. Grant noticed no wedding ring and realized this girl would be a good find for some lucky man. "Yes, I'm Abby's brother. Abby has left town without telling any of her family, including me, where she went or why. I thought maybe she said something to you about going away."

Mendy's expression changed to concern, a slight frown evident in the little dents above each dark eyebrow. "No, she never said anything about leaving." She drifted off into thoughts of old conversations, trying to figure out the mystery in order to satisfy her own curiosity, and to impress the young man standing before her. "All she talked about lately was Billy Rogers."

"Yeah, I know." Grant sighed. "Did she say anything about maybe running off with him?"

A slight smile came to Mendy's face. "No, but I know she was in love with him. I could tell by the way she acted. In a way I envied her. It's not very often that a girl gets that feeling about a man."

Grant noticed a movement in the heavy curtains behind Mendy and knew the old lady was eavesdropping. He didn't care. "Do you think she might have eloped?"

"Maybe," Mendy replied, her face growing serious. "She said he was some kind of speculator or something and that he traveled around a lot. She never mentioned leaving though."

"I see." Grant licked his lips, trying to think of more probing questions but couldn't. Obviously Mendy knew no more than he did. "Well, I'm sorry to have bothered you. Thanks anyway." He turned to leave.

Watching Grant's back, Mendy noticed the big square shoulders slightly hunched in despair. He seemed to be a kind and caring man, heartbroken by the disappearance of his sister. His face was honest with brilliant green eyes set wide above high cheekbones, his hair wavy, rusty-colored, and thick. The attraction she felt was only natural. "Grant!" she called suddenly, causing him to turn back to her. "You might check the train station. I just remembered, she said once she likes traveling by train."

Letting his eyes wander off to the side in thought, they came back to meet Mendy's. "That's an idea—I'll do that. Thanks."

"You will let me know, won't you?" Mendy asked, a slight hint of hope in her voice, inviting Grant's return.

"Yeah," Grant said, "I'll let you know."

The door closed behind him as Mendy stood innocently staring. Her mind slipped off into the world of make-believe. Abby had mentioned she had a brother and had spoken well of him, but she'd never said anything about his being so handsome.

"He's a looker," Isabella said. She had silently slipped up behind Mendy. "Those kind are usually heartbreakers."

Mendy gave the old woman a glance of disapproval. That wasn't what *she* was thinking, and she didn't appreciate Isabella's comment. Sighing deeply, Mendy returned to her work.

"Oh, to be young again," the old woman mumbled.

～

As the morning dragged on and gray clouds lingered overhead, an idea struck Grant. He hurried through the busy streets, now filled with the well-dressed and the less fortunate as they all scurried along the creaky boardwalks to escape the chilly wind. *I need a photograph of Abby*, Grant realized as his feet moved faster, his steps more sure now. *I think Mother has one.*

The door flew open at the office of *Western Magazine*, letting in a gust of wind and dust as Grant rushed in. Jennifer was standing nearby, dressed in a long blue dress with a long-sleeved white blouse, pages of white paper she'd been reading held in each hand. Her eyes darted to the commotion at the front door. Her face took on an expression of hope when she saw Grant, and she quickly dropped the papers onto a desk. "Did you find out anything?"

"I need a small photograph of Abby," Grant said with determination. "She had some portraits taken a while back. Didn't you get a small one?"

"Why, yes," Jennifer said, moving over to her desk. "This is it," she said, holding up a small photograph in a little silver frame.

Taking the picture from his mother, Grant looked at it carefully. It was an excellent picture of Abby that captured her well—the mischievous smile, the expressive eyes full of desire and alive with spirit. Unlike most photographs of the day, she wore her hair down in long and brown flowing waves instead of up. The picture seemed to almost talk to Grant, its expression showing a hungry, young woman eager to make a life for herself.

Grant quickly disassembled the frame and slid the picture out. "I'll be needing this," he said confidently and slid the picture into his shirt pocket.

"Good idea," Jason said. He had come over from his work and draped his arm around Jennifer's shoulder as they both watched Grant. "Any leads?"

Grant answered, "Billy Rogers hasn't been around here in a few weeks, so she couldn't have left on horseback with him. The only other way to travel that makes any sense is the train."

Nodding, Jason faced Jennifer, still holding her, the corners of his eyes crinkled with wisdom. "Don't worry, dear, I'm sure Grant will get to the bottom of this."

"I hope so," Jennifer fretted as she politely slid out from under Jason's arm and took a step, then stopped. She addressed both Jason and Grant. "I know I've always been a worrier, but this time it's a mother's intuition. I can't help but feel Abby is headed for danger. We must at least find out where she is—let her know we love her and that we'll always be here for her, no matter what she has done or what has happened to her."

In a single move Grant stepped forward and hugged his mother with his big arms. He looked down at her and promised, "I'll find her, Mother, no matter what it takes."

"There's a lot of country out here, Grant," Jason said in a serious tone. "But if anybody can find her, I believe you can." Jason said this because he knew Grant well—the boy who never turned and ran in the face of fear, the boy who had become a man at an early age. He had more than physical strength—he had the tenacity to hang on and tough it out. He was the kind of man who, once he made up his mind to do something, would keep working at it until it was done, like a bulldog with teeth clenched on a bone. Grant would never turn loose until a job was finished.

Releasing his mother, who now had tears in her eyes, Grant said, "I need to get over to the station. Somebody might remember having seen her." He rushed out, letting in another gust of dirty wind.

Jennifer returned to Jason's arms and clung to him in her moment of distress. "What if Grant takes off after her and I never hear from him again? What if something happens to him? What if I lose them both?"

"God knows where Abby is, and Grant can take care of himself," Jason said confidently. "He's strong, Jennifer. And he'll have the assurance of having the Lord with him, and that's the best kind of strength a man can have."

~

The 4-4-0 locomotive, known as the American, spewed and hissed steam as it chugged into the Leadville station, a cloud of ash and cinders lingering behind. The 102-ton engine squealed slowly to a stop near where Grant stood on the platform, the big diamond-shaped smokestack towering over him. The Denver & Rio Grande Railroad had won the Leadville route after a four-year war with the Atchison, Topeka and Santa Fe Railroad. Leadville had eagerly welcomed the first railroad, accessible only via the Grand Canyon of the Arkansas River, a notch 3,000 feet deep and in places said to be barely wide enough for a team of mules.

William J. Palmer, the Rio Grande's founder, and William B. Strong, the Santa Fe's general manager, were at times more like war generals in their strategies of takeovers and duress, having resorted to sabotage, hired gunmen, espionage, man-made avalanches, and shootings. No winner prevailed, because in 1880 eastern financiers ordered compromise in order to stop the violence. The Rio Grande got Leadville, the Santa Fe an exclusive route into New Mexico. Strong and Palmer could have reached such a solution bloodlessly, but as Palmer once remarked, "Amidst all the hot competition of this

American business life there is a great temptation to be a little unscrupulous."

Grant watched as passengers disembarked, some falling into the arms of long-lost loved ones while others went quickly on their way. Leadville was still in its heyday with promises of grand wealth bringing people from back east and over a vast ocean from distant Europe. The crowds soon dwindled, and another group began to board, a different kind of people—businessmen and others who had lost their hopes of instant wealth. They were the defeated, returning to their homes disenchanted and practically indigent.

If Abby had indeed taken the train, she would have been in a departing crowd, not because she was defeated but because she was letting her dreams carry her into the unknown, where chance is a way of life and hardships are the only certainty. For a woman it was even rougher, for reasonable jobs were limited, leaving only a few options Grant tried to keep out of his thoughts.

In a short while the big piston rods of the locomotive moved again with a *chug-chug*, like a great dormant animal awaking from sleep. The smells of oil and grease and wisps of steam and smoke filled the air until the long procession of cars slowly pulled away, carrying passengers and freight. Quietness fell upon the station as Grant meandered inside, searching for railroad employees who dealt with customers. He decided the ticket master was his best bet.

At the window, Grant laid his elbows on the counter, waiting to get the ticket master's attention. Finally the portly man with chubby cheeks and a heavy mustache noticed Grant and came to the window. "Can I help you, sir?"

"Yes. I'm looking for my sister. She's taken off without a word, and I think she may have taken a train out of here." Grant pushed the picture of Abby forward for the man to see.

"My, my!" the ticket master exclaimed. "She's a very attractive young woman." He brushed at his mustache with a cupped hand, his forehead furrowed while he studied the photograph. "Yes, of course," he responded with some enthusiasm. "Can't forget a young lady like that. She bought a ticket to Durango some days ago."

"Are you sure?" Grant questioned hopefully.

"Quite positive," the round man insisted. "She had several trunks. I saw to it personally that she was taken care of."

"Thank you very much!" Grant said happily as he took the picture back. "You've been a big help."

"Like to buy a ticket to Durango?" the ticket master asked, proud he was able to help.

"No," Grant replied. "Not right now."

Encouraged by the new information, Grant took off for the office so he could inform his mother of the news.

∽

"What do you intend to do now?" Jennifer questioned excitedly. "You'll need traveling money, but that's no problem. Do you have enough clothes? You can use my traveling trunks . . ."

"Calm down, Mother," Grant said flatly. "I won't be needing any of that."

"What?" Jennifer exclaimed. "How do you expect to travel?"

"I'm going to ride horseback."

Hearing this, Jason drew closer, deep concern on his face. "Horseback? Do you have a particular reason for riding when you could take a train and get there more quickly?"

"Yes," Grant said. Grant had already anticipated all the possibilities. "There's no guarantee she's still in Durango. She might have moved on, and if she's with that Billy Rogers, I'd suspect they've done just that. I can't be restricted by going only where trains travel. I need to have a horse."

"But the mountains, the trail—it's such dangerous terrain," Jennifer reminded Grant. They had all heard many stories of travelers in southwestern Colorado, the new frontier for silver and boomtowns. As usual, the boomtowns attracted not only miners and businessmen but all the parasites and scavengers that followed—thieves and robbers and the like. Desperation sometimes drove even honest people to adopt dishonest ways of life.

"I'll manage," Grant said confidently. "Look where I grew up, Mother, right in the middle of what you're worried about."

"But you've never crossed mountains on horseback," Jennifer argued. "I suppose you'll take Midnight."

Jason laughed at this, as did Grant. "No, Mother, I won't be taking Midnight. Not unless someone plans on following me with a wagon of oats. A thoroughbred wouldn't last five days."

"Then what do you plan on doing?" Jennifer asked anxiously.

"I'll buy a horse capable of crossing the high country, and a pack mule. I'll be all right."

"At least let us finance your trip and buy the animals," Jason suggested. "We want to help—we want to be part of this."

Grant moved over to the window and looked out onto the street. It was still gray outside. "All right, you can buy the animals, but I won't be needing to carry much money on me. That's a good way to get killed when some fool tries to rob me."

"But how will you manage without money?" Jennifer worried.

"With faith, Mother," Grant said sternly. "I'll have supplies, my gun, my horse, but mostly I'll pray that God will be with me. I'll take it one day at a time—that's all I can do."

Jennifer's face bore a mixed expression of sorrow, hope, and bewilderment. She looked at Jason as she had in the past when trouble faced them, seeking guidance and answers.

"He's right," Jason confided. "A horse will give him quick mobility to go anywhere. As for the danger from highwaymen, no one's better with a rifle than Grant. And as for the mountains, well, Grant learned respect for them years ago. He's right, Jennifer, you have to trust God to watch over him."

"Dear Lord," Jennifer prayed aloud, looking toward the heavens, "help me through this. Protect my children."

"Amen," Jason said. "Grant, if you need help getting things together, I'm right here."

"I'd better go and get cleared out of my rented room. I could be gone for a while. I'll bring my things over and put my stuff together from here."

"How long do you think you'll be gone?" Jennifer asked, still apprehensive.

"As long as it takes, Mother," Grant said. "As long as it takes."

~

That afternoon Grant made no bones about cleaning out his room and vacating the premises. He settled up with the owner, a modest man who wished him well, then moved his things to the back of the office where Jason and Jennifer couldn't help but watch curiously while Grant went about his business. The back room would serve fine for a night or two until he was ready to ride.

"I'm going to find a sturdy mount now," Grant stated when he had his things in place.

"I went to the bank," Jason announced as he approached Grant. "Here, take this, buy some good animals."

Grant accepted the bills Jason handed him and placed them in his wallet. "That looks like more than I need—I can't accept . . ."

"Keep it," Jason ordered. "You'll be needing it for supplies and such."

Old Willard was known as a fair dealer of horses, and after hearing Grant's plan to cross the Rockies, he suggested a certain horse. "His name's Mister," Willard said between missing teeth. He had a scanty short beard and wore suspendered overalls and a hat that was shiny with wear. Willard smiled and glanced at Grant, who stared at the horse with disbelief.

"That one?" Grant protested, pointing at the stocky animal. The horse was short, a dark solid bay with a big head. What set him apart from the other horses was the length of his fur—he looked like a buffalo; his legs were so heavy with fur, it looked like he was wearing pants.

"That's right," Willard said, now amused. He was smiling, making his rosy-colored cheeks swell into red lumps. "You won't find a tougher horse."

"Looks like a cross between a buffalo and a mule," Grant said with disgust. "What kind of horse is it?"

"It's a mustang," Willard informed Grant knowingly. "He can live on a cup of water and a handful of dry grass, and he's as strong as an ox and as sure-footed as anything."

"Looks kind of wild to me," Grant argued.

"He was once," Old Willard agreed. "Used to roam on his own. He don't miss a trick either. Good horse for a man to have around at night if you're campin' in the wilderness. He can sense danger a mile off."

"Let me take him for a ride," Grant said, now thinking in practical terms.

Willard threw an old saddle on Mister, bridled him up, and held the reins out to Grant. Confidently, Grant took the reins and lifted his leg to place his foot in the stirrup. When he did Mister just kept spinning away from him, making it impossible for the young man to get his foot in the stirrup. "This horse ever been ridden?" Grant complained. "Hold him steady for me, will ya?"

Willard did, and as soon as Grant got his foot in the stirrup and his leg over the saddle, Mister bucked, catching Grant off guard and almost throwing him. "Whoa, boy!" Grant cried. "Whoa, boy!"

Soon Mister calmed down and began a quick impatient trot around the corral, snorting his disapproval.

"I don't know about this one," Grant called down from the saddle. "He's a little wild."

"Why, a horse ain't worth a penny if he ain't got a little buck in him first thing," Willard stated. "He's got some spirit all right. Hold them reins up, make him hold his head up," Willard ordered.

Grant did as he was told and found that Mister responded well. "Open the gate, let me take him out."

Willard did, and Grant threw his heels into the mustang. Mister shot into a full run like a bolt of lightning, his head held high and his tail flying in the wind. Grant leaned into a tight turn, pulling the reins hard, and Mister almost sat on his rear, switching his direction in an instant and immediately returning to breakneck speed. Once more Grant reined the horse into tight maneuvers that would have agitated any other horse, but Mister seemed to enjoy it. When they got back to the corral Grant jumped down, landing on both feet in front of Old Willard. "That's a strong horse!"

"Yeah, and look, he ain't hardly winded either, barrel-chested rascal!" Willard said, holding his hand out. "His hooves are so tough, you hardly need to shoe him."

Grant decided he liked this horse, even if he was a bit strange. Haggling and typical horse-trade talk followed, which included a dark mule named Peaches, a mule that didn't seem to care about what was going on but minded well, an important asset for a pack animal.

Grant led his new outfit down to the livery where he kept Midnight, the thoroughbred stallion he'd owned since he was a youngster. Midnight raised his head, snorting for Grant's attention. He instructed the livery man to take care of the new animals and turned his attention to Midnight.

"How you doing, old boy?" Grant said soothingly as he stroked the horse's nose. Midnight bobbed his head and pawed with a front hoof, his way of saying hello. "Sorry, old boy, I'm going to have to take this trip without you. I'm afraid you wouldn't fare so well where I'm going."

Midnight nudged Grant with his muzzle, seeking more head scratching. "Could be a long trip, Midnight, very long."

Night was beginning to fall, the skies had cleared, and the jagged mountaintops were black silhouettes. The air was crisp with fall, and the temperature had already dropped, producing a noticeable chill.

Grant stopped in at a survey office and picked up some maps of the southwestern territory, then ambled on along, much on his mind. Suddenly it dawned on him that he'd promised to inform Mendy of his discoveries. Thinking of her pretty face brought a smile as he cut across Harrison, dodging horses and wagons until he reached the other side. He hoped it wasn't too late to catch her at work. When he came to the door of Isabella's, he reached for the handle, but the door opened before he could grab it. Mendy stood in the doorway, just as surprised as Grant, bundled in a sweater, a scarf over her head in preparation for the night air.

"Grant!" Mendy said, pleasantly surprised, her eyes greeting him warmly.

"Yeah," Grant stammered, "looks like I barely caught you."

"Any news?" Mendy asked, her face an expression of pleasure. She was indeed pleased to see Grant, for he was all she'd thought about all day long.

"I wanted to tell you, I went to the rail station and the ticket master—well, he remembered Abby. He remembered her quite well—said she bought a ticket for Durango." Grant was unknowingly fidgeting with his hands.

"What will you do now?" Mendy questioned further, afraid she already knew the answer.

"I'm getting my things together so I can go after her," Grant boasted bravely.

"You don't trust Billy Rogers to take care of her? They might have gotten married."

"I don't trust him for a minute," Grant admitted. "I know his type—I've seen too many like him. They take advantage of people under the guise of friendship and then they disappear."

As Mendy pulled the door closed behind her, Grant realized the polite thing to do. "Can I walk you home?"

"I'd be delighted, but it's a ways to the boarding house. I don't want to put you out."

Grant liked this innocent young beauty more and more every minute. "You don't have someone to walk you home? I mean, are you beholding to anybody?"

Bashfully, Mendy dropped her head, somewhat ashamed of the answer. "The men I've met here so far—well, they're not the kind of men I'm interested in." That was the best she could do for the moment, and Grant sensed this.

He had no idea later whether it was sincerity or just plain stupidity, but his heart spoke before he could think about it. "It's the same with the women I've met so far. They have no depth. What I mean is, they have no spiritual depth."

"So you're not attached to anyone?" Mendy asked uncertainly.

"No."

At this Mendy lightened her step, her gaiety obvious. "You mentioned spiritual depth. Would you mean anything to do with being a Christian?"

"Yes."

"Are you a Christian?"

"Yes indeed."

"That's wonderful. So am I," Mendy gladly admitted.

They walked along in silence for a moment, the people dodging them on the boardwalk. A man was up on a ladder lighting a gas lamp when they stopped beneath him to cross the street. Grant wanted to say more but found himself momentarily at a loss for words. He felt a little light-headed, and he realized the day had been so demanding that he had forgotten to eat.

"Mendy, would you care to have some dinner with me?"

Mendy looked at Grant, scarcely believing he had asked her to eat on the spur of the moment. This was like a dream come true. "I need to go back to my room and get cleaned up," she uttered, not knowing what else to say.

Grant looked at Mendy and began to laugh. "Are you serious?" he asked playfully, having no desire for anything but pure honesty. "You're the most beautiful woman I've ever met and you think you need to go fix up?" He laughed again, just wanting to say what he really thought. Silly courtship games seemed frivolous to him.

The remark caused Mendy to blush, her face hot in the cold night air, but she loved it nevertheless. "If you insist," she uttered quietly. She was a farm girl from the Midwest and had grown up with eleven brothers and sisters, a very close family. She missed the honesty they shared, the friendship, the love and devotion. She sensed these things in Grant as well, a wholesomeness, a love of truth. Words eluded her, but she knew how to speak in another way and placed her hand in Grant's as they walked.

Shortly afterward, seated in a comfortable little café, Grant realized he had never felt this way about a woman, and as they sat across from each other at the table, he gazed upon her face, so young and vibrant and innocent. Flames crackled in a nearby fireplace, and the light from the fire danced in her almond-shaped eyes. An uninhibited smile revealed her even white teeth. She appeared to be very happy.

"You seem young to be on your own," he said, making conversation, wanting to know everything about her.

The smile disappeared, and a vague pain took its place. "Father wanted to sell the farm, come out west, buy a mine, and get rich. So we all came. For a whole year, the mine produced nothing. We slowly became poor as our money ran out. Father died from coughing, some kind of disease in his lungs. We think it was from the wet and cold mining work. Mother died afterwards from heartbreak. My two sisters found men and married and moved away. One brother moved back to the Midwest to start another farm. My oldest brother was just like Father, a dreamer. He's probably in some new boomtown in the mountains. The others are scattered over the territory. I was the youngest—I'm twenty now."

All Grant could do was shake his head. How many times had he heard this story? It was sickening. Why did people give up something good for risks unknown? "I was raised in boomtowns," he said solemnly. "To this day I don't understand why men do such a thing. I've been studying it for years and I still can't figure it out. Maybe I'll never know. What's your brother's name? The one who went looking for treasure?"

"Warren—Warren Wheeler. He's tall and has black hair like my father did. He's twenty-six now. I haven't heard from him in several years." Mendy sounded sad at the mention of her separated family.

"A few make their fortune," Grant reminded her. "My family made it once and proved that money wasn't everything."

Mendy's smile returned. She liked what Grant had said, a reassurance he wasn't the foolhardy type to chase crazy notions, but instead was a solid man, just as she had thought.

Dinner in the cozy restaurant kept the world outside as Grant and Mendy shared their experiences with each other, some stories bringing laughter, some bringing sadness. It felt like they had known each other for a long time, and a keen fondness for each other rapidly developed.

After dinner Grant walked Mendy to the boarding house, a two-story affair on Chestnut. They stopped on the street in front of the building where the light was dim.

"Will I see you again before you leave?" Mendy asked with some worry. She had finally found a good man, just in time to see him leave.

"Yes, you will. I'll find you," Grant said, staring at her under the lights from streetlamps and nearby lighted windows. Her eyes were now a misty blue, happiness and sadness mixed together. He leaned a little closer, intending to kiss her, but then he drew back. She had been willing, but Grant realized that would only make it harder for both of them, for he had to leave, and as soon as possible.

Farewell

Before morning arrived, Grant was already up and packing his gear. A most important item was his Winchester model 74 repeating rifle, a rifle he'd purchased some years earlier. He removed the rifle from its scabbard and gave it a good cleaning with oil. The first lesson he ever had using a rifle had proved to be most valuable, a lesson offered by the notorious Lance Rivers many years ago when Grant was just a boy. One thing Grant had learned was that a gun was useless if a man couldn't shoot it accurately; so he had made it a regular habit to practice. As a result he could shoot clothespins off a wire at twenty yards. Having the rifle in his hands had come to feel as natural as the shirt on his back.

Grant still had to make his trip to the mercantile and worked on a list while waiting for the sun to come up. He would buy a few cases of cartridges for the Winchester, knowing that rounds for a rifle out in the wilderness could prove to be as valuable as pure gold. Other items would be needed as well—fresh jerky, canned goods, and other needed supplies. Being no fool about the fierce winters of the Rockies, he would dress in the warmest and most rugged clothes he could find—wool undergarments, heavy cotton shirts, rawhide outer clothing. A heavy duster might prove valuable as well to shelter him from rain and snow. He would need a pack saddle, a rawhide strap and rope—the items seemed endless as Grant ran his hand through his thick hair trying to remember everything.

Sitting at a small desk, biting gently on his pencil, Grant tried to imagine life on the trail on a day-to-day basis, trying to picture every little detail and the tools and items necessary for that kind of life. Whenever some particular item he didn't have occurred to him, he wrote it down.

The front door rattled, and Grant stood to his feet. He left the back room and turned on a light up front. Jennifer stood there holding a tray covered with a big linen napkin.

"I brought you a good breakfast," Jennifer said, setting the tray down. She lifted the napkin to expose a huge pile of scrambled eggs, thick bacon strips, and homemade bread caked with butter.

"You think you put enough on the plate?" Grant teased.

"Well, I don't want you to go hungry. This might be your last regular meal," Jennifer worried. "You are leaving this morning, aren't you?"

Grant sat down, put the napkin in his lap, and dug in. The eggs were still hot, and the bacon smelled like the smokehouse. "Yes, as soon as I can get everything together."

Standing over her son, Jennifer watched him eat, a pleasure a mother enjoys. Although Grant was a full-grown man, she still pictured him as a boy, inexperienced and innocent, unfamiliar with the harsh ways of the world. She could only imagine the tragedies and misfortunes he might encounter on his trip, and her thoughts caused her to sigh with grief. "I want you to be careful. Watch out for bandits on the trail—they'll rob anybody who has anything. And watch out for . . ."

"Mother," Grant pleaded, "stop it! You're getting all worked up. I can deal with whatever comes, with God's help. But think about Abby. How can *she* deal with such things?"

That statement caused Jennifer to shift her thoughts to her daughter. Grant was right; a woman alone could have a very difficult time. This reminder chased off her other worries, and she said, "What will you say to Abby when you find her?"

That's a good sign—she's thinking more sensibly now, Grant thought. "I imagine she'll be ready to come back by the time I find her. I doubt I'll have to say much of anything."

Jennifer realized anew that time could be of the utmost importance in rescuing Abby. After thinking about it all further, she had decided she had little faith in Billy Rogers to protect and care for her daughter and figured he would abandon her if the going got rough, leaving Abby to fend for herself. Billy Rogers was so typical of the young speculators she'd seen before—all talk with nothing to back it up. How Abby could have fallen for that kind of man was beyond her, but then she remembered—when she was young she'd done the same thing, not once but three times!

The sun was up and peeking through the windows when Grant finished his breakfast, wiped his mouth with the big napkin, and threw it on the plate. He came to his feet and said, "Mother, I have to get down to the mercantile. Thanks for the good breakfast." He leaned over and gave her a quick kiss on the forehead.

"Do you need money?" Jennifer questioned.

"Jason gave me more than enough, I'll be all right."

"Oh," Jennifer remembered, "Jason said he's going to bring you something to take with you."

"I'll be back before long—I still have to pack the mule, and it takes a while to do it right," Grant said as he put on his hat. Normally he didn't use a hat, but in the wild outdoors it was a necessary part of a man's gear, offering protection from the harsh sun, wind, rain, and snow. His hat had a wide brim, the edges rolled ever so slightly on the sides, typical of the hats worn by cowboys in earlier days.

Grant's walk was heavy on the wooden floor as he left, the sound of a big man on the move. He had reached six feet tall at an early age but only in recent years had filled out to fill his big frame, now weighing 200 pounds.

Watching him leave, Jennifer's thoughts depressed her. Her youthfulness, her beauty and passion for life, her love for her young children—all these things were growing distant. The change had been slow, but now there were crow's-feet at the corners of her eyes, and gray hair mixed with the dull auburn that had once been rich in brilliance. She saw herself as a mature matriarch who had once reigned but now had little influence on her adult children. But she also knew she had grown in several important ways.

Jennifer carefully considered the stranger she saw within herself. She nodded slowly, seeing herself as she entered a new part of the journey of life. Older now, she saw a wiser person, a woman who had survived difficult experiences and had learned from them, a woman now more settled and less attracted to flighty ambitions, a woman who had come to accept her station in life, acknowledging that she was no longer the young striking beauty she had once been. She now had strong roots and a strong faith in God, and a loving husband who was a good man as well as a smart one. A slight smile came upon her, and confidence returned. She knew, from experience and from a childlike faith, that everything would work out—God would keep watching over her and over her family.

~

Later that morning Grant returned with the assistance of a young storekeeper who helped him carry many packages. Grant gave the young man a tip and sent him on his way, then went and fetched Mister and Peaches. With Mister reined to a post wearing Grant's fancy saddle, the one he used on Midnight, Grant began the careful process of packing Peaches, an art he had learned from prospectors in the past. He knew a loose binding or an uneven load could lame a pack mule, rendering it useless. Jennifer and Jason looked on curiously in the glare of the morning sun as Grant performed the delicate work. The day had proved to be a more typical September day, with bright sun in a clear blue sky and crisp cool temperatures. Before long, Grant had completed his work, with Mister packed as well, Grant's rifle tucked neatly under the saddle in its protective scabbard. A bedroll including his duster was perched on the back of the saddle, a huge canteen on the front.

Jason stepped inside the office and returned to the street holding a package wrapped in brown paper. "Here, Grant—I want you to have this."

Grant unwrapped the package and saw a wrapped leather belt full of cartridges and a holster with a black, wooden-handled Colt revolver. "This is *your* gun," Grant said with amazement. "The gun you carried when you first confronted Big Ned back in Virginia City. I haven't seen you wear it since."

"I thought you might need it," Jason said proudly.

Grant's face turned serious as he handed the pistol back to Jason. "Thanks anyway, Jason. I know this gun means a lot to you, but I can't use it."

"Why not?" Jason asked, a little hurt.

"I've never learned to use a six-shooter. I have my rifle—that's all I need."

"I understand," Jason mumbled, "but there's one more thing." He handed Grant another small package.

Unwrapping the package, Grant saw it was an old Bible.

"That's from Virginia City too. Your mother gave it to me, and it did more good than any gun could ever do."

Nodding, Grant ran his fingers over the old worn leather binder. This was a special Bible, and Grant remembered it well. "This I'll take," Grant said, smiling as he took Jason's hand and shook it in a farewell gesture.

Feeling a handshake was inadequate, Jason hugged Grant, throwing his arm over the young man's big shoulders. "You take care, and bring your sister back home safely."

"I will," Grant said.

Jennifer stood watching, fighting the overwhelming fear within her. She wanted to be strong, to rely on the faith that had brought her through so many trials. She put her shoulders back, composed herself, and stepped forward. Grant leaned over and hugged his mother dearly, then kissed her on the cheek. "Don't worry, Mother. This is a job I have to do, and the Lord will see me through."

Blinking her eyes to fight away tears, Jennifer nodded, fighting off the emotions that were almost overpowering. She took a deep breath before she spoke. "Wire us when you can. Don't keep us in the dark."

"I'll stay in touch," Grant said as he put a foot in the stirrup and lifted himself onto the squeaking saddle. Mister snorted and bucked, kicking his hind legs high in the air, adding to the tension of the moment. Grant held on, tightening the reins and making Mister go in circles until he calmed down.

Unready for such an outburst, Jennifer jumped back and kept her hand over her mouth. Jason held Jennifer as he looked on with concern. "Are you sure that horse is all right?"

"A horse ain't worth his salt if he ain't got a little buck in him," Grant replied, smiling, then tipped his hat and spurred Mister into a trot down the street. Its ears perking up, Peaches followed the lead rope with quick little steps.

Jason held Jennifer as they watched Grant make his way down the crowded street. "He's grown into quite a man," Jason said.

Holding her face against Jason's chest, Jennifer fought back tears. "Yes, they've both grown up so much, but Grant and Abby are still my children—they'll always be my children."

~

Durango lay in the far southwestern corner of the state of Colorado, with Leadville almost in the center and many a mountain range in between. Grant would take the only route out of Leadville to the south and follow the Arkansas River down to Poncha Springs. From there he would have to head west over the Continental Divide.

But first he had one more stop to make. Grant threw a rein over the hitching post in front of Isabella's and went inside. Isabella sat smugly behind the counter adorning her fingernails, her flaming red hair piled high on her head. When she saw Grant, she assumed a defensive temperament.

"I need to see Mendy," Grant said abruptly.

"I'm sorry, she's busy. Maybe you can come back later," Isabella huffed.

"Now!" Grant said, slamming his fist on the counter with a loud bang.

Isabella jumped in fright and quickly scurried out of the little room.

In a few minutes Mendy appeared, a wide smile on her pretty face. "Hello, Grant," she said happily.

"Come outside—just for a moment," Grant said. He jutted his

chin toward the curtain he knew Isabella was hiding behind, sure she was eavesdropping again.

Once outside, Grant took his hat off and held it by the brim, rotating it in his fingers as he spoke. "Mendy, I'm on my way out. I don't know when I'll be back, but I had to see you before I left."

Mendy couldn't take her eyes away from Grant's face as she stood before him in the clear sunlight, her face looking up into his. She was for the most part a bashful girl. Life in the West had been hard and the days long and boring, until Grant came along. She'd thought that if she played her cards right, Grant might be the man of her dreams, the man she knew was meant for her. But now here he stood, saying good-bye, bravely beginning a dangerous journey, perhaps never to return. Mendy pushed her bashfulness aside—it was time for simple truth and honesty.

"I'll pray for your safety," Mendy said softly. She hesitated a moment and licked her lips as she searched for the right words, her eyes still holding Grant in her steady gaze. "Grant, I'll wait for you. I don't care how long it takes, I'll be here." She paused, thinking she had to say more than that. "I've never felt like this about any man before—it's all happened so fast and I barely know you—but then again, I do know you. I know the kind of person you are. I want to be with you as much as I can." She began to blush, for it was improper for decent women to be so forward.

Taking her hand, Grant understood her predicament. This was no time for beating around the bush. "It's all right, Mendy. This has never happened to me before either. I've never felt this way about any other woman. I want to get to know you—I think I'm already in love with you. I'll miss you while I'm gone, but I'll carry you in my heart and my mind—and I will return, if for no other reason but to come back to you."

They stood staring into each other's eyes. Grant figured the road would be long and hard, but it would be nice to have a memory of the taste of her lips to carry with him. Slowly he reached around her and pulled her to him until their lips met. It was a meaningful kiss, one that expressed his true feelings for this beautiful woman, confirming his assurance that this was the woman for him.

Mendy found the kiss something special as well. Time seemed to stand still, and yet she knew the moment had to end, though she held on to every dear second with all of her heart. Grant was the dream she had prayed for.

When they pulled away, Grant placed his hands on her shoulders and held her firmly in front of him. "I'll come back for you, Mendy. We have so much to look forward to. I love you!"

Mendy nodded, overwhelmed with the genuine emotions flowing between them. "I'll be waiting."

As Grant pulled away, she let her small hand slide down his arm and through his hand and out to the end of his fingers where she took a last little grasp. "Be careful," she whispered.

Mounting his horse, Grant took a last look at Mendy. Her pretty oval face stood out in the bright sunlight like it had a light of its own. She smiled a little and lifted her hand to wave good-bye. Grant would carry that picture of Mendy with him, and he knew it would bring him back.

～

The first days of the journey were uneventful as Grant traveled the rutted, well-used road leading south out of Leadville through the settlements of Stringtown and Malta. He encountered freight wagons, many groups of travelers, and an occasional stagecoach. The stage lines ran to remote places the railroads could not reach, bumping over the uneven and precarious roads, jostling their passengers into a frenzy. At times he passed the rattling wagons of medicine men and hardware salesmen eager to promote their goods.

"Need a bottle of Doctor Do-Good?" a salesman called from the perch of his roofed wagon. The wagon was painted with colorful signs, and the mule pulling it wore a straw hat. The little fat man had a thin mustache and wore a dusty, black, long coat. "This stuff will keep you warm on the cold nights on the trail—keep you regular too," he called out, holding a bottle aloft.

"No thanks," Grant answered as they passed each other heading in opposite directions.

The smile quickly left the salesman's face, and he slapped the reins on the mule's back.

The days were pretty but were growing shorter as Grant settled down in impromptu campsites night after night. As a precaution each day he stopped before sundown and built a fire, made dinner, then moved on along to a group of trees where he built no fire, which would signal his presence to unexpected or unwanted visitors.

After three days Grant moved onto the Santa Fe Trail through Buena Vista and worked his way along to Poncha Springs and a small serene town known as Fourteener Crossroads (referring to the 14,000-foot peaks), where north and south trails crossed the east and west trails. The first white man to visit the town had been Kit Carson, who said the Indians found the mineral waters spirit-filled.

While enjoying a hot mineral bath, Grant learned from another man in the bathhouse that the town had in effect cut its own throat. In its early days the town had elected to keep the railroad out in order to keep it a pleasant place. The Denver & Rio Grande laid tracks south to Salida, and the economy of Poncha Springs followed.

Turning southwesterly, Grant continued his journey. The climb was now steep, slow, and demanding as the road narrowed and ascended toward the huge peaks ahead of him. Up above, the Continental Divide dominated the scenery with huge and in some cases already snowcapped peaks. Fortunately, there was a mountain pass, one that Grant thought he needed to take in order to wind his way up and around the steep cliffs at hand. Mister labored on, his strength unwavering, his lungs strong in the high altitude.

By now Grant and Mister were becoming well acquainted. Never had Grant seen such a skittish horse, jumping at every little move, every little sound. Often Mister would stop and stare into a thick stand of spruce and pine, as if he heard something, forever cautious. Grant would have to wait until Mister was satisfied before spurring him on; otherwise Mister would grow disgruntled and state his disapproval by snorting until he calmed down again. Grant figured it was easier to let him have a look before moving on; besides, that gave the horse a chance to take a breather. Peaches, on the other hand, always seemed undisturbed, content to grab a mouthful of dry grass every now and then.

Unfamiliar with the countryside, Grant followed a trail upward, having no idea where it led, and finally had to admit he had lost his way. Not knowing what else to do, he continued on until he passed four men on the trail riding horseback. They had no pack animals and seemed out of place and were awful curious with their searching, beady eyes. They wore pistols in holsters strapped to their legs, desperation evident in their lean and mean appearance. Grant had no doubts these men lived outside the law, and an hour after they were out of sight Grant took the first decent animal trail he came across, a trail that appeared to head off to the south, skirting the Divide. He had no use for the men he had passed and felt sure they would double back, perhaps to try to catch him at night and relieve him of his animals and supplies.

The afternoon grew late as the slim trail wound around and around. Grant could see the mountain peaks off to his left, but the way the trail meandered, he felt like he might never reach them. Keeping a careful eye, he moved on, searching for another way and watching behind him as well, in case the men in question had tracked him.

With the sun already on the other side of the mountain, the high, thin air quickly grew cooler. Grant followed a ridge that gave him a good view. He was alone in an area where the going was risky for any traveler. But recognizing the possibly greater dangers of turning back, he kept climbing the wild heights of rock. Late-afternoon colors made brilliant patterns in the sky, reflecting downward to color the rocks and ledges as far as he could see. The mountains with their wild beauty and danger were obstacles, but inspiring ones. But for a young man who relished adventure, he saw them as wonderful challenges, foes to be conquered.

Grant stopped to take it all in. It was all new and fresh, and he wanted to remember it. He wondered what this great land had seen and wished it could tell him of the past days of Indians and Spanish explorers and the first mountain men—the secrets the great mountain range held—gold and silver and riches too great to imagine—

the abundance of wildlife in the elk and bear and deer. It was all right before him where he could reach out and touch it, and that made him feel tall in the saddle and strong in the heart.

"What do you think, Mister? Ever seen anything like this?" Grant whispered.

Mister cocked one furry ear back as if he were listening. The wild country had an effect on him too, for he was part of it. Horse and rider stood still on the rise overlooking a scene rare and grand. Indeed, they were part of that very picture.

A sudden pain struck Grant as he pictured Mendy looking up at him in the clean sunlight. He missed her more than he'd ever missed anyone or anything, but most of all he wished she could see and feel what he was seeing and feeling right now. It was a spiritual experience, the kind that sets a man apart from the regular order of things and makes him feel like he's on top of the world. The experience of the high country, and knowing Mendy was back home waiting for him—Grant knew this was what life was about—freedom and love and happiness. Only God could create such a life, and Grant was thankful.

Mister quickly perked his ears, and Grant felt a shudder run through his muscles. In an instant Grant pulled out his rifle and chambered a round. They stood still, listening, and then Grant heard what sounded like a man calling for help.

When Grant shook the reins lightly, Mister moved on down the trail, which descended to a small, narrow gully below. Again came the call, and it was indeed a man's voice. Grant moved closer to the stream-filled gully below. The sound of the water splashing over rocks grew louder until Grant was finally right at the streambed. The water looked like running silver in the dying light, reflecting the last light from above.

"Over here," called the voice.

Rifle in hand, Grant trotted Mister over another twenty yards of streambed until he came to a horse standing with his reins dangling on the ground. In front of the horse a man sat sprawled with his ankle in the fork of a piece of heavy driftwood. The man was old, his beard and hair long and white, his body stocky and short. Grant could see from the barrel chest and the size of the man's arms that he was strong for an elderly gent. Grant dismounted and surveyed the situation.

"Shore am glad to see you!" the old man said with pain in his voice. "I been here for two days. Thought maybe this might be it for me."

"What happened?" Grant asked. "It looks like you're in a real fix."

"Took a fall—my leg is out of sorts."

Grant reached down and gently removed the man's ankle from the fork in the driftwood.

"I wasn't strong enough to fix it myself," the old man complained. "I tried to use the fork in that tree. You see . . ." He stopped, coughed a spell, then continued, "You see, this has happened before. My leg has got to be pulled back where it belongs—it's mislocated, the bone that is."

"What can I do to help?" Grant asked.

"Why, son, you got to pull it, that's all there is to it." The old man shifted around on the ground and pointed at his leg. "There! Take aholt of that ankle and yank it with all you got."

"Are you sure?" Grant questioned. It was now quickly getting dark and cold.

"Yeah, I'm sure. Just do it," the old man pleaded.

Grant took the foot, made sure the old coot was ready, then snatched it toward him sharply.

The old man let out a howl like a wild wolf, shook his head until his eyes uncrossed, and then breathed hard. "Whew!" he exclaimed. "I didn't know you was going to try and tear my leg off! That's all right though," the old man said, holding his hand up in defense. "You done good, done it just right. Now help me on my horse."

Again Grant did as he was told and got the old fellow up on the animal.

"Follow me," the old man ordered. "I got a cabin just beyond that rise."

It was so dark now, Grant could not see any rise or hardly anything else. But Mister could, so Grant let him have the reins.

Once inside the small cabin, the old man found a lantern and struck a match to it, then found a cane he used from time to time. He produced a bottle of whiskey, set it on the table, and removed the stopper. "Take yourself a snort, you deserve it."

"I don't drink," Grant replied, "but thanks anyway."

"If'n you don't mind, I think I'll have a snort—kills the pain. I'm cold in my bones, and this here leg hurts somethin' awful." The codger took a hefty drink from the bottle, gave a good shake like a wet dog, then set it back on the table.

"You saved my life, young man. What's your name?"

Grant studied the old man and had to admit he was one tough old customer, having spent two nights on the ground with a dislocated leg, enduring what must have been tremendous pain. Grant couldn't help but admire the man. "I'm Grant DeSpain."

"God must have sent you, Grant. My name is Beuford, just plain Beuford. My house and anything I got here is yours. Make yourself at home, stay for a while."

"Thanks, Mister Beuford, but I'm on a journey to find my lost sister, so I won't be staying long. I need to get over the pass tomorrow."

Old Beuford leaned back his head and let out a hearty laugh, then took the bottle off the table and had another swig. "Most folks just knows me as Beuford, ain't no 'mister' to it. As for the pass, Mister Grant DeSpain, you ain't goin' over it or nowhere else fer a spell."

"Oh?" Grant said, surprised. "How do you figure that?"

"I smelt a blizzard in the air, one of them strange ones that comes a mite too early in the season. It'll blow in here tonight, guaranteed. But don't you worry yourself none—the snow don't last long this time of year. You'll be able to get on your way in good time."

"I didn't see a single cloud in the sky all day long, there's no wind, and I sure didn't smell any blizzard," Grant argued.

"Well, Mister Grant DeSpain, we'll see what you think in the morning."

"Call me Grant—enough of this mister business," Grant said, making fun of the old man.

Beuford laughed and said, "Grant it shall be," then turned his head and pointed to a dark shadow hanging in the corner of the cabin near the old stove. "That there is a smoked rump of elk. What do ya say we carve us off a chunk and have somethin' to eat. I'm well-nigh starved to death."

The men stayed up late eating and talking after Grant took care of the animals and put them in a shed. Grant learned that old Beuford was the end of a dying breed, a mountain man who led a solitary life. His old brown eyes still twinkled, and his stories of better days were intriguing. Sometime late in the evening Grant fell asleep right at the table and hardly moved the rest of the night. Only Beuford's rattling and banging the stove and getting a fire started the next morning brought Grant back to wakefulness.

Standing, Grant stretched his big frame in the low-ceiling cabin as best he could, then stepped to the door and opened it. Snow was halfway up the door and still falling!

A Lesson in Survival

D on't you worry yourself none," Beuford remarked, noticing Grant staring into the blinding white snow. "This here is one of them snowstorms that's lost and out of place. It'll blow on out of here directly."

Closing the door, Grant's disappointment was obvious. At least he had the good sense to be thankful he wasn't out in the storm. Warmth came from the old stove as the fire crackled and snapped into life.

"Can you shoot that there rifle you was a totin'?" Beuford asked.

"As good as anybody," Grant replied, trying to sound humble.

"That's good to know. There's a clearing on back of here that stays full of deer. After we get our bellies full we can step back there and drop some meat."

Grant nodded, sat back down at the little table, and watched Beuford hobble around on his cane while he put together the makings for a breakfast.

Later that morning the snow quit, and all was soft and quiet as the two men worked their way through knee-deep snow in a forest of stately spruce that opened onto a clearing.

"Right here," Beuford said as he squatted down, grimacing at the pain in his leg. "We oughta see a fat deer here shortly."

It appeared as if the forest were asleep under a velvety white blanket of heavy snow as the men sat still, their eyes searching. The wild country, white and wonderful, had a peace of its own. The dull gray clouds broke every now and then to let a shaft of brightness flash down onto the shimmering snow, causing Grant to squint in the glare. The air was cold and clean and could take a man's breath away.

Grant pulled his leather gloves tighter around his fingers so he could manage his rifle, its barrel pointed upward as he sat squatted and waiting. A distant movement caught the eyes of both men. Beuford nudged Grant and slowly pointed to the movement, then nodded, indicating Grant should take the first shot when it became available. Ever so cautiously, four large does stepped lightly through the snow, nibbling on the smaller trees, then stopping to hold their long, mule-like ears high, listening for danger. Content, they went back to grazing, their long white tails waggling.

The deer soon found themselves in the clearing, enjoying the warmth from the sunlight that appeared from time to time. Slowly Grant lifted his rifle and took careful aim at the doe in the lead.

A loud crack shattered the soft morning silence and sent three does scampering wildly in opposite directions. The fourth lay still in a scarlet contrast on a white background.

A while later, just as Beuford had said, the clouds parted and the sun shone brightly upon the woods. Near the cabin the deer hung from a tree limb as the men skinned and quartered it for the small smokehouse. It was a rewarding experience for Grant to live off the land like this. The two men found conversation natural and peaceful, and Grant told his new friend about his sister and the reason for his journey. Listening with a sympathetic ear, Beuford worked expertly on the animal, using his big knife in a professional manner and taking pains to keep his knife hand clean during the process.

"You got a good knife?" Beuford asked.

"I guess it's pretty good," Grant answered.

"After I get this here deer skinned and quartered, we'll hang her in the smokehouse. By the time you leave it oughta be ready enough you can carry some with you. In the meantime, there's a thing or two I can show you about stayin' alive."

"Staying alive?" Grant asked with some trepidation.

"Where you're goin', you'll need every advantage a man can have," Beuford said knowingly.

With the deer out of the way, Grant followed Beuford over to a woodpile and watched him stand a log on its end. Beuford then pulled Grant back twenty paces. "Stick your knife in that log—right in the middle."

Grant pulled his knife from its sheath and stared at it. He swallowed hard, having no idea how to throw a knife.

Beuford snatched the long blade knife from Grant's hand and studied it closely, then touched the edge with his rough thumb. "She's pretty sharp, not bad for a store-bought knife, I'd say." Then, as quick as the eye could see, Beuford hurled the knife and stuck it in the log. He glanced at Grant and removed his own knife, another long blade, and handed it to the young man.

Rearing back, Grant slung the knife at the log and watched it bounce harmlessly into the snow.

"That's what I figured," Beuford said. He went and fetched the knives and brought them back. Holding the knife by the blade, Beuford demonstrated to Grant the proper grip for knife throwing, then proceeded to show him how he controlled the rotations of the knife through the air in order to make it hit point first. They worked at this for a couple of hours until Grant started to get the hang of it.

"I can show you how to do this all day long," Beuford said, "but practice is what makes it perfect. You toss that knife of yorn every day until you get it right, then you'll have something you can trust. There's few things a man can trust, you know."

Taking this in, Grant realized the old mountain man really did know a thing or two. "Thanks, Beuford. I'll work on it."

"Let's get us somethin' to eat. There's more to do this afternoon."

After a lunch of biscuits, meat, and gravy, Beuford stumbled around in the dump behind the cabin, tossing bottles and cans into a pile on the side. He reminded Grant of an old, wise goat, his white beard shimmering in the sunlight.

"Take these here cans and bottles and line them up on that fence rail over yonder," Beuford called.

As he lined up the bottles and cans on the fence rail like soldiers,

Grant knew what was coming. This time he would surprise the old man at how well he could handle his Winchester. Before Beuford could even ask, Grant had his rifle and a box of cartridges out and ready.

Standing in back of Grant, Beuford said, "Let's see you hit a few of them there bottles."

Grant smiled knowingly. He lifted his rifle to his shoulder, took careful aim, and squeezed off a shot. The bottle exploded. Grant cocked the rifle and put it to his shoulder again. He squeezed off another round, and a second bottle shattered into a thousand tiny shards. Turning, Grant glanced at Beuford and smiled. "What do you think?"

"Fair," was all Beuford said. "Now hit this!" Beuford slung an old whiskey bottle spinning high into the air.

Quickly Grant cocked his rifle, chambered a round, and tried to put his sights on the sailing bottle, but it was too quick and fell to the ground before he could hit it. "I wasn't ready!" Grant complained.

"And you never will be when a man is gunning for you. It's instinct that'll keep you alive. That's what I'm tryin' to teach you," Beuford grumbled. "That's a good rifle you got there—maybe the best ever made. I got one just like it. Hand it here."

Beuford looked the rifle over until he was satisfied, then told Grant to pitch a bottle. Before the bottle reached the apex of its flight, Beuford shattered it in midair, shooting from the hip. Grant was impressed.

"Unless you're making a mighty long shot, you need to learn how to shoot this here gun without aiming down the sights," Beuford said. "You need to learn to shoot it quick too. Now throw two bottles at once."

Two bottles flew into the air like doves, and Beuford shot them both, causing a shower of glass. "That's the idea behind a repeating rifle," Beuford said. "You can cock it fast and shoot again as fast as a flutter of sparrow wings. First," he went on, "we got to get you some old barn boards lined up behind them there targets so you can see where your bullets are hittin'."

With everything set up, Grant began practicing shooting at still targets from the hip. He was embarrassed at how bad he was.

"Think about where the bullet is hittin'!" Beuford ordered as he watched. "Don't be lookin' at the barrel or worry about the rifle. Just watch where them bullets hit, and make your corrections from there!"

Grant felt nervous practicing in front of his expert teacher, but he soon settled down and began to hit cans and bottles. "I know I need practice," Grant offered, "but I can't be using up all of my cartridges."

"Don't you worry about that none," Beuford said, scratching under his arm. "I got more shells than a tradin' post. You keep that barrel hot while I go rest a spell. This here leg ain't what it used to be."

Following orders, Grant did as he was told, occasionally taking a break to think over what he was doing and trying to decide if he was improving. Soon he began counting the rounds and hits to see if his average was improving, which it was.

Afternoon rolled on as Grant practiced. He found it useful to take a fifteen-minute break every now and then, putting the rifle down and giving his mind and eyes a rest. During the quiet few minutes of one break, Grant took a good look around. Old Beuford had a pretty good setup for a man living alone in the wilderness. The sturdy log cabin appeared solid and warm. His horse had a shed and small corral. There was a smokehouse and privy, and tools and gear hanging on almost every wall. The entire affair was settled on a flat spot with a forest of giant spruce forming the background, with aspens filling in the sparse openings; a stream ran down the mountain nearby.

But Grant knew he could never be happy here because of one missing element—Mendy, the lovely girl who continued to grow in his heart and in his thoughts. The more he reflected on her, the more wishing and thinking he did. To have to leave a new and wonderful relationship behind had been distressing. Yet had it not been for Abby's disappearance, Grant knew he might have never met Mendy.

"Strange how things work," Grant murmured as he picked up the rifle and reloaded it.

⌒

"I have a hankerin' for some fish!" Beuford said the next morning as he snapped his suspenders.

Grant watched Beuford as he strutted around wearing pants over long johns that had been white a long time ago. The old man found enough clothing hanging on the walls to get dressed for the day.

"Reckon I'll be taking off today," Grant said matter-of-factly.

"I reckon you won't if you got any sense atall," Beuford said matter-of-factly.

Surprised, Grant asked, "How come?"

"If'n you give a hoot about your animals, you'll wait. You see, when there's a heavy snow this early, well, the sun comes out the next day and melts the top down some. Then night comes, and that top freezes into a sheet of ice, and this happens several times before the snow melts away. You try to ride a horse through that, and the top layer of ice will cut his legs down to the bone—take the hide right off." Beuford let Grant absorb this, knowing the boy understood little about traveling through the mountains.

"Oh," Grant uttered sheepishly, thinking what a tragedy it would be to make his horse lame due to stupidity.

The cabin was small for two men, the walls darkened from smoke and grease. The smell of smoked meat and burnt wood and Old Beuford reminded Grant of an old buffalo robe. He was ready to get out into the mountain-fresh air and see what Beuford would be up to next.

Like a little kid, Grant followed the old mountain man, carrying his rifle under one arm, until they came to a spot in the mountain stream where the water rushed and gurgled, sparkling clear between snowy banks and boulders. Beuford pulled out his knife, cut a couple of aspen saplings, and stripped the limbs from them, making two small poles. Grant watched curiously as the old man pulled some fine twine from his pockets and tied it to the ends of the poles, then fished around and produced some small hooks with tiny bird feathers tied to them.

"Do fish eat bird feathers?" Grant asked.

"No, but they think they're bugs," Beuford said, squinting as he tied the hooks to the lines. "Now, it's bright out, and we want to stay low when we get near the crick—don't never let your shadow on the water 'cause them fish can see better than you think they can."

Crouching, the men eased close to the stream, and Beuford swung the line out, letting the water carry it past him, then did the same thing again. "See that pool there? Well, I'm tryin' to get that little rig I fixed to float by it—there's always a couple of good ones in there waitin' fer somethin' to float by that they fancy."

On the third try the tiny feather disappeared, and the line tightened and buzzed through the water sideways. Beuford pulled back, and the sapling in his hand bent double.

"Oh boy, I got a good one!" Beuford wrestled the pole and line and finally backed away from the bank and dragged the flopping fish onto shore.

Always ready to help, Grant grabbed the fish, about fourteen inches long, before it could bounce back into the water. His heart beat hard from the excitement.

"Couple more like that and we'll have a fine dinner," Beuford said, coming over to remove the small hook. "Give it a try yourself. Right over there is another pool that's got a big one in it."

"How do you know?" Grant asked.

"Why, I see his eyeballs stickin' up," Beuford said playfully.

Sneaking up slowly, Grant did his best to imitate the old man. He crouched over and kept back from the water as best he could, trying to work the line to where the bait would float by the pool. He discovered it wasn't as easy as it looked, and he had to try again and again until he got his fishing rig to cooperate.

When Grant least expected it, a fish almost jerked the pole out of his hand. Panicking, Grant held on tight, not sure what to do.

"Keep the line tight!" Beuford called. "Keep that pole up in the air—don't point it at him!"

Grant was so excited, he could hardly follow Beuford's orders but managed just the same until he pulled the stubborn fish onto the bank, then watched it flop around in the snow. The slippery creature almost escaped back into the stream after Grant removed the hook, but with a little luck the young man managed to pin him down.

"I couldn't have done it better myself," Beuford said, looking on. "Nice fish."

As the morning warmed, each caught another fish, enough for a satisfying meal, then settled back, slipping into easy conversation, only halfheartedly fishing.

"I noticed that many of the things you have are store-bought," Grant said. "There's a store near here?"

"I wouldn't call it near," Beuford lazily replied, sitting on a big boulder, leaning back and soaking up some sun on his weathered and leathery face. "There's a tradin' post a ways over the pass—a day's ride in good weather."

Grant thought about this for a minute, then asked, "What do you use for trading? Hides, meat, or what?"

"Gold," Beuford said, never moving.

"Gold?"

Beuford turned and looked at Grant. "Yeah, gold. You're sittin' right next to a load of it."

"Really," Grant said, now looking at the stream in a different way. "If there's as much as you say, why, you could be a wealthy man."

"I am a rich man," Beuford bragged. "The good Lord provides everything I need right here. That's why I live here."

"You believe in God?" Grant asked.

Old Beuford couldn't keep from laughing at Grant. "Shore I do. Just take a look around you. Where do you think all this come from, some generous politician back east? Take a look at the stars tonight, look at these mountains, look at the animals and these fish, the forest and the size of this place—it's grand, ain't it, son?"

"Yes, it is," Grant admitted. "Why did you tell me about your gold? Most men would keep that a secret."

"'Cause you ain't like most men," Beuford said, becoming more serious. "I know you're searching, like so many that come through, but you ain't lookin' for gold or silver. And I ain't talkin' about searchin' for your sister neither!" He readjusted his position and sat up straight, stroked his white beard once or twice, then continued,

"I was like that once, always lookin' and not knowin' what I was lookin' fer. Didn't find it 'til my old age, and what I found was right here, halfway up to heaven on the side of a mountain. I hope you find what it is you're lookin' for, Grant. Some men never do, and they roam aimlessly their entire lives. But you seem the stubborn type, so I think you'll end your search soon, sooner than you think."

Impressed with the old man's wisdom, Grant sat silently, watching the stream flow by rapidly just like the previous few days had. "This is a nice place, real nice. How do you get the gold out of the stream? Do you pan?"

"That's the easiest way I know of," Beuford claimed. "I once found a nugget the size of a chicken egg. It was more than I needed, and it was so perty I threw it back for some other time."

Grant shook his head but smiled. Old Beuford was something else. "I've been in gold and silver boomtowns all my life, and I never learned how to pan gold," Grant told Beuford, half ashamed to admit it.

"That's 'cause gold don't mean nothin' much to you," Beuford surmised. "I'll be glad to show you how, ain't nothin' to it."

The coat Beuford was wearing was a long leather coat with many pockets, some on the inside, from which he produced an old pie pan. "Always got my pan with me," he said as he slid from the boulder and stood gently to his feet. "Right over here I can usually scare up a nugget or two."

Another lesson began. "I gotta knock that top gravel away," the prospector said, leaning over the stream where the water was just a few inches deep. Using his big rough hands he dug some of the gravel out of the way. "Gold is heavy, and it sinks down some." Several inches down, the stream clouded from the disturbance.

"That should do it," Beuford said as he pulled up a handful of wet muck and dropped it into the pan. "Next we dip the pan in the water and tip it back and forth—that gets rid of the cloudy stuff so we can see what we got."

Grant watched, and sure enough the pan became free of the cloud and now contained big and little rocks.

Bringing the pan out of the water, Beuford picked out all of the big rocks and threw them back. "Now we're gettin' somewhere," he said as he dipped the pan into the stream and came up with more water. As he tipped the pan back and forth, many of the small rocks fell over the side along with some water. "You can be rough with it—won't hurt it none," he said, repeating the process. "Gold is heavy, so it'll stay in the bottom 'til you get enough cleared out of the way to get at it." He kept repeating the process until there was only what looked like very small rocks and black sand in the bottom of the pan. He scooped up just a little water and swirled it in the pan scattering the residue over the base of the pan, then handed it to Grant.

In the bright sunlight the gold was easy to see. Most of it was just tiny specks, but a few small pieces stood out. "That's incredible," Grant said with amazement.

"Spend a few hours down here and you can come up with more than you need," Beuford said, unimpressed. "Most of the time I prefer to find just one respectable nugget. That way I don't have to mess with all that small change there like you're holdin'."

"Can I try it?" Grant asked.

"Help yourself."

Imitating Beuford, Grant produced a nugget the size of a peanut on his first try. He held it up in the light, mesmerized by its beauty. "Would you look at that! It's beautiful! Mind if I keep it?"

"Be my guest," Beuford said, eager to be generous. "I'm beholdin' to you anyway for saving my life."

"I never thought of it that way," Grant said, panning another handful of streambed.

"Save that nugget for that special girl in your life. Tell her you found it yourself."

Grant thought about Mendy. Time seemed to stand still in Beuford's mountain paradise, and during those days Grant almost forgot his goals for the journey. This place seemed to be far away from all stress and worry. But as wonderful as it was, it wasn't perfect. And a new sound made that clear.

At first Grant wasn't sure what he was hearing. It sounded like a *huff-huff* above the noise of the stream. Curiously he glanced up one side of the stream and saw nothing. But when he glanced the other way he saw a huge bear galloping straight at him and Beuford.

Out of instinct, Grant grabbed his rifle and aimed the barrel in the direction of the bear that was now within ten feet. Beuford's big hand swatted the barrel down just as a shot rang out, sending the bullet into the ground right in front of them.

"Run!" Beuford shouted as he swung his bad leg into a crazy, stiff-legged gait. "Don't shoot—run!"

Grant didn't have to be told twice. Agile and young and strong, Grant was right behind Beuford as they both crashed through the underbrush back to the trail. Glancing behind him, Grant slowed down some and was glad to see that they weren't being pursued by the bear. Beuford, now winded, slowed down as well, wheezing through his missing teeth.

"I think that bear's eating our fish," Grant said, peering back but unable to see anything.

"I'm sure she is," Beuford agreed between breaths.

"What about our gold?" Grant asked.

"I doubt she'll eat that," Beuford said.

"Why didn't you let me shoot it?" Grant inquired, a little irritated. "I could have hit it right between the eyes, as close as it was."

Now completely stopped and out of danger, Beuford caught his wind while leaning against a tree, then gave Grant some more information about getting along in the wild. "First off, that would have been bad judgment. A shot between the eyes of a bear looking straight at you won't work. You see, the way their skull is built, that bullet would have just bounced off, leaving her with a terrible headache and awful mad at you, in which case she might have decided to tear you to pieces. Second, we should know the powerful smell of fish carries a long ways, and the sensitive nose of a hungry bear will bring her right to the fish. Last, old Maybelle only has one front tooth, and I reckon she needs those fish. Besides, we can always catch more."

"Maybelle?" Grant questioned.

"Yep. She lives in a cave not far from here and comes to visit from time to time," Beuford said as if he were talking about another human being.

Grant shook his head, dismayed, then looked back at Old Beuford. "If she's a pet, why'd we run?"

"I weren't sure how she'd take to you," Beuford answered, tickled at his prank. "And we ran cuz we was standin' between her and the fish."

～

The fall days passed at a leisurely pace, and the weather warmed back to its normal state for that time of the year. Grant continued with his practicing and lesson-learning until the snow melted away enough for him to leave.

"Can't say I ever had a better time," Grant said, extending his hand to Old Beuford. "Thanks for all the lessons. I'm sure they'll come in handy."

"I at least owed you that," Beuford said, taking Grant's hand in a manly shake. "You're a good man, Grant DeSpain. You watch out for yourself, and find that sister of yours so you can get on back to that girl I know you been thinkin' about."

"I will," Grant said as he swung into the saddle. Taking the trail out, Grant turned in his saddle and waved at the old man who was watching him leave. "What a fine old coot," Grant mumbled through a smile as he rode in and out of the shadows of the great spruce trees.

After a while it dawned on him—he'd never mentioned anything about Mendy or any girl or anything else along that line. How did Old Beuford know? Was the old man that sharp, or was it just painfully obvious that Grant was a young man in love?

~ 5 ~

The Western Slope

Taking Old Beuford's advice, Grant decided not to cross the Continental Divide just yet. Beuford showed him on his maps where it was easier traveling south, skirting the La Garita Mountains until he came to South Fork, where he could take the pass over to the other side, a branch of The Old Spanish Trail. Then he would have a long, somewhat flat ride over to Durango.

Navigating the big country was not as easy as Grant had thought it would be. It looked simple enough on the maps, but determining his exact position was generally no more than a guess. His best bet was to base his sense of direction on the fact that the sun swung over the southern hemisphere this time of year and the mountains were to the west. Information from strangers along the way was easy to obtain, for everybody seemed to like giving directions, although sometimes their directions were confusing.

The days blended into one another, and Grant pressed on, noting that the weather had settled into warm and sunny days and cool and clear nights. The mountains seemed to be able to generate weather systems that could vary radically from day to day, but for now Grant was content with the pleasant fall atmosphere.

~

Grant stumbled into the town of Bonanza by sheer accident.

Grant had heard about Bonanza before—a booming town of 5,000, he'd been told. But more importantly in many people's eyes, it had thirty-six saloons and seven dance halls, along with many fine restaurants, pool halls, drugstores, livery stables, and hotels. News of one famous mine, the Rawley, had reached Leadville, and Grant remembered reading about it.

But despite its high reputation and its glorious past, Grant saw before him now a town in which buildings leaned on each other for support, a town where the only thing that stirred up and down the street was a silent breeze. Bonanza had obviously seen better days and was now in decline. Riding slowly down the street now nearly void of people, Grant searched for a store where he could replenish his supplies. It felt eerie to see a place that had once thrived but was now decaying in silence, a town left behind for better prospects elsewhere.

One store remained, its façade weathered gray, the wooden front porch swaying under its own weight. Grant tied Mister and Peaches at a water trough where they gulped their fill. Glancing up and down the deserted street, he saw no signs of life except for two men wearing long black coats and wide-brimmed black hats. They stood down the street a ways in the shadows, watching him like two hungry wolves. Knocking the dirt from his boots, Grant stepped inside.

In the remnant of a general store a slim man sat perched on a stool behind the counter. His head was bald and shiny, his face round and supporting a full growth of whiskers. His apron, worn and tattered, hung sloppily. He smiled and came to life, a look of hopefulness in his dull eyes. "Howdy, friend, what can I help you with today? We don't get many folks in here anymore—pickin's are a little slim, but it might be I can take care of your needs anyway. Plan on stayin'? There's plenty of riches left in these hills, you know. Some say Bonanza is coming back into her own. I suspect she will. That's why I'm still here, me and the missus. Most folks left, which I guess you can see. Some say even the chipmunks left. Least, that's what the *Denver Times* reported. Me? I prefer to wait it out, although the missus don't always agree."

During the man's lengthy greeting, Grant searched the mostly barren shelves for canned goods but saw few. Obviously this man was starved for company, the way he kept rambling on.

"It ain't true, you know," the man said.

"What's not true?" Grant replied.

"The chipmunks. They didn't really leave. There's a lot of 'em left."

Grant nodded as he picked up two cans of peaches. "You have any bacon?"

"I'm sorry, sir," the man apologized. "The last pig was kilt some time ago. Might I interest you in some marmot? Some say they taste like pig."

"I don't think so," Grant said, repulsed by the idea of eating a rodent. "How about some salt?"

"Yes, sir! Salt I have. One block or two?"

"One will do," Grant said, reaching for his money. When he opened his wallet the storekeeper's eyes widened, and his mouth opened so far that Grant expected him to drool. Grant didn't understand the man's reaction since he didn't have that much money.

"What else can I get you, sir?" the bald man asked excitedly.

"That'll do," Grant answered, eager to leave the strange place.

"No whiskey? Tobacco?"

"No."

"There's women here too."

"No."

The man's face fell into dejection as he took the bills and made change from a dusty cash box that screamed of neglect. Grant took his things and walked outside, where the two men in black coats and hats were inspecting his animals. Setting his sack of goods on Peaches, Grant placed his foot in a stirrup and flung a leg over Mister.

"What's your hurry, mister? Where you goin'? We ain't even got acquainted yet," one of the men said forcefully. He had a thin, long face and a big black mustache. His partner looked much the same except he was a much bigger man with a hunger for fighting, judging by the scars on his face.

"Just passin' through," Grant said calmly.

"That's not very gentlemanlike!" the man taunted, his voice

whiny. "A gentleman would take a stake in a game of cards and have a drink with us. Ain't that right, Earl?"

The big man, Earl, just grunted, his expression irritated as if he'd slept in a cactus patch.

"No thanks," Grant said soberly.

The small man grabbed Mister's reins as Grant tried to pull away. His other hand shoved his long coat back and rested on a holstered pistol. "I said stay and have a drink!"

Grant pulled out his Winchester rifle and pointed it in the man's face, all in one quick and confident motion. "Drop that pistol in the trough. You too, Earl. Now!"

The two hesitated, wondering how Grant got the drop on them, wondering if they were good enough to draw their guns before he could fire. The man turned Mister's reins loose and swallowed hard, his Adam's apple bouncing in his skinny throat. His hand sat limply on the pistol at his side, but the muzzle of the Winchester was too close to risk making a move. The two slowly removed their pistols, dropped them in the wooden tank, and stared at Grant with intense hatred.

"That's better," Grant said as he pointed the rifle toward the sky. He backed Mister away a few yards, then turned the horse on his heels and galloped out. Peaches ran along behind hee-hawing in protest.

Once out of town, away from his first serious confrontation, Grant began to shake, and his stomach felt queasy. After a while he got over it, thankful he hadn't grown jittery in front of the desperate roughnecks. Old Beuford had been right—it would be a long, hard road and Grant would likely encounter more trouble before his journey ended.

∽

In the days to come the trail south dragged through a long and open mountain valley that resembled high, flat prairie lands. The mountains to the west were distant and hazy. Grant was beginning to wonder if he'd taken the wrong trail, wondering if it would ever turn back west. But finally it did, following the Rio Grande Canal to the Rio Grande River and then on to South Fork. A warm wind off the flat land brought the smells of a dying summer—sunburnt grass and dry dust. Herds of pronghorns played nearby but were careful to stay out of range of the Winchester. Mister dropped his head and scooped a mouthful of grass at every chance, for once content with being on the open flats and being able to see all around him for a safe distance. The days were lazy, and the riding was easy, but that would change soon.

With the San Juans rising before him, Grant took the long and steep rise out of South Fork, climbing at a steady rate. The rutted road was nasty and treacherous, winding around rock slides and steep cliffs, crossing over streams and falls slick with wet stones and mud. Sometimes Grant found himself leaning with all of his weight in one stirrup, leaning toward the safety of the earthen side of the trail, for on the other side, far below, lay a vast openness dropping to what seemed like a miniature world of green valleys and rivers.

The temperature steadily dropped, and the nights were freezing as Grant neared an altitude over 10,000 feet. He was steadily climbing, being especially careful with his animals and watching Mister's every step. The progress was slow and the rider cautious; few passed him on the trail. It was nearing the time of year when most travelers wouldn't take a chance over such a high mountain pass, for a blizzard could strand a man until he starved or even froze, not to be discovered until the following year after the snows melted.

Grant finally made it safely to the summit—the Continental Divide in the glorious San Juan Mountains. From there, where pockets of snow sat dirty white in the shade, snows from previous winters, Grant could see seemingly forever in all directions. The many jagged and massive peaks, some bare and some covered with perpetual snowcaps, were so big and far-reaching that Grant was nearly overcome with the grandeur of it all. The thin, dry, cool air chapped his lips and reddened his cheeks.

This was the top of the world, where all of the rivers began, where mountains touched the sky, where God must have had most of His fun in creating the lands of the earth, the young man thought to himself. Grant sat still on his horse, trying his best to take it all in, to make a picture in his mind so he would remember it forever. Yes, this was God's country, big and bold and full of the Lord's presence and power. Some thought God was mean and vindictive, but in this great mountain range God played and painted and decorated in His own delightful way. Here He had purposely created beauty to astonish and bewilder the vanity of the humanity He had created. This was the kind of place where a man could get lost and not give a hoot, but just live off the land and be happy, like Old Beuford was doing, except these mountains were even bigger and prettier. It was the most majestic sight Grant had ever seen.

That night he camped at the timberline and built a nice fire to ward off the bone-chilling cold. A can of hot beans and venison jerky made a pleasant meal. The night was crystal-clear, and the campfire died down to embers when he awakened to the long call of a wolf emanating from deep shadows far below. From the other direction another wolf sang its lonesome song.

Sitting up, Grant threw back his heavy blanket and pulled his Winchester close to him. The rifle, fully loaded, felt good in his hands, the safety of blazing power right at his fingertips. He hadn't forgotten Old Beuford's teachings, practicing frequently. At times like this he realized the importance of knowing where his bullets would fly without having any light but starlight.

As the treetops made a silhouette against a starlit sky, Grant glanced upward into the vast space above. It was the biggest sky he had ever seen, with a parade of stars across the center. Other stars shone brilliantly, twinkling with hues of red and blue, each in its own brilliance, all of them appearing closer than he ever remembered seeing them before. He almost felt as if he were no longer viewing the sky from below but now sat among the heavenly bodies themselves.

At that exalted moment it occurred to Grant that God had been trying to reach him, trying to show him the way, for the sights of the recent day and that night seemed almost supernatural. He felt like he was part of what he saw, the moonless sky revealing the universe in incredible brightness.

Mister shuffled his hobbled feet nearby, sensing that Grant was awake, and neighed as if he too felt a supernatural quality in the night sky. Grant noted the black shadows of Mister and Peaches, then lifted his face back to the heavens above.

"What is You want of me?" Grant asked in a calm voice. He waited but heard nothing. The air was still and cold and fresh in the high, dry altitude. "I'm no preacher, You know. I believe in the Bible, but I can't go around preaching—not me, Lord. I'm not good at talking like that."

A streak brightened the northern sky, leaving its trail shimmering white for only a brief second, the long and graceful arc stretching before Grant's eyes in a wondrous spectacle unlike any he had ever witnessed before. Grant had an idea of what God was trying to tell him. Like the falling star, he would teach others by his example—not by words, but by actions.

"Of course," Grant mumbled. It was as if God had laid a hand on him, light as a feather. Something of His patience and calmness passed into Grant, who sat with his knees up and his arms crossed over them, the rifle now lying beside him, forgotten.

"I'll do what I can," Grant said as he gazed into the seemingly endless universe, proud that God had called him to cherish the true Word of God and to do his best to show others the way.

Gathering his blanket back around him, Grant rested peacefully, relishing the night with its mystical serenity and a spiritual warmth that filled his very soul.

The next morning the sun came forth boldly, accompanied by a spectacular show of colors. The blinding resplendence came from the mountain range far to the east, the light of a new day rising above the horizon like a miracle from on high. It was a new beginning for Grant—not just a new day but a new life, one that he knew with certainty had a special purpose. There were no doubts in his mind that he had experienced a life-transforming encounter with the one true God.

∽

The Old Spanish Trail wound down wildly for many curving miles until it leveled off in a valley, at the edge of which Grant encountered a herd of elk. Two bulls bugled, competing with each other, their calls echoing through the hills as the cows looked on. Each had a rack of antlers that spread far over his back, his head held upward as the shrill sound of the call came forth. Grant watched for a while in amazement at the beauty of the wild creatures, each as large as a horse, each prepared to defend his dominance. Mister took a genuine interest as well, his furry ears alert, his head held high, his muscles tense.

Moving on, Grant made his way at a steady pace with Peaches prancing along behind. He had made it to the Western Slope, where the atmosphere was vastly different from what he was used to, where the air was thinner and riper with the wildness of the outdoors, where the sun shone warmer and the wind carried scents of sage and pine. The San Juans were by far the greatest mountains he had ever seen, their peaks jagged and massive, regal mountains that could be seen for a hundred miles, their outline purple against a cavernous and shockingly blue sky.

According to his map, the town that lay just ahead was Pagosa Springs, where hot sulfur springs filled the air with a rotten egg smell that was already evident to Grant. With plenty of daylight left, he casually rode through the town, gazing at the people who were looking curiously at the wanderer. Pagosa Springs had once been the home of the Ute tribe, who named the springs "Pagosah" ("healing waters"). Much later the U.S. Army came and established Fort Lewis to control the Utes, bringing an influx of white settlers—miners, tradesmen, and businessmen. But the railroads neglected Pagosa Springs, and the army camp moved west to the banks of the La Plata River, as did most of the settlers, leaving the small town for travelers and those seeking the healing waters. It seemed to be a calm and settled town, lacking the craziness associated with boomtowns.

The road west traveled up and down through a thick pine forest and rock cliffs. It was not uncommon to see a huge boulder sitting where it appeared no boulders should be. Grant was finding his travels intriguing, constantly changing from one kind of terrain to another, the trail sometimes wide and well used and at other times hard to determine. Many a traveler used the road Grant was on now, the wagon ruts deep and passersby frequent.

Afternoon settled in as the sun lazily approached the treetops to the west. Grant had given little thought to making camp just yet, thoughts of the night before still occupying his mind.

Suddenly two long-bearded men stepped out of the thickets into the road right in front of Grant, each pointing a rifle at the rider. One shouted, "This is a holdup!"

Startled, Mister reared, giving Grant the brief second he needed to slide his rifle out and lever a round into the chamber. When Mister's feet came back down, Grant reined him to the side and held his rifle on the two men holding rifles on him. A careful look at the two men revealed they were not typical highwaymen; their drawn faces revealed their desperation, and Grant knew that desperation leads men to do things they wouldn't normally do. Their clothes were tattered and their hats ragged, and Grant noticed the scared look in their eyes and the nervous way they handled their rifles.

"Drop it, mister. There's two of us and one of you," one of the robbers said.

Grant fired a shot into the ground at the feet of one of the robbers, sending dirt and debris up into his face, then quickly fired another round sending the other man's hat flying in the air. Both men screamed in fear as they dove for the woods. That confirmed to Grant that these men were not outlaws by profession. They were just scared and probably broke and out of sorts with the world, like so many after arriving in the mountains where they expected to find instant riches.

That thought gave Grant an idea. Having seen a multitude of deer tracks back just a ways, he doubled back and found the deer trail leading off into the woods. He rode Mister into the forest, pulling Peaches along, until he came to an ideal spot to tie his animals and let them graze. Following the trail a little further, he found a big opening beside a running stream, the stream's banks covered with the hoofprints of deer. He hid and waited.

The wait was short, for deer were plentiful in the area, and soon Grant shot a big buck. Doing just like Beuford had done, Grant made short work of field dressing the kill, went back and got Mister and Peaches, loaded the deer, and made his way back to the trail. Light was growing scarce when he found the place where the men had tried to hold him up. Their trail through the woods was easier to follow than the deer trail, and in a short time their camp sprawled out before him. Grant saw dilapidated wagons with busted wheels and languid women and children with no shoes on their feet.

Grant rode in so quietly and easily that at first no one even noticed him, but suddenly the group panicked with fear, calling to one another that a stranger had entered the camp. Two men with long beards appeared, one holding a rifle, the other an ax—the same two men who had attempted to rob Grant.

"I brought you something to eat," Grant said as he let the big deer fall to the ground.

Mouths fell open as the two hurried forward and squatted down to inspect the animal. "This here's a fresh kill, Rupert," one man said excitedly.

The other man stood and took a better look at Grant. "Say, ain't you . . . ? Why'd you do this, mister, after what we tried to do to you?"

"Let's just say that because of a recent experience I look at things a little differently," Grant replied.

Women and children curiously came closer, their big eyes staring hungrily at the deer. The other man came to his feet, waved an arm, and ordered the women to get to work on the deer and make supper with the gift. In an instant the starving children and feeble women were on the carcass like flies. The man turned his attention back to Grant. "We'd kill our own, but we ain't got no bullets," he said meekly. "There weren't no bullets in our guns when we tried to rob you either. Mister, we're powerful sorry. It's about dark—break bread and stay the night here with us, please."

Grant decided that since he was so tired, and since he had no fear of these people, he would accept their invitation. While enjoying a tasty meal around the campfire, Grant heard the same story he'd heard so often before, a tale of disappointed expectations told by disheartened people with gaunt, hollow-eyed faces. They had come from farming country back east, expecting easy money and easy living in the West where gold and silver were certainly abundant. They had sold everything and invested it all in the trip, jeopardizing everything they owned and even their lives. It hadn't taken long before all was depleted, and not knowing how to get along in the West, they soon became stranded and desperate. It was a sad story of despair brought on by hunger, greed, and a sense of adventure that had led only to squandered dreams and a sense of hopelessness.

The next morning Grant gave the men plenty of cartridges and went on his way. "Now don't rob anyone with these bullets," he urged. "That would be wrong. And besides, you're not very good at that."

"Oh, we won't do that—not never again!" Rupert said. "You scared us away from any such notions."

Traveling on, Grant felt good about helping those less fortunate than himself. He had explained to them that he was no preacher, but a servant of God just the same. He was glad he'd been a blessing to the poor, and they had been thankful.

~

Grant pushed westward on The Old Trail, passing Chimney Rock, two pinnacles of tall rock that resembled chimneys. The Anasazi Indians, or "The Ancient Ones," had had a thriving civilization there almost a thousand years earlier, leaving intriguing evidence of their presence in the form of ceremonial structures called kivas and pueblo-like residences.

The days rolled along like the long and rolling hills Grant encountered after descending the last mountains. And yet before him spread the long and majestic range of the southern La Platas, mountains that drew closer ever so slowly.

The days on the trail had worn Grant down at first, but eventually he became stronger, growing used to the ways of living in the outdoors and taking meals when he could take them. Shaving had become a nuisance since at times water was scarce and a face chapped from biting winds found no pleasure in a cold, steel razor. In time the short, red beard grew full and thick and shielded his face from the wind and the cold. His green eyes now shone brilliant from a sun-darkened face; his shoulders, arms, and back were stronger than ever from the rugged work of riding the high-country trail.

His spirit renewed, his senses sharpened, his shooting skills finely honed, his confidence full, and his spirit high, he was a different man than the one who had left Leadville what seemed like ages ago. Lean and muscular in the saddle, he felt a new harmony with the wild and beautiful country of Colorado. Just ahead the La Plata Mountains grew larger before him, now clear in his sight, only a day's ride away. He hoped he would find Abby in Durango.

Durango

The town of Durango actually owed its existence to the railroad. Denver & Rio Grande officials originally intended to extend the line to Silverton from Animas City, but the residents of Animas City asked too much for the land the railroad would need. So Denver & Rio Grande executives smartly decided to bypass Animas City and establish their own town to the south. After a Denver & Rio Grande director named Alexander Hunt returned from a trip to the Mexican city of Durango, he chose that name for the new settlement. Once Durango was established, many of the townsfolk of Animas City moved there, realizing the business profits the railroad would certainly bring with it.

Riding into town, Grant quickly saw that Durango was a congested place on the La Plata River with all the modern conveniences of a fully functional town. A huge chimney bellowing smoke was the site of the San Juan and New York Mining and Smelter Company. A streetcar busily clanged its way up and down Main Street, giving Mister a scare. The railroad station was at the east end of Main, grand in appearance, but not as grand as the new hotel further west on Main Street, the Strater.

The Strater Hotel was a sight to behold, and as Grant rode by he stared at its architecture, which combined Renaissance, Italianate, and Romanesque styles. He had to admit Durango was one of the best looking little towns he had ever seen, and the scenery around it was just as pleasant.

Knowing he had to take care of first things first, Grant decided to find a livery for his animals. "Give them something good to eat," he said to the blond-haired boy at the livery. "Those animals just made a long trip, and they deserve it."

"I got some sweet grain," the young boy said in his high-pitched voice.

"That'll do fine. Don't give them too much though. Say, where's a good place to stay and get cleaned up?" Grant questioned as he unpacked his horse and mule.

"Gonna be stayin' long?" the boy asked, his eyes curiously searching Grant, who definitely did not look like the typical customer. He had the look of a man on the cover of a dime novel. Maybe he was even an outlaw.

"I might," Grant answered, not looking at the boy.

"There's a boarding house on Main, a big one. I'm sure you can get a room and meals there—and the food is good too."

"Thanks," Grant said. "Please put these things away for me," he said, indicating the saddle and packs. He carried his personal items in a pack thrown over his left shoulder, carrying his Winchester in his right hand.

The stable boy watched him leave, knowing the grit in a man like that was something to be admired. The way the stranger walked, the way he carried that rifle, the way he carried himself—the boy was sure he must be somebody important.

Walking down Main, Grant could see that Durango was a hub of activity. He heard the train whistle and wondered if Abby had walked through that very station. He'd get settled in and get something to eat, then scout about and ask some questions, using the photograph he had so carefully protected all along the way.

～

Eager for information, Grant began stopping people in the busy streets and showing them the photograph, ducking into stores and showing store owners the picture, but everywhere he went he got the same response. A sad shake of the head indicating they had not seen this woman, or a pleasant, "I'm sorry."

After sending a telegram to Leadville to tell his mother he had arrived in Durango and had begun his search, Grant continued walking through the town questioning almost everyone he came in contact with, but nobody had seen the missing woman. Even no one at the train station recalled seeing Abby, and he asked almost everyone who worked there.

"We get a lot of people through here," a conductor said while eating lunch on a station bench. "Just because nobody noticed her doesn't mean she didn't come through." He wiped his mouth gingerly, then tried to encourage Grant. "You ought to check the hotels and boarding houses. She had to stay somewhere if she was here."

"I already tried that," Grant said, growing discouraged. What if Abby had never come to Durango and the entire trip was a wild-goose chase? Yet he couldn't stop searching. But he was running low on money too, so he decided to find a job to replenish his funds.

Durango was the home of several newspapers, and Grant got a job at the first one he walked into, *The Durango Herald*.

"Can you read?" asked a man wearing glasses and having short gray hair and gray sideburns.

"Yeah, I can read."

"Can you write?" the man asked, his bushy gray eyebrows rising at the prospect.

"Yes, I can write . . ." Grant was anxious to tell the man he'd been associated with newspapers all of his life, but the man was too quick for him.

"You're hired. Can you start right now?"

"Uh, I guess so," Grant answered.

"Good! Take that stack of newspapers over there," he said, pointing, "put them in that canvas bag, then take them to these places and leave a pile at each." He handed Grant a list, mostly the names and addresses of businesses.

"All right. Say, what does this job pay?"

"Enough to keep you honest," the man replied.

"What's your name?"

"Sorry, I get in too much of a hurry sometimes. My name's Henry Pitts. I don't own the paper, but I run the show. We all do everything around here and jump on a news story like firemen on a fire. Hang around, you might get the knack of it; it kind of gets in your blood."

Grant just smiled. Grabbing the canvas bag, he filled it with newspapers and slung the shoulder strap over his beefy shoulder.

"That should keep you busy for a while. When you get back, there's plenty to do around here." He smiled at Grant, his eyes creased with crow's-feet.

Delivering the papers took Grant to places he hadn't been to yet, and at each place he not only delivered the papers but showed Abby's picture. Unfortunately, most people quickly answered they hadn't seen her, except for one man who studied the photograph for a long time. He was a heavy-set man wearing a very expensive black coat, tie, and derby. His hair was black and slicked down neatly on the sides, his clean-shaven face pudgy and round.

"You know, I could swear I have." His forehead wrinkled into a frown as he thought and thought. "A young lady this pretty would be hard to miss, but I can't seem to place when and where it was I saw her."

"Was it in Durango?" Grant asked.

"I'm sure it was. By the way, I'm the mayor here."

"Oh," Grant mumbled in surprise. "Well, thanks for your help. If you remember anything more, I'm working at *The Durango Herald*."

"Yes indeed," the mayor said. "Good luck with your search."

∽

As the days passed, Grant went from sweeping floors and cleaning equipment to setting type for the newspaper, even pointing out corrections that articles needed.

"My word!" Henry said, astonished. "How long have you been doing this kind of work?"

"Ever since I can remember," Grant replied, proud of his newspaper skills. "First in Virginia City, Nevada, at *The Miner's News*, then in Black Hawk and Central City with *The Advertiser*, then in Leadville with *Western Magazine*."

"Your credentials sound better than mine!" Henry said playfully. "You must have started mighty young."

"I did," Grant replied. "Newspaper business has been in the family ever since I can remember."

"I would have taken you for a man of the outdoors, a trapper maybe. No, let's see . . . When you first walked in, I thought you might be a rancher—that's it, a rancher. A strapping young man like yourself, dressed like you were, I never would have guessed you were so, ah, let's see, literate. Yes, that's it, literate!" Henry remarked with enthusiasm. "Goes to show you can't judge a man by his looks."

"I suppose not," Grant agreed.

"In that case, I think you deserve better than starting pay. Perhaps you can show me a thing or two."

"Perhaps," Grant answered, reflecting back on the modern ways and equipment of *Western Magazine*.

Days turned into weeks and the onset of fall brought Durango and the surrounding hills into flaming colors like Grant had never seen. The mountains were bright yellows, golds, oranges, and reds, as if someone had gone wild with a paintbrush and painted the setting to bring the mountains to life in a brilliant kind of way. It was a wonderful sight, like viewing a beautiful flower. Grant tried to look at the panorama as often as he could, for he knew it would soon end.

Work at *The Durango Herald* proved to be interesting and joyful. The others there liked Grant's company and his stories of the wild boomtowns he was raised in, especially the story of his family striking it rich. The job was easy, but challenging enough to keep him busy.

"You're a fine young man, Grant, and a hard worker!" Henry stated one day in the middle of the afternoon. "There's something I want to talk to you about—business, that is—but not here. How about we discuss this over dinner at the Strater Hotel tonight? I think you'll find my offer interesting."

"The Strater?" Grant remarked with bright eyes. "That's a little rich for newspaper blood, don't you think?"

"Nonsense! We'll have a fine time," Henry reassured Grant.

That evening the two men sat in a crowded dining room, Grant and Henry both enjoying tea, for Henry did not drink alcohol either. The place was lavish, with white tablecloths and hand-carved trim, royal drapes, and fine silver.

"What I propose," Henry began, wasting no time, "is to offer you a real position with this newspaper. This town is growing fast, and so is the newspaper. With all your experience from raw boomtowns, you can help us report on the towns north of here where the boom is still going—places like Animas Forks, Silverton, Lake City, Ouray, and a new discovery in Creede. I'm sure you've seen the towns like them before."

"Oh, yes," Grant said. "As a matter of fact, I know such a phenomenon very well. Ever since we left New Orleans, I've been right in the middle of the gold and silver rush."

"Splendid!" Henry said, growing more excited, his expression full of anticipation.

Their waitress came to the table, a pretty young lady with a pleasant smile, her dark hair up. "You gents must be thirsty. Would you like some more tea before you order?"

"Yes," Grant and Henry answered together.

"With your background and knowledge of the new machinery your family has in Leadville, I'm sure you can go far with this newspaper. We've been needing a man like you, somebody with some gumption," Henry continued enthusiastically.

"There's more to it, I'm afraid to say," Grant said, pulling the photograph of Abby from his pocket. "This is my sister Abby. She ran off from Leadville thinking she was in love and followed a man here. At least that's what the information I have suggests. The problem is, the character of the man she followed is questionable. I have my doubts he can look after her, and I know what kind of trouble she could get into. She's too stubborn to admit she may have made a mistake and probably too embarrassed to contact any of our family."

"I see," Henry said, disappointed, his ego deflated. "So you'll be moving on in search for her?"

"Possibly. So far I can't find anyone who knows she was here for certain," Grant said with some regret. "It's like I'm looking for a ghost."

"Yes," Henry agreed, his smile gone. "I was hoping you could stay. A man like you could end up owning the *Herald*, and that could lead to much bigger things, politics even!" He continued looking at the picture. "Your sister is very pretty."

The waitress returned and poured more tea into the empty glasses. As she stood over Henry, her big brown eyes drifted to the photograph.

"That's Abby!" she said happily. "You know her?"

Henry shrugged his shoulders and handed the picture back to Grant. "I think you just hit the strike you were looking for."

"Do you?" Grant questioned, rising in his seat with expectation.

"Sure, I do," she said. "Abby stayed here for weeks, took all her meals here. We did some things together—shopping and so on, you know. How do you know her?"

"I'm her brother."

"Is something wrong?"

"Maybe, maybe not," Grant said, giving this girl his strict attention. "I need to find her, to talk to her, that's all. It's important. Do you know where she went?"

"Why, sure. She went to Silverton some time back. Took the train."

"God bless you," Grant said, feeling great relief. "I've come a long ways and so far I've found out nothing—until now."

"Well," she said cheerfully, "I get off shortly. We could talk."

"I'd like that," Grant said, smiling.

As the girl walked away, Henry looked at Grant with a look of complete astonishment, as if he'd found a great fortune and had been sentenced to prison at the same time. "This has to be one of the most remarkable evenings I've ever spent. First I'm excited about making you a great offer, then disappointed by your answer, then brought to a thrilling high point by what I just witnessed. I'm simply amazed. Tell me, is it always like this for you? I mean, do things like this happen frequently?"

The smile on Grant's face showed genuine happiness. "I don't recall life ever having been too dull, if that's what you mean. But come to think of it, yes, interesting things like this happen all the time, like some creative author was writing my life."

"I have to tell you—it's been most enjoyable having you around," Henry complimented. "As for that pretty waitress, you watch out. I don't think she only wants to talk about your sister."

"What do you think she wants to talk about?" Grant asked seriously before he gave way to a smile.

Henry shook his head and smiled as well. "I suppose you'll be leaving for Silverton."

"Just as soon as I can," Grant admitted.

After dinner, Grant parted with Henry, wishing him a good evening, and waited for the pretty young waitress in the lobby. She soon came along, wearing a different dress and having rearranged her hair so it hung down in the back, dangling over her shoulders. Her big brown eyes were quite becoming, set in an oval face with a finely chiseled nose, her mouth always smiling. "My name's Kate." She extended her hand, and Grant took it.

"I'm Grant."

"Yes, I know. Abby spoke of you. She thinks very highly of you."

"Not highly enough to tell me she was running off."

Kate laughed. "You men just don't understand, do you? Abby couldn't tell you or anyone else she was running off because she knew you would disapprove and try to stop her. That's not very complicated."

Turning his head aside, Grant realized this was true, though he hated to admit it. "How was she? Is she doing all right?"

"A little bored maybe, waiting for her man to send for her."

"Send for her?"

"Yes. She arrived here, and he had paid for her room and meals in advance, said he would be in touch, that he was on to something and had to move on. She was here for weeks, not knowing what to do. I think she began to worry." Kate was caressing Grant's hand now.

"What happened next?" Grant asked, noticing what Kate was up to.

"Well, she got this letter with a train ticket to Silverton and some money in it. She was very happy."

"How long ago?"

"It's been several weeks now." Kate moved her face closer. "I suppose you'll be off for Silverton."

"Yes, early tomorrow," Grant said, his mind occupied with plans for getting his things together.

Pulling her hand back, Kate's expression revealed her disappointment. It wasn't often she met a man she cared for; so many were occupied with selfish ambitions or crazy notions of striking it rich. Grant was different. He had an inner strength she was attracted to immediately, and now he was going to get away before she even had a chance. "Well, good luck." She paused, letting her eyes drift off and then looked at him again. "If you ever come back this way . . ."

"I'll be sure and look you up," Grant said politely. "Thanks for your help. Without you I wouldn't have known where Abby went."

Turning to leave, Grant moved out the front door and closed it gently behind him. The Strater was the only hotel he hadn't checked to see if anyone knew of Abby. He thought it was far too elegant for his sister to have stayed at, a mistake he wouldn't make again.

As for Kate, she was very nice and an attractive woman, the kind who simply wanted a decent man and probably a family, the kind of woman who was lonely and had inviting eyes. But Grant's heart was with Mendy, and he wondered how she was doing, if she thought of him at all—she was so far away.

⁓

The next morning Grant had a lot to do but managed it in a reasonable time and by mid-morning was riding north. Mister and Peaches, both feeling rested and well-fed, were obviously glad to be outdoors and on the trail again. The sun had made the morning warm and pleasant as Grant rode past a long, steep cliff that shot straight up from the ground to his left. The strata in the rock wall were slanted and colorful, as if a piece of earth had been pushed upward to reveal an artistic cross section of what lay below. Off to his right black smoke rolled into the sky as a train whistled by, filling the valley with its musical signal. Heavy freight wagons pulled by mule teams carried supplies in both directions, squeaking and grinding, mingling with lighter buckboards driven by farmers transporting their goods. In the Animas River Valley, wide and beautiful, long and flat, farmers had settled to plant their hopes and chase their dreams.

Mining had become the primary industry, as it had in so many places in the Rockies, but it took more than miners to make a community. Businessmen brought in and sold food, clothes, and tools, and lumberjacks cut trees for the mining operations that required lumber and logs in great quantity. A need for lumber to build stores, homes, and implements was supplied by those who invested in sawmill operations. Grant had noticed at least three sawmills along the busy road, all with their thumping steam engines and whining saw blades, making boards for a new world.

Grant estimated the trip to Silverton to be around forty-five miles and had no intention of trying to make it in one day, knowing how foolhardy it would be to arrive in a boomtown at night. The day was enjoyable, the Animas Canyon being easy traveling for horse and rider under a pleasant sun with only a few clouds smeared lightly into the deep blue of the big sky.

Stopping that afternoon, Grant camped on the River of Lost Souls. Deciding to catch some fish, with a great deal of patience he worked the rig Beuford had set him up with. At first he had no luck, but as the sun lowered, he caught two trout. In a camp snuggled in a thick stand of spruce trees, he pan-fried the fish and had his fill. The fresh river trout tasted as good as any delicacy in even the finest restaurants.

Making sure Mister and Peaches were unloaded and secured properly, Grant returned to the campfire and prepared for the evening, knowing cold nights were part of living in the higher elevations. He arranged a nice pile of sticks and branches beside him to toss on the fire as needed. Resting back on an elbow under a heavy blanket, he checked his rifle next to him to make sure everything was in order. The high-mountain woods grew dark as the sounds of night birds came over the treetops. The mint-like smell of spruce freshened the air, and the flowing river nearby sang its constant song.

Glancing up, Grant could see the black trees folded over and around him, and through an opening in the treetops the stars gleamed brightly. Again he felt the exhilarating presence of an all-powerful Maker. In this he felt a comfort like no other, an appreciation for life, the certainty of faith.

Just before dropping into a deep and restful sleep, Grant let his thoughts turn to Mendy, the wonderful and pretty girl he was sure he loved. He imagined her as his own, imagined them living together every day for the rest of their lives, imagined the children they would raise, imagined a love so great no man could defeat it or take it away—all special gifts from a loving God. And in all this he found great happiness.

～

By 1890 Silverton was a sprawling municipality, overlooked by Sultan Mountain, which rose mightily over the town. Residents of the many smaller nearby towns had moved to Silverton, now a railroad junction for the many mines and mills of the surrounding valleys. It was a bustling place where everyone claimed to own a mining stake or at least a piece of one. The talk always centered on new strikes, bigger, richer, and wider veins of precious metal, and grand plans of what to do with the wealth that would follow.

As always, the lure of money attracted all kinds of people, and many decided Silverton would not be outdone, building places like the Grand Imperial Hotel featuring all-night balls and exotic foods in expensive French restaurants. With money pouring from the surrounding mountains, the mills and businesses flourished, and the elite set out to make Silverton famous.

But there was another side as well, like the notorious Blair Street, open every hour of the day and night every day of the year to satisfy miners who came down off the hill. The two-block-long area was lined with nearly forty saloons, gambling houses, and dance halls. The red-light district was also located here, and more than sixty girls worked the parlor houses or walked the streets. Silverton did have one rule—the women of the evening did not venture uptown, and the daughters and wives of the men of the town did not venture to Blair Street.

Grant rode in from the south, following the train tracks right up to the train station on Blair Street. He was hungry and tired, but before he could dismount, he heard the crack of gunfire and the screams of frightened women. Glancing down the street, he saw a crowd huddled around a man lying in the dust. Soon the man was dragged away, and it appeared things were back to normal, business as usual.

Grant realized this was the kind of town where he would always need to have his rifle with him, where he would have to be cautious and sleep light, where it would be difficult to track down Abby.

PART TWO

DESPERATION

Chasing Dreams

The Strater Hotel in Durango was nice, very nice, and Abby DeSpain loved the luxuriant atmosphere. This was the kind of life she was meant for, a life of being wealthy and affluent and worrying about things like what to wear and where to eat. She had lived the opulent life at an earlier age and tasted its glorious obsessions, but all too quickly it had been taken away. Since then she'd been determined to regain what had been lost, and her hopes for this dream were renewed in a man named Billy Rogers.

He'd blown into her life like the wind and swept her heart up in a whirlwind of love. Billy could persuade even the shrewdest businessmen to invest in a venture, for he had a gift with words. The friendly swagger and ever-present smile he used so wisely pushed him up the ladder of success. Always dressed in the nicest attire, enhancing his youthful and handsome face, he could buy a kingdom with a smile. He had a friendly and likable face, an honest countenance that assured everyone he would never lie. He was the kind of man who would go far, maybe even in politics; perhaps someday he would be a governor or maybe even the President of the United States. That was how Abby saw Billy Rogers, the love of her life.

Unfortunately, not everyone agreed with Abby's views of her new love, especially Jennifer, Grant, and Jason, who had learned the hard way about questionable characters and their ways.

"He's likable all right," Grant had said mildly. "I'd say he's good at what he does, very good!"

Sensing a dislike, Abby questioned, "But you don't like him, do you?"

"I didn't say that," Grant said. "I like him just fine. I just don't trust him."

"What's that supposed to mean?" Abby stormed.

"I don't know," Grant said. "It's just a feeling."

They had all been that way, warning her and telling her to be careful, saying men like that could talk a goat out of its horns.

Abby's heart had made the ruling decision when Billy told her of his grand speculations in the new boomtowns. He would have to hurry off to see about his investments and would send for her as soon as possible. They would be rich and have a big and wonderful wedding—that was the plan.

Having no doubts, Abby had patiently waited for word from him, determined to show the rest of the family how wrong they were. She would leave without a word and go do as she wished until she was ready to reveal her wealthy and wonderful life to the skeptics. Billy was the only man who ever showed her the courtesy of respect and promised her the world she wanted.

When the money and the train ticket came, Abby had stolen silently away. It was a dream come true; she had found true love.

The train ride was long and torturous until it finally ended up in Durango. Dirty, dusty, and tired, Abby's spirits lifted in anticipation of seeing Billy standing on the platform waiting for her, something she'd pictured in her mind a thousand times, the coming together of two lovers who had been separated. But he wasn't there, and in his place a porter led her to the Strater Hotel where she opened the letter he had left her.

My Dearest Abby,

I'm sorry I couldn't meet you, but the smell of silver has called, and there are great riches to be had. I must follow my instincts and make the fortune you deserve. In the meantime I have provided you with room and board at the best place in town. I miss you and miss seeing your lovely face more than ever, my darling.

Love,
Billy

Abby found the contents of the letter thrilling, deeply touching her emotions. Only Billy could do that with his kind words and considerate ways. She missed him so and wanted to see him badly; waiting was so hard. But she would do anything for Billy and decided to make her visit pleasant until he sent word.

When her trunks arrived, Abby removed the contents, including her dusty clothes, and hung everything up. She would have to get her clothes cleaned and take a bath as soon as possible in order to maintain the dignity of the well-to-do. Then she would go downstairs to the restaurant and have dinner. Certainly this kind of waiting could not be too hard.

Evening came, and during an elegant meal Abby met another pretty girl, her waitress, Kate.

"You're from Leadville?" Kate asked curiously. "I hear that's a beautiful place."

"Depends on where you're looking from," Abby informed her. "It's a good place to be if you're wealthy."

Kate smiled. "Must be nice to be wealthy like yourself—stay in the nice places, buy nice clothes like you're wearing."

Abby smiled at Kate's misconception. "Fact is, I don't have much, yet. But my fiancé sent for me, and he's going to be rich."

"Oh? Where is he now?" Kate questioned, wishing she too had a man with a future.

"He was supposed to meet me here, but he said he had pressing engagements in some boomtown north of here," Abby bragged, her eyes dreamy like a girl in love. "What boomtown is north of here? Do you know?"

Kate laughed an honest laugh. "Honey, there must be one every twenty feet, the way I hear it. Mines everywhere and men galore, all looking for the same things—silver, whiskey, and women."

"I know what you mean. I've lived in boomtowns all my life, and you're right. But Billy's different. He's trying to establish something permanent so we won't have to worry when we get married, so we can travel and enjoy life." Abby's dream showed in her glowing face.

"So how long will you be staying here?" Kate asked, wanting to see more of Abby.

"I'm not sure right now—until I hear from Billy, I guess."

"I only work evenings," Kate began. "During the days I'm free. We could do some things together. There are some nice stores here in Durango—we could go shopping."

"That sounds like fun," Abby said, happy to have a friend to show her around.

"I'll look you up tomorrow," Kate said. "It's more fun to go around with a friend than by yourself."

"I'll be expecting you." Abby smiled politely.

⁓

The next day was typical of Durango fall weather—perfectly beautiful and warm and dry. The day had started off well when a knock came at Abby's door—a porter with coffee and coffee cake, a daily order Billy Rogers had left with the hotel. She drank from a silver coffee cup and ate from a silver platter decorated with white lacy napkins. The coffee cake was an apple strudel as good as any Abby had ever tasted, including her own.

What a wonderful way to wake up, Abby thought. *Billy thinks of everything!*

Abby took her time getting dressed, making sure every little thing was perfect, her hair exactly in place. She heard a light tap at the door and called, "Come in."

Kate stepped inside, looking sharp herself. She wore a blue dress tight at the waist, a smart, light blue top, and a jacket that matched. The small hat on top of her dark hair worn high made her look older than she was.

"You look very nice," Abby complimented. "How old are you, Kate?"

"Promise you won't tell?"

"Of course I won't tell," Abby assured her.

"I'm twenty."

"You could have fooled me. I thought you were at least my age."

"Thanks. How old are you?" Kate asked, pleased that she looked like a lady.

"I'm twenty-five," Abby said, as if that was the limit for waiting to find a man. "I'm glad Billy came along or I'd be an old maid."

The girls laughed together, their friendship and confidence in each other growing quickly.

The morning was no more than a tour of downtown Durango, but it was enjoyable nevertheless.

Abby had a delightful time as the two pretty girls saw the sights, flaunting their good looks, every man tipping his hat to the young ladies and smiling. One man in particular made it a point to greet them.

"The only thing prettier than this nice day is the two ladies before me," he said cordially. He was a portly man wearing an expensive black suit and derby hat. His black hair tucked neatly in place, he smiled, waiting for a response.

"Mayor, you say that to all the ladies," Kate said.

His eyes darted back and forth quickly between the two young women, his smile genuine. "It's my duty, ma'am, to promote beauty and prosperity, a duty I enjoy very much. Good day."

"Is he always like that?" Abby asked, her hand covering her mouth.

"Oh, he's a ladies' man all right. The stories I could tell you," Kate said mischievously.

Admiring the goods in the store windows was fun, but neither young lady had money to spare or spend, at least not on fancy or expensive items. Abby's cash was strictly limited; all she had was the little amount she had saved, money she guarded closely.

Durango was a neat and clean town with permanent, well-built buildings, unlike the surrounding boomtowns of clapboards and tent canvas. The people were proud of their town, and the respect showed; for the most part the rough and rowdy blew off their steam elsewhere.

"This is a pretty place," Abby complimented after the girls had walked through the downtown area. "Looks like a good place to live."

"If you have the means," Kate added. "Nothing a good man wouldn't solve."

"Yes," Abby agreed dreamily, her thoughts shifting to Billy. She wanted to see him badly and wondered what he was doing. In her mind she pictured him in a business office with other well-dressed men signing and looking over papers, buying stock in mining claims, or sitting in a bank discussing investments with the banker. He was everything she'd ever wanted in a man.

~

Although Abby's tab was open at the hotel, where she could stay and eat without worrying about the bill, there was little to do. Her room was nice but soon felt small and confining. Her window overlooked Main Street, and she often sat and daydreamed, staring down into the street like a doll perched in a store window. She was free to move about town, but without money to spend that was rather pointless. What seemed like a long walk would only kill an hour or so, and boredom quickly returned. The days were long and depressing, and her hatred of being poor grew to overwhelming proportions.

"Will he ever send for me?" she spouted one day, throwing her coat on the bed. Her growing anger was becoming more than she could control; her patience, generally in short supply anyway, was running out. Her time with Kate had been enjoyable, but walking around town was only interesting the first couple of times, and she was running out of things to do. She stomped her foot and in frustration decided to take a walk outside anyway. She knew that a pretty young woman walking the streets of Durango could give the wrong impression, but she didn't care, and soon a predator made an effort at stalking his prey.

"A nice day, isn't it?" a slender man said, stopping in front of Abby and tipping his hat. He was older and obviously well off financially, judging by the suit he was wearing. His face was cordial, but something . . .

"Yes," Abby replied politely, waiting for the man to state his business since he was blocking her way.

"I have a wonderful suite. Perhaps you'd like to see it," he said, pretending to be the perfect gentleman.

Abby's mouth fell open when she realized what he was suggesting.

"If you're concerned about the money," he continued, "I have plenty."

A streak of anger flared in Abby, distorting her face in vicious wrath. "You don't have enough money!" she seethed as she stomped away.

That's it! she thought. *I can't sit in that little room like a prisoner, and I can't even go out for a walk!* With her money dwindling, she realized sadly that she would have to seek employment. Another option—to contact her family—was not an option as far as she was concerned. In a way she wanted to reconcile with them, but her stubborn pride stood in the way.

Looking for a job in a town where she had only one friend proved to be a trying task. Kate said the hotel had all the employees it needed, and anyway it would appear strange to be living in an expensive room and eating in the fine restaurant at the same hotel where she worked, with her pay less than her room and board.

Very few jobs were open for women, most of them menial and degrading, like washing and ironing or other work as a maid. She searched the east side, for the west side had only saloons and the like. A small bakery had a worn-out sign in the window: *Help Wanted*.

Bakeries always need help, Abby thought with disgust. *That's because the job is horrible, and the pay is practically nothing.* But the fact remained that a job would give her something to do, and the added little bit of money might come in handy as well. So she went inside.

An old wiry women ran the place, her salt-and-pepper hair up in a tight bun, her face looking like a white prune. "You know anything about working in a bakery?" she asked tiredly.

"I guess I do," Abby answered, smiling, trying to win the woman over with a little charm. "I've been working in one for years."

"Oh? And where might that have been?" the old woman pried, examining the pretty young girl closely and with skepticism.

"In Leadville," Abby said boastfully.

"What are you doing so far from home?" the woman asked as if she were accusing Abby of ill will.

Abby's charm suddenly went flat, intimidated by the old lady's questions. "I do have years of experience in a bakery. Do you need help or not?"

The old woman's head shook uncontrollably, and her eyes no longer maintained that distrustful stare. "When can you start?"

"Tomorrow," Abby said in a milder tone.

"We start at 5 in the morning," the woman said with no hint of expression one way or another. "The job pays a dollar a day."

Abby smiled at the thought of that much money. "I'll be here," she said cheerfully. "Thank you."

The old woman grunted in response as Abby walked out. At first it had been insulting to think of looking for a job, but now she felt better about everything. Her whole world looked brighter, refreshing her spirits and hopes, giving her a place to be and something to do. Anyway, she knew the situation would be short-lived because at any time Billy could send for her.

The next day instead of making the delicate and fluffy pastries she knew so well how to bake, Abby found herself in the back performing the hard chores that took their toll on her back, arms, and feet. Mixing and weighing flour from fifty-pound sacks, lifting and pouring from five-gallon containers, fighting fifteen-pound balls of heavy dough, this was her workday. In addition, work like this made an extreme mess, which she was responsible to clean up. The kitchen was hot, the big ovens beside her radiating their dry heat and making the temperature almost intolerable.

The old woman's name was Henrietta Burks, and she had owned and operated the bakery as long as anyone could remember. She had a sour temperament, was hard to get along with, and had never been married. She was only able to stay in business because her pastries and pies were incredibly delicious.

Because Abby wasn't used to doing such hard work—others did

that part in the family business, she was a little careless. Puffs of flour spilled onto her clothes; milk splashed here and there. Pretty soon strands of hair protruded from beneath her cap and hung down in her sweaty face, splotched with white flour.

Henrietta looked on critically. "You should clean up as you go—you're making a mess. Are you sure you've done this before?"

"I'm not used to doing this part," Abby blew out in a hard breath. "I used to make the delicacies and tend to the customers."

"Humph!" Henrietta grunted, turning back to her work. As she made the pastries, she muttered to herself and concentrated on her tasks. Abby thought she looked like an old mother hen as she hovered over her work.

When the bakery closed for the day, it was almost 5 in the afternoon. Abby had certainly earned every penny of her dollar and walked back to her room too tired to even think about having dinner. When she got to her room, she collapsed on the bed and fell into a deep and untroubled sleep.

When Abby returned to work the next morning, she felt as if she'd just left a few minutes earlier. The second day's work was even harder as the old mother hen looked over her shoulder and watched every move she made. Abby was starving from having had no dinner the night before and no breakfast that morning, and before long Henrietta caught her eating a donut.

"The help is not allowed to eat the goods!" she snapped sharply. "If I catch you again, it will come out of your pay."

"I had to sample the product," Abby said weakly, "to make sure it was up to your standards."

Henrietta stood like a scarecrow with her hands on her hips. "I've been doing this long enough to know what it tastes like without eating up the profits."

Embarrassed and irritated, Abby attempted to defend herself. "Well, Miss Burks, to tell you the truth, your donuts aren't nearly as good as the ones I'm used to fixing."

Angry but recognizing there might be a bit of truth in Abby's criticism, Henrietta sat down in confusion. Finally she said, "What's wrong with them?"

"They're too heavy, too cake-like," Abby said.

"And what would you recommend?" Henrietta inquired snobbishly.

Abby knew well the New Orleans recipe her mother had taught her for light and fluffy donuts. "I can't tell you, but I can show you," Abby suggested, smiling through a flour-smudged face.

Later Henrietta picked up one of the new donuts and sampled it. She was determined to put Abby down, to degrade her for wasting time and pursuing such foolishness. But to her own surprise, her dried-up old face broke into a smile. The donut was light in her mouth, a culinary pleasure unlike any she'd ever tasted.

"Where did this recipe come from?" Henrietta asked, reaching for another donut.

"New Orleans," Abby said, sensing she had begun to establish rapport with the old woman.

"They're delicious—so different. How did you get this recipe?"

"I was born in New Orleans," Abby said. "My mother once worked in a bakery there."

Abby told her story, and then Henrietta told about how as a young child she had come west across the prairies in a covered wagon. Abby found Henrietta's story moving. Her fiancé had been killed by Indians, and she'd never fallen in love again. By mid-afternoon Abby and Henrietta were like old friends, reminiscing and laughing at oddities of the past.

Life became easier for Abby then, and her work became easier as Henrietta shared the labor, constantly talking, opening up like a mysterious underground cavern. Abby learned much from her about the history of the Southwest—the Ute Indians and their nearby reservations, the coming of the railroads, the way towns sprung up literally overnight. When Abby told her how her family had struck it rich but squandered their wealth, Henrietta went into a fit of uncontrollable laughter, then had to tell a similar story she had witnessed.

"I used to give handouts to this poor man who hung around the garbage in the back digging for something to eat," Henrietta said. "One day he disappeared, and I thought he'd died or moved on. Later he came back in a lacquered carriage pulled by matching bays and came in here and gave me a hundred dollars. A few years later I found him out back scrounging in the garbage again and looking something awful. I gave him something to eat and asked him what had become of his wealth. He said, 'I do attest, ma'am, it was too slippery to hang on to.'"

Abby laughed at the animation with which Henrietta told the story. "Who was he?" she asked curiously.

"His name was Warren Wheeler. Last I heard, he was successful again up north of here in Aspen."

"It's funny how things can change so drastically, so quickly. You never know what's around the corner," Abby mused

"The only thing that's consistent," Henrietta said, "is change."

One afternoon Abby came back to the hotel from work and was stopped by the desk clerk. "Miss DeSpain, a letter arrived for you." He held out the envelope.

Abby's heart jumped with anticipation. Nervously, she thumbed it open and found a train ticket and a generous bank draft inside. A hand-scribbled note accompanied the ticket and money.

My Dearest Abby,

Forgive me, but things have been a blur. Please come to Silverton at once. My escapades have escalated faster than I imagined, mining investments are at a premium, and it's all I can do to keep up. I'll be at the Grand Imperial Hotel.

Love Always,
Billy

Abby rushed up to her room and began to pack. Once that was done, she put on one of her nicest dresses and went down to have dinner. Although she wasn't really very hungry, she was eager to tell Kate her news.

"He sent me a letter and a train ticket," she announced enthusiastically.

"That's wonderful," Kate said, though disheartened she would no longer be seeing her new friend. "When you're rich, remember me."

"Oh, I will," Abby assured her. "I'm going to meet him in Silverton."

Kate was happy for Abby but grew serious. "You be careful in Silverton—that's a rough place."

Abby waved her hand in front of her face, brushing such thoughts away. She'd been around, and she felt like nothing could surprise her. "I'll be all right—don't you worry."

"I'll miss you. It's hard to find a good friend."

"I'll miss you too, Kate," Abby said sadly.

～

The next morning Abby had her trunks taken to the railroad depot and checked out of the hotel, where she was pleasantly surprised to find she had a refund of $60. Decked out in her finest, she went to see Henrietta.

"He sent for me," she announced excitedly.

"That's wonderful," Henrietta said, happy for Abby. "I'm sure you'll do just fine, a young and smart girl like you. May the wind be at your back and good luck before you."

They hugged. Abby thought she saw a tear in Henrietta's eye. "I've enjoyed working for you and especially your stories of the old days. Maybe someday I can come back."

"I'll be here," Henrietta said as if she were an immovable and permanent fixture. She moved over to the counter where she filled a sack with pastries. "I want you to have this—you'll get hungry on your train ride."

"Thank you for everything," Abby said with emotion as she left, regretting she might never see Henrietta again. The old woman had been like a grandmother to her, sharing her life and offering advice. Abby would miss her.

The train ride to Silverton was not what Abby had expected. Sitting beside a window, the view scared her to death as the train clung to the edge of the mountains and wound around them, with a rushing river far below at the bottom of the gorge. She couldn't understand how the train managed to stay on the tracks, so narrow and so high up, curving and climbing, the engine rumbling and shaking. But the view was spectacular with changing scenes of peaks and valleys, the colors of fall just beginning to show, making the mountainside appear to be on fire. Overcoming her fear, she enjoyed the sights. She wondered how people had crossed such awesome country before, how they had built the railroad through such rugged terrain, how men had come to discover riches in such out-of-the-way places.

Whistling into Silverton later that morning, the train puffed slow breaths of steam as it squealed to a halt. Passengers quickly piled out, eager to be about their business. Abby went into the crowded station and made arrangements to have her trunks taken to the Grand Imperial Hotel. Then she politely asked directions as to how to get there herself.

"It's walkin' distance, ma'am," a man told her. "Cross Blair Street here, and go straight up Twelfth—you'll see it."

As she walked, Abby noticed the big mountain standing right over the town, the wide-open sky. She knew she was high in the mountains—her ears had been popping on the ride up, and the air was obviously thinner.

A catcall and a whistle caught Abby's attention as some rough men waved for her to come over and join them. Ignoring them, she stuck her nose in the air and marched onward toward the hotel.

At the hotel Abby quickly approached the desk, her heart racing. "I'm Abby DeSpain. Mr. Billy Rogers is expecting me."

"Oh yeah," the little man said, bending over out of sight. He popped up with an envelope and handed it to her. "Mr. Rogers said to put you in the room he was in."

All of a sudden Abby felt her hopes waver—the room he *was* in? Opening the envelope, she saw Billy's handwriting.

> I've gone and done it, my dear love—I bought a silver mine lock, stock, and barrel. I wanted to wait for you but had to get to the mine immediately. It's a long trip, but I shall return. Please don't be angry—my love for you is greater than ever, and our day will come!
>
> Love,
> Billy

Abby's disappointment was overshadowed by the fact that being a mine owner meant she might soon be rich. Billy was smart and knew how to make money, and he certainly wouldn't buy a mine if it weren't a good one. As she walked to her room, she couldn't help but recall her family's days living in the Chevalier, a stately mansion full of servants. Hardly able to believe her good fortune, she let her imagination run wild as she pictured living a life of luxury with Billy—bossing around servants, throwing parties, going to plays with rich friends. It was all just around the corner, and she could feel it; the air in Silverton tingled with excitement. It had been a long time since Abby had had a case of gold fever.

∼ 8 ∼

A Link from the Past

Adelightfully pleasant morning greeted Abby as she opened the curtains and let in the warming sunlight. Her future bright, she began getting dressed and making herself pretty, taking her time, enjoying the lavish comfort of her surroundings in the privacy of her hotel room. The mirror told her story. Blue eyes that now had a sheen of emerald reflected a happy inner soul alive with anticipation. The oval face expressed a lively confidence, the smile evidence of a happiness she could not confine. She brushed her long, wavy black hair, pleased with her appearance.

The sounds of Silverton coming through her window indicated the arrival of a regular business day, the streets filled to capacity with all kinds of people, creaking wagons, and braying burros. Abby had not seen so much activity since the days of early Leadville. Silverton, a strong and booming town, was new to the scene of big-city life with permanent buildings and a higher class. It was a town destined to make its own history, a town bent not only on survival but on establishing a way of life far above its neighbors. But even with its unique and grand appearance, the rough side was still present—the tough fighting men, the gamblers and drinkers, the con men, the unruly miners, and of course the immoral women.

With this in mind, Abby decided to hide her money, a precaution especially needed when she was on the street, where pickpockets worked in teams, one distracting while the other did the dirty work. Searching for a clever place, she slid the dresser out and examined the back side. She could see the backs of the drawers, dusty and full of tiny cobwebs. She slid the folding money into a tight crevice out of sight, even from the back. Sliding the dresser back into its normal place, she took the few dollars she kept unhidden and stuffed them into her handbag.

Hungry for a good breakfast, she hurried downstairs and was soon seated in the restaurant. Abby picked up a menu, thinking of eggs and ham—until she saw the prices. "A dollar for an egg!" she blurted out.

"That's right," said a young waitress who had suddenly appeared beside her. "You know how it is in a town surrounded by silver mines—everybody is supposed to be rich, so prices are high."

"That's ridiculous," Abby complained. "No chicken egg is worth a dollar!"

"May I suggest the toasted bread and hot oatmeal?" the waitress said.

To Abby, that was livestock food, but she ordered it anyway, too stubborn to pay exuberant prices for a single egg.

After finishing her meager breakfast, Abby decided to take a walk—on the good side of town, of course. The air was refreshing and pleasant, replacing the offensive odors of the city with the smell of the high country. Women moving across the wide avenue lifted their dresses slightly and stepped carefully to dodge the manure. Men in finely tailored suits and bowler hats frequented the boardwalks, tugging at cigars and engaging in conversation. Money announced its presence in fine clothes, the smell of expensive tobacco, and clean carriages and groomed horses, all a part of the life of the elite.

This is the kind of life I'm going to live, Abby thought. *The life of leisure and good company, buying only the finest, attending balls and plays, counting the money that comes out of the silver mine. Billy and I can go wherever we want and do whatever we want.* Smiling and lost in her daydream, she made her way past the many shops and stores, all showing their goods in big glass windows, all of it very expensive.

Stopping, Abby cupped her hands on a window and looked at

the women's wear inside. Mannequins wore ball gowns, and fine hats sat perched on their wooden heads. One hat in particular caught her eye, one with colored feathers, the kind a lady of class would wear. Shades of green made it stand out, and the curves of its brim were quite attractive. After careful consideration, she decided she just had to have it, for her hats were old and out of style. Besides, Billy would be back soon and would expect her to look nice when she accompanied him. It was an easy decision; confident in her taste, she went back to her hotel room.

A tingling excitement ran through Abby as she slid the dresser out. The hat was expensive enough to make her have second thoughts, but thinking of how she would look wearing it chased away all doubts. Reaching into the back of the dresser for the wad of money, she felt nothing. Dropping to her knees, she reached further, her hand now frantically searching, scratching desperately. Perhaps it had fallen out. She quickly searched the floor and underneath the dresser but still found nothing. Abby angrily went around to the front of the dresser and ripped out all of the drawers, spilling their contents. Her fingers ran through every crack and crevice, and she began to feel ill with irreplaceable loss, a feeling she knew all too well. Growing despondent, she shuffled over to the bed and fell onto it face first.

Feeling like a child separated from her mother, she grieved, though no crying came. Someone sly and experienced in evil had broken into her room and robbed her. They must have been watching her and knew where she would likely hide her money. She was mad at herself. She should have known better. What would she do now?

～

"How many days are paid for?" Abby asked the desk clerk. She had demanded compensation from the hotel, but they had been quick to tell her they could not be responsible for their guests' possessions. "You should have had your money put in our safe," the manager advised. He had seen this before—inexperienced travelers trying to be coy, not knowing they stuck out like black sheep.

Bringing a ledger to the desk, the clerk looked up Abby's room number. "You're paid up through Friday," he said kindly.

"That's tomorrow," Abby uttered, frightened.

"Yes, ma'am."

Turning away, the look on Abby's face was childlike, innocent, and frightened. She was near panic, her options slim, as she trudged upstairs to her room, apprehension a heavy burden on her slumped shoulders.

Abby had no friends, nobody to turn to, no way to leave town, nowhere to go. All she could do was wait on Billy, and who knew how long that might be? And how would he find her if she was fending for herself on the streets, or sleeping in back alleys or haylofts, or eating from garbage cans and begging for food? How quickly things had changed! What would she do with the trunks that held all of her earthly possessions? Her promising life had turned into a dark, demanding nightmare, an ever-lurking presence of fear and oppression.

"Can you at least store my trunks for me?" Abby pleaded as she checked out of the hotel the next day. "I'll be back for them soon."

The manager wrinkled his brow, feeling sorry for Abby. A middle-aged man, he looked on her with regret. Such a pretty young girl. A married man, he entertained no thoughts of immorality, but he wanted to do something to help her. If there was a job available in the hotel, he would offer it to her, but . . . "We have a cellar—I'll have your things put there. I wish I could be of more help."

"Thank you," Abby muttered. "Do you know where I might find work?"

He shook his head. "There are so many people here, jobs are hard to come by. Some folks are so desperate, they're willing to work for next to nothing. I wish I could do more."

Abby left the hotel and began walking down the street. Her clothes decent, her hat snug on her head of thick hair, she carried her biggest bag strapped over her shoulder with items she thought she might need. The streets that had appeared happy and friendly just a few short days ago now had a distant and unappealing nature, and she felt the eyes of strangers glaring down on her like she was a disreputable transient.

With so many stores lining the streets, Abby hoped she could find some kind of job, anything. Putting her pride aside, she stepped into almost every store, trying to be cheerful and polite. With little or no experience in the jobs she applied for, it was easy for the owners to turn her down. She applied at two bakeries, where Abby felt at home with the smells of rising dough and sugar and spices. Both places brought back better memories, giving her hopes of camaraderie with the owners.

She had no luck in the first bakery. A German family ran it and spoke very little English. "Very little room here—can feed no more mouths," the father explained vehemently.

The two old fat women who ran the second bakery were sisters, judging from their appearance. "Hire a hussy like you?" the first woman said rudely. She laughed, and her big sister with her. "You must be crazy. What do you think we're running here anyway, some dance hall? I'm afraid not, honey. You better get on over to Blair Street where you belong."

Insulted, her feelings hurt, Abby kept going but had no success anywhere. As darkness came, a different kind of people began roaming the streets.

Abby had approached almost every business she could find on the so-called good side of town. Languid and hungry, her feet hurt as she pushed closer to the noisy district of rambunctious crowds, dance hall music, and women's laughter.

"I guess I could work in a saloon," she mumbled morosely. "But I'd just serve liquor, and that's all I'd do." She knew about the rowdiness and coarse talk, the flirtatious drunks and their grabbing hands, the long work hours requiring great stamina and patience. She suddenly remembered when she was a child and they first arrived in Black Hawk. Her mother and Jason had bought an old bar to make into an office, and the bar where whiskey had been served remained. She remembered jumping up on the bar and kicking her legs, saying, "I want to be a dance hall girl!"

Grant had quickly grabbed her and taken her down, saying, "Abby, you don't know what you're talking about."

How prophetic that was, she thought sadly. She wondered if Grant missed her, or if he even cared, for she'd always tried his patience. She wondered about her mother too. Surely she must care, but what could she possibly do for Abby now? Her thoughts saddened her as she walked toward a street filled with lights, horses and mules, and men.

Before she even got to the first saloon she heard, "Hey, babe, what's a perty thang like you doin' out here? Why don't you come on with me—we'll have a good time!"

The stumbling man threw his arm around her neck, his breath foul with whiskey. She stumbled under his weight when another man abruptly pushed him away. He was drunk too. "C'mon, Bart! You're too drunk to take care of a lovely lady like this." He turned his whiskered and dirty face to Abby and said in a low voice, "Don't you worry none, honey, old Uncle Amos will take care of you."

About then the man called Bart spun Amos around and crashed his fist into the man's teeth. In an instant the two were rolling in the dirt, trading blows and cursing, each too drunk to realize what he was doing. Abby hurried away from them, finding herself on Blair Street.

Boldly entering a busy bar where men sat drinking and playing faro and a variety of other games, Abby proceeded across the smoke-filled room to the bar and signaled the bartender. The balding man with a big mustache and long sideburns came over to her, his expression one of surprise. "Yes, ma'am?"

"Who runs this place? I need to talk to him."

"He's right over there," the bartender said, pointing at a lean man with gray hair sitting at a table playing poker. "His name is Clark—Mister Clark."

Approaching the men at the table, Abby was a little nervous, but stubbornness and determination gave her strength. "Mister Clark?"

The man turned away from his cards, folded them in his hand, and took immediate notice of Abby. He was older, with gray hair, his face hard, cold, and wrinkled; but his light blue eyes were very alive. "What can I do for you, honey?"

"I need a job," Abby forced out.

Clark turned to the men at the poker table and smiled. "What do you think, fellas? Think she'll cut the mustard?"

"I reckon so," one of the men answered, "she's good lookin', Clark!"

Without warning the old man grabbed Abby's arm with an iron grip and pulled her closer, then turned her, like he was inspecting a piece of hanging beef. "You could put on a little meat," he noticed. "Come here!"

To Abby's shocking dismay, he pulled her onto his lap and held her steady in his iron grip. "You got a place to stay, honey?"

"No," Abby uttered, ashamed.

"I'll tell you what—I'll put you in a fine room upstairs." He turned his head away for a minor coughing spell, then back to her. "I'll be finished with this game here shortly, then you and me can talk upstairs. That good enough?"

Feeling nauseous, all Abby could do was nod. He released her, and she stood to her feet. "What's your name, girl?"

"Abby," she said meekly.

"I'll tell you what, Abby, you go on up to room 3 up there, and I'll be along after a while."

Nodding, Abby turned away. The men laughed boisterously behind her. As quickly as she could, she grabbed the bag she had left at the end of the bar and ran outside. Tears flooded her eyes as she stomped rapidly down the boardwalk, daring anyone to get in her way.

The shock of it all began to settle in at the same time that fatigue came over her like a rushing bull. She ached all over, and she was hungry, but sleepiness persuaded her to search for someplace to rest her pretty head. Down on the west end of Blair Street the crowd thinned, and most of the noise was behind her. She saw a stable with a low roof. There was a front room and a lantern burning in the window. The man who ran the stable evidently lived up front.

Slipping silently around the back, Abby found a small corral and waded through the fresh manure. The barn door opened easily as she crept in and felt her way along, finding an empty stall with a pile of hay near the feeding trough. She was so tired, she lay down and let her head rest on the end of her bag.

A loud squeal startled Abby, and she heard bumping and snorting as a disgruntled sow in the next stall let her protest be known. The smell of the pigsty reeked with a sour, rotten odor strong enough to gag a mule.

"You're a wonderful God!" Abby said bitterly. "You don't want us to sin, but now I'm forced into it or die! I'd rather die! And if You're any God at all, You'll let me die!"

Exhausted, she fell asleep.

～

The big hog squealed, bringing Abby out of a peaceful dreamworld and back into a world of harsh reality. She rubbed her eyes and glanced up. Standing before her was a skinny old man wearing suspendered overalls and a straw hat, with the astounded look on his face as if he had just found a pig with wings.

"Are you all right, lady?"

Disgusted and starving, Abby vented her anger. "Does it look like I'm doing all right? Do you find ladies in here every morning?" She stood to her feet and brushed the straw from her full and rich hair, then brushed off her wrinkled dress. "Oh yes, I'm doing just fine. I prefer to sleep with stinking hogs in filthy hay out in the cold."

"I'm sorry, ma'am," the old fellow drawled. "If I'd've known, you could have used the extra cot up front where it's warm. Are you hungry?"

"Yes, I am," Abby sighed, the thought of food mellowing her anger.

"All I got is bacon and bread. Will that do?"

Abby almost choked as she tried to answer. "Yes," she said again, grabbing her bag and following the man.

The old man's name was Shoo, Dermit Shoo, an old hog farmer from Kentucky. The stable Abby slept in wasn't home for any horses but rather for the hogs Dermit Shoo raised and sold for a living. He'd never had any trouble with vagrants since most folks were satisfied to sleep in an alley rather than in the hog pens. He watched Abby gorge herself, happy he could be of assistance.

"I come out here thinking I could find gold and silver," he sadly reported. "Didn't work out that way. But turns out I can make more money raising hogs here than I ever could back in Kentucky, so it ain't so bad."

Finished eating, Abby felt as filthy as the pigs she'd slept with, but at least the hunger was gone, temporarily. "Do you have somewhere I can wash up?"

"Course, I do," Dermit said. "Right there. See that washbasin?"

That wasn't what Abby had in mind, but she did the best she could. At least washing her face improved her spirits. "I'm sorry I was rude before," she apologized to the old man.

He simply smiled. "'Tweren't nothin'.'"

Opening the solid wood door, Abby squinted at the bright light of day, the sun already up over the southern horizon. "Thanks," Abby said, then went on her way—but to where, she had no idea.

~

"We got people washing dishes for free right now—can't pay their debt!" the big fat man wearing a white apron said laughingly. He held a cigar between his teeth. "A girl that looks like you ought to—"

"That's enough," Abby said, shouldering her bag and moving on. The day proved fruitless, and she found herself in the same desperate situation as the evening before. Night moved in with its scary and unpredictable ways, with men forgetting they were men and acting like animals. Tired from walking and searching for a job all day, Abby leaned against a light post, clinging to it for support.

Two ladies of the evening strolled by, decked out in loud colors, their heavily made up eyes staring at Abby as they passed.

"There's one for you, sister."

"Sure is, Elvy. Don't look like she'll hold out much longer."

"It's always the same, ain't it? They think they're so sweet and pure, too good for the likes of us. Next thing you know here they are, working right beside us!"

Both girls giggled and pranced away, pleased with the venom they'd spit upon their victim.

Not knowing where else to turn, Abby thought about knocking on Mr. Shoo's door and asking him for a handout, or at least for somewhere to rest. He seemed harmless enough. But she knew she would have to pay him back somehow, and the idea of slopping and butchering hogs brought little comfort.

In the shadows before her a man was packing his mule, his horse tied to the hitching post. The man kept his head down, his hat covering his face; he seemed oblivious to the world, minding his own business.

Abby stood gloomily like an injured animal knowing she would soon be sought out by predators. She had hardly any strength left.

A stranger walked across the street, a large man almost as wide as he was tall, a big and happy smile on his face. His suit was in perfect order, his belly protruding from beneath his vest, his coat hanging open, a diamond stickpin glittering in the street's light. His hands were wide and strong, his demeanor confident and full of cheer.

"My lovely young lady, you look a sight. You must let me offer some assistance, no matter what you think."

Abby blinked at him, untrusting.

"Let me introduce myself—I'm Harvey Strickland. I own a big place down the street, plush as a feathered pillow. Let me take you there, get you something to eat. You can clean up first if you like." He smiled graciously, exposing a gold front tooth.

Realizing what kind of man this was, Abby mustered up the strength to speak her mind. "I'd rather die."

In an instant Harvey turned shrewd, his smile gone. "Let me tell you how it is, honey. In a matter of days you'll be so far down and out nothing will matter to you anymore. And believe me, nobody is going to let you die, not when you have something marketable. So face the facts, your fate is inevitable."

Abby stared coldly back at the man, his big body close, his wide hands forming fists.

"I'm not like that," she mumbled. "I won't do those kind of things."

Harvey put his big meaty palm on Abby's shoulder and pulled her under his arm. "Trust me, honey, in a few days you'll be looking like a diamond, and you'll have a nice room and plenty of money. Why fight it?"

"Get away from me!" Abby spouted, struggling to escape his grip.

In the shadows the man who had been packing his mule was ready to ride away. But when he saw what was happening, he stepped over. "Leave the girl alone. She said she wasn't interested."

Turning his heavy mass, Harvey spit tersely. "Butt out, friend. This doesn't concern you."

"I'll decide what concerns me," the man said evenly, coming closer, his face still in the shadow of his hat. He looked like an old cowboy half Harvey's size.

With a quick move for a big man, Harvey sent the cowpoke flying on his back, having caught him in the jaw with a ham of a fist, his entire massive bulk behind the blow. He turned back to Abby impatiently. "You're causing a scene, miss. Now let's go." He reached for Abby and grabbed her arm.

"I said leave her alone," a voice demanded, and Harvey turned just in time to catch the butt of a rifle right in the mouth. He went down in a heap, expelling a huff of air, and was out cold. His gold tooth landed right beside him, gleaming in the dirt. The cowpoke picked it up and dropped it into his shirt pocket. "Sorry, ma'am. I can't tolerate a man with no manners."

Abby stared, perplexed and unsure of herself. In the light of the street lantern the line of the man's square jaw looked vaguely familiar, but the rest of the face was hidden in the shadow of the hat brim. The voice sounded like one she'd known, but she couldn't place it. Her heart pounding, she searched her memory and finally remembered. "Butch! Butch Cassidy!"

Butch quickly put his hand over Abby's mouth. "Ssshhh!" he whispered. "You'll get me hung!" Backing away, he examined the face before him, studying it closely. "Abby? Is that really you?"

"Yes," she cried. Tears came freely as Abby hugged the boy she'd loved who had become the man who'd just saved her from certain doom. "What are you doing here?"

Butch laughed. "I think I should be asking that question of you." He stared at her. "Abby, you've grown up—you're beautiful."

Abby smiled and wiped her dirty face with the back of her arm. "I'm not beautiful, and I'm not grown up. I'm tired and broke and hungry, and I have no idea what I'm going to do."

Butch made one of his funny faces and pawed at his jaw where the big man had popped him, his mind busy. "I'll tell you what you're going to do—you're coming with me. I've got a place up in the mountains—it ain't the Grand Imperial Hotel, but it'll do."

Helping Abby over to his horse, he pushed her up into the saddle, took her bag, and hung it on the mule, then sat behind her. Dreary and cold, Abby found comfort in cuddling up to Butch. She spoke softly. "I've read about you, Butch. They say you're an outlaw."

"That's just some newspaperman's idea," he said playfully. "They want to blame me for everything they can't figure out. It sells papers, you know?"

Butch kicked the horse into a rapid trot down Blair Street and into the darkness and on out of town.

"Abby," Butch said, as if something was bothering him, "when was the last time you had a bath? You smell like a hog pen."

A sharp elbow poked Butch's side and confirmed that he had indeed found the Abby he'd known years before. Only now she was older—and much, much prettier.

A Mountain Hideout

Butch Cassidy and Abby arrived at his mountain hideout late that evening, an abandoned mine site with a few cabins around the mouth of the tunnel. Sliding off the horse, Abby was stiff, sore, and exhausted. Lights from the cabins shone through the windows, casting yellow squares on the ground as a haze of wood smoke floated in the cool air.

"Home sweet home," Butch said cheerfully as he climbed down from his horse.

Staring around in the dim light, Abby could see the old place was dilapidated, the shacks leaning over from days of heavy snow and high winds.

"That you, Butch?" a man's voice called from somewhere in the darkness.

"Yeah, Matt, it's me," Butch said a little aggravated. "You should have noticed me coming in a long time ago. What's the matter—were you asleep?"

"Why, no, Butch," Matt said as he came closer, holding a rifle in his hand. "I could see it was you. Who's that there you got with you?"

"This is Miss Abby DeSpain," Butch announced proudly. "At least I think the last name is DeSpain. You haven't gotten married, have you, Abby?"

"No," Abby said softly, shaking slightly from the cold.

"What are you doin' bringin' a woman up here, Butch? You know all that's gonna do is cause trouble."

"You let me worry about that, Matt. Put these animals up, and bring in the supplies I brought. C'mon, Abby, let's get inside—I'll introduce you to the gang," Butch said, taking her gently by the arm and leading the way. "By the way, that was Matt Warner."

Inside, the cabin was warm and cozy, the stove glowing orange and a cast-iron pot simmering on top. The steam coming from it carried the heavy aroma of meat stew. A lantern hung over the table, where a group of men sat playing cards in their stocking feet. They turned their attention to Butch when he entered, but were caught off guard by the woman.

With every one's attention focused on Abby, Butch said, "Fellas, here's a fine lady I want you to meet, Miss Abby DeSpain. Abby, this here is Bill and Tom McCarty. That there is Silver Tip Maxwell, but his real name is Bill Wall. And that fella over there is Indian Ed Newcomb."

Tom McCarty stood and came a step closer. His eyes had a worried look. "Butch, you know the rules—no women in the hideout."

"That's right," Butch agreed, "and I don't ever want to see any of you fellas breaking the rules either."

Abby stood still and silent, embarrassed by her appearance and scared of the outlaw gang.

"I want you to know," Butch continued, "this ain't no regular woman. We was friends when we was kids." He turned and set his saddlebags on the table, poured a small shot of whiskey, and gulped it down as his listeners waited patiently. "I run into her in Silverton, and she was in a bad way. You might say I rescued a damsel in distress." He laughed, but nobody else did. "Anyway, fellas, I couldn't just leave her there for the wolves; that wouldn't be gentleman-like."

Tom sat back down at the table, shaking his head. "I swear, Butch, you have a way of twisting things around to make people side with you. So now what are you going to do with her?"

"First off, Ed, I want you to bucket up some water from the stream and heat it and get the tub ready for Abby. I'm sure she would appreciate it. We'll all have to bunk up over here and let her have the other cabin for a while," Butch said, his mood playful as usual.

A groan came from a few of the gang as Ed got up, put his boots on, and went to draw the water. Secretly the men were delighted to have a pretty woman to glance at for a change.

"You still didn't say what you were gonna do with her," Tom reminded Butch.

"Well, I guess it's up to her," Butch said, removing his hat and scratching his head. "Look after her for a while, I guess."

Abby was tired of being talked about like she wasn't present. "I just need a bath and some rest for right now. Can't we talk about this later?"

The men nodded affirmatively. Silver Tip and Bill McCarty got up to leave, pulled their boots on, and went to get their things from the other small cabin. They figured they'd better straighten up the place for Abby.

"Be sure the fire's warm and the water's hot over there, boys," Butch said politely.

"Don't worry, boss, we'll get it fixed up," Bill said on his way out.

"Forgive my lack of manners, Abby. Would you like a shot of whiskey to warm you up?" Butch asked, trying to be the perfect host.

"No," Abby said. "But I am hungry."

Butch moved quickly over to the wooden stove and removed the lid from the simmering kettle. "Sure smells good. I don't think it's a good idea to ask what's in it though. Like some?"

Abby nodded, and Butch dipped her out a bowl. "Dig in. No need to be bashful."

Sitting down, Abby ate like a starved orphan as Butch watched with a gratifying smile. Even with her clothes dirty, her hair a mess, and her exhaustion evident on her face, he thought she was gorgeous. He pulled up a chair, sat down beside her, and watched her eat. Abby, glad to have a good meal, chose to ignore Butch's curious eyes.

"So tell me, Abby, how'd you end up in such a fix?"

"Later," Abby said between bites.

Butch nodded. He felt like a man who'd hit a gold strike, having discovered Abby when she especially needed his help. After so many days on the trail, living in hideouts, always running, he'd almost forgotten what it was like to be in the company of a pretty lady. He had no fears about her safety, for he was the unchallenged leader of the gang, and anything he said was the rule. The way he figured, it would do the men good to have a spunky gal like Abby around; it might cheer them up a little.

When Abby finished her stew, Butch took her over to the other cabin, where the men had swept the floor and had a steaming hot metal tub of water waiting for her. The fire in the potbellied stove cracked and popped and sent firelight dancing on the walls.

"Here you go, Abby," Butch said, leading her inside. "Make yourself at home. I'll see you in the morning."

With Butch gone, Abby peeled off her filthy clothes and slipped into the hot tub of water. Her body tingled with the warmth. She hated to admit it, but getting rid of the filth made her feel like a snake shedding its skin, starting out all new again. The bath acted like a sedative as well, sending her into a dreamy state of mind as she leaned back and relaxed. She thought back to the days of living in Black Hawk and remembered how much she'd admired Butch and what a good friend he'd been. At times she'd thought she was in love with him, but now, looking back, she realized a girl that young had no way of knowing anything about loving a man. Nevertheless, she saw Butch as a hero for saving her, and he was still wise and witty and always smiling. She wondered why he chose to live on the wrong side of the law, someone so talented, someone whom everyone liked, except of course for those being robbed.

After her bath, Abby blew out the lantern and climbed beneath a pile of heavy blankets. High in the mountains on a cool night, the air sweet and thin, the bath a luxury she thought she might never enjoy again, the bed comfortable and her belly full, Abby felt at peace, at least for now.

~

The next morning Abby awoke to the smell of breakfast cooking—sausage and scrambled eggs—and her stomach growled in response. Her eyes felt swollen as she kicked off the blankets and crawled out into the cold air of the cabin. Searching through her bag, she found a fresh dress, although it was badly wrinkled. Kindling, stove wood, and matches sat beside the stove, and she managed to get a fire going under the water kettle. As she brushed her hair and worked on her face in a cracked piece of mirror that hung on the wall, the cabin slowly warmed up, and the water began to boil. She held her clothes over the steam and watched the wrinkles fade away, then slipped her warm dress on over a thick cotton blouse. It wasn't much, but it was the best she could do.

If it weren't for her circumstances, Abby would have found the clear and sunny morning delightful, the view from high on the mountain wonderful, the air fresh and clean and crisp. She stepped onto the front porch of the cabin, but her mind was on her worries, and uncertainty and fear clouded her thoughts.

She saw Bill McCarty crossing the yard. He had been tending the horses. He was a tall, dark-haired man about her age; he had a friendliness in his tone that she felt covered up some dark secret. "You have a pleasant night, ma'am?"

"Yes, I did. Thank you." Abby squinted in the sunlight.

Bill's eyes stayed on her a moment too long before he said. "Go on in, they're all up. Breakfast is ready."

Gently knocking on the door, Abby slowly pushed it open. The first thing she saw was Butch leaning back in a chair with his foot up on a table covered with dishes, reading a newspaper in his lap.

Glancing backwards, Butch said, "Good morning, Abby. I hope the bedbugs didn't bite."

"I slept well, thank you."

"You look a sight better," Butch said jokingly. "Sit down, eat something." He plopped his chair down and swept the dishes over to one side of the table. "Ed, don't just stand there, fix this woman a plate."

Quietly Ed did as he was told, and Abby sat down.

"Maybe you can explain this to me," Butch said, interested in the newspaper he waved, then began reading out loud. "It says here: 'Butch Cassidy and his gang attempted a robbery at Delta, but were foiled by the sheriff, who happened to be in the barber shop next door. Shots were fired, but the gang escaped unscathed. A sheriff's posse was assembled but lost the gang's trail several miles outside of town.' Now, Abby, I ain't never been to Delta—none of us have!"

"Newspapers write what sells, Butch. Besides, if the men wore masks, how could they know it wasn't you?" Abby responded defensively.

"If it was me, we would have been successful!" Butch said, slapping the newspaper down on the table. "They should know that! I ought to go rob Delta just to prove my point!"

Abby faced him with an expression half soft and half hard, and he knew he couldn't reason with her. She was set in her ways, and he knew she'd never approve of his outlaw ventures, so he let the subject go.

The men moved out of the cabin to look after chores and keep a steady lookout for unwanted visitors, leaving Abby and Butch alone. After finishing breakfast, she shoved her plate aside and looked over at Butch, who seemed about to burst with questions.

"So what have you been up to for, let's see, over ten years at least?" Butch asked, his blue eyes lit up in anticipation.

"I usually don't like a lot of nosy questions, Butch," Abby said firmly. "But what I've been through makes a good story, so I'll tell you."

Butch jumped up, grabbed the blue metal coffeepot, refilled their cups, and hurriedly sat back down, eager to listen. Abby began with Butch's leaving Black Hawk and told the story of their gold mine and all it had led to until finally they ended up in Leadville with nothing, how prayers had saved them, and about the responsible life they'd been living ever since—that is, until Billy Rogers came along.

Reluctantly, making excuses for Billy, Abby told how she had followed him west and how she'd been robbed and ended up on the streets while waiting to hear from him.

"You really love this fella, Billy?" Butch pressed.

Abby nodded.

"Abby, you didn't even give me a chance!" Butch stormed, coming to his feet. "I got feelings for you too, you know."

Halfhearted, Abby gave Butch an understanding but strict glare. "What am I supposed to do—marry a robber, live in hideouts, raise a family on the trail with a posse behind us, watch you get shot or hung? What a lovely life that would be."

"Aw, c'mon, Abby, I don't plan on doing this forever. A couple of big jobs and we could be fixed for life—go to Chicago and live it up, or I could take you to San Francisco—you always wanted to go there, remember?" Butch walked in circles, waving his hands as he talked. "We could live like kings, eat at the best places, stay in the finest hotels, whatever you want."

"And when the money runs out, then what?" Abby debated.

Butch shrugged his shoulders as if that would never be a problem. "All I would have to do is make another withdrawal from the bank."

Abby laughed. Butch's way of thinking seemed so simple, but it was all backwards. She wished he could see that. "No sale, Butch," Abby said. "All you would do is break my heart."

Calming down some, Butch sat back down and folded his hands in front of him on the table. "Abby, I never dreamed you would end up so pretty. I mean, you were pretty before, but it's different now—you're grown-up." He hesitated and looked off to the side, searching for the right words. "How can I say this . . . Abby, I'm crazy about you. I always said we'd meet up again."

Coolly admiring Butch, Abby reached over and placed her hands on top of his. "Butch, you could be a good man—not robbing banks and the like, but instead doing something decent with your life. The story always ends up the same for those who live outside the law, and you're smart enough to know that. Why don't you change your ways?"

The question made Butch nervous, and he pulled back and gazed at Abby. "I don't know how to do anything else. Anyway, I'm good at what I do. They'll never catch me!"

"Famous last words," Abby said sadly, almost lecturing. "When have you ever met an outlaw who thought he would get caught?"

"I don't guess I ever have," Butch admitted, biting his fingernail. He stood and paced back and forth a bit. "Well, at least you know how I feel; maybe that means something. I have work to do. Make yourself at home, do whatever you like. If you need anything, just holler." He grabbed his hat.

Abby stood and drew closer. "Butch, it does mean something. I never said I didn't care about you."

"Thanks," Butch said. He smiled his contagious smile, his blue eyes shining. "Maybe I can cash that in sometime." He left the cabin, looking for something to do.

~

By the middle of the week the men had grown accustomed to Abby's cooking and cleaning as she tried to earn her keep. Scolding them for coarse talk when they were around her, the men's manners improved, and soon there wasn't even any belching at the table. More often than not, the men went out of their way to be courteous and helpful. All was well except for one small incident when Abby was returning to her cabin one evening. Bill McCarty caught her at her front door as she was about to enter.

"Hello, Abby. Can I build a fire for you—it's cold out."

Abby recognized his intentions immediately. "I'm quite capable, thank you." She reached for the door handle, but his hand rested on top of hers.

"I said I'd like to build a fire for you," he insisted.

"Forcing yourself on me isn't going to do any good," Abby said with warning in her voice.

"I'll decide what's good," Bill said in a low and husky voice. Pushing the door open, he shoved Abby inside. "I'm just trying to be friendly." He went to the stove and began making a fire.

Abby stood with her back to the wall. She wished Butch was around.

When the fire was going, Bill shut the iron door and walked over to face her. "You're a fine looking woman, Abby. It's hard for a man not to take notice."

"This isn't the way a real man acts," Abby informed him.

He leaned over and put his hands on the wall behind her, trapping her between his arms. Abby stood stiff as a board, her heart beginning to race. "You and me for a little while—that's not such a bad thought, is it?" Bill said smoothly.

Abby was shaking now. She frantically looked around for something with which she could defend herself.

"Bill!" a voice called loudly from outside. It was Butch. "Bill, come out here. We need to talk."

Jumping away, Bill went to the window, pulled the curtain aside, and saw Butch and the rest of the gang standing in the twilight. He went to the door, opened it slowly, and took a step onto the porch. Abby sighed a breath of relief as she followed curiously.

"Come on out here, Bill. I'm not gonna hurt you," Butch said, motioning with his hand. Bill stepped down into the yard, facing Butch while Abby watched from the porch.

"Bill, it's not nice of you to be in there bothering Abby. That's rude." The rest of the gang chuckled at Butch's antics.

"I don't see where it's any of your business," Bill retorted.

"Oh yes, it is," Butch insisted. "Now, I want you to apologize to Abby and go on to bed. Then everything will be all right."

"Or what?" Bill said.

"Or I'll have to give you a whippin'," Butch said, growing impatient.

"I can whip you, Butch, you know that," Bill responded.

The gang watched quietly as the tension increased. Abby stood on the porch, her hand tightly gripping the post.

"I don't know that," Butch said teasingly. "You never whipped me before."

"I don't know why we need to fight—nothing happened."

"I wasn't planning on fighting," Butch added. Then in a swift move he spun around with his fists clenched together and brought them down on top of Bill's head, using all the weight of his body in the blow, like he was swinging a sledge hammer, causing Bill to collapse to the ground.

Bill felt too dizzy to get up. Finally, raising up on one hand, he held his other hand up in defense. "That wasn't fair, Butch—to hit me while we were still talking," Bill groaned.

"I'm sorry," Butch said. "I apologize. You see how easy that was? Now you apologize to Miss Abby."

"I'm sorry," Bill moaned, rubbing the top of his head. "It won't happen again."

Butch reached over and pulled Bill to his feet, then put his arm around his neck and pulled him close. "C'mon, pardner, I'll pour you a drink." The men moved toward the other cabin as Butch glanced back and winked at Abby.

Shaking her head, she went back into her cabin thinking about what a character Butch was. He was so high-spirited. A natural leader, he was always convincing in an easygoing sort of way. Forgiving his shortcomings, Abby saw Butch as a man with great potential, but she dreaded the day he would be captured, dreaded reading about his inevitable fate if he didn't change his ways.

~

"All right, Abby," Butch agreed a few days later, not caring for the idea. "I'll take you back to Silverton so you can find your lover."

"He's not my lover, Butch," Abby answered resenting the insinuation. "He's my fiancé. We're going to be married."

"Whatever you say," Butch added, his face clouded with regret. "But what if he doesn't show—what if you end up back in trouble again?"

"He'll come for me," Abby said with confidence. She refused to believe anything else.

The afternoon was still and warm, the fall weather holding just a tinge of a chill, indicating winter was not far away. The colors were alive in the mountains, with the bright yellows of the aspens smeared like gold across the mountainsides, the oranges and reds of the scrub oaks striking against a background of evergreens. Butch and Abby stood a distance from the camp on a ledge overlooking the grand beauty of vast spaces and brilliant colors, the sky a deep and dark blue.

"Makes you feel kind of small," Butch commented, gazing at the view.

For once Abby was able to think about something besides her

troubles. A bluebird rustled through the brown grass before them, then fluttered up into a spruce tree. Taking a deep breath, Abby could feel the return of her old feelings for Butch. She would miss him and his entertaining ways, and she knew from his half-satisfied stare that he was holding back his emotions, wishing he could make something of what they'd once had.

"It sure is beautiful," Abby said, breaking the silence.

Kicking his boot in the dirt, apparently trying to come to a clear decision, Butch reached into his pocket and handed Abby a wad of bills.

"What's this?" Abby said.

"About 300 dollars—you'll need something to live on."

"I can't take your money," Abby said.

"Think of it as a wedding present," he said, trying to be convincing. He pushed her hand away. "It's the least I can do. You can't expect me to leave you in that town of wolves without money, can you?"

Abby recognized the truth in what Butch said. Silverton had its cruel side, and exploitation of others was a way of life there. Overwhelmed with appreciation, Abby placed her arms around Butch, pulled herself closer, and kissed him, holding on a little longer than she'd planned. A mixture of strong emotions flooded over her—the hurt in her heart, sadness, love, a desire for things lost, and a desire for a more tender and innocent way like when they were children. The young faces, the great dreams, the wistful peace of another time and another place all flashed before her in a moment.

Butch wished that moment could last forever. Abby was the only woman he'd ever considered anything more than a one-night stand. Abby was a permanent resident in his heart, the kind of girl he thought he'd marry, if he ever married. But at the same time he knew the kiss was just Abby's way of saying farewell, her way of letting him know he was special and that she did love him as a friend she'd never forget. Nevertheless, the kiss made him wonder if he should give up his wild ways for a more honest life. But he decided, again, that dreams like that were for someone else, not for him. He pulled away.

"A fellow could get used to that," he said, licking his lips, trying to be humorous in order to hide his embarrassment.

Abby had a dreamy look on her face. She straightened Butch's collar carefully and said, "We'd better get our rest. We'll have a long ride in the morning."

"Yeah," Butch said. "Besides, I could get into trouble hanging around you."

~

By first light Butch and Abby were headed down the winding trail, the horses' hooves sliding on the steep incline as they descended. Abby followed as Butch led the way, carefully guiding her horse where he had gone, trying to dodge the loose gravel and shale. The horses grunted under the strain, taking each step cautiously until they were safely in the valley below. The sun was climbing now, warming Abby's cold hands and chilled face.

"I didn't know you could ride so well," Butch said once they were on safe ground.

"I can't," Abby admitted, relieved that the perilous descent was over.

"Well, we're safe now. The rest of the way we just follow the road."

"Aren't you scared somebody will recognize you in town?" Abby asked.

"Naw. Nobody knows what I look like," Butch answered in his carefree way. He'd been thinking of how much he hated to see Abby go. Her good-bye kiss had stirred memories, and he had dreamed about her and his days in Black Hawk all night. "I was glad to hear that Jason and your mother linked up," he said. "I always thought they were made for each other. He's a fortunate man."

Abby calmly answered, "Mother is a lucky woman."

Butch laughed. "I wish I was so lucky," he said, thinking out loud.

Declining to comment, Abby let his words drift into the breeze behind them.

Changing the subject as they lazily rode along, Butch said, "How's Grant these days? I always liked him."

"He's the same as before," Abby said, "except a lot bigger. He works with Mother and Jason mostly."

"Never got married?"

"Not yet."

They rode a little further, and Butch said, "You and Grant get along?"

Hesitating, Abby realized she missed her brother and their heart-to-heart talks. She tried not to think about him because she felt guilty about leaving without telling him good-bye. "We were very close," she answered, wishing she had confided in him before she left.

"That's good," Butch said and let it rest, realizing he was invading private territory.

In Silverton Butch helped Abby down from her horse and into the Grand Imperial Hotel, where she was eager to see if there had been any message from Billy.

"I think there is a letter for you here, Miss DeSpain," the clerk said, putting on his glasses and searching though a bundle of mail. "Yes, here it is. It came in the other day."

Taking the envelope, Abby quickly ripped it open to read the contents.

My Dearest Abby,

I'm here at the mine, and she's a beauty! Sorry, I didn't realize Creede was such a far ride from Silverton. You must come at once. A stage runs from there to Lake City and then on over to Creede. There should be enough money in here to take care of you until you get here. I miss you with all of my heart.

Love always,
Billy

"Good news?" Butch questioned innocently, already knowing the answer by the look on Abby's face.

"Yes," Abby said, her heart beating more rapidly. "He's in Creede, and he wants me to come at once."

Butch forced a smile, envious of Abby's love for another. He did his best to be polite. "Sounds like you're following the Silver Thread."

"The Silver Thread?"

"Yes. That's what some call the trails that hook these towns together—they're all silver towns, you know."

"Oh," Abby breathed. She felt as if she'd been holding on by a thread. She turned her attention away from the letter and the dreams it promised and looked at Butch. "How can I ever thank you enough? You saved my life and took care of me . . . Will I ever see you again?"

Bashfully, Butch shuffled his feet and shifted his weight. "Abby, you don't owe me a thing. You brought some happiness into my life, and that's priceless. I mean—" He turned his head away and looked out toward the street.

Abby reached over and hugged him as he stood there speech-less. He reached his arms around her and patted her on the back. "You be careful—take care of yourself."

"You too, Butch."

Butch jumped in alarm. "Who's Butch?" he whispered.

"Oh! I'm sorry," Abby said realizing her mistake.

They both laughed a little, trying to soften the pain of parting.

"I'll be seeing you," Butch said as he backed away and turned to leave. At the front lobby door he turned around to have one last look at Abby. She blew him a kiss.

Rose's Cabin

Wasting no time, Abby located the hotel manager and had her trunks moved to the stage line down the street. Kropps & Simms stage lines were going through hard times due to the arrival of the railroads. To compensate, they advertised travel over the rugged terrain through the Rockies to out-of-the-way places for a cheaper price.

"Yes'm, the railroad runs to Animas Forks from here, but not to Lake City, unless you want to go the long way around," the limber and lean man said as he checked the tag on someone else's trunk and shoved it back out of the way. He looked weathered and beaten like an old wind-whipped tree, his skin sun-darkened and as tough as bark. He was as skinny as a rail and wore a tall cowboy-style hat with a large brim, which made him look taller and thinner than he was. His mouth was hidden behind a large, bushy salt-and-pepper mustache, and his faded eyes drooped with sadness. Appropriately, his name was Slim, and like the stage line itself, he was a dying breed.

"But can this line take me all the way to Creede?" Abby inquired, eager to be on the trail.

"Weather permittin'," Slim replied, then spit a stream of brown tobacco juice into the dirt.

"Why should the weather be a problem? It's beautiful out," Abby said, repulsed by his tobacco spitting.

Slim chuckled. His lifetime of experience in the area was not to be taken lightly. "It's fall, miss, and snow's likely at any time. It might even snow enough to block the trail on the high passes."

"When does the stage leave?" Abby asked, refusing to be deterred.

Slim moved over to the back of the clapboard shack and looked out a window into the corral where the horses were kept, then came back to Abby. "When do you want to leave?"

"Don't you have a schedule?" Abby asked, growing worried at the lack of organization.

"Not anymore," Slim said. "Not many folks take the stage from here. They might even be closing this office soon."

"I'd like to leave as soon as possible," Abby said. "I need to get to Creede quickly—it's very important."

"I see," Slim said. He rubbed his heavy mustache as his pale blue eyes sized up Abby. It was his guess she didn't know a thing about life in these parts. "I can have the horses hitched up and ready in an hour. You got the fare? It's forty dollars."

"Yes, I do," Abby said, digging out the bills and paying him.

Slim counted the money and stuck it in his pocket. "I'll get the horses hitched," he said. "It'll take a little bit."

"I'll wait. Those are my trunks right over there."

Slim nodded and got to work. Abby sat down, impatiently tapping her foot.

When Slim pulled the stage around, Abby was appalled. The old stagecoach was listing to one side, and the doors were tied closed with leather straps. The stage looked like it had been dragged out of a wash after being abandoned for years. Needless to say, the small, narrow old rig had seen better times.

Slim hopped down from the driver's seat, locked the stage office door, untied the coach door, and swung it open. After loading the trunks, he offered his hand to help Abby in.

"Is this the best you've got?" Abby questioned critically.

"It's the only one we've got," Slim said. "Hop aboard."

Reluctantly, Abby stepped up and into the dusty old coach, swept the dust from the seat with her hand, and sat down. Slim tied the door, crawled into the driver's seat, and snapped the reins. The coach lurched ahead. It was going to be a rough ride.

Slim whipped the horses along the northeast trail, the road dry and flat and dusty, and on up the canyon toward Animas Forks. Abby noticed there was a large hole in the front floorboard of the coach, worn through from rot, rocks, and debris from the horses' hooves. It was so big she could crawl through it if she needed to, but a bigger problem was all the dirt and dust coming in through the hole. Abby held her head out of the window for a breath of fresh air but found that no better, thanks to the pounding hooves of the six horses.

"Hey!" she yelled up at the driver. "Stop the coach!"

Slim brought the rig to a halt and climbed down. "What's the matter? Something wrong?" he asked, craning his neck inside the window of the coach.

"Yes!" Abby fumed. "See that hole? All kind of dirt and rocks and dust are coming in here! I can hardly breathe!"

"That's funny," Slim said "Nobody ever complained about it before."

"I can't ride in here," Abby griped.

"I don't know where else you'd ride," Slim drawled.

"Up top with you!" Abby persisted "Let me out of here!"

"Well, if you insist. I ain't never had no lady ride up top before though." He leaned over and spit.

Once out of the coach, Abby dusted herself off. At least she was dressed properly for the hard ride, wearing a heavy cotton dress with cotton leggings and a heavy canvas jacket.

Slim had to help her up to the top, pushing from behind. He liked her spunk. "What's your name, miss?"

"Abby. What's yours?"

"Folks call me Slim."

The view from up top was incredible and the air clean. Abby felt much better, content to be on her way with what she felt like was a competent man. He was obviously from the old days, when things were wilder and harder. She guessed his age was around forty, but it was hard to tell how old a man was when he'd lived in the dry heat of the Colorado sun and in the cold biting winds of the mountain winters. Though she wasn't sure why, she liked Slim and trusted him.

Ahead of them a cable stretched between two mountains. Ore buckets traveled along the moving cable, swinging wildly up and down and side to side, the cable flexing and singing in the wind. To her surprise, a man waved from one of the dancing buckets far up in the sky, his arm small and his face just a speck.

The trip to Animas Forks was relatively short, and they arrived by noon, Slim slowing the stage to a crawl as they passed through town. "I got to water the horses," he said, pulling the reins. "Won't take long."

Abby kept her seat, her eyes roaming about the small town. It was right in the middle of what appeared to be a wild and harsh country, surrounded by towering peaks, located at an elevation of over 11,000 feet, Slim had told her. Animas Forks had boomed in the 1870s with the discovery of lodes along the timberline, but now decline was apparent in the empty and rundown buildings surrounding the main street. Oddly, Abby noticed an unusual number of dogs lying about or sniffing around, a conglomeration of mutts.

Slim climbed back aboard after watering the horses and glanced at Abby with his sad eyes. "You ready, Miss Abby?"

"This is a strange place," Abby observed. "In a way it's like a ghost town."

"Winters are severe here," Slim told her. "Most of the people who work here have already left for the winter. You see that tall pole in front of Frank Thaler's Saloon? See that top notch? That's how deep the snow got here one winter. Twenty-five feet."

Abby couldn't begin to imagine snow that deep. "What did people do?" she questioned. "How'd they get by?"

"The entire town holed up in the saloon and waited it out playing poker."

"An entire town?"

"Well," Slim had to admit, "there was only a dozen men and three women here at the time, and maybe twenty dogs or so."

"The dogs are still here," Abby noticed.

Slim leaned over the side of the coach and spit, then popped the reins and got the coach rolling again. "There's two passes we can take. One is shorter than the other, but it's a harder trail."

"Take the short one," Abby ordered, keeping her eyes ahead.

Slim glanced at her and noticed her jaw out and her head held high. He liked this girl—she was tough and stubborn and determined, the only kind of gal that could make it in this kind of country.

～

The traveling became tough as the stage horses labored up an increasingly steeper incline, leaving the Animas River drainage behind. The trail grew horrendous, high above the timberline, at times the coach wheels sliding sideways on loose rock. The distance to the lower valley seemed like miles as Abby gripped the seat handles with white knuckles. If the coach were to fall . . . The air had grown cold, and Abby gulped in the thin air.

"Whoa!" Slim cried, riding the brake with his foot and pulling back at the reins. It was easy to see the horses were nervous, the whites of their eyes showing as they stomped and snorted.

"What are you stopping for?" Abby asked, her throat tight and her stomach in knots.

"Got to stop about every fifty yards for a while," Slim said knowingly. "Not much air up here, and the horses have to get a breather. Wouldn't want 'em gettin' exhausted and falling down now."

Abby sat still, trying to force away any mental pictures of a horse slipping or falling. She felt slightly dizzy as the big country whirled around her. She decided she would jump if she had to rather than going over the edge with the coach.

"Let's go, boys," Slim called as he took his foot off the break and inched the stage forward.

Sitting on the high top of a flimsy coach did little to calm Abby's fear as they climbed to even higher altitudes. But Slim was a skilled driver, taking care to be slow and gentle with the uneasy horses.

After a while Abby grew used to the heights and their wondrous scenery. Feeling like she was on top of the world, she became so fascinated with the high country that the perils of the trail frightened her less.

From her perch she could look down on the mountains below and far beyond them to the golden plains dancing in the fall sun. She found the view of distant heights and depths exhilarating. Her senses were sharpened by the piercing chill of the cold wind.

Abby's hair was blowing wild and free in the breeze, reflecting the way she felt in her soul. She felt inconsequential among these physical immensities. Her spirit soared in the awesome power of a supernatural presence who was all around her, and she felt for the first time in a long time genuine humility. The burden of oppression had lifted, and her previous misgivings flew away like a flock of birds, leaving her thoughts clear and undisturbed. Her deep blue eyes were calm as they scanned the steep slopes of timber far away. She felt a deep inner peace.

"You scared?" Slim asked, interrupting the silence.

"No, not anymore," Abby said softly. "This is wonderful."

"We're at the top of Engineer Pass. It's downhill from here, but the trail is still tricky in places."

Abby nodded as they moved on cautiously, the wheels creaking and groaning under the strain. The old coach had traveled these heights and these kinds of roads many times, and that had taken its toll. But Slim knew the capabilities and limitations of the horses and the coach. He was a man who knew what could be done and what could not.

Stopping again, the horses wheezed after only a short distance. The going was slow.

Slim stared into the distance, holding the reins loosely in his hands, his face worried.

"What's wrong?" Abby asked, not wanting anything to interrupt the euphoria she'd been feeling.

"I don't like the looks of them clouds yonder," Slim said, jutting his chin toward the northern sky, which they could now see clearly from the top of the pass.

Abby saw a dark mass of gray clouds rolling their way. The northern sky looked big and dark and cut a clear line across the blue.

"Is it a storm?"

"I'm afraid so, and we're in a bad place," Slim confessed, then spit over the side. "This ain't no place to get caught in a blizzard, I'm telling you."

"Can't we hurry and miss the storm?" Abby suggested, uncomfortable with the way a new onset of fear was replacing the wondrous tranquillity she'd been feeling.

"Can only go so fast up here. Once we get down the other side of this rascal, I maybe can pick it up a bit." He shook the reins, and the lead horses neighed as the group began to move.

Going down was about as bad as going up, Abby soon discovered. It seemed like the entire weight of the coach was pushing against the horses, and Slim placed all of his weight on his left foot, pushing hard on the oak lever of the squealing brake.

The sky darkened, and the clouds engulfed them, making it look like they were in a thick fog. Big, soft, wet snowflakes seemed to form before their very eyes, floating down like leaves from a tree. Neither Abby nor Slim said a word as he worked the horses skillfully, winding through the switchbacks, swinging the coach wide to stay away from the edge. The road became slick and the wheels caked with wet snow, causing the brake to slip. Fear gripped Abby as she pulled her jacket over her head like a turtle retreating into his shell.

"It's not much further," Slim said, trying to comfort her.

By the time they reached a safe and reasonable grade in a protective spruce forest marking the timberline, the snow was as thick as oatmeal, the white flakes sticking to everything in sight. Visibility was poor, and the horses' backs turned white and began to steam.

"We're going to have to hole up," Slim said, his black leather gloves wet and slippery on the reins.

"Out here? In the middle of nowhere?" Abby protested in fear.

"There's a place right up here called Rose's Cabin. We can stay there 'til this blows over and the road clears. Storms this time of year are crazy and unpredictable."

Abby huddled even tighter in her coat, the snow starting to cover her.

Distinguishing the road became a problem for the lead horses and for Slim, and he had to back up once, having trailed off too far to the side. The coach bounced and jerked over rocks and boulders he would have missed had he been able to see them. One time Abby thought she was going to fall off, but Slim's strong hand grabbed her arm and steadied her.

A loud crack suddenly broke the silence, and the coach fell to one side. Slim quickly halted the horses. "I think we just lost a wheel," he said, tying off the reins and jumping down. He waded through the snow, already a foot deep.

"We ain't going no further in this rig," Slim said, coming back to the front. He held his arms up to help Abby down.

When her feet landed in the snow, she instantly felt wetness creep into her socks. "What are we going to do?"

"We have to leave the stage behind. I'll walk the horses in front of me. You can ride on old Jess." He pointed at the appropriate horse.

Abby let Slim help her onto the horse's back. "What about my things?"

"We'll have to come back for them." Slim saw the sorrow in the young girl's expression and the fear in her eyes. "Just hang on, Miss Abby—I'll have you inside and warm in no time."

As they moved forward, the only sound they heard was the animals' breathing and their hooves crunching the soft snow. It was as if they'd been covered in some kind of blanket and everything had become still and silent. Slim worked the reins from behind, keeping the horses at a slow pace.

First Abby smelled smoke, and then a big building came into view. The log cabin was three stories high and had a steeply pitched roof. It sat in the middle of nowhere, like an answered prayer.

Slim found a place to tie the horses off, then came for Abby. Gently letting her down, he said, "Let's get inside."

Pushing the door open, Slim and Abby gladly felt the warmth coming from inside. Slim stepped ahead of Abby and removed his hat. The room, resembling a saloon, was crowded with men holding mugs. A fire burned in a huge iron stove. The place smelled of unbathed men, smoke, and cooking food. The walls were shiny with old grease and were stained with soot.

"Slim! My friend, come on in here, make yourself warm," a big man said, approaching Slim with his heavy hand extended.

"Abby, this is Mr. Corydon Rose, a good man in a storm."

Abby was amazed—Rose was a man! He was a stout man with dark and curly black hair, though graying some now, and he had a healthy black mustache. His face was round and cheerful, just like his dark eyes. "You've been away too long," he told Slim.

"We might be stayin' a spell. The coach has a busted wheel a ways back," Slim said, removing his gloves to warm his hands at the fire. "My passenger here will need accommodations too."

"Why do you think I built this inn?" Rose asked jokingly. "I put *everybody* up. The snowstorm—she brings us all together."

"I reckon we better get the horses stabled," Slim said, slipping his gloves back on.

"I'll help you," Rose offered. He turned his head and called in a loud voice, "Margaret! See that this lady gets a room!"

Abby stood still and silent with every eye in the room upon her. They were rough and hearty working men with wide backs, big arms, and strong hands. They didn't smile or make any expression; they just stared. She felt like a lamb in the midst of wolves.

A wiry older woman appeared, the kind who always seems in a hurry. She had her gray hair pinned back; her face was full of wrinkles. "Come this way, deary. Right up the stairs over here." She walked so fast, Abby thought she might have to break into a trot to keep up with her, but soon they came to the right room.

"Here you go," the lady said, opening the door. "I'll be serving dinner after a while. You just come on downstairs and join us—there's plenty." She pulled the door closed, and Abby could hear her little feet patter away.

Going to the window, Abby could barely see out, the snow falling heavier than ever. She sat and watched for a while disbelieving. She felt like she'd been in two separate worlds on the same day—one sunny and warm and the other a high-mountain winter blizzard. Shadows outside turned into men as Slim and Rose came back from the stables, having tended to the horses.

Turning around, Abby set her big bag on the bed. It had some things in it, but not much. It was cold, even inside, and she decided to put on additional clothes. Digging through the bag, she picked

through her things and dressed accordingly. The day had been trying and exhausting, and now dreariness came upon her like darkness
at the end of the day. The bed was a feather bed, plush and soft and
covered with thick quilts. She let herself down slowly, relishing the
cozy comfort and softness, and went to sleep.

～

Abby's dream was troubling. A man with a gold tooth was yelling
at her, frightening her, and when she pulled away she saw the man
dragging off some young girl by the scruff of her neck. Then Abby was
in Leadville at the bakery, waiting for Billy, who never seemed to show
up. Then she was whisked to a high mountaintop, where she looked
down on the tops of the clouds. Butch Cassidy laughed at her as he
told her he would never get caught. But when Butch turned around,
a man was holding a gun on him and began firing. *Bam bam bam!*

Opening her eyes, Abby heard it again. *Bam, bam, bam!* "Miss
Abby," Slim's voice called from behind the door.

Jumping to her feet, Abby opened the door, still in a daze.

"Miss Abby, they got dinner ready downstairs. I thought you
might be hungry."

"Thank you, Slim," Abby said sleepily. She left the door open as
she dampened a washcloth and wiped her face. The water was cold
and invigorating, and the chill reddened her face. She brushed her
hair and went to the window, but the ice and snow blocked her view.

When Abby came downstairs, the talking stopped, and all eyes
were on her again. The same men were there, still sitting and drinking in the same places as when she first saw them. If she hadn't been
so hungry, she would have gone back to her room.

"Young lady," the older woman called, "come on over here and
let me fix you a plate."

Grateful for the woman's attention, Abby went over to the
stove, ignoring the staring men. Talk resumed, and Abby came back
with her plate. She saw Slim sitting at a long table and an empty
place on the long bench next to him, so she went and sat there.

"This is good," Slim said, nodding at her plate. "It's elk."

Abby was so hungry, she wouldn't have cared if it was porcupine.

She began to eat, keeping her eyes down to avoid eye contact with onlookers.

"Like I was sayin'," Slim said to a white-haired, red-faced man sitting across from him, "we come over the pass, and there she was, plain as day, a fall blizzard. I told Abby here we might be in trouble, but she held her head up and rode right on beside me."

"What?" the red-faced man said. "You mean to say she was a-ridin' up top?"

"Yep, pretty as you please," Slim bragged.

"I ain't never heard of no woman ridin' over Engineer Pass on the top of a coach! Is that right, ma'am, or is he pullin' my leg?"

"I rode on top all right," Abby said as she chewed. "It was real pretty until the storm came."

Two old miners picked up their mugs and moved closer, wanting to hear better and get into the conversation.

"You wasn't scaret?" one asked.

"Scared of what?" Abby boasted.

"Wooo-weee!" a man named Old Swede screamed. "Hey, fellers, we got us a live one here!"

At that, all the men in the room came over and gathered at the long table, most of them elderly. They were all miners, most of them working their own small claims, some working together. They either had a stake somewhere nearby or had been caught at Rose's Cabin when the storm blew in. Either way, they were frequent visitors to the inn, which during the hard winters practically served as their second home. They very rarely saw a pretty young woman.

"Here, look at this," a bearded man said, holding out a gold nugget in his palm. His name was Ernest Miller, and he was an old hand at mining. "It's pure gold, it is."

Abby found the nugget to be unusually heavy, and the way it sparkled in the light made her smile. "Is it real?"

"I'll say it is!" Miller bragged. "Got it out of my claim, I did, right up the mountain here."

"Sit down, you old fool," a man named Freddy Hopper said impatiently. "You show that same nugget to everybody, and it didn't come from no mine around here." Hopper was an expert with years of experience and knew there was little gold in the area. "You have to pardon him, ma'am—he don't know what he's doin'."

"I got a real mine," a squat man with sideburns boasted.

Another man, Henry Rowell, could stand no more and said, "But ain't none of you got snow snakes at your place, and I do!"

"Snow snakes?" Abby giggled.

"That's right. And they get as big as a South American python."

"Nobody ever seen one but you, Henry! Must be drinkin' some of the good stuff," a miner mocked. They all laughed.

Corydon Rose kept the mugs filled while everyone tried to outdo the others to see who could impress Abby the most. All were gentlemen and watched their language and kept the stories clean. It was an all-night kind of party, but Abby had to cut it short around ten o'clock, yawning sleepily. "You've been fun, but I have to get some sleep."

"If'n you need anything, you just call out," Old Swede said.

"That's right," everybody said in agreement.

Slim knew all these old coots and liked every one of them. They were all good, honest, hard-working men living a rough and rugged life in hopes of making a dream come true. Probably one of the best things that had happened to them for a long time was for a storm to hit at just the right time, trapping a beautiful woman at the inn with them. This was a dream come true itself, and there wasn't a thing any one of them wouldn't have done for Abby. In a way Slim felt responsible for Abby's welfare, but he wouldn't worry about her as long as they were at Rose's Cabin.

Back in her room, Abby had to face the fact that they would be stuck at Rose's Cabin for days, maybe weeks. She thought of the funny old men and smiled. They were making fools of themselves over her, but unlike young men they never let it go too far. Each in his own way wanted her to like him best but knew things wouldn't go any farther than that. After all, they were dreamers; that was what kept them going, what kept them alive, what made their lives worth living.

CHAPTER

~ 11 ~

Delayed

Morning came and Abby came to life, and she could see her own breath in the near-darkness of her room. She thought about getting up but wasn't ready to face the shock of the cold, not just yet. She heard a gentle knock at the door.

"Who is it?" Abby called from under her mountain of blankets.

"Old Swede, Miss Abby. Me and Henry was a-wonderin' if you want us to build you a fire in the stove."

Smiling, Abby pictured the two old men waiting outside the door, eager to do something for her. She decided it would be nice to get up in a warm room and said, "The door's open."

The two old fellows stumbled in, and when they saw her in the bed they quickly turned their heads the other way and focused all their attention on the stove. Crouched on their heels beside the little parlor stove, they talked without looking at her, knowing it was improper to look at a woman while she was still in bed.

"You got the kindlin'?" Old Swede asked.

"You see me holdin' it, don't you?" Henry barked back. "Get out of the way so I can open the door."

"I've got the coal oil when you're ready," Old Swede said. "Miss Abby, we'll have this thing goin' in just a minute, you wait and see. It won't be long at all."

"Oh, shut up!" Henry snapped. "Give me a match."

With a nervous old hand, Henry struck the match, carefully lit a small piece of newspaper, and placed it under the oil-soaked kindling. Both men watched as if they'd never seen a fire started before, smiling when the flames began happily lapping up the sides of the stove.

"There, that ought to do it," Henry said. "Let's go, Swede." He left the door open just enough to speak through. "Miss Abby, there's some real coffee down stairs. I'd be happy to bring you a cup."

"I'd like that," Abby said, now wide awake and hiding her giggles from the silly old men.

"I'll be back as soon as I can," he said, closing the door behind him.

Abby could hear the two arguing as they went away, fussing about something, she didn't know what. Before the room had a chance to warm up, she heard the clumsy footsteps return and another knock at the door.

"Come in," Abby called coyly.

The door eased open, and Old Swede and Henry stood there, both trying to hold the big cup of coffee. "Get your fat hand away!" Henry said angrily. "It was my idear."

"You shakin' old fool, you'll dump it all over her," Old Swede warned. "Let me do it!"

Eagerly, both men came over to Abby, now sitting propped up on plush pillows. They both handed her the hot cup very carefully.

"Thank you," Abby said, smiling.

The two old coots just stood there for a moment, their eyes looking everywhere except at Abby, their hands fidgeting.

"That'll be all. Thank you so much," Abby said primly.

"Yes'm, Miss Abby," Old Swede said as they backed away, stumbling over each other's feet. "You just call us if you need anything."

Henry quickly added, "The way you call us is to stomp on the floor so's we can hear you downstairs."

"I'll do that," Abby said, sipping the boiling hot coffee.

They closed the door and ambled away, still bickering and bellyaching.

~

Abby couldn't remember ever having a more entertaining morning. Even when she went downstairs, she wasn't allowed to do anything for herself; everything was done for her. She almost grew tired of all the attention. She was surprised they let her walk with her own feet or feed herself with her own hands! She knew what it was like to be rich and have servants, but this was ridiculous—it was as if she were royalty!

"Put that plate down! I'll get it fer ya, Miss Abby," an old-timer named Thomas Williams said after Abby finished her breakfast.

Abby laughingly protested, "I have to do something for myself! I can't just sit here!"

"That's all right, Miss Abby. You jest rest your pretty self we'll take care of everythin'." Williams grabbed her plate and wiped the table with a damp cloth he'd been holding just for this moment.

The front door swung open, and in came Slim, snow-caked. Removing his hat, he shook it out and brushed off his shoulders and stomped his boots. "Don't look like she's gonna let up today," he complained. "Must be pretty near three feet of snow." He had gone out to feed the horses and check the weather.

"Well, ain't that too bad," one of the old men cackled. "We's all stuck in here."

Stifled laughter came from most of the group. Being stuck here meant they couldn't go back to work and had to just stay and eat and drink and look at Abby. They'd known worse days, that was for sure.

Just because they were old didn't mean they weren't smart. They knew how to entertain and pass the time, how to make light of being snowed in. A codger named Andy Ballantine, his hair gray and curly, his beard cropped short, his eyes clear and mischievous, sat across the table from Abby and gave her a smug smile. She noticed that most of the men were smiling, like something was up. Andy placed a deck of cards right in the middle of the table.

"You know how to play poker, Miss Abby?" Andy asked, still grinning.

"I know how it's played, but to answer your question, no, I don't play poker."

"Humor me," Andy said. Andy was well educated, judging by his proper and precise use of the English language. "Cut the cards—we'll just pretend."

Doing as she was told, Abby cut the cards. Without picking up the deck, Andy dealt her and himself five cards one at a time.

"Now look at your hand," Andy said.

The group had crowded closer to watch the show, looking over Abby's shoulder to see what her cards were.

"Do you have a good hand?" Andy asked.

"I guess so," Abby answered, which generated laughter from behind her, for they could all see she had four kings and a queen.

"If you were a poker player, would you bet on that hand?"

"I suppose," Abby answered.

Andy placed all his cards on the table faceup—four aces and a queen.

Amazed, Abby said, "How'd you do that? I cut the cards, and you never picked up the deck!"

"You ain't seen nothin'," a voice said from behind her.

Andy smiled and picked up the cards. The show was on. He could do the most unbelievable things, including shuffling a deck of cards, fanning out the entire deck, making them fly almost a foot in the air to his other hand and landing neatly stacked there. It was as if he made them come alive, and they obeyed his every desire. Abby sat completely enthralled and entertained at the remarkable tricks Andy performed. It was like watching a magician who made things appear out of thin air.

All the old-timers had seen the tricks a dozen times, and of course none of them would ever play cards with Andy. They were enjoying watching Abby, not Andy. To see the expressions and wonderment on her young and pretty face, to see the excitement in her flashing blue eyes, to hear the music of her laughter—that made their day. Morning quickly turned into afternoon.

But Andy wasn't the only man with special talents, and soon Old Swede came in carrying an accordion. He had a little trouble getting warmed up at first, but once he had a few drinks under his belt he played well. He played songs they all knew and could sing to, which they did until everyone could sing no more.

At one point Slim whispered to Abby, "These old fellers are really something—they can carry on like this for some time."

"I'm having fun," Abby said. She'd never been the center of a party before, never had so much attention, and for the moment all of her troubles were forgotten and far away.

"What I was tryin' to say was, if you get tired, you don't have to sit here just to be polite," Slim added.

"I'm fine," Abby assured him.

It all went on hours and hours, and the evening ended late, leaving an impression on Abby that she would never forget. In the roughest part of the country she had found decent men, good companionship, and happiness in old-fashioned fun. And it cost nothing in the way of money. If only everybody could get along this way, she thought, taking what life had to offer and making the best of it, the world would be a better place.

When she went to bed that night, Abby noticed that her jaw muscles were sore from smiling and laughing, something that had never happened before.

∽

The next day the sun was full and bright. Outside, the spruces were laden with heavy snow, their branches drooping. The mountains were white and shimmering in the sunlight. Pretty soon melting snow began to drip off the roof, the damp air getting warmer every hour.

"We're ridin' over to the coach," Slim said once Abby was downstairs. "Gonna bring that wheel back here and see what we can do with it. Old Henry was a wheelwright—he'll know what to do."

Abby nodded. "I hope my things are all right."

"They're fine," Slim reassured her. "You're in good hands here, and we'll be back directly."

With old age comes wisdom, and as a few of the old codgers watched Abby eat breakfast they noticed that something was bothering her. They didn't want to pry, but they did want to help her with any problem she might have. They whispered among themselves until a delegate was elected to approach Abby and find out what was wrong. Old Swede was their choice.

Walking in measured steps, he came over to where Abby sat listlessly, his worn hat in his hands, his face long. "If yer not feelin' well, we got a recipe for tea that would perk you up, Miss Abby."

"It's not that—I feel fine," Abby said, no smile on her face.

"Yes, well, uh, it occurred to me and the fellers that you looked a bit sad today. We was wonderin' what we could do."

He seemed so sweet and honest and helpless, Abby actually felt sorry for him. A glance back revealed that the others looked the same. When she was sad, they were sad.

"Oh, it's silly, I guess," Abby admitted, "but a long time ago my family had a gold mine, and from that mine my stepfather, Jason Stone, had a gold ring made for me. It's nothing fancy really, but I was attached to it, and now it's gone."

"Gone?" Old Swede said, wondering if she meant it had magically vanished. "You mean you lost it?"

"No," Abby said. She noticed the others were leaning toward them, trying to hear, so she spoke a little louder. "Last night when I went to bed, I took it off and set it right on the dresser. This morning it was gone."

Old Swede had a serious look on his worn old face, and then a smile slowly formed. "Fellas," he yelled behind him, "come on over here. Miss Abby put her ring on the dresser last night, and this morning it was gone. Now who do you reckon stole that perty ring from her?"

They all chuckled, nodding their heads in agreement that they all knew for a fact who the thief was.

Abby wasn't sure how she felt about being left out of something they all knew about.

"You take this, Miss Abby," Andy said, holding out a small but brilliant little clear stone.

"I don't want your diamond," Abby said.

"It's not a diamond—it's only a piece of quartz crystal. It might be pretty, but it's worthless. Now, you take it and put it where you left your ring last night, and tomorrow morning your ring just might be back."

"If this is one of your tricks, Andy, I don't like it," Abby said bitterly.

"It's no trick," Andy said, holding his palms up. "Just do as I say."

A glance at everyone revealed they all agreed. Abby wished she knew what they were thinking.

~

That afternoon warmed up, producing a wet and melting mess. The sun was high and bright; the treetops swayed in a gentle breeze. Abby had returned to her room feeling like a fool but placed the little shiny stone where her ring had been as she'd been instructed. Hearing a blacksmith's hammer on an anvil outside, she went to the window and saw Henry, peeled down to his undershirt, working on the busted wagon wheel, with Slim's help. With the weather so nice, she decided to go outside and pay them a visit.

When Abby walked up to the two men, Henry stopped what he was doing. "Afternoon, Miss Abby. 'Twern't much left of this wheel."

Abby saw the old wheel disassembled and lying in pieces on the ground. Henry was forming new iron rings for the hub on a small forge smoking next to him. "Mind if I watch?"

"You go right ahead." Henry smiled.

Slim winked at Abby. After Henry finished the hub rings, he grabbed some oak strips, sat on a stump, placed the strips between his knees, and began pulling a spokeshave up the strip. Slivers of oak curled off and landed at his feet. Henry held up a perfectly rounded spoke and inspected it. "Grain runs good in this one," he said to himself and set it aside. He cut the tapered pieces for the hub and spoke tops with a funny-looking saw.

Watching an artisan work was relaxing for Abby. He made it look so natural and easy, not a move wasted on extra effort. Pretty soon he had re-formed the wheel, most of it now made with fresh lumber.

"How'd you learn to do that?" Abby asked, running her fingers over the smooth work.

"My father was a wheelwright and a blacksmith in the old country," Henry said, his small eyes looking back in time. "We come over on a big ship, then settled down in Philadelphia. Pop started a shop, and I was his apprentice. We once made wheels for a carriage that was going to the White House—fer the President to use."

It dawned on Abby that she hadn't been in the company of foolish old men but in the presence of a world of experience. They had come from everywhere, bringing their trades, their secrets, their knowledge. She could only guess at the stories they could tell, what their wise old eyes had seen, including the making of a country and the settling of the wild west. It was a humbling experience to be among such men, the kind legends were made of, men who braved danger often and thought nothing of it.

"You all come on in." Rose waved from the inn. "Eb talked Margaret into letting him into the kitchen, and he's been cooking all afternoon—that meat pie he makes. Come on!"

"I reckon I can ring this wheel tomorrow," Henry said, studying his work and pulling his overalls back up over his undershirt. The sun had met the mountaintop, and it was already growing cold.

"We've put in a good many hours. Let's call it a day," Slim said, removing his hat and wiping his forehead.

Everybody was lined up for dinner holding their empty plates, eagerly waiting for something special. They pushed Abby to the front of the line, her plate in her hands, and right into the kitchen where Eb stood over his preparations. "Here you go, Miss Abby—let me heap a mess of these fixin's on your plate."

Abby held out her plate. "Where'd you learn how to cook like this?" she asked, delighting in the heavily spiced air of the warm kitchen.

The meat pie was covered with a delicate crust, and when Eb dipped the ladle into the pot, a ball of steam rolled up, releasing a delicious aroma. "My maw taught me how to make it when I was just a boy."

"What's in it?" Abby asked. "It smells good."

"I can't tell that," Eb said with a mischievous smile on his thin lips. "I only got one secret, and this here's it."

The entire gang ate until they were full and fat and sassy. Most leaned back and lit a pipe or built a smoke afterward. Abby just sat with her hands in her lap, feeling warm and comfortable. Slim sat next to her, his belt undone to allow for his protruding stomach.

"That was one of the best meals I've ever had," Abby commented, growing sleepy-eyed.

"He does that every now and then. Takes him most of the day," Slim mumbled.

"Wonder what was in it?"

"Nobody knows. Some say they seen Eb out wandering through the woods diggin' up things. I know fer a fact he puts mushrooms in it—I could see them."

"Wild mushrooms? I thought they were poisonous."

"I hear tell that most are. You got to know the right ones to pick or you could kill yourself," Slim added.

"I feel sleepy," Abby said. "I wonder if it was the mushrooms."

"Probably just ate too much," Slim chuckled.

Droopy-eyed, Abby said good night and went upstairs to go to bed. She locked her door, fearing somebody might have intentions of snooping around, something to do with her missing ring. She glanced at the clear little stone sitting on the dresser and shrugged the matter off. Thoughts of her trip and Billy were beginning to come back to mind. She had enjoyed her new friends' company, but she was ready to be on her way.

～

The next morning Slim and Henry finished the rebuilt wheel and carried it back up to the coach, taking the team of horses with them.

Abby was slow in getting up but pushed to get herself awake. She noticed that her gold ring was back on the dresser and the worthless rock was gone! Quickly she slipped it onto her finger. She figured she was the butt of somebody's joke and intended on getting to the bottom of it. Checking the door, she found it still locked, but that meant little. As clever as these old fellows were, they could probably slip in and out of her room easily.

Downstairs, Abby was having coffee when Old Swede and Andy came over, their faces alive with amusement.

"I see you got your ring back. That is it, ain't it?"

Abby glanced at the ring smugly and back at them. "I don't like these kinds of jokes, nor do I like anybody coming in my room while I'm asleep."

"The feller that come in your room traded your ring back for that rock Andy give you," Old Swede said.

"Who would do a thing like that?" Abby asked. "That's ridiculous."

"Weren't no Tommyknocker." Swede laughed. "It was a little bitty feller with a long tail."

"What?" Abby coughed, spilling her coffee.

"Some call it a pack rat, some call it a trade rat," Andy explained. "He collects things."

"You mean I had a rat in my room?" Abby asked with disgust.

"Not exactly," Andy continued. "He's really not a rat or a mouse. Some say he's closer related to a kangaroo."

Abby shook her head to make sure she was thinking and hearing clearly.

"You see," Andy went on, his face animated, "he likes to collect pretty and shiny little things to put in his den to attract female pack rats; but usually when he takes something, he leaves something else in its place—that's why they call him a trade rat."

"How'd you know he'd bring my ring back and not something else?" Abby asked.

"We didn't," admitted Andy. "But we did know he would like the stone better and would try to find something he thought was equal in value."

"This is the craziest thing I've ever heard," Abby said, bewildered.

"I find little things missing and little things I didn't have before in my cabin all the time," Old Swede said. "They's a busy bunch, them pack rats."

"Well, I'm glad he brought my ring back," Abby said, admiring the ring on her finger. "I certainly won't leave it lying around anymore."

"That's a good idea," Old Swede agreed. "But if you're ever in a tradin' sort of mind, you might like to see what kind of things they like to trade."

"I don't think so," Abby said. "There are enough two-legged rats in the world to worry about already."

~

By noon Slim was back with the coach and was ready to resume the journey.

"Miss Abby, we can make Lake City this afternoon—it's only about eleven miles. We'll have to stay the night there. It's a fifty-mile stretch from there to Creede, and half of it is straight up. We can start that trip tomorrow morning."

"I'm ready," Abby said, feeling a new excitement. Rose's Cabin had been a delight and a unique experience, but she was getting anxious to catch up with Billy.

"Grab your things, and we can be on our way," Slim said, turning to make sure everything was in order.

Word spread quickly that Miss Abby was leaving, and all the old men quickly gathered around the coach to see her off. When Abby came outside, she was astonished at the reception awaiting her.

They all started talking at once. "You come back anytime you like, Miss Abby!" "We shore are gonna miss you around here." "Ain't gonna be the same around here without you." On and on they gushed.

Abby made her way to the coach, where Slim was ready to help her up into the driver's seat. She turned and faced all of the old gentlemen as they grew quiet. "I just want to say this is the nicest place I've ever visited. You were all wonderful, and I won't ever forget you."

Smiles broke out on all their faces, and they nodded and mumbled among themselves, some lifting their old hands to wave goodbye.

"You have a safe trip there, Miss Abby. You're in good hands with Slim," Andy said, looking up at her.

"Good-bye, everybody," Abby called, waving as the coach pulled away from the big cabin.

"That was an experience," she said loudly to Slim over the clopping of the horses' hooves and the rattling of the coach.

"Them old men back yonder," Slim said, watching the road, "they'll talk about you and your visit from now 'til kingdom come, and a little will get added to the story now and then, a little changed here and there, and in time it will become legend, at least among themselves. I've been in these mountains a long time, and believe me, what folk say is true—legends outlive the facts."

"Legends?" Abby queried.

"That's right, Miss Abby. That bunch will be talking about you for a long time."

The stage passed a busy mill that stretched straight up the mountainside. The grade broke into a flat about three miles later, and the road became wide and easygoing. Abby could see buildings in the high valley ahead, apparently some kind of small town.

"Is that Lake City?"

"No, that's Capital City," Slim answered.

"What's it the capital of?" Abby questioned.

"Nothing," Slim answered.

As they drew closer Abby could see that the place had some industry—a smelter and some saloons. She saw a big brick house in the distance over by a creek. It all sat in a lovely valley of golden aspen with leaves that flickered yellow in the sunlight.

"So why do they call it Capital City?"

"You see that big brick house yonder? It belongs to George Lee, a powerful rich man and politician. He had big dreams of this place being the capital of Colorado."

Abby thought about that for a moment. "But this is so far away from everything," she said. "Who would want this to be the capital?"

"Apparently some did. When they voted between Denver and this place, Capital City only lost by one vote."

"Amazing," Abby said as they rode through and she got a closer look. This was yet another town in decline, with unkempt buildings and little activity as far as she could tell. She knew some men's dreams were bigger than others, and she could see that George Lee had been a big dreamer. But in reality, the dream was growing old and was turning to ruins.

The coach was soon following Henson Creek, a river with white froth and rapid, crystal-clear mountain water. It ran in a deep gorge that the river had carved out of stone thousands of years earlier. The scenery was beautiful in an entirely different way, the bright yellow aspens the center of attention. Dark rock walls rose from below, met the road, and rose higher. The rocks were moss-covered and green and purple; some were striped with white lines, making artistic designs pleasant to the eye. A fresh smell seemed to come from the water below. Abby saw deer and other wildlife and game trails. She couldn't help but be moved by the forest's beauty and the rushing river that grew louder as they moved along.

Suddenly a man stood before them in the middle of the road, holding up his hand to signal them to stop.

"What's going on here?" Slim called, braking to a halt as the man stepped aside.

"Dynamite!" the man said. "We're starting a mine, and there'll be fire in the hole in a minute."

Slim turned to Abby. "Want to hop down and stretch your legs?"

"Sounds like a good idea," she said, although it was actually her back that was sore.

Slim helped her down, and they walked up to the man who had stopped them. "Just breaking ground?" Slim asked.

"We're only about fifteen feet, running a horizontal tunnel," the man said. He was small, strong-looking, and all business, like a man who well knew the workings of mines.

"What do you call it?" Slim asked.

"The Hard Tack."

About that time Abby felt a rumble and saw smoke and rocks shoot across the road, over the cliff, and on down to the river. Then she heard the blast, which startled the horses. Quickly Slim grabbed the bit in the lead horses' mouths and talked to calm them down.

"You can go on up there now. They'll have the road cleared pretty quick since they've got plenty of muckers workin'."

"Thanks," Slim said as he helped Abby back up. They moved

ahead, and when the men saw them they rushed to clear the way. Once they were done, the coach eased on through, all the workers taking a good look at Abby.

After that the going was rough and beautiful at the same time, the road hanging to the side of a rock wall over Henson Creek until it finally came down level with the water. Abby imagined the river beside them was full of fish that were tasty and as wild as the countryside.

Afternoon was setting in, and the sun seemed to go down early, thanks to being surrounded by tall mountains.

"Just around the bend," Slim said, "is Lake City."

Lake City

Henson Creek widened into a small river that rushed right through the middle of Lake City, opening into the Lake Fork Valley. Late that afternoon the coach made its way around a shoulder of rock, offering Abby a view of the entire town. A smoky haze hung over the sprawled-out community surrounded by mountains rising thousands of feet, hiding Lake City in the security of a protected mile-wide valley.

The mining depression of the 1880s had brought many a boom-town to its knees, some abandoned and forgotten while others hung on by sheer will and determination. Though the 1880s had been tough on Lake City, thanks to the long expected arrival of the Denver & Rio Grande in 1889, Lake City was enjoying a second boom, mainly due to the silver and lead from the Ute-Ule mine. Word of a second mine, the gold-producing Golden Fleece, carried far and attracted many others. Lake City had again become pros-perous, and expectations ran high much as in the late 1870s.

Slim brought the horses to a slow walk through the town of exquisite architecture. It appeared many were remodeling. The first construction boom of the early days had resulted in retail and mer-chandising stores with basic block fronts and a manicured façade, celebrating the preference of civil order over unsightly tent roof affairs. By the late 1870s buildings were constructed of finished stone and brick, the architecture mainly of Victorian influence with inherent qualities of Gothic, Italianate, Greek-Revival, and Romanesque, all of which formed a jumbled mixture pleasing to the eye.

Coming to a halt in front of the Hinsdale House, Slim set the brake, spit, and turned to Abby. "This is a good hotel for the night. You'll be safe here." He broke his speech as if thinking of the trip ahead, then let her in on his thoughts. "We should leave as early as possible. The first half of the trip is hard on the horses. Once we get over Slum we ought to be all right."

Having confidence in Slim's opinions, Abby was agreeable. "I can be ready whenever you want. Where will you spend the night?"

"We don't have an office here, but we do have a place to rest and feed the horses. I'll be stayin' over there." Slim felt he had to say a little more, having appointed himself to oversee Abby's welfare. "Lake City is a nice place for the most part, but it still has its share of lawlessness. If I were you, Miss Abby, I'd get me a bite to eat, then just get some rest in my room. It probably ain't safe to be roamin' around."

"Now what would I be roaming around for, Slim?" Abby quipped. "I'll be ready in the morning by the time you are. Now help me down."

"Yes'm," Slim said as he jumped to the ground. He came around and helped Abby down. As she brushed the road dust from her dress, Slim rolled the canvas back for her so she could fish a few things from one of her trunks and put them in her large bag. "Well," he drawled, "I reckon I'll see you in the mornin'."

"I'll be waiting," Abby assured him. She detected the worry in Slim's voice and was well aware he had adopted her for the time being. Even if he was far from polished, he was a kind and decent man, not to mention toughened by the ways of the wild and experienced in dealing with all kinds of misfortune. She had to admit that when Slim was around, she felt well-guarded and safe.

The Hinsdale House was a popular hotel, as Abby discovered upon entering the two-story structure, a place where visitors sat in the lobby in friendly discussion over coffee or tea and scattered newspapers. It was a big hotel for a small town, but primitive in comparison to the Strater Hotel in Durango or the Grand Imperial Hotel in Silverton. Accommodations were pleasant and agreeable, her room small and efficient with everything neat and tidy and in its place.

Once settled in, Abby changed clothes. The grit and grime of travel was like a coating that darkened her face and hands and dusted her clothes. Using the pitcher, washrag, and washbasin, she cleaned up until she felt refreshed. Darkness replaced light at the window, so she pulled down the shade and lit a lantern; the oily odor of kerosene filled the room. The conveniences of electricity had yet to reach this remote town, reminding Abby that her trip was taking her further into the wilderness. She wondered what Creede would be like. The boomtown would probably have even fewer of the modern things she was used to. But she had survived worse, and she decided she was as tough as anyone else, and just as determined to reach her goals.

~

A grinding hunger sent Abby a block away to Delmonico's Restaurant, where she enjoyed a beefsteak and mashed potatoes and gravy. A pretty young woman having dinner by herself attracted the eyes and curiosity of many, but she ignored them all and was on her way in a short time. The town was busy with life and gaiety from the saloons on Silver Street, the music of pianos penetrating the cold night air. Men on the streets were generally well-mannered, most of them businessmen of the district. The miners frequented a separate area on the western bluffs of Lake City where the red-light district overlooked the town. It was commonly referred to by the men as "Hell's Acres" and was not referred to at all by the proper ladies of the community. The district was located on Bluff Street, and the young ladies of class were strictly forbidden to even speak the street's name.

In front of the hotel, Abby paused to take in the pleasant night air. A group of gentlemen were doing the same not far away, lost in conversation about their ambitious plans. All she could think of was how close she was to reunion with the man who loved her. Perhaps tomorrow she would see Billy and his smiling face. The trip had been long and trying and at times a true test of her stamina, but all her troubles disappeared as she envisioned future happiness.

"Pardon me, don't I know you?"

Abby turned quickly at the sound of a woman's voice who spoke with a genteel British accent. The voice did not match the woman at all. She must have been forty at least and wore a frilly, feminine dress. She was short, stocky, and round-faced and clenched a smoking cigar between her teeth.

"I don't think so," Abby replied nervously, not sure what to expect from a character like the one standing before her.

"One wouldn't forget a face like that," the woman said politely as she studied Abby's countenance, drawing closer. She removed the cigar from her mouth so the smoke no longer hampered her vision. "Yes, deary, I've seen you before. Have you ever been in Leadville?"

"Why, yes," Abby admitted, half-mumbling. "I lived there for years."

"That's it!" the woman said, then stuck the cigar back in her mouth, grinned, and offered Abby her hand.

Reluctantly Abby shook her hand, noticing that, unlike her appearance, her hands were soft and delicate. Her dainty manners contrasted with her crude mannerisms, but her friendly grizzled face smiled with enthusiasm. "My name's Alice Duffield. I must have seen you in Leadville—I lived there for five years, until my husband, Frank, died in a mining explosion."

"I'm sorry about your husband," Abby said timidly. "I'm Abby DeSpain."

"Don't feel sorry for me," Alice said boastfully. "So it's Abby, is it? A fine name in the old tradition. Me? After my hubby died I learned a trade of my own—played in the best parlors in Leadville."

Fearing Alice was a soiled dove, Abby bashfully withdrew. Then a thought came to her as she vaguely remembered stories of a British woman and her uncanny trade.

Sensing Abby's dismay, Alice laughed and said, "Honey, I'm not what you think. I play poker for a living." She turned and glanced across the street as if she were addressing all of Lake City. "This has been a good town, but it's time for me to be on me way. I've played the saloons here and made me mark, and now there are few who'll play against me."

"I remember you now," Abby said. "You're Poker Alice."

"That'd be me." Alice smiled. "I hear there's a new town over the hill just brimming with money. Be me guess it's fine pickin's for a woman of me trade." She puffed at her cigar, now growing short, and continued, "The stage came in this afternoon, and I'm told it'll be going over the hill in the morning."

"The stage to Creede?" Abby questioned.

"One and the same, deary," Alice acknowledged.

"I'm going to Creede myself," Abby boasted. "My fiancé is waiting for me—he owns a silver mine."

Alice smiled at the thought of youth and love and days when she was younger and prettier and had such high hopes. "It's a fine thing, having a man around. I wish my luck with men was as good as me luck with cards." She took the cigar from her mouth and smashed it under her boot on the boardwalk. "Nice to meet you, Abby. A bit o' company on the stage will be nice."

"Good night," Abby said, her eyes following the curious woman as she gently strolled away.

Abby thought about what she'd heard about Poker Alice. She had come from England, and her family settled in Virginia where she attended an elite boarding school for young women. Later her family came west to join the gold rush, and Alice married. Bored to tears during the long, cold winters, she amused herself with the game of poker and became quite good at it. When her husband died, she searched for a job teaching school, but since there was no school in Leadville, she turned to what she knew best—playing poker. She never worked for the sleazy saloons of Leadville, but rather the most luxurious and lavish parlors where she played against men of class and wealth. From what Abby heard, the stakes were high, and Alice often cleaned out the best. But like any exceptional poker player, she had to keep moving and soon vanished from Leadville.

Her eyes fixed on a sky filled with stars, Abby tried to hold down the gathering excitement, so she wouldn't toss and turn all night. Making her way up to her room, she decided to put herself to sleep by reading Psalms from her old Bible. To Abby, God was a distant entity, too distant to contact and certainly too big and powerful to go to with her woes. She pictured Him as mean and insensitive, even cruel, and she believed the most accurate passages in the Bible were the ones telling of His wrath. There had been times of encouragement in her life, times when God seemed caring; but those were days long gone and almost forgotten. She sometimes thought about God but hadn't prayed in years, even in church. Her mind drifted to present matters, swayed by the influences of the day. Nevertheless, she found the poetic feel of the Psalms relaxing and melodious, a way to set her mind at rest.

~

Abby heard the jingling of the horses' bits and jumped out of bed. Running to the window, she peered down into the street and saw Slim and Poker Alice talking beside the coach. Apparently they were about ready to leave. She had overslept! Shoving the stubborn window up, Abby leaned out and called, "Slim! Hold on—I'm coming!" Then she disappeared into the darkness.

Slim shook his head and chuckled at the energetic young Abby. "You know that girl?" Poker Alice asked.

"Yes, ma'am," Slim bragged, his sad eyes turning to Alice. "She's quite a young woman. A bit green maybe, but I believe she'll make it."

Alice had paid Slim and to his astonishment even helped him load her things. "I met her last evening—she seems young to be traveling these parts."

"I guess we all were at one time or another," Slim defended. He spit a small puddle of tobacco juice into the dirt and added, "She's got to start somewhere."

Not offended, Alice removed a cigar from her handbag and struck a match to it, squinted through the smoke, then cleared her throat. "I hear Creede is a rough town, all new and full of vinegar. Might be a hard place for a young lady to get along."

"Yeah," Slim worried. "I been thinkin' about that too. I hope the man she has there is a good one, somebody who will look after her."

Bustling down the stairs and rushing outside, Abby was a bit winded, her hair slightly unruly, her face gleaming with anticipation. "I'm ready, Slim. Let's go!"

"I want you to know," Slim pointed out, opening the coach door, "I fixed the hole in the floor."

Poker Alice crawled in, Abby right behind her. They had the small coach to themselves. "At least I don't have to worry about falling out," Abby teased, making fun of the old coach. "We still might be safer walking."

The older woman grinned around her cigar. Abby's flighty mood was almost contagious in the brilliant morning sun, setting a notion in Alice's head that the day would be a good one. Fall mornings in the mountains of the western slope were inspiring, hindering even the most sour moods. The thin air, sweet and bracing, was cool enough to flush a cheek or nip a nose. The wind stirred softly and unpredictably, carrying the aromas of wood and rock and stream.

The old coach rolled to one side with Slim's weight as he climbed up into the driver's seat. He leaned over the side and called to the passengers, "We're on our way!" He whistled shrilly at the horses, and the coach rushed forth to meet the new day and its hazards.

The coach headed south on a route that climbed above the deep and mysterious Lake San Cristobal, the largest natural body of water in Colorado and one of the most beautiful. Hundreds of years earlier half a mountain had moved in a giant mud slide that dammed the Lake Fork River, forming the lake Abby was staring at with wonder now. In the orange of the morning sunlight, the lake, still as glass, reflected the glorious colors of the mountain range like a giant mirror, casting a spell on its onlookers. Slumgullion Pass in turn exposed the red colors of the dirt and sand of the geographical wash, its trail winding up steeper and steeper to Windy Point. Abby gazed far back to the tiny city below, now resembling a setting in miniature.

On the distant horizon the majestic and jagged peaks of the Matterhorn and Wetterhorn sat like kings over a domain. Named after mountains in Switzerland, they had the wild and airy look of peaks that showed off heights no man could conquer. From afar it appeared their snowcapped summits tore the clouds to pieces, smearing the remnants in a pastel white against a clear and dark blue background. Their massive range spread over what looked like hundreds of miles of impassable terrain that reached up to and became one with the sky. Proud in their glory and dominance, they said more than words could convey in their distant silence.

Abby sat back and exclaimed, "This country amazes me everywhere I go!"

"Yes, it's beautiful," Alice agreed, for she too had been watching the majestic scene through a window. "God had a grand time here, making these mountains."

The grade was long and progress slow, winding higher and higher through thick spruce forests, the sun casting shafts of light through the dark woods like bright bars of gold in caves of darkness. An occasional glimpse of a deer standing in the forest, wiggling its long ears and watching the coach pass, filled Abby with a sense of being part of all she saw. Little ground squirrels darted about, their cheeks fat with tiny seeds. Scurrying marmots in their heavy brown winter coats, issuing their high-pitched warning whistle, blended with the mysterious festiveness of this place, so remote and surprisingly different. A strong smell of spruce and fir followed them as the coach wheeled into and out of shadows of strong greens and browns.

The unburdened and innocent world all around Abby filled her with the happiness of freedom and a vision of controlling her own fate, as if the unreachable illusion was finally coming to pass. She wondered how long it had been since she'd felt this way. She recalled a time when the precious feeling had been tortured—when her father died, and then again when the childish feeling had been dealt its fatal blow—the loss of her family's wealth and status, reducing her to the hardheaded, everyday work of common people. She recalled the strange sensation of loss and vowed to never go through that again. Now that love and wealth were in sight, she was on top of the world and all was within her grasp.

～

"I'd say it's about time for a bite, missy," Alice said as she bent over and rooted through her baggage. She came up with items wrapped in grease-stained brown paper. "Like some? It's a thought I had this morning—bacon and cheese in bread."

The mention and smell of the food reminded Abby of how hungry she was. "I never even thought about lunch until now," Abby confessed. "Your idea sounds good."

"I've got apples too," Alice said, unwrapping the sandwiches.

The coach bounced along as the women ate lunch, spilling crumbs of dry bread everywhere.

"I guess I haven't been very talkative," Abby apologized.

"I can see you've got a lot to think about—your head is in the clouds," Alice mused. Her face was hardened from rough living, but kindness was revealed in her expression. "It's a fine time in life when a young woman comes to a time when everything seems lovely and wonderful, when the future holds nothing but promise."

Abby chewed and listened, realizing Alice had some deep regrets. "I used to see life like a rainbow—all the colors and even the pot of gold. Now I know life can throw anything at you, deal you a hand you don't expect—it's all in the cards, Abby."

Abby didn't believe in cards or luck or much of anything else except that Billy was on the other side of the mountain and she would find him and they would be married and live wealthy lives of happiness ever after.

The summit of Slumgullion Pass was long, smooth, and flat. Slim stopped at a small creek that ran into a large pool beside the rutted road. "Got to water the horses, ladies," he called. "Might want to stretch your legs—we got a fer piece to go yet."

Taking advantage of the opportunity, Abby and Alice climbed out and walked around, bending over and stretching their backs. It was midday, and the sun sat high above them, a white and blinding spot in the sky.

"How much further?" Alice asked Slim.

Slim put his hand over his eyes and checked the weather. "We ought to make it by dark—it's all downhill now. That's if we don't encounter any obstacles."

Alice nodded and continued moving her feet and stretching her back. Abby thought she looked older in the bright sunlight, her hair graying, pulled back and put up tightly in a bun, her face dry and wrinkled, her lips thin. Slim wisely kept his big-brimmed hat on to provide himself with a little shade, his facial expression hidden by the shadow.

"We better be gettin' along," Slim finally said, pulling the horses back around. He courteously helped the ladies in and took a long step to climb back up on top, then whistled at the team. They were on their way again.

~

Abby grew weary as they rode along miles and miles of winding road. As the speed of the coach picked up due to the descent, she bounced around like a loose pebble in a shoe. Alice held on tight. They both sighed in relief when Slim called out, "Whoa, boys!"

Looking out the windows, the two women saw they were in the middle of a big valley, with mountains off to one side. Abby stuck her head out the window and saw about a half a dozen Indians motioning for Slim to bring the coach to a full stop. She pulled back inside, her eyes wide and full of fear. "Alice," she cried, "there are Indians out there!"

Alice immediately removed a .38 pistol from her garter belt and checked to make sure it was loaded. "No Indian is going to mess with me!" she said vehemently.

When the coach rolled to a stop, the women heard Slim and the Indians talking but couldn't understand what they were saying. One of the old Indians came close to the coach and stuck his dark, weather-beaten face in the window. His face was morose and unyielding, expressionless and cold. Only his big dark eyes moved, looking the women over like they were cattle. Alice palmed her pistol, ready to fire at the least provocation. Abby was afraid to utter a sound. The sight of the old man's face in the window was as scary as hearing a bear try to knock down a cabin door. Fortunately, the Indian quickly withdrew.

Soon the coach rolled on once more, and Abby looked out to see the small band on their way again, walking down the road. "Hey, Slim!" Abby called.

The coach stopped, and Slim leaned down. "Somethin' wrong?"

"What was all that about? They scared the tarnation out of us down here."

Slim stretched so far from his seat he was practically leaning through the window. "Sorry, ladies. They meant no harm. Just a bunch of starvin' Utes that was wonderin' if I had anything I could give 'em."

"What'd you tell them?" Abby questioned, still frightened.

"Well, I didn't have nothin' for them to eat, but I had a good rope of chewin' tobacco and gave 'em some of that. Told 'em it would hold off their hunger until they got up on the pass where we seen plenty of deer." Slim just stared, waiting for more questions.

"Oh," Abby said, then stared at Slim staring at her. "Well, let's get goin' then."

Leaning back in her seat, Abby watched Alice replace the gun in the garter belt. "You always carry a gun, Alice?"

"Always," Alice replied.

~

It was almost dark when the coach came rolling into Jim Town, where the rail yards and bridges straddled Willow Creek, beyond which stood the Gateway Cliffs and Willow Creek Canyon, including the town of Creede. The creek wound like a corkscrew for almost two miles. The town had been discovered by Nicholas C. Creede, a wandering cowboy searching for riches who found an outcropping of silver in 1889. Quickly selling his claim, word leaked out, and the rush was on. The town soon turned into a tent town with a population of some 10,000.

Poker Alice leaned forward eagerly to see this famous town located near the headwaters of the Rio Grande River. Vertical rock walls enclosed the town on two sides, forcing it to run up the canyon deeper into the mountains. At places it looked no more than a hundred feet across. Already Creede had earned a reputation as one of the West's richest and wildest mining camps, the folk there ruthless and contemptuous, a lawless no-man's-land because of disputable county boundaries. Efforts to bring law to the area were useless, and

Shotgun Hill, the local graveyard, filled up fast. The only order was maintained by the camp bosses, self-proclaimed venturers bent on exploitation and profit.

Unknown to either Alice or Abby, one of these bosses was a small weasel by the name of Bob Ford, a ruthless man who had killed the notorious Jesse James. Watching the approaching coach in the dusk like a snake watches a mouse, Ford was curious about the new arrivals. He was delighted to discover that two of them were women.

PART THREE

~

LOST SOULS

~ 13 ~

In the Den of Sin

Daylight grew thin after Grant found a livery for Mister and Peaches. He unpacked the things he would need, put them in a canvas bag, slung it over his shoulder, and carried his Winchester in his free hand. The rest could stay at the livery, locked out of sight. Entering the street, he could see Silverton was a boisterous place. Night was here in full swing, and the rowdies were already partying. Like most boomtowns, there was a delicate balance between the respectable side of town and the not so respectable. Having limited money, knowing he needed a cheap room, he decided he would take his chances on the rough side.

Fortunately, Grant found a room on Mineral Street, one block over from the notorious Blair Street. The Gray Bear Saloon was small and down on its luck and rented the few rooms upstairs by the night. Two men stood at the bar, and a few more played cards at a lopsided table. There was no piano and no girls.

"I saw your sign out front," Grant said, dropping his gear to the floor. "Got a room?" He was tired and hungry and wanted to make this as easy as possible.

"Yeah, I got a room," the bartender said. "Ain't much." He looked like he had seen his better days as well, being old and out of sorts, slow and lethargic. Like so many, his face was sunken and his neck thin; he had a look of malnutrition about him.

"How much?" Grant asked.

"Two dollars a night. Will you be stayin' long?"

"Maybe, maybe not," Grant answered as he paid the two dollars. "I'm looking for a girl—here's a picture."

The old bartender looked at the photograph, the edges crinkled and worn. He shook his head. "Might be hard to find a girl here."

"I know," Grant said, picking up his things. "But I have to find this one—she's my sister."

Handing him the room key, the bartender said, "Room 3, up the stairs and on the right. Good luck trying to find your sister."

Grant climbed the stairs, glancing back at the barkeep and seeing his dull eyes following him. He knew the old man probably figured he was the kind of man who was always in, or causing, trouble—big-shouldered, wearing the rawhide of the outdoors type, a rifle in one hand, thick auburn hair, piercing green eyes, and a wide jaw clinched tight. Grant tried to erase that impression with a smile and walked softly to his room.

Another two-bit room in another boomtown—nothing more than a large closet with a bed, a chair, and a dresser, and thankfully a washbasin, pitcher, and washrag. Grant stripped to the waist and cleansed himself of the grit from the trail. The reddish beard could stay, he figured, as long as he kept it trimmed.

Standing by the window later, he had a view of the town below. He had caught the smell of it at first entry. There were the usual wood smoke and livestock odors, but the smells he noticed most were those of whiskey and cigar smoke and sweet perfume, typical of the rustic boomtowns, along with gambling and drinking and prostitution. He prayed Abby hadn't turned to such a desperate life to survive.

Grant had little or no trust in Billy Rogers, a wise and witty greenhorn who thought he could outsmart the best. He was the kind of young man who would end up in a tight corner, and then his true colors would show. Grant had no doubt Billy thought only of himself; anyone else was expendable, including Abby.

Smelling a sizzling beefsteak reminded Grant he was hungry. He valued his good health and made it a point to eat well if he could, unlike many who wasted away their lives through immoral living and whiskey.

Night had set in by the time Grant found a place to eat, a long and narrow building on Blair Street that advertised beefsteaks. He found a table and pulled out a bent wood chair and sat down. The smell of beef roasting over a fire made him hungry. The ceiling was stamped tin, the walls made of square hewn logs, the tables covered with red-checkered oilcloths.

"Yes, sir?" a small, thin woman said, looking at Grant with big brown eyes.

"I'll have a big steak, red in the center," Grant said, guessing the woman weighed ninety pounds at the most.

"Rib cut?"

"Yeah, that'll do fine. Bring whatever comes with it."

While Grant was waiting for his steak, two ladies came in and sat near him, dressed in a way that advertised their trade. They were both young, but rough living had made them appear much older than they were. Every time Grant glanced over, he caught one or both of them looking at him, but they quickly turned away.

Must be off duty, Grant thought with some amusement. *I guess they have to eat too.*

The steak was hot and big and juicy, and Grant made his best effort to show some manners while he gorged himself. Just as quickly as he had come in, he was leaving, passing the two girls. "Evening, ladies," he said, touching the wide brim of his hat.

They smiled, giving him the eye. They didn't usually end up with a strong and handsome young man like him.

Pushing his way through the crowds of Blair Street, Grant realized that searching for Abby in this town could last for weeks or even months. In fact, he might not ever find out anything. Satisfied from the good meal but worried about his lost sister, he made his way back to his room, noticing all the details of his surroundings. A bullet hole in a wall, a girl on the corner under the streetlamp, a fat man in a fancy suit. He stored it all away for possible use later. He would get some rest; maybe things would look better in the morning.

～

Dawn was normally the quietest time in Silverton, but this

morning Grant was abruptly awakened by gunfire. From his window he could see a drunk staggering down the street, his pistol raised, firing into the early-morning air. Moving away from the window, Grant pulled his leathers on over his cotton underwear and got ready for the day. It would be a long day of searching, asking questions, trying to find a clue to Abby's whereabouts.

The morning's fresh air contrasted sharply with the streets' mud, litter, and manure. The odors of the overcrowded town were unmistakable. Some of the bars were still busy, but for the most part traffic on the streets was light. As he walked, noting the layout of the place, Grant saw a pig farmer at the end of the street slopping his hogs, his bucket clanging in one hand, his apron soiled and dirty.

He wondered where he should start his search. Remembering his mistake in Durango, Grant decided he would start in the upper-class district. Obviously, Billy had been funding Abby's trip quite well and putting her in the finest places, though Grant expected that ploy would be short-lived. He again felt uneasy about Abby traveling alone. Something wasn't right about the entire picture. Abby was chasing a fantasy, but why?

The Grand Imperial Hotel was big and imposing, sitting on Greene and Twelfth Streets like a stone castle. The traffic out front was mostly carriages and fine horses. This area was almost like a different town, a complete opposite of Blair Street. Here buildings were big and glorious, and the upper class flaunted their wealth.

Entering the lobby, Grant noticed the stares, the disapproving eyes looking at him like he'd crawled off of a manure wagon. Caring little about what others thought, especially the well-to-do, he approached the desk clerk, a small man with a big head, a pointed chin, and a blank expression.

"I'm sorry, sir, we're all full," he said blandly, a practiced speech for the unwanted.

"Glad to hear business is good," Grant said, overlooking the man's snootiness. "Listen, I'm looking for my sister. She's missing, and I think she might've been here a short while back." Carefully, Grant removed the photograph from its protection in his leather wallet and handed it to the nervous little man.

The clerk cast a glance at it, not really caring about this stranger or his sister, not really looking at the picture. He just wanted to do his job—discouraging any riffraff from frequenting the lobby. "I'm sorry, sir," he said, blankly staring at Grant, hoping he'd get the message that he should just go his way.

Replacing the picture, Grant turned to leave without another word. The manager came up to the clerk inquiring, "What did he want?"

Proud of how he'd handled the situation, the small man said, "He's just some lost mountain man who thinks his sister might have stayed here." They both had a brief laugh and forgot about it.

The other hotels, restaurants, and stores all gave Grant the same helpless reply. One lady at a dress shop pointed out the certain futility of Grant's efforts. "Do you know how many lost or homeless girls come in here looking for a job? Why, I bet I get four or five a week, and they're all the same. They think because they sewed something once they're qualified to work here. No offense, mister, but you might try looking over on the side of town where they *can* find a job!" She spun quickly and went back to her business, leaving Grant standing there alone.

After a few days of searching, Grant began to realize the truth of the woman's words. As horrible as it made him feel, he knew he had to start looking on the bad side of town, just in case. It was by no means an easy job to ask questions about someone in a place where everyone was secretive. When Grant showed the picture to a group of men outside a saloon, one of the men, who was slightly drunk, grabbed it and stared at it hard. "Well, she's nice lookin' all right," he said, handing it back. "Let me give you some advice. Don't be wastin' your time lookin' for her 'cause she'll just run off again if you do find her. You're only hurting yourself, friend, so give it up. It's like this—women is like the stagecoach, they come and they go."

Disgusted, Grant could see he was getting nowhere. Since he and Abby didn't have a strong resemblance, some people didn't even believe she was his sister, thinking instead she was his wife who had run away. They thought he was a fool for chasing after her.

His money quickly ran low, for prices were high. With no other clues as to where to go, Grant figured he needed to get a job so he could stay around and continue his search for his sister. He went to *The Silverton Standard*, a newspaper office on Greene Street.

"I like your qualifications," the editor said, a man with receding black hair and a dark black mustache. His eyes were dark but honest. "I really don't have much work available right now, other than delivering papers."

Grant nodded and gave it some thought. Jobs were hard to find, and some he could find didn't pay enough to get by. "I'll take it," he said. "Never know what might come up."

"That's right," the editor agreed, thinking Grant was referring to the rewards that come from hard work.

Grant actually meant that he might be able to find out something about his sister if he stayed around town. The job took him all over town and into almost every place of businesses. He kept hoping that he'd meet someone who could help him find Abby.

Generally Grant wrapped up his day by early afternoon, having started at five o'clock in the morning. As the editor had insinuated, it paid little, but it was enough to cover Grant's overpriced two-dollar room and some simple meals. As he went about his routine day by day, he carefully observed every small incident, memorizing every face. Oddly, nobody said a word about the newspaper being delivered by a man toting a Winchester rifle. Stranger sights had been seen in Silverton.

∽

A late-afternoon wind whisked the smell of autumn down from the high country, bringing with it a chill that tightened wraps and overcoats. Grant was done with the newspaper for the day and stood on the corner of Blair and Tenth Streets, watching. Week by week people came and went, but some remained—the regulars, the business owners and operators, the working class, including the ladies of ill repute.

Again Grant saw the two young girls he had seen at the restaurant and many times since. They were about the same size—healthily plump—and wore the frills of their trade. One had dark brown hair, and the other was a dirty blonde; both had blue eyes and round and plain faces. On a hunch he decided to question them to see if they had seen Abby.

"Excuse me, ladies," Grant said politely, stepping in front of the girls as they approached. "I was wondering . . ."

"It's about time," one of the girls interrupted. "We were the ones wondering—wondering when you would come around."

Grant's face reddened, an emotional giveaway he despised but couldn't help. "You don't understand . . . I'm not requesting your services—I'm looking for my sister—she's missing." He held out the photograph, and both girls quickly took it in their small hands and looked it over, then looked at each other. Stories like this interested them, for they had been in the same predicament at one time—on their own and going through hard times, turning in desperation to a way of life that at first repulsed them.

"Isn't this the one we saw loitering over there on the street corner?" the girl with brown hair asked her friend. "Remember? She looked like she was on her last bit of luck."

"Oh yes, I remember, several weeks back. That Harvey Strickland was comin' at her." The wind whipped a strand of long blonde hair into her face, and she gently shoved it back with her gloved hand, then flashed her eyes at Grant. "We seen her all right. When a girl gets in that shape, usually one of the pimps picks her up and takes care of her for a while."

"Then she has to repay him," the brown-haired girl added with disgust. "And after that, a girl never gets out of debt—always workin' for the same man."

"Have you seen her since?" Grant asked, breathing heavily. The idea of having found someone who had seen Abby elevated his hopes.

The girls looked at each other and back at Grant and shook their heads.

"Who's this Harvey Strickland?" Grant questioned further.

The girls made faces at each other, expressions of obvious disapproval. "He's a no-good so-and-so," one of them said. "Runs a parlor down the street here. Nice place, but he's mean and vicious, always beating his girls and takin' things from them he shouldn't be takin'."

Grant knew about those kind of men. Every town he could remember living in had its red-light district with sad girls and their sad stories.

"You say this Harvey Strickland approached Abby, my sister?"

"We was walkin' by and noticed her, down-and-out like she was. Then we seen Harvey pushing his way through to get at her, and he was talkin' to her. We ain't seen her since then."

"Do you think she might be down at his place?" Grant asked, growing impatient and trying to restrain his temper.

"She might," the girls agreed.

"How will I know this Harvey Strickland?"

"You can't miss him," the blonde said. They both laughed. "He's a big fat man dressed like a penguin; black suits is all he wears. He's got a gold tooth right in the front, right up here," the other girl said, putting her finger on a front upper tooth.

Grant found the girls warm and human, with emotions just like everyone else. The life they were living wasn't right, but they weren't worse than anyone else. He knew that women of their trade had been exploited and manipulated into pushing any natural feelings down beneath an impenetrable outer shell.

Touching his hat brim, Grant said, "I sincerely thank you both. You've been a big help. Anything I can do for you, just give me a yell."

The girls giggled, and one said, "You could come callin' on us."

Grant smiled and shook his finger at them, then headed for the end of the street. He felt sorry for the young girls, recalling that sometimes a man would come to town and take a liking to one of the soiled doves and marry her. Sometimes it worked out, but sometimes after a week or a month of being stuck in a mountain cabin, the girl would return to town and take up where she'd left off, preferring the immoral excitements of city life to the loneliness of rural or wilderness living.

Walking swiftly, Grant's mind busily thought about Harvey Strickland. If this pimp had pushed Abby into his employ or had harmed her in any way— Grant gritted his teeth as he pictured the beating he would give the man.

At the end of the street he saw a quaintly painted house with white lace trim and a white picket fence around the front. A sign hung in the front saying: Gentlemen Welcome. This was surely Strickland's place.

Grant shifted his rifle to his other hand, unlatched the gate, and walked softly up to the front door. He knocked with the barrel of his gun. He saw the window shade move as if somebody was peeking out; then the door gently opened. An older woman wearing makeup as thick as a coat of paint stood there, her brilliant red hair piled high above her head. She held a cigarette in one hand. "Please, do come in," she offered with a smile, opening the door all the way.

Grant was immediately assaulted by the smell of strong perfume. The dimly lit parlor was exquisite, crowded with heirloom-quality Queen Anne chairs and davenports, luxurious lamps hanging from gold chains, and exotic furs draped over a grand piano. Golds, reds, and violets were predominant. A silver-plated parlor stove made popping noises. As his eyes adjusted, he could see several women sitting in seductive poses and smiling at him. They wore low-cut dresses of lace and velvet; their hair was adorned with soft-floating plumes of feathers.

"Can I get you something to drink?" the older woman who'd answered the door asked, her voice soft and alluring.

Turning to her, Grant said firmly, "I'm here to see Harvey Strickland."

Instantly, her expression fell and was replaced by a hard stone face. Her painted eyes dropped to the rifle in Grant's hand. She stared coldly at Grant's eyes, eyes that had become as cold as steel. "May I tell him who's calling?"

Out of the corner of his eye, Grant noticed that all the girls in the parlor had scampered away, like mice when a lamp is lit. "My name isn't important." The woman turned her back on Grant and rushed through a door, closing it securely behind her. He could hear a man's angry voice, then heard some shuffling sounds.

Then the door opened, and Harvey Strickland stood there looking like a gorilla in a suit. He had broad shoulders and big muscles and must have weighed nearly 300 pounds. His hair was black and well-groomed, his eyes dark and deep-set, his nose flat above a wide, stubborn mouth. He glared at Grant, determined not to budge an inch on any matter that brought a man to his door demanding to see him.

"Can I help you, sir?" Harvey asked coldly, obviously not really wanting to be any help at all.

His bulk was enough to intimidate most men, but Grant refused to let fear keep him from doing what he had to. This was a man who exploited and beat women, and Grant simply would not back down from such an evil coward, though he wouldn't act impulsively either. Grant was sure the bulge in Strickland's pocket was a small pistol.

Confidently, Grant stepped right up to Strickland. "I'm looking for a particular woman, my sister. I understand you may have talked to her." Grant held out the photo, beginning to show wear and tear from the trip.

Exhaling with some relief, Harvey took the little picture in his wide hand and looked at it long enough to think of what he was going to say. The woman who had let Grant in now stood behind Harvey, her arms crossed, the expression on her face severe.

"I've never seen her," Harvey snapped. "Now, is there anything else I can do for you?"

Grant noticed a gold tooth, and he was certain the two young girls had told him the truth about Abby and Harvey. "That's not what I was told," Grant challenged

Harvey's eyes turned into slits, and his brow furrowed. His mouth formed a slim straight line across his wide face, and his wide hands turned into clenched fists. "Are you calling me a liar?"

"Yes, I am!" Grant fumed.

For a big man, Harvey moved fast, and he grabbed the front of Grant's coat and slammed him against a wall. But Grant had been ready, and he sent a heavy blow into the big man's stomach, making him double over with a coughing spasm. Harvey stood with his hands on his knees, trying to get his breath back, looking up at Grant with eyes of rage. He barreled forward like a bull on a rampage, his arms extended to grab Grant and pin him to the floor. But Grant was quick as a cat and sidestepped the locomotive-like lunge. As Harvey passed him, Grant helped him along with a push from strong muscles and sent the man crashing through the front door and out into the dirt yard.

Grant was right behind the big man, jumping on him like an angry badger. Harvey slapped a huge hand at Grant's ankle and took his foot out from under him, forcing Grant to tumble to the ground, losing his hat and dropping his rifle. Harvey hoped to take advantage of his bulk in order to pin the young man down.

What Harvey hadn't planned on was the quick agility and the extreme arm and shoulder strength possessed by the young man. Grant's fist came up, catching Harvey under the jaw with a loud *pop*, causing the gold tooth to fall onto the ground and forcing Harvey to fall on his back, his mouth bleeding. The big man exhaled, his arms spread-eagle, his head spinning in pain.

A crowd had gathered, always hungry for a fight, cheering the men on for more. But after they saw Harvey drop like a shot bear, they lost interest and dispersed. Up on the porch all the girls stood in their fancy colors, glad to see Harvey get a taste of his own medicine. The older woman stood at the front, glaring at the scene in the shadows of dusk, her expression tight and unyielding.

Grant came to his feet and dusted himself off, then picked up his rifle. He stood over the ailing Harvey, looking down at the miserable hulk. Grant wisely reached into the villain's coat pocket, removed the small pistol, and tossed it to the side. "I'm going to ask you one more time—when did you see my sister? And what did you say to her?"

Out of breath, Harvey lifted himself to his elbows, then ran one of his huge hands across his bloody mouth. He felt the hole where the tooth had been, then looked around and saw it lying in the dirt. He picked it up, stared at it sadly, and whimpered, "Second time that's happened lately. Can't seem to keep these things in my mouth." He turned his attention to Grant, his head pounding, but now willing to tell his story rather than get another beating.

"I saw her on the street," he breathed heavily. "I see lots of girls like her—dirty, out of luck, nowhere to turn. I offered her a bed and a bath, somewhere to stay until she got on her feet again."

Grant heard the girls on the porch giggle at such nonsense.

"But she'd have nothing to do with it," Harvey continued. "I tried to convince her she was being silly, tried to tell her how things really are." Harvey paused, trying to find words that wouldn't incriminate him.

"Keep going," Grant said, nudging Harvey under the chin with his rifle barrel.

"Well, there was this man, some cowboy, trying to butt in. I turned and shoved him out of the way, told him it was none of his business. I had my back to him, talking to the girl, and he came up behind me and coldcocked me. He knocked my tooth out too." Harvey blinked, realizing he was a mess, his mouth bleeding onto his fancy clothes. "That's all there is to it. I don't remember anything after that. I haven't seen the girl again either. She must have gone with the cowboy."

Grant digested this while deciding if Harvey had told him everything. He extended his hand and pulled the big man to his feet. "You could have told me that to begin with, saved us both a lot of trouble."

Harvey produced a white handkerchief and rubbed at his busted lip. He nodded at Grant, defeated, and marched up the steps and into the building. The older woman followed him inside. Watching him go, Grant picked up his hat and slapped it against his leg, then placed it on his head. He turned to the young ladies on the porch, now making flirtatious gestures at him, their eyes glowing, wearing big smiles.

"Evenin', ladies," Grant said calmly and slowly moved away. *So she rode off with a cowboy*, he figured. *Wonderful!*

~

Another two days passed, and Grant was unable to learn anything new about Abby. He was running out of money, and his job didn't pay enough to live on. Besides, since he now knew Abby had moved on to parts unknown, there was no reason to remain in Silverton.

So one morning, with Mister saddled and Peaches packed, Grant took to the mountains, putting Silverton behind him. Clouds blotted out the sun, and the air was calm and cool as Mister snorted and broke into a trot. Living under the sky would be easier and would cost him nothing while he decided what to do next. Unsure which direction to take, he took the road north past the long mills that ran up the mountains, their roofs big and flat and angled downhill parallel with the mountainside. A trail cut up to the east, and he took it, rising into higher elevations, glad to leave the stench of the town far behind.

After climbing awhile, the trail dwindled to nothing, the spruce forest thick and dark green and offering plenty of shelter. Grant picked a good place to make camp. A mat of pine needles gave off a fresh fragrance. A stream gurgled nearby, the tranquillity relaxing after a rowdy town with constant noise.

Dismounting, Grant could see the mountains across the wide valley far below, mountains dotted with mines and their tailings. He went over to unpack Peaches when he heard a twig snap under heavy weight.

"Hold it right there—let that rifle drop to the ground," a man ordered.

Mister jumped and snorted, frightened by the intrusion. The soft pine needle mat had enabled someone to sneak up on Grant and his horse. As he lowered his rifle, he turned to see two men with their pistols drawn—they had the drop on him.

∽ 14 ∽

The High Trail

His hands tied behind his back, Grant was helped up onto Mister, whose reins were held by the man riding up front, leading the way. The other man rode behind, pulling Peaches along, a rifle ready in his hand in case Grant tried anything foolish.

Grant could feel the big knife he carried, the one Beuford gave him. It was in his belt in the middle of his back, right under his hands, covered by his leather coat. At the first opportunity, he would slip it out and work on the ropes that bound his wrists. In the meantime, he was trying to figure out why the men were taking him somewhere, and why they hadn't simply shot him and taken his goods. The men were no amateurs, and they weren't the desperate type with a crazy look in their eyes. These were the kind of men who truly worried Grant—they were professionals.

Before long the trail widened and came to an abandoned mine with small cabins at the tunnel opening. The men rode in casually, in no hurry.

Two men came out of the cabin to inspect the find. "What we got here?" one said, looking Grant and his animals over.

"Found him sneaking around just off the trail. Looks like he might be workin' for somebody." The speaker dismounted, then helped Grant down to the ground. "Come on inside, pardner. I'm sure the boss will have some questions for you."

The inside of the cabin was dim and smoky. They backed a chair up to the wall and sat Grant down so they could watch him. One man went back out, leaving three in the cabin with Grant. Ever so casually, he slipped the knife out and worked it around in his hands until the blade was on the rope. He lightly sawed with the blade while he tried to make conversation, drawing attention away from any movement he was making. "You fellows always kidnap people, take a man and his horse and mule?" Grant's voice was low and calm.

One of the men who sat at the table before him was rolling a smoke, his eyes on what he was doing. Another shuffled a deck of cards, and the third glanced at Grant and said, "Ain't nobody got any business up here unless they're snooping around. And we don't take kindly to anyone snooping around our camp."

"I didn't even know this camp was here," Grant said. "I thought this was free country." The ropes were loosening as Grant worked the blade. He was already considering his next step. The man talking to him had his pistol lying on the table in front of him. Grant would throw the knife at him and then seize the pistol. He wasn't sure that would work, but it was the only plan he had. He'd stumbled into a nest of robbers, and now that he'd seen them and knew where their hideout was, he doubted they would let him go.

"Just shut up and keep your seat," the man said rudely. "The boss will be along directly. He'll find out who you are and what you're up to."

Grant knew he had limited time. He untied the rope and held it in one fist, the big knife ready in his throwing hand. Now he just had to decide the best time to catch them off guard.

Boot steps sounded loudly on the front porch, and the door swung open as two men entered. "What kind of mangy horse is that out there?" one asked jokingly. "Looks like something out of a book I once saw—a prehistoric horse. I thought they were extinct!" He laughed, then came directly over to Grant. "What kind of horse is that anyway?"

"It's a mustang," Grant said, in no mood for joking.

"See there, fellows," he said, turning to address the rest of the group, "a mustang just might be the descendant of that primitive horse I saw in that book."

When the man turned his back, Grant sprang from the chair and put the razor-sharp blade to his throat. The others instantly had their guns drawn, but Grant held the leader in his grasp.

"All I want is out of here," Grant said calmly. "I don't mean nobody no harm."

"Whoa, hold on now," the man Grant held said carefully, the big blade at his throat. "I'm sure we can work this out—no sense in getting upset."

"What'll we do, Butch?" one of the men asked, holding his pistol on his boss and looking helpless.

Grant caught the name instantly, and his thoughts began to race. He pulled the man to the side better so he could see his face in the dim light. "Butch Cassidy?"

"All right, so now that you know my name, what are you going to do? These boys aren't going to let you escape if you kill me."

"Butch?" Grant said again, releasing his grip and putting the knife away. "Don't you remember me? Grant DeSpain."

Butch turned, rubbing his throat, and looked at Grant closely until his eyes lit up. "Well, stick me in the pickle barrel! Is that you, Grant? I didn't recognize you under that red fur on your face. Blow me over!" He turned and looked at the boys, who still had their guns drawn, bewilderment on their faces. "Put those things away before somebody gets hurt! Get the whiskey out!"

Grabbing the chair and dragging it over to the table, Butch pulled Grant into it and then sat down himself. Butch poured a glass and shoved it at Grant, then poured one for himself. "Good thing you told me who you were, I might have had to kill you. I sure hope you're not working for the law," Butch said.

"Nothing like that," Grant said, relieved.

"This is a real surprise," Butch acknowledged, then cocked his head to one side and decided maybe it wasn't such a coincidence. "Wait a minute—I bet you're lookin' for Abby."

"How'd you know?"

Butch leaned back and laughed like he always did, then slapped his palm on the table. "She was just here—right here in this camp!"

Grant sat taller in his chair, his ears perking up at the news. Had

God brought him to this place? "How is she? Was she all right? Where is she now?"

"Calm down—drink your whiskey," Butch urged. "I tried to talk her into stayin'." He smiled, thinking of Abby. "Of course, she's way too smart for that." He looked at Grant a little more seriously. "I can't believe how pretty she's grown. I mean, she's beautiful!" The other men grunted, agreeing with his statement.

"But to answer your questions, she's doin' good. Wasn't doin' so good when I found her down in Silverton though. Some big old hoss was getting ready to make a meal of her, so I loosened his jaw a little and brought Abby on back up here. She stayed a while, then had a notion she had to get back to Silverton to see if some slicker she's in love with had sent for her."

"Did you take her back?" Grant asked.

"Yeah, I did. Even gave her some travelin' money. She had a letter waitin'. The fellow wanted her to meet him in Creede."

"Creede," Grant repeated under his breath. "From what I've heard about Creede, that's no place for a lady."

"That's the truth!" Butch said. "I tried to tell her, but you know how thickheaded Abby is."

Nodding, Grant had to agree. "How long has she been gone?"

"A few days or so," Butch thought, then gestured at one of the men. "How long has she been gone, Matt?"

"A week," Matt replied.

Grant was taking all of this in, sorting it out, trying to decide what to do and when to do it.

"You sure grew into a big fellow," Butch said happily, grabbing Grant's shoulder. "Feel those big muscles, would ya? Must have been Lita's cookin' you was raised on."

Grant shrugged. "I just sort of grew, maybe because of the work I do."

"It's a good thing I showed up here—you might have killed all my boys, and then what would I do? I'd have to start all over, and let me tell you, a good gang is hard to find—men who can ride and shoot and all." Butch was enjoying seeing an old friend.

The boys loosened up, trusting Butch's judgment. The sky grew dark outside, and it was only the middle of the afternoon. Snowflakes were beginning to fall lazily, silently floating down. Missing nothing, Butch told Grant, "Looks like you might be stayin' a while, at least until this blows over. You'd be a fool to try to take off after her right now."

Looking out the window, Grant realized Butch was right. He would be staying at the hideout for a while whether he liked it or not. His drink of whiskey sat untouched in front of him as he pondered the future.

~

Butch had grown restless since Abby's departure, thinking about her frequently, wishing he could have done more for her. He often pictured her pretty, laughing face, the silly frown she made when he teased her, the fury she expressed when she was angry. She was the woman he'd always wanted. So he came up with a plan.

Over breakfast the next morning Butch told the boys to shut up and listen while he explained to Grant exactly what they would do. "Now you take me," Butch began, finishing a biscuit with jelly, "I never do a robbery or anything else without a plan." He licked the jelly from his fingers as he finished his biscuit. "I don't know this buzzard Abby is after, but I figure he'll abandon her at some point. Otherwise, why wouldn't he be with her now? I know if it was me, I wouldn't send for her and have her travel across country like this with all these dangerous people lurking about. Why, there are robbers and murderers and all sorts of wicked people out here—this is a dangerous place!"

The gang sat around like sons listening to their father, eager to hear Butch's plan, partly because cabin fever was beginning to set in.

"Here's what we'll do, Grant." Butch pulled out a map and pointed to where they were. "We're right here. The best way to get to Creede is through Animas Forks and Capital City and on over to Lake City. I hear Lake City has a nice fat bank, ripe for pluckin'. We'll go there and lay low while I scout the layout. We'll hit the bank and hightail it over the pass to Creede. There we'll find Abby and see if she needs rescuing. I'll get a good look at the layout on the bank there too. We'll rob it before they know what hit them, then head on up to Utah, get out of this state for a good while. Those rich mining town banks up there are bound to be busting at the seams with plenty of money. What do you think?"

The gang all banged their fists on the table and agreed that it was a good plan.

Grant felt otherwise. "It's a bad plan, Butch. What you're proposing isn't right. And besides, how are we going to save my sister with the law chasing us? What kind of sense does that make?"

Butch stirred and came quickly to his feet, waving his hands. "You don't understand. We'll save her all right—we'll just hit a few banks in the process."

Though uneasy about Butch's plan, Grant chuckled at Butch's antics. The snow outside was steady, covering everything; the cabin was warm and comfortable. "I can't throw in with you, Butch. I'm not an outlaw and don't plan on becoming one. And if something went wrong, I might never catch up with Abby."

"Why must you always be so practical, Grant? You were always that way, and sometimes I find it downright depressing. Suppose this and suppose that! What if this and that. I can't be a successful outlaw and worry about what ifs." Butch was angry though he still had his silly grin.

Shaking his head, Grant realized he could never convince Butch the chances of his plan working were slim. Butch was a wild spirit, untamed and impetuous, a man who just didn't understand about the Lord or about right and wrong. He had his strong points—he was friendly and humorous and sincere; but his finer qualities wouldn't save him from a lynch mob someday if he didn't change his ways.

～

Leaning back in a chair next to the stove, Grant soaked up the heat and let his mind wander. He thought about Mendy—her golden hair, her honest blue eyes, her sunshine-sweet smile. He wondered if she was thinking about him. He tried to imagine being married to her, living in a town, and having a family. Mostly he reminded himself of her soft kiss. Would he someday return home and see her again? He reflected on the perils of the high country and the wild towns in the valleys between the mountains, the perpetual danger of evil men. What if he got killed and never returned? The thought sickened him, but the sound of Mendy's voice in his mind brought him new hope. It seemed like so long since he'd seen her misty blue eyes.

"Wake up, Grant. You've got that dead man stare," Butch said, jostling Grant's shoulder. "What do you say we do some target practice off the porch. Ain't gonna be nobody out in this weather to hear us, so I don't think we'll be giving away our position."

Grant needed a good practice session. Coming to his feet, he found his rifle and cartridges and joined the rest of the group on the porch. Butch was out in the snow stomping around, his arms full of cans and bottles as he lined them up on a log sixty feet away. He came rushing back to the porch and slipped his belt and holster on, his pistol loaded and ready.

"I'll go first," Butch said and drew his pistol and fired. The bullet kicked up snow five feet in front of the bottles. "Takes me a minute to warm up." He fired again and again, hitting all around the cans and bottles until he had fired all of his rounds. "I didn't hit one! I never was any good with these things," he said, holding the smoking gun out in disgust. "Hope word don't get out that I can't shoot. I'd rather talk my way through things anyway. It's the idea of a gun that scares 'em, you know."

Matt Warner drew and fired and rapidly sent five cans up in the air and spinning off behind the log. He carefully reloaded his pistol and placed it back in the holster. "Don't reckon I've lost my touch," he bragged.

Tom McCarty tried to imitate Matt but did a lousy job of it. He reloaded and took his time, and this time he hit every target.

"Let's see you use that rifle," Butch suggested.

"Cans and bottles are no match for a rifle," Grant said. "Besides, they're sitting still."

"Course they're sittin' still!" Butch cried. "What do you expect them to do, get up and run?"

"I need somebody to throw them up in the air," Grant said.

Butch made a funny face. "This I got to see!" he said. "Ed, get out there and toss them bottles up, will ya?"

Ed went out in the snow and gathered up some of the long-neck bottles. He glanced back at Grant, who stood on the porch holding his rifle with one hand, the barrel pointed down. "Throw 'em!" Grant called. "Fast as you can."

Ed slung the bottles high into the air. Grant bent his knees and fired the repeating Winchester from his hip, exploding the bottles in a rain of glass. Ed held his arms over his head and came running back to the porch, cursing for all he was worth. The rest of the gang sat with their mouths open, awestruck by Grant's display of shooting talent.

"Well, scald a skunk! Would you look at that!" Butch cried out and then whistled. "I don't believe I've ever seen anyone shoot like that. Where'd you learn that? You've got a job with us if you ever want one!"

Grant smiled, reloaded his rifle, and leaned it against the wall. "An old mountain man taught me. It's really not that hard, once you get the hang of it."

Always thinking, Butch had an idea. He reached into his pocket, pulled out a silver dollar, and sailed it up into the air. "Bet you can't hit that!"

Grant grabbed the rifle and fired, all in one move. The coin zinged as soon as the bullet hit it.

"That's what I call pure instinct!" Butch boasted. "No man can *learn* to shoot like that—he's got to have it in his blood."

The rest of the boys felt like they'd been shown up, and they didn't like it. A man that good with a rifle was more dangerous than a man with a pistol because he could shoot further, shoot more times, and reload faster. On the other hand, they felt some comfort about the possibility of Grant becoming one of them; at least they wouldn't have to oppose him in a gunfight.

"Can you do that every time?" Ed asked, brushing glass out of his collar.

"Yes," Grant said.

"Ever killed a man?"

Grant looked at Ed and noticed that the rest were waiting for an answer. "No."

Ed nodded, and Tom, Bill, and Matt seemed to share a silent mental confirmation. Target shooting was one thing; shooting at a man was another. Men shot back. With this in mind, they felt they held the upper hand, since each of them had killed at least one man. Except for Butch.

"Enough of this," Butch said, feeling uncomfortable at the turn in the conversation. "Let's go inside and play some cards. Ed, get something cooking—I'm getting hungry."

～

The next morning the snow had stopped, but the sky remained gray and the weather cold. Grant decided it was time to continue his trip.

"Reckon I'll be pushing off," Grant told Butch after breakfast. An hour later they stood beside the small corral as Grant prepared the horse and mule to continue the journey.

"That trail going down will be mighty slick," Butch warned. "If you ever get to slippin' and slidin' you'll never stop until you reach the bottom."

"This rogue I ride is like a mountain goat," Grant said, slapping Mister on the rump. "He's too stubborn to slip and fall."

"Suit yourself," Butch said, not happy Grant was leaving so soon. "You and Abby are both in a hurry." He hesitated, unsure whether he should express what was really on his mind. Rarely did he show his true feelings.

"Grant, I have something to tell you . . . I'm in love with Abby. Ever since she left, she's all I think about." He stopped for a moment. "I'd do anything for her, you know that. I tried to tell her when she was here, but she only has thoughts for that other guy. What can I do?"

"You could punch him a few times," Grant suggested teasingly.

Butch kicked his toe in the snow, aggravated that Grant would joke at a time like this. "I wonder if she'd accept me if I stopped being an outlaw. You know, do something normal. I like banks—I could be a bank president or something like that. Do you think she'd consider me then? I could dress in those nice suits and wear an expensive hat, grow a mustache . . ."

Grant stared helplessly at Butch. The thought of Butch being a bank president was comical, and Grant had to bite his lip to keep from laughing.

"She's the prettiest woman I've ever seen," Butch rattled on. "If I'd known she was going to turn out that pretty, I would've told Uncle Mike to go on ahead and take off without me—I would've stayed in Black Hawk!" He shuffled his boots around in the snow, making a pattern with his toe and then erasing it and starting over again. "Dagnab it! Why don't nothin' ever work out?"

Obviously frustrated, Butch tried his best to tell Grant how much he loved Abby, while Grant was wondering why'd he met the love of his life just as he was leaving on a trip he might not ever return from.

"Life's just that way," Grant mumbled. "Love is kind of funny sometimes. I guess only the good Lord can make two meet and know they're right for each other and stick together for the rest of their lives as their love grows and grows."

Butch felt like he was being cheated by life again. "Well, when she left, she took my heart with her. I feel like an invalid or something."

Grant couldn't restrain himself—he just had to laugh at Butch. "Haven't you ever heard that time heals all wounds? Besides, you might meet some other good woman and live happily ever after."

"I'll probably end up with a schoolteacher," Butch mocked, still irritated.

"Well, Butch, I wish you the best. Take care of yourself," Grant said, reaching out to his friend.

Shaking Grant's hand, Butch looked sadder than ever. "Don't be a stranger. Drop in and see us sometime."

"Sure, I'll do that," Grant promised. He stepped up and sat in the saddle, and Mister bucked in a circle, snorting like a hog until Grant settled him.

Butch was again his laughing self as he watched Mister. "I still think that's some kind of prehistoric horse, with all that fur all over him like a buffalo."

"He's all right," Grant said, patting the horse's neck. "So long."

"So long, Grant. When you find that pretty sister of yours, you tell her I still want to marry her," Butch called.

~ 15 ~

The Visitor

Once back down in the valley, Grant traveled on toward Animas Forks, the gray clouds overhead swollen and threatening with snow. The snow-covered mountains on either side of him were smoothed over in a slant of bright white, the rough edges and rocks covered in a velvet blanket of smooth drifts. The well-used trail was rutted and packed and mixed with mud and slush, but Mister plodded on, bouncing his head as he took high steps.

Passing through Howardsville and Eureka, Grant could see that the weather had not so far deterred the smelters and mills, as evidenced by the steam and smoke. The aerial trams were a fascinating sight, with big ore buckets hanging in the sky on a cable and traveling miles back into the mountains to retrieve ore from the mines and then bring it back to the mill.

Animas Forks had the look of long neglect as Grant rode in. Ideas of a hot meal gave him the notion to stop and see if he could find one in a place where the only signs of life were in the saloon. Tying his animals near a water trough, Grant surveyed the town, a small place with only about a dozen houses, some run-down and empty hotels, a few businesses, a small jailhouse, and a mill. The valley was surrounded by imposing snow-covered peaks.

Inside Frank Thaler's saloon, Grant moseyed up to the bar. Nearly all of the tables had been shoved out of the way and had chairs piled on them. A piano sat under a coat of dust with the lid closed over the keyboard; the mounted head of a huge elk hung on the wall above. Several yellowed photographs covered the walls, pictures of busy mills and mines of an earlier day. Three people were sitting at a table when he walked in, a woman and two men. The woman got up and came over behind the small bar. "What can I get for you?" Her eyes were searching Grant for some sort of clue as to why he would be in Animas Forks this time of year, when snowstorms were likely.

"I was wondering," Grant said, smiling, doing his best to be polite, "is there any way a fellow could get a bite to eat—something hot?"

The woman blinked and stared. She was wiser from her years, having seen the heydays of big business and the melancholy that settles in a town when its time is over. She had seen the wildness of the miners and all that the lure of money attracts, and she had seen what happens when the money is all gone. The wrinkles around her eyes and at the corners of her mouth and the gray strands of hair outnumbering the brown testified to all this. Now she sat ready to wait out another hard winter, with spring long in coming. She expected nothing in return from the dried-up town. But her faded eyes still had some life in them, and it was nice to see a handsome young stranger come in out of the cold.

A slight smile on her lips, her hands spread on the bar, she said, "I don't get enough customers to try and sell meals." Her fingers were long and thin. "But I do have a pot of elk stew going in the back, along with some corn bread."

This made Grant's mouth water. "I'd sure be glad to pay for a portion," he said, a wishful pleading in his voice.

"I'll see what I can throw together," she said and moved off toward the back of the long, thin building.

Leaning on the bar, Grant turned and glanced at the two men at the table, sitting idly, not saying much. "How are you doin'?" Grant asked.

The fellows looked older than they were, humpbacked from the strain of working the mines, their faces etched with the despair of poverty.

"We're gettin' by," one of them said. As the man moved his arm up to the table, Grant noticed he was missing a hand. He slowly sipped his beer; his face had the bristly growth of three of four days.

The other man never moved, keeping his hand on his beer, hunched over the table, staring into nothing, frozen in time. Grant was of the opinion a blast from a stick of dynamite wouldn't make him blink.

"Heard anything about the pass?" Grant asked.

"What pass?"

"The one that goes over to Lake City," Grant replied.

"There's two passes. Which one do ya mean?" The man waved his stump in the air. "There's Engineer, and there's Cinnamon."

"Which would you advise?" Grant questioned.

"You don't want to take Engineer in this weather. Any snow up there won't melt 'til next July, and I imagine it's deep already. Take Cinnamon, you'll have a better chance."

"Thanks for the information," Grant said.

The woman showed up with a heaping plate of steaming brown gravy, meat, and potatoes. A wedge of corn bread sat on top. She placed the plate in front of Grant and said, "Come on over to the table, sit with us."

All four sat at the table while Grant ate.

"My name's William Crofield," the man with the stump said, holding his only hand out to Grant. Shaking his hand, Grant went back to eating. William kept talking. "I used to be a miner up here, but I lost my hand—mostly do odd jobs now. I help Mary here whenever I can."

The man who sat quietly never moved or blinked, but just sat there staring with his hand cupped around his beer. Mary seemed pleased to have Grant's company—somebody new to talk to.

"So are you prospecting these parts?" she asked.

"No," Grant said. "I'm on my way over to Creede."

"Creede?" Mary said. "We hear that's a real treasure hole. You plan on staking a claim there?"

"No, I'm no miner," Grant admitted. He thought for a moment, wondering if he should tell them about his sister, then decided there was no harm in it. The story was growing old for Grant, having repeated it so many times, but he told it and finished by saying, "She may have come through here on a stage."

Mary straightened as if something had come to her. "What does she look like?"

Reaching for his wallet, Grant removed the photograph and showed the woman. She seemed interested and eager to help.

"A stage did come through here a few days ago, and a woman was riding on top with Slim. I didn't get a good look at her face, but I recognize the hair. Yes, I believe this is the same woman."

Grant smiled as he finished his plate. "I guess I'm on the right trail then. You say Cinnamon is the way to go to Lake City?"

William piped up, now also eager to be helpful. "Yeah. You'll see the high trail, winds right up the side of the mountain here. Soon as you pass the first switchback, you'll come to a second. Take the fork to the right, otherwise you'll be headed for Engineer. Cinnamon should be all right, don't you think, Mary?"

She nodded and added, "You know about these snowstorms up here, don't you? Could get in a pretty bad fix if you ain't prepared."

"I learned that the hard way," Grant said, "years ago. I imagine I can get by."

"It's early yet for any real snow," William said, basing his facts on years of living in the area. "On the other hand, every time a fellow gets to thinkin' he knows the weather up here, it surprises him. I've seen it snow in July."

"Who's Frank Thaler?" Grant asked, thinking of the name of the saloon as he glanced around at all the old items on the shelves and walls, icons and implements of the mining industry.

"This is Frank sitting right here," William said, pointing with his stump.

"How you do?" Grant said.

Frank sat like a statue, his mind far away.

"Don't mind him," Mary said. "He's not being rude; he just don't say much anymore."

Grant looked at the man and could barely tell that he was alive. He reminded Grant of a steam locomotive he'd seen once. The engine had broken down and was so old the railroad company simply pushed it off to the side, where it sat idle forever, a monument of days past.

Reaching in his pocket, Grant pulled out a few silver coins and set them on the table. "This should cover it. That was an excellent meal."

"Maybe it'll stick to your ribs for a while," Mary said, pleased by the compliment.

Standing, Grant looked at the two he had been talking to and again at Frank. "I better make some time while I can," he said. "Thanks for the information."

"Good luck," William offered. "Be careful in Creede."

"I will," Grant said as he walked outside. The trip looked much better with a full stomach, and he climbed on Mister and trotted up the street to the road that skirted the mountain above. When he came to the second fork, he veered right, climbing, unable to see the country he was headed for until he reached the summit.

~

To his surprise, the sky cleared and opened up into the deep blue of the high country. Grant thought he had seen all the basic scenes of the mountain ranges, but he found the first leg of his new journey excitingly different. The going was fairly easy over the high and open meadows that stretched above the valleys. Log cabins dotted the trail along with mining works and more aerial trams stretching their cables from peak to peak. The ore buckets hung idly in the sky, swaying slowly back and forth in a slight breeze, the long cables silent. Some of the log cabins appeared to be boarded up and abandoned for the winter.

"Looks like they closed for the winter," Grant said out loud.

Mister responded with a snort, indicating he could care less.

The rounded summits dipped and ran past shaft houses and silent mills and down through the settlements of Sterling, Tellurium, and Argentum, the small mining camps of White Cross, and on down the shelf road past Sherman, where the trail met the Lake Fork of the Gunnison River. White Cross appeared to have a population of around 300, Grant guessed, judging by the men and their families living in cabins and tents. Some watched him ride through, probably curious about Mister, whose legs had grown shaggy and thick with fur, while others just went about their work.

Dropping down, enjoying a bird's-eye view, Grant could see the camp of Sherman, where the streets and cabins and business buildings, one of which appeared to be a hotel, were arranged in orderly rows, as if they were anticipating a big and busy city in the future. From what he could see, there were few people about and little activity. He moved on through swampy land and through clumps of evergreens where the roadbed was spongy with tree loam and pine needles.

Grant could feel the bigness and loneliness of the country, where the only sound was the wind moving through the treetops. Perhaps people would return in the spring to bring such places back to life, but these towns were so remote that even if they did have producing mines and good ore, it would be difficult to get it to a railroad. He wondered why men pursued the idea of establishing towns in such places at all.

Following the edge of the abyss, with the streambed looping far below, Grant felt like calling it a day. Although he hadn't traveled that many miles, the going had been tough and demanding, in some places treacherous. Mister showed signs of exhaustion, and Peaches was tired as well, hee-hawing for an end to the traveling.

A cutoff swung above the trail, and Grant turned Mister up the grade to find a level spot with the protection of thick spruce trees. The ground was soft with needles, and within a hundred feet a meadow of grass poked up through thin layers of snow.

"This looks good," Grant said, stepping down. Mister turned his head at Grant and then back to the grass nearby. "Don't worry, Mister," Grant said, comforting the horse, "you can eat all night if you want to."

Once the animals were unsaddled and unpacked, Grant hobbled them, and they immediately dropped their heads into the tall grass.

A fire was made easily, using the branches and needles lying about, and soon the clean high air abounded with the rich aroma of coffee. It was a peaceful afternoon, the sun dropping out of sight over the mountaintop above and the temperature falling accordingly.

Grant made a comfortable bed from a pile of needles and then spread his heavy blanket over it. The fire was about right by now, full of glowing red embers. He had fashioned a nice pile of wood next to him to toss on the fire as needed. In this neck of the woods at this time of year travelers were few and far between, and he had little worry of being ambushed or robbed. The thought of a warm fire on the cold night was a welcome idea anyway, and since he was in a thicket, the light from the fire wouldn't be easy to detect.

The night had come quickly, and the silence was remarkable. Grant could hear his animals grazing not far away, their jaws and teeth crunching rhythmically. His meal had been a can of beans and elk jerky boiled in water to make it tender again. Coffee boiled as he freshened his cold cup and bent over by the fire. The heat felt good on his face.

Again the stars showed themselves with an incredible brilliance, the clear mountain air making them appear remarkably close. As far as Grant was concerned, this beat any hotel with its small and confining rooms that made him feel like he needed to open a window. Out here the beautiful night sky was the window, and he took it all in gladly. Reaching over to the saddlebags, Grant removed the Bible Jason had given him for the trip. Snug in his blanket, he thumbed through the worn pages in the firelight until he came to the Beatitudes in the book of Luke.

Grant read, "Blessed be ye poor: for yours is the kingdom of God." He stopped and thought for a minute, trying to decide whether he was poor. As far as material wealth was concerned, he had very little. But he was rich in health and rich in his spirit and had a love for life. The Bible always got him to thinking, offering solitude and peace. He continued reading, analyzing each verse as best he could, until his eyelids grew heavy and he fell asleep with the Bible open before him.

~

Mister neighed, waking Grant. By now he was familiar with Mister's noises, and this one meant there was an intruder. He froze, sitting perfectly still while his eyes searched the shadows. The fire was nothing more than a pile of embers, the coffeepot sitting off to the side. Maybe it was a deer or an elk or some small animal of the night, but he heard nothing unusual. Reaching over, Grant piled dry sticks on the fire until a flame jumped and then another. In a few minutes the bark of the spruce trees nearby reflected gold in the firelight.

Waiting, watching, Grant picked up his Winchester, his eyes darting, scrutinizing every shadow until he came to one tall one. At first it appeared to be a bear standing on its hind legs, or maybe it was just a tree in the darkness. He couldn't tell, but he kept staring at the figure until he saw light from the fire glint in its eyes.

"Who goes there? Show yourself!" Grant shouted.

Moving very slowly, the figure took a step closer, then paused. Grant held his rifle ready, certain he could protect himself from the easy target. Out of the shadows stepped a man wrapped in many layers of skins, so bulky he was almost round. He came closer, a rifle hanging limply across his folded arm. He stopped again at the edge of the firelight in plain view. It was an Indian.

The two stared into each other's eyes, sizing up one another silently. Grant was almost hypnotized by the dark eyes with wrinkles of wisdom surrounding them. The newcomer looked like a tall and powerful man still youthful and vigorous in his middle years, a rock-like dignity in his calmness. Most evident, Grant thought, was the severe pain in the man's wise old eyes, the kind of pain it takes a lifetime to accumulate. Because of this and the fact that the Indian had not ambushed him when he had the chance, Grant felt surprised but unthreatened.

"Don't just stand there—come on in, sit down," Grant said with an easiness unusual for a man having been disturbed late at night at his campsite. He reached over and shook the coffeepot, making sure it had enough in it, and set it on the fire. "You like coffee?"

The Indian sensed a kind of peace in Grant; he saw it in his young green eyes—the kind of settled peace many spent a lifetime looking for and never found. He knew from those bright young eyes the man would not shoot him unless provoked. Moving closer, he squatted down beside the fire and relaxed, still watching Grant curiously. "Coffee sounds good," he said in surprisingly good English. "I smelled it earlier, and it brought me here."

"Traveling alone?" Grant asked, not wanting to be surprised by any more Indians popping out of the darkness.

The man nodded. "Yes. I'm on a journey. What about you? Are you here to seek wealth from the mountains?"

"No," Grant said. "True wealth is not in the minerals from the mountains."

Smiling, the Indian understood this very well. Grant took the only cup he had, a metal one, poured hot coffee into it, and handed it to the Indian. The man accepted it with both hands and sipped at the hot cup carefully. He wore a fox skin over the back of his head, but his black hair jutted straight up over his forehead. His face was round and his nose well shaped, his mouth wide and straight. The strings of white beads he wore appeared delicate and finely crafted.

"You have a name?" Grant asked. "My name is Grant—Grant DeSpain."

The man lowered his eyes to the cup and savored its flavor once more before answering. "My name is Joseph, Grant DeSpain."

"Grant will do. I haven't seen many Indians on my trip," Grant said. "And most of the ones I have seen were poor and hungry and appeared to have no home. You don't look like them."

"Those you see," Joseph said, "are the walking dead. They have no spirit and wander uselessly, begging and suffering."

"And you?" Grant questioned.

"I am on a spiritual walk, a quest if you will. Some consider me a renegade, even some of my own people, but I'll return after I'm finished here."

"Who are your people?" Grant questioned, his interest growing rapidly.

"I am Nez Percé," Joseph said proudly.

Grant straightened up immediately, wide awake, his senses acute. "Then you must be Chief Joseph."

Joseph nodded.

"I am truly honored," Grant said. "I know all about you and the plight of your people—the wars, the terrible camps and reservations. I've been in the newspaper business for years, and believe me, many newspapers and much of the public are sympathetic to your cause. Especially because of your speech in Washington, D.C."

Joseph, astonished by this young white man named Grant, was impressed by his knowledge of him and his people. "Yes, much has happened, but it has been quiet for many years now. My people have lived in oppression for five years. Some were sent to the Lapwai reservation in Idaho, but I and 150 others were exiled to the Colville reservation in Washington Territory. I fled not long ago to come to this high country we consider sacred, to find the Great Spirit and talk to Him. My home is in the Wallowa Valley, and I want to go back there to live. My mother and father are buried there. If I could only return . . ."

"This is a fine place to talk to God," Grant said. "Not many nights ago I talked to Him, and He showed me the way I must go."

The chief understood this well and had no doubts of its truth. His eyes saw the book open beside Grant, the Bible he'd been reading before he fell asleep. "You read The Book of Heaven."

"Yes," Grant said. "It is truth."

"What part do you read, and what does it say?" Joseph asked.

Grant picked it up and started reading aloud the Beatitudes he'd read earlier from the Gospel of Luke. "Blessed be ye poor: for yours is the kingdom of God. Blessed are ye that hunger now: for ye shall be filled. Blessed are ye that weep now: for ye shall laugh."

Chief Joseph held up his hand for Grant to stop. "This is the God of white men speaking."

"This," Grant said, holding up the book, "is the God of *all* men."

"What does it mean, 'Blessed are ye that weep,' for my people weep, but I do not see how that is a blessing."

"It means to have faith, to trust in God, Chief Joseph. Men who suffer come to know God better, for through their suffering He comes to them and shows them His love. You and your people suffer now, but you can live with God in heaven where there is no suffering."

Joseph seemed befuddled by this but wanted to hear more, for it was good news. "How does one come to know this God of all men?"

"I'll do my best to explain it," Grant said. "For many years God tried to tell man how to live, but men were sinners, committing crimes and breaking the laws set down by God. For this the punishment was death, eternal death, when a man's spirit lives in agony forever. Then God sent His only Son, who became a man and lived among men and taught them how to live. But men hated Him and persecuted Him and hung Him on a cross to die. But He was God, and so, to show His love, He died on that cross bearing the sins of all men, so that they might be forgiven and live forever in heaven. While He was here He said, 'I am the way, and only through Me does a man come to heaven.' So when a man accepts the Son of God, Jesus Christ, as his Savior and asks Him for deliverance from evil and forgiveness for his sins, a man comes to know God, the Great Spirit."

Chief Joseph set his empty coffee cup down, his face showing grave concern about Grant's words. "I have heard this story of Jesus Christ, Son of God, but I have never heard it taught so I could understand it. I have come far to this high country seeking the Great Spirit, seeking advice. Perhaps I have found it in a young man who shows no fear. His spirit is strong. I was never a war chief but instead a civil chief. My people have looked to me for guidance, and I have had none to give them. I never hated the white man but only asked that we live by laws together and abide by them. This did not happen. Maybe now I can return and guide them with hope of a better world to come."

"Can you read English?" Grant asked, holding up his Bible.

"Yes," Joseph answered. "I read well."

"Then take this. It is God's Word, a message from God to us so we can understand the truth."

"This is a great gift, my friend, Grant. I will read it and try to understand it; perhaps I will learn something."

"You are a ruling leader of your people. It is your job to be their spiritual leader as well. Show them the way, Chief Joseph. Show them there is hope, for all men are treated fairly by God, even those who are living in oppression."

Chief Joseph had always believed in a Supreme Being and in a spiritual life after death. He thought that perhaps what he held in his hands might very well hold all the answers he was seeking. For this great gift he felt he owed Grant a gift in return. "Have you come to this land of the Great Spirit to search as well?"

"Yes. I'm searching for my sister," Grant admitted.

The chief smiled, a smile that transformed his stone-like face. "Not only for your sister. You are searching for answers like I am."

Dropping his head, Grant realized Chief Joseph was intuitive and had understood him correctly. "I guess I am," he confessed. "I don't understand men and their ways, the way they give up a perfectly settled life to come take their chances out here expecting to get wealthy overnight. It almost never happens that way—why can't they see that? They risk everything—their families, all of their possessions, even their lives—and for what?"

"You have searched for the answer to this for a long time, I see," Joseph said, his eyes black. "Now it is my turn to give you a gift. You have been searching in the wrong places. The answer lies within— look within yourself."

This came as a shock to Grant. How could he possibly hold the answers within himself? He brought his eyes to meet those of Joseph and held them there. "How could that be? How could *I* know the answers?"

Chief Joseph closed his eyes, his leadership and strong character evident, his authority subtle and durable, his unswerving devotion to duty and principle obvious. When he opened his eyes again, Grant could see the conversation had ended.

Slowly coming to his feet, Joseph placed the Bible in a large deerskin bag he carried over his shoulder. Grant stood too, watching the great chief with his slow and deliberate movements. Joseph stared at Grant a moment, then turned and walked silently away. Grant watched, his eyes following the tall man's form until it became a dark shadow and blended in with the night. He sat back down and went over it all again. He had been in the presence of a very famous and a very great man.

From what Grant remembered, Chief Joseph had never wanted to fight with the white man, but when the likes of General Howard

and Colonel Gibbon forced him into battle with hundreds of caval-
rymen and infantrymen, Chief Joseph and his men showed them up
badly, outsmarting them every time with his few braves, at one time
facing six to one odds. But the U.S. Army persisted, bringing more
and more men, driving Chief Joseph and the Nez Percé into unfamiliar lands, where the women and children froze and starved. Finally
Joseph called for an end to the fighting and handed over his rifle.

Afterwards, the Nez Percé were led from forts in the Dakota
Territory to Fort Leavenworth, Kansas and to different reservations
in Kansas, with the Nez Percé dying all the way of diseases like
malaria. The plight of the Nez Percé had become a national issue,
and the next year Congress, bowing to the sympathetic public and
press, authorized the Secretary of the Interior to do with Joseph's
people as he saw fit.

In 1885 the Nez Percé were moved to the Pacific Northwest,
where they were split into two reservations, one in Idaho and one in
the Washington Territory. Joseph was kept under a watchful eye at
the Colville reservation in the Washington Territory, for the army
feared his military genius. Somehow he had escaped and made his
way to Colorado, searching the high mountains to bring him closer
to the Great Spirit. And by some act of fate, Grant had run into this
great man and shared ideas with him.

Reclining again, his shoulder on his saddle, Grant stared into the
fire, where a spray of sparks swirled up into the night as if to join the
magnificent stars bright in a black background. He felt elated, even
privileged, at having shared company with Chief Joseph of the Nez
Percé. It had been like a wonderful dream, but the chief's last words
haunted him—"Look within yourself."

CHAPTER

~ 16 ~

Creede

"Would you look at all the people!" Poker Alice stated as the coach rolled in between the Gateway Cliffs and into the heart of Creede, Colorado. She casually removed a cigar from her handbag, clenched it in her teeth, and struck a match to it, tugging on it until it grew bright red.

Alice's cigar smoke choked Abby and made her eyes water, but she said nothing, her focus on the town outside. It was a boomtown in its wildest state, new and raw and full of money and all kinds of men. Two-story buildings crowded the narrow main street, packed together like stacked firewood without an inch to spare. Piles of green lumber and sawhorses sat in the road, an avenue crowded with men who had to part to let the stage through. Even in the late afternoon light it was clearly evident the place was full of all kinds of activity, including the din of competing conversations and music and hammers and saws. It was a boomtown at its height of discord. Any kind of order was lost in an excitement that flowed through the deep ravine like electricity. A place of raucous and unrestrained behavior crowded into a thin gulch with towering walls of rock on each side—this was the red-hot town of Creede.

"Could be hard to find a place to sleep," Alice noted wisely, for the throng of people obviously surpassed the capacity of the established hotels advertising room and board.

Abby's immediate concern was finding Billy, and judging by the overcrowded streets, that looked like an impossibility. She realized it would be hard, if not dangerous, for a girl like her in a town like this, where the men probably outnumbered the women a hundred to one.

"Whoa!" Slim cried from above, bringing the stage to a stop in front of The Western Cafe. He set the brake and jumped down, then came over to the coach door and stuck his head in the window. "We're here, ladies."

As Slim opened the door, Alice and Abby stepped out, turning their heads to look up and down the street. The layout was unusual and cramped. A shortage of building space had apparently forced builders to take advantage of every square inch, making one feel they were in a roofless tunnel.

"Miss Abby," Slim said, "we don't have a stage office here, and there ain't no room to stable the horses or put the stage either. What I got to do is take the rig up yonder." He pointed at the ridge above. "To the little town of Bachelor. It's the only place that's got room. What I'm gettin' to is, we got to find somewhere to put your trunks."

Abby glanced at Alice, who wisely traveled light. "I don't know where, Slim," Abby uttered, her eyes wide and disbelieving at the spectacle all around her.

"No problem," a small man said, stepping up. "I couldn't help overhearing you." He addressed Abby and Alice. "You won't find a room for rent in this town—not right now, you won't." He wanted this information to soak in, and to accurately place fear where it would do him the best, then said, "I'm Bob Ford, at your service." He bowed politely, a courteous gentleman. "I own The Exchange," he gestured at the saloon with his small cigar, "and that building over there." He pointed across the road at a two-story affair. "I have rooms upstairs you can stay in—as good as any hotel in town."

Slim threw a cautious glance at Abby, making certain she understood how the game worked. Abby already knew and glanced back at Slim, assuring him she could handle this small man and take care of herself. "How much is a room?" she asked.

"Since you're new here, I can make you a deal for five dollars tonight. Tomorrow we can discuss business," Ford said cordially, pushing his black derby hat back on his head. He had a boy's face and seemed eager. His hair was short and neatly groomed; he had no facial hair at all. His smile inviting, he had the demeanor of a friendly businessman.

"For now that will do," Poker Alice said. She had been sizing up the young man and decided she liked him. "I'm a poker dealer. Need any help at your saloon?"

"Indeed I do, madam," Ford announced happily. "It's always good for business to have a woman dealing, provided she knows the game."

"I probably know it better than you do," Alice said without a hint of vanity.

Bob lifted his eyebrows at her boldness. "And what's your name, madam?"

"They call me Poker Alice."

Bob smiled heartily now, proud of his discovery. He had indeed heard of Alice. "This is good news! Now Creede Lilly and Kilarney Kate will have some competition. They work for my competitors." Bob turned his attention to Abby. "Your name?"

"Abby."

"And what do you do, my dear? Dance? A gal with your looks could fetch a pile of money dancing on stage."

"I'm here to find my husband," Abby lied, fearful of the small man and his boldness. The way he handled himself suggested he had money and power.

"I see," he said. "May I show you to your rooms?"

Slim unloaded the trunks and hauled them over for Abby. "You be careful, Miss Abby," he said softly. "I don't trust that there fella."

"I'll be all right," Abby insisted. "At least I have somewhere to stay tonight."

"All right then, Miss Abby. I got to get goin'. I'll check on you tomorrow before I leave here, make sure everything's all right," Slim said, then turned to leave.

The rooms were small, nothing fancy, but they had the necessities. Ford kindly showed the women where everything was, then left them to themselves.

Alice quickly got settled in, then knocked at Abby's door. "I'm rarin' to get goin'," she said, a new cigar fresh in her mouth. "I'm goin' over to that young man's saloon and skin a few of these slickers. You probably won't see me again tonight unless you come over to the saloon."

"I think I'll pretty much just stay here, Alice," Abby said. "It's dark out, and I'm not going searching for Billy this late. Besides, I'm tired. That was a long, rough ride."

"Yeah, it was," Alice agreed, though she was a tough old customer and had barely noticed the ride being rough.

Abby pulled the shade over the window and began removing what felt like an inch of grit, shaking sand out of her clothes in disbelief. Cleaning up with a dishpan of water and a washrag wasn't nearly as satisfying as a bath, but it served its purpose. She changed into a common dress, one that was clean, a cotton outfit that felt much better. She thought next about getting something to eat when she heard someone approaching her door outside. The arrival knocked lightly.

"Who is it?" Abby asked, a little fearful.

"It's me—Bob Ford. I brought you something to eat—figured you might be hungry."

Abby opened the door, and Ford stepped in carrying a tray covered with a big checkered napkin. "This is on the house," he said, uncovering a plate of roasted sliced beef, potatoes, and beans. "I didn't think you would want to be wandering around out there at night if you got hungry."

"That was nice of you," Abby complimented. "I am starved, and you're right—I don't want to be roaming around a town where I don't know anyone."

"Tell you what I'll do," Bob volunteered happily. "Tomorrow morning we'll have breakfast, and then I'll escort you around, and we'll find your husband if he's here."

"Really?" Abby questioned, happy to have his help.

"First thing in the morning," Bob said. "Well . . ." He stood looking at Abby, wishing he had more to say, more to offer, but that would come later. His eyes enjoyed the curves of her figure, then rested on her face. "I'll see you tomorrow." He gently closed the door behind him.

Abby attacked the meal. That Bob Ford was an interesting character, so eager to be helpful, a real gentleman. Yet there was something about him she didn't quite trust. She wondered if he had underlying motives. She'd have to keep an eye on him.

∼

Abby got hardly any sleep at all with people hollering, horses galloping, wagons creaking, plus all the hammering, pounding, sawing, and shooting. Creede was a town that never slept, with the businesses open all night every day of the week. She crawled out of bed and put her hair up, then made herself ready for the day. She picked one of her nicer dresses, hoping to impress Billy when she found him. Tired and still sleepy, anticipation soon took over, and she adopted a sweet smile and an eager attitude. She had finally arrived in Creede, and it was time to locate Billy.

Good to his word, Ford walked Abby over to breakfast at The Tortoni, a hotel with a dining room that seated 200. Horses trotted around the corner pulling the small stage, and Slim came to a stop in front of the hotel.

"Mornin', Miss Abby. I'm takin' the rig on back to Lake City. Seems everyone is a comin' here and nobody leavin'. Everything all right?"

"Perfectly fine," Abby said. "Glad to have known you, Slim."

"Well," he said, crunching his tall hat down tighter on his head, "I guess I'll be seein' ya around."

Abby thought she noticed a slight sadness in his voice. "Thanks for everything, Slim," she said with a smile.

"Any time, Miss Abby. Any time!" Slim called to the horses and moved on out, his figure visible above the crowd in the street as the coach disappeared around a bend.

"Nice man," Ford observed and led Abby inside.

Hungry businessmen and miners half filled the place as Ford showed Abby a table, then politely pulled out a chair for her. "I'll be right back," he said and quickly disappeared.

Abby checked her makeup, ignoring the curious eyes following her every move. Her small, handheld mirror revealed a face of innocence, painted to look pretty. To the men around her, this was almost as good as going to a theater.

Ford returned and sat down with two plates of eggs, biscuits, and bacon, then went back for two cups of coffee. The beverage was hot but watered down and weak. "So tell me, what name does your husband go by?"

"Billy Rogers," Abby said quickly. "He owns a mine here somewhere."

"Did he leave word as to where we might find him, or the name of his mine, or something else to go by?" Ford pried.

"No," Abby admitted, disheartened. "But I know he's here."

"Lot of people in this town," Ford pointed out. "Could take a while to locate him. I know a good many people here in spite of the confusion—we'll go see them and spread the word that we're looking for Billy Rogers. Sooner or later somebody is bound to bump into him."

After breakfast, dressed like a dandy, Ford proudly escorted Abby around, doing his best to show her off. The morning was overcast with low-hanging clouds passing over the gulch, the air chilly and smoky. They spoke with a few people Ford knew, and he made a good show of presenting Abby's problem. What Abby didn't know was that Ford had a group of toughs working for him, a dozen at least, and the men they approached were all part of that group. He had previously given orders to locate Billy Rogers and to keep him away from Ford's end of the street. Ford planned on taking care of Billy later on, for he had discovered a find greater than any silver strike as far as he was concerned—namely, Abby.

By noon they had walked both sides of the street and Second Street too. Fortunately for Bob Ford, Billy Rogers was nowhere around. Next he took Abby to show off his saloon, The Exchange.

"Come on in, Abby," he said, pulling her inside. "Don't be afraid, everything is going to be just fine." The saloon was full of men yelling and drinking and gambling and only a few women, all of whom were employees serving drinks and wearing colorful, revealing outfits. The women appeared rough and untamed, seemingly as tough as the men themselves.

"There's Alice," Ford motioned, pointing her out. "She's been at it all night, giving those rascals a regular house cleaning."

The long bar was packed, men standing shoulder to shoulder, and a piano player sat with his back to the crowd hammering out old melodies. A sign on the wall above the piano player read, PLEASE DON'T SHOOT THE PIANO PLAYER—HE'S THE ONLY ONE WE HAVE. A thick layer of heavy cigar smoke hung like a cloud, and the place stunk of unwashed men and liquor. Games of faro and poker attracted most of the crowd, though a roulette wheel also spun nearby, the numbers flying around in a blur. It was an impressive sight despite being filthy, and Abby guessed Ford was raking in the profits.

Leading Abby back outside, Ford wanted to show her more. "This way," he said, leading her down the street to a small building with bold letters on the front that read, FORD'S THEATER. Unlocking the door, Bob escorted Abby inside, where it was dark and dank. He lit a lantern and walked up the small steps to the stage. Abby could see that the backdrop resembled the inside of a plain, everyday house.

"You have shows here?" Abby asked. "I mean, do acting companies play here?"

"Not exactly," Ford said, grinning. "We do one play, and I play the main role. We have a full house every time."

"I'll have to come see your performance," Abby said politely. She was letting Ford have his way, showing her around and bragging about all that he did and all that he owned. He was obviously a man full of himself.

"Is there anything you'd like to do, something you'd like to see?" Bob asked as he locked up the small theater.

"I could look some more for Billy," she said. "You don't have to come along."

Suddenly Ford put his arm around Abby's neck and pulled her close to his face, speaking in confidence. "Abby, I'm sure you're aware of how pretty you are. This town knows nothing of manners, and there aren't enough women here to satisfy a fourth of the men. Most of these men are rough and crude and will do just about anything to spend time with a beautiful woman. And there's no law here to prevent them from doing as they wish. Are you getting the picture?" He turned her loose and stood back, his eyes convincing.

"You're probably right. You've certainly been here longer than I have," she said. "What should I do?"

"You're welcome to spend time with me," Bob offered, holding his hand out in invitation. "I have my regular duties, but that's about it. It would be nice to have you around."

Abby realized Ford was doing his best to win her over. "Thanks for the invitation, but I got no sleep last night—this place is so noisy! And I'm getting tired. I think I should go get some rest. Maybe some word will come about Billy's whereabouts."

For an instant Ford's young face looked hurt, but he quickly recovered, masking any emotion. "I'll walk you back to your room."

"Thank you," Abby said, sensing he was offended but not sure how to feel about that.

~

Bob Ford was more than simply interested in Abby. He was a shrewd if not ruthless opportunist. What he saw in Abby was a young and innocent girl of great beauty yet to be ruined by the ways of a town like Creede. If he didn't take advantage of the situation, somebody else would, another town boss like Soapy Smith. For now he pretty much had the run of things, having the most money and the most hired toughs to see his deals through.

Abby could raise him a notch in his kingdom if he owned her. She could bring in all kinds of money if he could talk her into doing a small show in which she danced and wore a skimpy costume. Best of all, he figured, she could command a king's ransom from certain rich men just for accompanying them for the night, and he would get 80 percent of that, just like he got 80 percent of the profits from the other soiled doves he owned.

The problem of Abby's having a husband seemed minor compared to convincing Abby of her abilities. If necessary, Ford could order Billy Rogers done away with, and nobody would ever know the difference. He already had the man pegged for a fool, coming to Creede and sending for his wife to join him in a place where she would be swept up by predators in an instant. Ford kept a man posted at the west trail and one at Wagon Wheel Gap, men who were paid to watch for women coming and inform Ford of their arrival. Like looking over livestock, he wanted to have first pick.

As a last resort, Ford could be very convincing with Abby. He was hoping she'd be cooperative, malleable in his hands, but he was beginning to get the idea that she might be stubborn. He had dealt with stubborn women before and knew how to handle them, pressuring and frightening them until their will was broken. He would use no physical abuse—they had to stay pretty to earn a wage. His ways were more subtle and involved games of mental warfare in which he always emerged the victor. Like horses, once their spirit was broken, they were easy to handle. He hoped it wouldn't come to such means with Abby, but he had to have her, and if he had to get drastic, so be it.

Abby slept all afternoon, unaware of the noisy world outside. When she woke up, the sun was already out of sight. Because the town sat in a steep-walled canyon, the sun didn't shine very long anyway. She jumped to her feet and peered out the window, again seeing a cluster of animals, men, and wagons, all making noise. Uncertain of what she was going to do, she fixed herself up. She didn't want to stay pinned up in her room when she could be out looking for Billy.

Ford's light knock came at the door, and Abby recognized it. "Yes?" she called.

"I thought maybe you'd like to see me on stage," Ford called through the door. "The show starts in half an hour. I want you to be my guest—front row seat."

For some reason this appealed to Abby. Professional entertainment was rare, and nobody passed up a free ticket to a show. She moved over to the door and opened it. "You can walk me over—I'm almost done here."

Ford smiled with enthusiasm. Perhaps this young lady was smarter than he gave her credit for and was coming around to his way of thinking. After all, he was young and rich at only twenty-nine years of age, a decent-looking and astute businessman. What more could a woman want?

～

Ford happily escorted Abby to the theater, where people were already crowding in. He led her to the best seat in the house, a bouquet marking her reservation. Picking up the flowers, he handed them to her. "For you!" he said, then quickly departed up the steps to the stage and exited behind the curtains.

Abby felt strange accepting the flowers, but she had no choice. Holding them in her lap, she patiently waited for the theater to fill up and the show to begin.

When the lanterns were dimmed, the front curtain rolled up like a window shade. Bob Ford and other men were dressed in loud suits in a place that looked like a politician's fancy office. The man sitting behind the desk was introduced as the governor of Missouri, Thomas Crittenden.

The actors were overly melodramatic as Bob said to the governor, "Yes, sir, I know Jesse James, and I can get him for you, Governor."

"If you can do this for the state of Missouri, acting for the people of the state, I'll give you a reward of 5,000 dollars."

"Consider it done," Bob bragged loudly, then pulled out his sixshooter and held it in the air for the audience to see.

The play lagged as Bob imitated a man traveling with a duty to perform for the state. Abby thought his makeup a bit exaggerated, his eyebrows and hair a heavy black; his powdered face looked sort of humorous.

Finally the scene changed to a house she had seen earlier that day. Bob Ford and a man playing his brother, Charlie Ford, began to enter the house.

"Good to see you, old friend," Bob yelled for the audience to hear. "Jesse James!" He let the audience grasp the fact that this was indeed the notorious outlaw. "So now you go under the name of Howard, hiding in this small town."

"Be quiet, it's a secret," Jesse James said, letting the two men inside.

The man playing Jesse James was wearing a fake beard that kept sagging, and he had to keep readjusting it. Abby enjoyed the play as if it were a comedy, which it wasn't, and she held her hand over her mouth to keep her smile from being seen. Based on the fine plays she had seen in Leadville, this show was definitely amateurish.

"We have come to join your gang, old friend," Bob said.

"You're welcome to stay," Jesse said, and the curtain dropped so the scene could change.

When the curtain went up again, it was the same backdrop, but the men were sitting as if it was a later date, all wearing pistols on their hips.

Jesse acted restless and then jumped to his feet and challenged Bob Ford. "I know your scheme—you want to turn me over to the law."

Bob jumped to his feet. Both men held their hands over their guns.

"I represent the state of Missouri," Bob said, "and I'm asking you to come along peacefully."

Jesse James made a slow play for his gun, and Bob pulled his and shot a loud blank, filling the stage with smoke. Jesse James fell to the floor.

Instantly the crowd was on their feet, screaming and cheering and clapping. Abby thought the show a farce and didn't understand why the crowd was so appreciative. The acting was bad, and the story had been poorly written and poorly acted. She stood anyway, ready to leave.

From behind her an angry man yelled, "That ain't the way it happened! That ain't the way it happened!"

Abby turned to see the man just as he pulled something from his pocket—a piece of ore. He threw it at the stage and almost hit Ford. "You coward—you shot Jesse in the back! He didn't even have a gun!"

The crowd grew silent and gave their attention to Ford to see how he would react. Angrily, Ford pulled out his pistol and began firing at the man. Of course, his gun was loaded with blanks, but the smoke and the noise caused the audience to scramble for the door. Abby ducked back down in her seat until the theater was empty.

Seeing her, Bob immediately came down. "Sorry about that. We get one in here like that every now and then. So, how'd you like the play?"

"I didn't understand it all," Abby confessed.

"I'm playing myself in a true story," Ford said, enlightening her.

"What?" Abby said, confused. Then she began to understand. "You mean to say you really did kill Jesse James?"

"I sure did," Ford gloated. "Shot him dead as a hammer, one shot."

All of a sudden Abby felt ill. Jesse James had saved her brother's life once, and Grant said he was a fair man. She turned to look behind her where the man who protested had been sitting, then turned back to Bob. "Was that man right—did you shoot Jesse in the back?"

Ford laughed, but his laugh sounded forced. "Of course not. That man is just an old fool. Let me go change and wash this stuff off, then I'll take you to get something to eat," he said graciously.

"No," Abby murmured. "I don't feel well. I'm going back to my room."

Glancing at Ford, she saw that he had a crazy look in his eyes and was glaring at her. But just as quickly as it came, the look went away, and his face appeared calm and normal again.

"Fine, Abby," he said with a twisted smile. "I'll walk you back."

Half scared to death, Abby walked beside Bob Ford through the crowd of men on the street. Ford still wore the ridiculous makeup from the play and the suit and gun belt with the gun still in it. His hand gripped her arm tightly, causing her pain, but she didn't complain and moved along, anxious to be away from this man.

Once they were at her room, Abby unlocked the door and quickly stepped inside, trying to put the door between her and Ford, but he stuck his boot in the way, preventing it from shutting. The room was dark except for the dim light coming through the window.

"I'm not leaving!" he said forcefully.

Abby's heart jumped into her throat, and her stomach felt nauseous. "You're not staying!" she said with as much courage as she could muster.

"I'm staying until I get what I want," he said and shoved her onto the bed.

Before Abby could stop him, Ford was on top of her, the black makeup smearing on her face as she tried to turn her head away.

The ferocious temper Abby had tried to control her entire life surfaced as an angry wildcat. She slapped at him with surprising strength, then reached down and pulled the heavy pistol from his holster. She slapped him on the side of the head with the barrel. Ford went sprawling to the floor, holding his head with both hands. Abby jumped to her feet and stood over Ford with the pistol ready to strike again. Scrambling, he made his way for the door, coming to his feet as he did so.

Pulling the door open, he looked back at Abby and growled, "Have it your way for now! Soon enough you'll be begging for mercy!"

The door slammed, and Abby could hear a key working in the lock. She ran for the door, terrified, and tried to open it, but it was locked tight. She was a captive! With her energy quickly waning, she dropped the pistol and wandered over to the bed, where she fell in a heap and began to sob.

Captive

The horrible incident caused Abby to cry herself to sleep, withdrawn into a world of dreams safe and far away, fear keeping her from waking into the nightmare she had left behind. In the cloudy vagueness of her dreams, Bob Ford lurked in the darkness, but she pushed the phantom behind a curtain of images of other times and places where things were more pleasant.

A loud banging caused Abby to sit straight up, her heart pounding in her ears, her eyes wide open and searching for the danger. The walls were shaking, and the banging persisted, hammering and pounding loud enough to send a chill of fright through her like the piercing point of a big knife. Jumping to her feet, she hurried over to the door and tried it, but it was still locked. Spinning around, she saw a shadow at the window, a window half dark and growing darker as somebody placed yet another board over the outside and began pounding again. Quickly she ran to the window and opened it. A man was even with her second-story window. His bloodshot eyes looked in different directions. The grizzled, bearded man held nails in his rotten teeth as he stood on a ladder, boarding up the outside of the window.

"What are you doing?" Abby screamed, her temper rising.

"What's it look like I'm doing?" the man jeered through

clenched teeth as he raised another board, blocking the view of his ugly face, and began to hammer it into place.

Abby pushed at the lumber with her hand, but it wouldn't budge an inch. The man outside chuckled, his laugh sounding like that of a crazy man. "You must be a wild one!" he said sadistically.

"Stop it!" Abby cried, her stomach beginning to sink into an empty and nauseating feeling of fear and helplessness. "I'll scream!"

"Go right ahead," the voice said from behind the planks. "That ain't nothin' new."

In a last effort of fright and tempered nerves, Abby picked up a chair and threw it at the window. Glass smashed, and the chair bounced off harmlessly to the floor. The futile effort ended up looking like nothing more than an emotional outburst, a simple childish fit. The man on the ladder vanished, and the room grew darker without the daylight from the window, Abby's spirits darkening as well. She sat on the bed, breathing hard, staring at the slats of light coming in between the planks the man had nailed up.

A variety of emotions swept through her, from anger to dismay, from melancholy to anxiety, until she settled down enough to think. *There must be some way to escape this dreadful tomb,* she thought, her blue eyes searching the obscure shadows. On the floor she saw the pistol Ford had left the night before, its pearl handles and silver-like finish shining brightly. Scooping it up, Abby opened the cylinder and slid the cartridges out, some already spent—all blanks, a dab of wax where the bullet should have been in the remaining live rounds. Holding the gun by the barrel, she imitated swinging it like a hammer. *This might do,* she pondered, then took the pistol with her over to the door. Using the gun butt as a hammer head, she swung it at the doorknob. She swung again, harder, each time bending the knob a little more, until the imitation pearl handles busted off the pistol and fell broken to the floor. The doorknob protruded at an angle but showed no signs of surrender. Swinging harder, she hit the knob again, this time breaking the pistol into two pieces, doing little damage to the door lock and mechanism.

"Cheap junk!" Abby said, throwing the broken gun on the floor. Bending over, she peeked through the keyhole and could see the small hallway and the door to the room where Alice was staying. She would have to listen for Alice, and when she came, she'd call for her and ask Alice to go for help.

Moving back across the small room to the window, Abby peered through the cracks in the lumber. She could see only a slice of the street below. If she moved her eye around she could see most everything, but not all at once. She could see The Exchange across the street, where a number of men stood on the boardwalk talking. The street below was busy and packed and noisy with the day's confusion, though for the moment there was no sign of Bob Ford. She knew she would have to come up with some way of escape before things turned even worse.

～

Thinking way ahead of Abby, Bob Ford had already moved Alice to a room over at The Exchange, a nicer room above the saloon. She was about the best poker player he had ever seen, and she'd made him a fine profit in a few short days. Alice could win straight up or she could fool the suckers at the table. Almost always smoking her cigar, she played long hours into the night, taking a break every now and then to limber up her back.

"I'm glad you're playing for the house," Ford said to Alice. "Otherwise I'd have to ask you to leave."

"For the house, for myself—it doesn't matter as long as I make good money," Alice replied around her cigar.

"It's a crime the way you clean those suckers out of their money," Ford complimented, smiling.

"It's a crime not to take a sucker's money," Alice retorted.

Ford backed up to the bar and leaned against it. "Your new room upstairs all right?"

"A bed is a bed." Alice frowned around the cigar smoke. "But it's nice having one just up the stairs, real convenient."

Ford nodded as Alice returned to the players awaiting her at the table. He would keep her around for a while, do what she asked, make her happy, as long as she was raking in the cash.

Regardless of whether he wanted to think about Abby or not,

she kept coming to mind—her pretty blue eyes and luxurious long hair. It made him furious that she had rejected him and stirred up his volatile anger, but his plan would soon tame her. Others had resisted too, and they had all come around eventually. Some still worked for him, which gave him an idea. Lulu Slain might be able to talk some sense into Abby before things got ugly, tell her what she was in for, how things would be easier if she cooperated. Leaving the bar, Ford took off down the street at a hurried gait.

~

Abby took out her steel nail file, long and pointed, and began working at the keyhole in the door. It didn't fit right until she bent the tip so she could maneuver it in the keyhole. Tired of squatting, she pulled over the chair she had thrown earlier and sat in it fidgeting with the lock. With an unrelenting patience born of desperation, she worked and pried for several hours, sometimes stopping to rest her hands, then going back to work. She could see the mechanism inside somewhat but couldn't get the lock to open. And unfortunately the door was a well-built, solid door with massive hinges nailed in place; breaking it down was out of the question. Abby knew that picking the lock was her only way out. She had no idea if she could really get the lock open, but at least her efforts would keep her mind and hands busy.

Late that afternoon Abby heard footsteps scuffling up the stairs. Quickly she removed the chair and hid the file, picked up the remnants of the broken pistol, and sat on the bed holding the pistol barrel tightly under her dress. *If it's that little runt, I'll hit him again!* she thought, her fury growing.

A key was inserted into the keyhole, and Abby held her breath, her heart beginning to race. The door opened, and a woman stood there, carrying a tray. She stepped inside, then turned back to a man standing behind her and mumbled something. He shut the door behind her, and she came forward, holding the tray out.

"So your name's Abby," she said matter-of-factly. "My name's Lulu. I brought you something to eat." She looked around for somewhere to set the tray. "Why don't you light a lantern? It's beginning to get dark in here."

Lulu set the tray on the chair. Pulling a match from somewhere in her hair, she struck it to the lantern and adjusted the wick for the best light. "You look a sight, honey."

"You would too if you were locked in here," Abby fumed, yet knowing she needed someone to talk to. Having an ally would improve her chances. "You work for Ford?"

Lulu nodded, standing before Abby with her arms crossed over her chest. Her hair was long, black, and stiff, her face hardened, her eyes dark and empty. She had the look of the town about her—ruthless and unbridled, sort of a wild animal quality. Her frilly and revealing red dress was evidence of her trade. "Him!" she said vehemently. "Like I have a choice! If I tried to hide or run off, he'd have his henchmen on me like dogs on a cat. There's no escaping, honey. You'll eventually wear down, no matter how strong or how stubborn you think you are."

"Never!" Abby protested, her face livid. "I'll kill him if he ever tries to touch me again."

A slight smile on her colored lips, Lulu blinked knowingly. "I felt the same way once. I would have killed him for a nickel. We were kind of going through the same thing you and him are. It took a while before I came around. At first it was horrible, but a gal gets used to it."

Abby was devastated at the thought. "Can't you see what he is? He's a murderer, and he's—he's evil," Abby argued defensively, her voice quivering. "I could never go along with somebody like that."

"The men are all like that—at least in this town," Lulu said sadly. "If it wasn't Ford, it would be someone else. We women don't have a chance in a place like this. What's a gal like you doin' here anyway?"

Hanging her head, Abby told her story. She ended by saying, ". . . my husband Billy has a silver mine here. If he knew what was going on, he'd take care of Bob Ford!"

Lulu came closer and said nervously, "You better stop talking about your husband or Ford will have him killed. If you really care for him, act like it was all a lie, say that you really aren't married, that you don't know any men here."

This hit Abby like a stone wall. It hadn't occurred to her that she might have put Billy in danger. "But he's the only one who can save me," she whimpered.

"Is he good with a gun?" Lulu asked.

"I don't think so. I've never seen him carry a gun."

Lulu turned her head in disbelief before she turned back to Abby. "Girl, you've got a lot to learn about this place. Let me tell you what's going to happen. You can sit up here caged in this room like an animal until you're almost wasted away, half starved and itching for a bath, or you can cooperate, see things Ford's way. If you decide to work for him, he'll see to it that nobody bothers you, and you'll probably have more money than you've ever seen before. It ain't so bad. You'd be surprised what a person can get used to."

"I don't care about the money!" Abby responded, surprised at her own words. Hadn't it been the lure of money and riches that had brought her here? She felt like she was falling down a deep, empty well. Lulu was right—she wouldn't be able to hold out forever; it would get to the point where she simply didn't care about anything except survival. That was the game Ford was playing.

"I can't give in to *him*!" Abby insisted. "He makes me sick to my stomach."

Running low on patience, Lulu decided it was time to leave. "Well, you'll have plenty of time to think it over," she added, turning toward the door. "Though I can't stand Ford, working here ain't all bad. The gents treat you fair, most of them anyway."

"I will not be a prostitute!" Abby shouted. "Never!"

"We'll see," Lulu answered, opening the door and stepping outside, locking the door behind her.

Feeling weak and defeated, Abby lost whatever appetite she had and let the meal sit on the chair untouched. The walls were unpainted boards with no pictures, the ceiling the same—nothing to look at except rough-cut lumber. The lamp's yellow glow revealed how dismal her surroundings were—just like a prison cell. It occurred to her that she'd made a mistake by coming to Creede, that maybe she should have sent word for Billy to come to her instead. Looking back, it was hard to make sense of the events that had put her in the worst fix she'd ever been in.

Her thoughts ran wild as she tried to think of ways to escape. She could concede, tell Ford the deal was on, then, once she was set free, run away. But his henchmen would just bring her back; they'd probably even beat her to punish her rebellion. Every idea that came to her was too risky and dangerous. If only Billy knew she was here, maybe he could do something. And now her stupidity had put him in danger too, though he didn't know it. Everything seemed to be collapsing around her, and she was doomed to a life of slavery. Sickened by it all, she fell into a deep but troubled sleep.

～

Her stomach growling, Abby was suddenly wide awake. She had no idea what time it was or how long she had been asleep; it could have been several hours, perhaps more. Going to the tray Lulu had left, Abby uncovered it and saw a pile of cold, fried pork chops, corn bread, and a big glass of water. She grabbed the glass and drank its contents with an intense thirst, then ravenously ate the pork chops, not even bothering to use the eating utensils. When she was done, she wiped her mouth with the towel that had covered the plate. She was shocked at her behavior. Her hunger had been so severe, she'd eaten like an animal, neglecting any semblance of manners. How much more like an animal would she become before it was all over?

Looking through a slit between the boards covering the window, Abby could see it was dark out. No longer sleepy, she felt like a captive wild animal, anxious to escape. Pacing the small room, she felt her anger build even further. What if the next time somebody came to the door she attacked them as soon as they got inside, knocked them out of the way, and ran away with all of her strength? What if she used the chair to knock them out of the way? Or what if she hid and pounced on them from behind, using the pistol as a hammer? The enraged thoughts dominated Abby's mind as she paced back and forth, growing more desperate with every step.

The seething anger soon wore itself out, and Abby sat on the bed, watching first light come through the window in narrow strips. Her earlier brave thoughts now seemed foolish. Even if she did get out of the building, she could never escape the town since Ford's men were everywhere. Leaning back on her pillow, she put her hands behind her head and tried to think reasonably, something that was becoming harder and harder to do. There must be something she could offer Bob Ford in exchange for her freedom, something besides doing immoral work for him.

Suddenly Abby had an idea. Billy had a silver mine and by now should be making a good profit. Money! That was an asset he should have plenty of; he could pay Ford off, and they would both be rid of him. The next time somebody came to the room, she'd tell them all about it. Then they would be forced to find Billy, and he would come and save her from a horrible fate. In her frantic state it didn't occur to her that they would probably just find Billy's mine and then kill him and keep her in the same dilemma she was already in.

~

Far away in Leadville, in the early hours of the morning, Jennifer tossed and turned in her bed, moaning with dreams she couldn't understand. At first there was a voice calling her as she searched and searched, but she couldn't find the caller. She seemed to be running, but something was holding her back. So she crawled, dragging herself along. She recognized the urgency in the young girl's cries. Coming to a huge black chasm, far on the other side through the mist she could see the young girl, holding her hand out to Jennifer, calling and calling. Jennifer fought for control, trying to see what was happening, trying to make sense of it all.

"Wake up—you're having a nightmare. Wake up, Jennifer," a calm, reassuring voice said.

Awaking, Jennifer saw Jason sitting next to her, his warm hand on her shoulder. His face was sleepy but concerned. "You were having a bad dream," he said. "Everything's all right now—it was just a dream."

Jennifer felt like crying. The dream had emotionally drained her, leaving her limp and sweating. "Jason?" she questioned.

"Yes, it's me, you're fine," Jason consoled.

Wiping her eyes, Jennifer slowly recognized Jason and her room and the light from the lamp next to her bed. All seemed safe and cozy in the security of their home, the windows still dark with night. "That's the worst dream I've ever had," she mumbled. "It was so real!"

"Do you want to talk about it?" Jason asked, wanting to be all the help he could. It was uncommon for Jennifer to have nightmares.

"It's hard to talk about something so crazy," Jennifer said softly. "It was like— I don't know what it was like. A little girl was calling me, and I couldn't reach her, I couldn't save her." As she recalled the sketchy images, she could see the girl in her mind. It slowly became apparent that the girl was Abby.

"Jason!" Jennifer said, sitting up and grabbing his arms with both of her hands. "Abby's in trouble!"

Staying calm, Jason looked deeply into his wife's beautiful, loving, and caring eyes, eyes now overcome with worry. "That just might be," he said. "But I don't know what we can do about it—we have no idea where she is."

Clutching Jason, Jennifer felt now like she had in the dream— helpless. "We have to go find her. We must leave at once."

"But where will we go?" Jason asked. "Grant has already gone to do just that. He'll find Abby."

They both sat in silence for a long time, the yellow light from the electric bulb flickering slightly. The more alert Jennifer became, the further away the dream seemed as reality took its place. She wanted to keep the dream close, to see Abby, to reach her, to touch her. But the dream was already fading, quickly becoming just a fantasy of the mind.

"The feeling was so strong, Jason. It was like Abby was in trouble and needed me, and she was only a little girl. I felt so helpless— I couldn't do anything to help her. Do you think she's really in trouble, or do you think I'm being foolish?"

Jason smiled with understanding. "You're asking me if I think you might be foolish? That's a foolish question in itself."

Jennifer smiled too, appreciating her husband's ability to make a little joke to ease her troubled spirits.

"But then again I have heard stories," Jason said, "about a close relative knowing when another relative is hurt or in trouble, and then finding out their intuitions were right. So it's hard to discount your worries about Abby. Grant felt this way from the very beginning and did something about it without delay. If anybody can help Abby, it's Grant."

"You're right, but I don't know if I can stop worrying about her," Jennifer admitted. "She's a grown woman, but I still think of her as a child."

Enjoying the soft light on Jennifer's face, Jason watched her blink her sleepy eyes. She was more beautiful than ever. Like her mother, Abby had to test the waters herself, make mistakes and learn from them, see what it was like to fall in love, having no idea what the man she loved was really like. Like a child learning how to walk, she had to go her own way, falling at times, but learning to get up and start over.

Abby's stubbornness and determination could work against her, but Jason never considered these as entirely negative assets. Those attitudes had enabled her to survive a hard life and keep going, had given her strength when she needed it, and kept her spirits up when many people would have given up. That all reminded him of Jennifer in the past.

"Do you pray for Abby?" Jason asked softly.

"I pray for Abby these days more than ever," Jennifer answered. "Since Grant left, I pray for him a lot too. There's no telling what kind of things he's having to deal with. The last letter from him said he was very close to Abby, in fact right behind her. But what worried me was where the letter was from—Silverton. The stories we've heard about that place—so much danger there."

Smiling, Jason moved his hand to Jennifer's face and traced the graceful outline from her cheek to her jaw with his finger. "You act as if your children are being thrown to the wolves by being in places like Silverton. Did you ever stop to think they might know their way around a boomtown? Seems to me I remember a few wild boomtowns they've lived in since they were youngsters—Virginia City, Black Hawk and Central City, Leadville in its early days."

"But back then I could always keep an eye on them."

"But they're grown-up now," Jason reminded her.

They looked into each other's face for a long moment, communicating feelings of love and understanding in a way that can only be said with the eyes.

"Jennifer?"

"Yes?"

"Let me ask you a question," Jason said quietly. "Of all the crazy things you've been through, all the rough towns, the misguided relationships, the hard times of poverty and wealth, the times of loss, now that you can look back, has God ever let you down?"

Jennifer's face clouded over, then her eyes brightened. "No," she answered and pulled Jason to her, hugging him with all her might. "No, He never has."

Mister

Morning came, and Grant awoke feeling like he'd emerged from some kind of mystical dream. He had slept like a rock, and it was now late, the sun having already cleared the peaks that cut a jagged edge across the great blue depths. He sat up, trying to shake away the sleep that lingered like the smoky smell of a fire. Had he indeed had a visitor in the middle of the night, the famous Indian leader Chief Joseph?

Grant recalled the conversation, the darkness, the man's chiseled face. Yet it seemed so much like a dream that Grant came to his feet and searched the ground around the fire looking for traces of his visitor's presence. At first glance it appeared nothing had been disturbed—no footprints, no evidence of even a twig having been moved. He began doubting the reality of the experience again, thinking of the otherworldly euphoria the high country brought, the effects of fatigue on a man's thinking.

Wanting to be sure, he took a closer look, on his hands and knees, but still found no trace of another's presence. Of course, he realized that an old Indian knows how to travel in harmony with the wild, leaving no evidence he's been present. The coffeepot sat undisturbed, the metal cup sitting next to it. Looking through his things to see if anything was missing, Grant found everything in its place. Mumbling to himself, he began gathering his gear for the day's travel. Suddenly a new thought crossed his mind, and he began rummaging through his things once again. His Bible, the one Jason had given him, was nowhere to be found.

~

The trail above the Lake Fork of the Gunnison River was set in gold, a sparkle accenting the early-morning dew. Mister plodded along, satisfied with his surroundings, his furry ears cocking this way and that, catching every little sound. He was a solid mount, stocky and strong, his mane long and wavy. Grant couldn't have been more pleased with his selection, for the horse was accustomed to the steep grades and tricky footing. Similarly, Peaches's long hooves stepped into Mister's prints with as much grace as any burro.

Mesmerized by the scenery, Grant rode loose in the saddle on the shelf road as it proceeded lower and lower until it reached the flats of the river. He let Mister have the reins, the beast wisely picking his own way for the easiest travel as the morning sun warmed rider and animals. Almost dizzy, Grant still felt the spell of the night before, his eyes sleepy, his body relaxed as the riverbed widened and opened into a huge valley. Veering left with the trail, he saw Lake San Cristobal, the expanse of glassy water so bright he had to squint.

The side of the mountain going down into the lake was covered with loose rock, and Mister slipped and caught his balance frequently, often snorting with disapproval. Grant tried to shake off his lethargy and help Mister by putting his weight in the stirrups. Below, the waters sparkled, small waves rippling on a pleasant fall morning, the air soft and cool.

Mister suddenly halted, his big head turned toward the mountain above, his ears perked. Grant cast a glance, and for a second he thought he was going to lose his balance, maybe even fall off his horse. It appeared as if the entire landscape was moving. Then he heard the rumble of a thousand small rocks coming down the mountainside right at him. Before Grant could think, Mister lunged forward with an incredible display of strength, almost causing Grant to topple off behind him. Peaches brayed with fear, trying to keep up. As the slide built momentum, Mister raced down the precarious trail full of sharp stones, Grant holding on tight. After fifty yards at break-neck speed they were out of harm's way, and Grant pulled the reins taut. Mister was breathing hard, his muscles quivering, his eyes wide and white.

"Good work, boy," Grant said, patting the horse's neck, trying to soothe him.

Peaches, right behind them, was braying and tossing his tail, aggravated and frightened. Turning in the saddle, Grant looked back. The slide had brought down perhaps a ton of flat rocks. He looked down to the water's edge and the steep bank there. Had they been caught in the slide, the animals could not have kept their footing. They would have tumbled several hundred feet down into the icy water. They would certainly have been killed.

Wide awake now, Grant's heart was pounding hard. Mister's alertness and instant reaction had saved his life. He knew the horse was strong, but the burst of energy he'd displayed was nothing short of miraculous.

"Good boy!" Grant said, patting Mister's neck. "Good boy."

Leaning forward, Grant saw Mister bobbing his head and limping. Dismounting, he looked at Mister's right front hoof. The shoe was fine, but blood was coming from the center of the hoof. Evidently he'd hit a sharp rock during the run, being unable to pick his steps carefully.

Pulling the reins over Mister's head, Grant led him and Peaches along for the last few miles to Lake City

～

"Looks like a bad bruise," said a blacksmith named Eric, a short round man with great strength. He let Mister's hoof down and stood up to speak directly to Grant. His short black beard and ocean-blue eyes made him look like a sailor. "You'll have to stay off him a few days, give him a chance to heal up. I'll keep strong liniment on it until then, and after that I'll have to put a pad on."

"A pad?" Grant questioned.

"Yeah. I take off the shoe and cut a thick leather pad the size of his hoof, then clamp it on with the shoe. That way, won't be nothin' gettin' up in there to make the injury worse. That'll give him some protection too."

"All right," Grant said, glancing out the door. "I guess I'm stuck in Lake City for a few days."

"It's a good town," Eric said. "It's settled down some since the wild days of Injuns and mob lynchings."

"Is that right?" Grant said. "I've heard very little about Lake City. I heard a lot more about Creede."

"Creede's wild as fresh killed game, just now goin' through the motions of becoming a real town, what with all that silver they're findin'," Eric said. "But you take Lake City now, why, she's been around a while, knows the ropes. We got some good folks livin' here."

Grant grabbed his bag and his rifle. "I'll check in on you later," he said, walking out.

Lake City was a pretty town, the main street lined with cotton-woods, the colorful buildings mostly blue paint and blue stones. Henson Creek joined the Lake Fork of the Gunnison River right in town. The streets were smooth and wide, the houses and buildings of a more permanent nature. Every now and then there was a vacant lot in between buildings as a result of fire or some other tragedy, the scene resembling a smiling mouth with a missing tooth. People on the street appreciated the pleasant fall atmosphere, walking about in no hurry, taking care of daily routines.

A strong hunger drove Grant to The City Restaurant, where he enjoyed a fine steak dinner with all the trimmings. Full and satisfied, he meandered out front to the covered boardwalk lined with chairs. An old codger with a long gray beard sat there leaning forward, both hands resting on a cane that stood straight as a stalk before him. Grant sat down to let his meal settle.

"New here, ain't ya?" the old man inquired.

"Just passin' through," Grant mumbled. A good steak in his belly and the light air made him feel lazy. He propped his Winchester rifle on the wall behind him and relaxed, watching the people pass by.

"That's what I said the first time I came through here. Of course it weren't nothin' but willow-covered beaver ponds back then," the old man said, reminiscing.

"That must have been a while back," Grant guessed.

"1874. I worked with Enos Hotchkiss on his road-building crew. He built a toll road for Otto Mears all the way from Saguache, discovered a claim down by the lake called the Golden Fleece."

"You been here ever since?" Grant asked, enjoying talking to the old fellow.

"Yep," he said, moving his cane aside and removing a pipe from his vest. He loaded it carefully, then put a match to it and took a few gentle puffs.

"Look out for that old man," a gentleman said to Grant as he stepped out of the restaurant. He wore a suit and looked like a banker or a lawyer. "Once he gets started, he goes on forever." He smiled.

The old man squinted at the man who made the comment and said, "I done forgot more than you'll ever know, so maybe you ought to write what I jest said down and take it over to your bank and put it in the safe so you don't forget it."

Still smiling, the man looked at Grant, then gestured at the old man with a pointed finger. "He's not only known for being cranky, he's the town historian. Been here since that mountain over there was just a small hill." He laughed at his own joke and proceeded across the street.

Grant turned back to the old man. "Town historian, huh?"

"Henry Finley," he said, extending a hand.

Taking his hand, Grant felt strength in the man's grip. "I guess you've watched it from beginning to present. I've often wondered, what makes men come way out here all the way from back east, giving up everything they ever had for a chance at striking it rich?"

"Lying newspapers is what done that, sonny," Henry said, then took a mild puff on his pipe. "They said there'd be plenty of gold for those who wanted to come pick it up."

Grant was familiar with the newspapers of those days and the lies told to attract people to western towns. But he felt like no intelligent man would ever believe those kind of stories, much less pursue them with intentions of gaining great wealth.

"I was in the Californy rush of '49," Henry added. "'Bout the same then too—men comin' from everywhere expecting to pick up gold and get rich quick."

"Lake City seems like a settled town," Grant said, thinking out loud. He picked at his teeth with a toothpick, thinking this was maybe the nicest little town he'd ever come across. "Still some mining going on around here, I guess—saw it on the way in, several mines. I like to got in a rock slide that would've have put me in the lake. Hurt my horse's foot."

"That's been a dangerous spot for a good many years, right out by the mine. I almost slipped down it a few times myself. Things got a mite slow in the 80s 'round here," Henry began. "The train comin' in last year opened things back up again, and now they're all back out yonder workin' in the mines. Now they've got a way to get their ore out. But you take the 70s now—them was the days. News spread like wildfire about the claim me and Enos staked, and here they come, all wantin' a cut of the action."

Henry's old eyes were looking into the past. It was fine with Grant to sit here and take it easy while the old man reminisced.

"Lake City has had her share of lawlessness and the wild side, back in the days when you had to stand your claim or someone would come along and pull up the stakes and claim it for themselves. Once our sheriff got killed, old Campbell. If he'd been a better shot, he might still be alive. What happened was, he was trying to apprehend a couple of crooks, George Betts and James Browning, who owned a dance hall here, while they were breakin' into a place. They kilt the sheriff and run off. Before they got far they was captured and put in jail, but that ain't the good part of the story.

"Late that night, soon as the moon went down and it got good and dark . . . I ain't mentionin' no names, but a group of fellers went over to the jailhouse with sledgehammers and banged their way into the jail. They got them two men and dragged them over to the Ocean Wave Bridge over the Lake Fork and strung 'em up. The next day they let school out and marched them children down there to look at them two hanging with their eyeballs bulgin' out."

"Nothin' like vigilante justice," Grant said, remembering similar situations in his own past.

Henry rearranged himself in his chair and tugged at his pipe, facing Grant. "That story ain't much. I got one better. Five prospectors hired a guide to lead them over the San Juans to find gold, and they took off out of Ouray against the advice of Chief Ouray, for winter was coming, and nobody knew better than the old chief how rough it could get in the mountains. It was just a year before me and Enos staked our claim that these fellers found themselves at the foot of Slumgullion Pass, snowbound.

"Now these prospectors should've known better 'cause they hired this guide after they bailed him out of jail and paid his fine. He was in for counterfeiting and was a known liar, bragging he knew all about the San Juans. Well, it was too late when they realized he didn't know a thing—and it was an unusually bad winter with heavy snow and temperatures below zero. Game was scarce, and their supplies soon ran out. They even boiled their moccasins and ate them."

Henry smiled as he patiently reloaded his pipe. He knew he had Grant's utmost attention and deliberately took his time, as any good storyteller would do. "Six weeks later the guide showed up at Los Pinos Indian Agency, seventy-six miles from here, and he looked fit as a fiddle. He told them he lost his companions and had no idear what happened to them—said he barely made it out alive hisself. Funny part was, he was mainly interested in getting a drink, not in havin' something to eat. Had plenty of money with him too. Some evidence was found of foul play, they say, but not much come of it 'til they found the five men—all partly eaten, with strong evidence of cannibalism.

"The guide's name was Alfred Packer, and he disappeared before they could arrest him. Took 'em nine years before they found him up in Wyoming, then brought him back, right here to Lake City, for a trial. They convicted him and sentenced him to hang. I was helpin' build the gallows, but they claimed somethin' was done wrong in the trial, and Packer got forty years of hard labor instead.

"I think it might have had somethin' to do with Judge Gerry when he sentenced Packer. The judge said, 'You man-eatin' rascal! There was seven Democrats in Hinsdale County, and ya ate five of 'em! Therefore I sentence ya to be hanged by the neck until you're dead, dead, dead—as a warning against reducing the Democratic population of the state!" Old Henry laughed. He loved telling that story.

Grant laughed too. The story was absurd, but the way Henry told it, it was funny.

"I better get on out of here," Grant said, standing. "It's getting a mite deep."

"I swear that's a true story," Henry said, holding his palm up in oath.

"If you say so," Grant said, grabbing his rifle and his bag. "I've got to find a place to stay. I'll see you around."

~

After his nights high in the mountains sleeping under the stars, Grant found the hotel room confining and cramped. He wondered if he was growing wild and uncivilized, preferring the outdoors to city life.

Mister nodded with a sense of familiarity when Grant walked into the stable the next morning, tossing his head with excitement. "How's he doing?" Grant asked Eric.

"Looks like he's glad to see you. Once I got his hoof cleaned out, it didn't look so bad. I think he'll be all right tomorrow. That's one tough horse. Don't see many like that," Eric said, stroking Mister's neck.

"He's a mustang," Grant said. Now the phrase had become more of a boast than a simple statement.

"I don't suppose you'd be interested in selling him?"

"Not after yesterday," Grant said, patting Mister's nose. "He saved my life."

Eric understood, also being a man who grew attached to animals.

"I'll be back tomorrow," Grant said and moseyed on.

After a good breakfast, Grant walked through the town, noticing the fine architecture and several impressive churches with tall steeples. The people were for the most part civilized and well-dressed, unlike the boomtowns he was used to seeing. Lake City even had telephones, a gadget he'd never used. A train coming in was an impressive sight, the big locomotive whistling to a stop at the station. For some reason Grant felt at home in Lake City.

That afternoon Grant sat in front of a drugstore eating a peppermint stick and thinking of Mendy. He allowed himself to think about Mendy only on certain occasions, like rationing a good thing so it can be savored. Lake City, at least to him, seemed like the kind of small town he and Mendy could live in, raising a family and enjoying life. An easygoing town, Lake City had all of the things the big cities had, just on a smaller scale, a town isolated and far away from the worries of the world.

After visiting the mercantile to pick up supplies, Grant watched as the sun settled behind a mountain to the west, though it was only early afternoon. He'd never quite gotten over how the mountains shortened the days in certain places because of their tremendous heights. He guessed it was around 3:30 P.M., and he still had some time to kill before getting dinner and retiring for the night.

Ahead of him a woman dressed in the fashion of the day crossed the street, her hair up and her face pretty. She looked slightly older than Grant, though it was hard to tell from the way she'd fixed herself up. Just then he saw something shiny drop to the ground. Rushing over, Grant picked it up and looked at it; it was a diamond earring. He glanced up to see the woman heading down the street, away from him.

"Madam!" Grant called, taking off after her. "Madam!"

Catching up with her, Grant called to her again.

When she turned around to glare at him, Grant saw that she was a very attractive and distinguished lady. "Can't I even walk down the street without being approached for immoral purposes?" she asked with disgust.

"But . . ." Grant said, pointing to the earring in his hand.

"You are rude and inconsiderate," she lashed out, interrupting him. "Calling to me like I was a horse or something! I would think a man of your appearance would have some character. At least learn some manners, won't you?" She turned and stomped away.

Grant moved quick as a cat and stepped in front of her. "If you'd give me a chance to talk, you might change your mind," he said forcefully. "You dropped this in the street back there."

Taking the earring from his hand, she blushed, her cheeks rosy. "Oh my . . ." she said softly, her voice now friendly and alluring. "I'm so sorry I treated you like I did."

"Don't worry about it," Grant said easily, accepting her apology.

"As expensive as these earrings were, I always have trouble with that one falling off. If I don't get it fixed, I'm going to lose it some-day. These are very special to me. Thank you so much," she said, her eyes friendly and persuasive. Still feeling uneasy about the way she'd treated him and wishing to make amends, she said, "Walk with me a ways, will you?"

Grant fell into step beside the lovely woman. "What's your name?" she asked.

"Grant DeSpain. What's yours?"

"I'm Clara Ogden. You're not from around here, are you?"

"No," Grant said, enjoying her company. However, he noticed that people were watching them with eyes of contempt. Clara either didn't notice or ignored the stares. "I'm from Leadville."

"Oh, I hear that's such a big city, high in the mountains and full of rich people and big parties," she said with obvious admiration for that kind of life.

"It's all of that," Grant agreed, "and more. Where are you from?"

"Back east," was all she said.

"Are you married?" Grant asked.

"I was once."

"It didn't work out?" Grant inquired curiously.

"It's not that," Clara said reflectively, her eyes looking especially pretty. "I married an older man back in Delaware, and he was good to me. We had a good life, but I was young and foolish and I thought money brought happiness. We were supposed to inherit a fortune— his father owned a lumber company; but when he died, we had noth-ing but debt. I ran away, thinking I could make a fortune out west because I'd heard about the bountiful gold and silver here. It just hasn't turned out to be what I thought."

"I know what you mean," Grant said, thinking of all the stories like this that he'd heard and the many times he'd actually seen it. Suddenly he suspected he'd heard this story before, this exact story. "I don't mean to be nosy, but what did your husband do for a living?"

"He taught college—chemistry," Clara said.

Grant stopped in his tracks, apprehension on his face. "Is your real name Charlotte Potter?"

Clara looked as if she'd seen a ghost "How could you know such a thing? That was so long ago."

"I used to work for your husband. He's an assayer in Central City. At least he was the last I heard," Grant informed her.

Clara placed her small hands on Grant's chest, gripping his lapels as if she were trying to pull something out of him. "How is he? I've thought of him so often."

"He's doing well financially. He lives in a big house, has a house-keeper, and still thinks about you—he told me so. He stands at the back door and stares into the sky every now and then, wishing . . ." Grant noticed that her eyes were moist.

Barely audible, she said, "I should have never left."

Trying to cheer her up, Grant observed, "Looks like you're doing well."

"No, I'm not." Clara was ready to tell Grant the truth. "I'm a prostitute, though I sometimes pretend otherwise. The only way out of this wicked life of mine is suicide."

Shocked, Grant found her words hard to believe. Clara had completely fooled him. Now he understood the passing eyes glaring at them, the disapproving looks from other women.

Grant took her small hands in his. "No, that's not the only way out. Pray to God, and He will forgive you and give you a new life."

Clara replied despondently, "It's too late for that. God would never forgive someone like me."

"Yes, He would," Grant promised. "There's a story in the Bible, about the woman at the well, a woman like you. Jesus forgave her. All you have to do is ask."

"You're a rare man, Grant. I must go now, but thank you for everything. I won't ever forget meeting you." She moved off slowly into the darkening afternoon.

Grant watched her go, thinking how amazing it was that he had bumped into Charlotte Potter. No wonder Mr. Potter was so troubled over her disappearance. She was a lovely woman, another person who had discovered that the riches she sought were not to be found. She had looked in the wrong place. He felt sorry for her and hoped she would take to heart what he'd said.

～

An early-morning mist hung over Lake City as Grant took the road out. Mister was eager to be back on the trail, slightly favoring his front foot. As Grant climbed the road that overlooked Lake San Cristobal, he watched the sun rise in all its bright orange glory, the lake placid and still, deep and mysterious. During the long climb over Slumgullion Pass, Mister never wavered, trudging forward after his brief rest in Lake City. The spruce forest crowded the road with a sweet scent and cool shadows. The road had its share of traffic, men walking with packs on their backs or riding on wagons or horses, most of them on their way to Creede. Over the pass Grant went, following the winding road until it finally leveled off into the rolling meadows of a big valley. The traveling was easy now, and he made good time the whole day in the saddle until he saw the lights of his destination. Above Creede stood the Gateway Cliffs over and beyond Wagon Wheel Gap.

"So this is it," Grant said. Mister twisted an ear to hear his rider as they approached the smoky town. "The end of a trail called The Silver Thread."

PART FOUR

REDEMPTION

CHAPTER

~ 19 ~

Chaos and the Petrified Man

Darkness had already fallen when Grant rode into downtown Creede. The main street was well lit with fires and lanterns, and the people bustling here and there reminded Grant of moths swarming around a lantern. Creede was like towns he had seen before—Virginia City, Black Hawk and Central City, and Leadville when they were in their heyday. The difference was, Creede was crowded into a confining small gulch and spilled out of it like a river into the flats. Sitting on his horse, he could see far down what looked like an endless street winding like a corkscrew up the gulch, a street lined with unpainted clapboard buildings, the people so thick it seemed the town would bust at its seams.

Outside of the Vaughn Hotel a throng of people pressed against the doors trying to get inside, the excitement at a peak.

"What's going on in there?" Grant shouted down at a man from his horse.

"Why, they found a petrified man buried out by Farmer's Creek. No tellin' how old he is. Only cost twenty-five cents to see it," the man said, a typical miner, overwhelmed with enthusiasm, his eyes flashing in the dim kerosene light.

Moving on, Grant found nowhere to stable his animals and had to turn back and make the trip back down the overcrowded street. Mister snorted and jerked, disliking the confinement and the fact that Peaches was pushing him forward, being disgruntled as well. Grant finally came back to where the canyon opened to the rail yards, packed with boilers, crates, bags, and beer kegs. Spread out to the side was the lower part of the camp, known as Jim Town. After a prolonged search, he finally found a place to stable Mister and Peaches.

"Is it always like this in town?" Grant asked, paying the livery man in advance.

"Like what?" the man asked, lifting bushy eyebrows.

"I could hardly ride my horse down the street," Grant complained.

The man chuckled and said with a wheeze in his voice, "No place for a horse up there. I had to move down here. Couldn't throw the water out of the washbasin without hitting someone—and that's as good a reason as any to get shot."

Throwing his bag over his shoulder, Grant held his rifle in his other hand, ready to hike back to the melee. "Take good care of that horse—he's been a real friend," Grant said with great seriousness.

"Yes, sir, sure will. You take care of yourself up yonder."

Grant nodded and left, making his way by the lights cast from windows, street fires, and kerosene lanterns hanging here and there. Creede was yet to see the likes of electricity or any modern conveniences, and being there gave Grant a sense of stepping back in time. Gazing at the sights as he made his way back into the heart of Creede, he wondered if the place wouldn't burn like a kerosene-soaked rag if a spark ever got loose. The way it was all crowded together, all that would be left was a black spot.

"Reckon a man could find a room here?" Grant asked a passerby.

"There must be a hundred hotels here," the man in a dark suit answered, quite serious. "But if you can find a room, I want you to stand beside me for luck when I roll the dice." He moved on.

"Great!" Grant mumbled as he strolled on through the thickening crowd.

He suddenly heard gunfire at the end of the street up ahead and more gunfire from behind, in the area he had just come from. Grant kept his Winchester handy, wondering whether he should start searching for a place to sleep or go get something to eat. He came back to the excitement at the Vaughn Hotel, where men stood in line with their money in hand, eager to see the petrified man.

Grant wondered what a petrified man looked like, what his origins were. On a whim he got in line, fumbling in his pocket for a coin. As the line moved slowly toward the entrance, imaginative conversations escalated the drama. "Could be a caveman from thousands of years ago," one furry-faced man said. "Might just be some Injun," another added. "He's got to be old to be petrified," a third said with some authority.

The line moved inside, and Grant paid the fee and soon had a glimpse of the spectacle. Under a couple of flickering kerosene lamps the petrified man lay on his back on several straw-filled burlap bags. Standing off to the side, one of the town bosses, Soapy Smith, answered questions. "Yeah, J.J. Dore found him buried in mud by Farmer's Creek. We think he might have been a member of the Freemont party that explored these parts back in '42." Soapy was answering a man's questions, the little man scribbling on a pad as fast as he could."

"What'd he look like when you found him?" the man asked, hesitating with his writing.

"Covered with mud—wasn't sure what it was at first. Got to throwing buckets of water on it and it come clean—hard as a rock!" He tapped on the carcass with his cane to prove his point—*tap-tap!*

Men looked on in awe as Grant stood motionless, staring at the thing before him, wondering what stories the man would tell if he could talk. It was intriguing to let his mind wander and speculate. But upon a second look, Grant wondered if the item was genuine, for the man was frozen in a strange position—lying on his backside with his knees up, completely unclad and lacking any details.

"What do you think?" Grant asked the little gentleman scribbling notes.

"Don't matter what I think," he answered quickly, barely casting a glance at Grant as he scribbled with his pencil. "It's news, and that sells papers. I'm calling him McGinty—he's got to have a name."

"You a reporter for the newspaper here?" Grant questioned, hungry to know more.

"I *am* the newspaper—Cy Warman, the *Chronicle*," the fellow answered briskly.

"I'm a newspaper man too," Grant stated.

Stopping his work, Cy looked Grant up and down and decided he didn't fit the picture of a newspaper man. "You don't look the part. What paper are you with?"

"None right now," Grant admitted. "I work for a magazine back in Leadville. I'm here searching for my sister—she's missing."

Warman took an immediate interest. "Missing? And you think she's in Creede?"

"Yes, I do," Grant answered.

Taking Grant by the arm, Cy pulled him aside, his voice lowered. "A woman missing, and she's in Creede . . . Hmm, there might be a story here."

"Why's that?"

Cy made a face at him as if he were a novice. "A woman alone has no business here unless she knows what she's getting into. If she doesn't, that's where a story would begin. You see, there are thousands of men here but only a handful of women. Seems they either survive to become famous or wind up dead in a hurry. Either way, it might be a story. Sorry, I didn't mean to scare you."

"Well, you did," Grant admitted. "Maybe you've seen her." He removed the picture and showed it to Cy, who shook his head.

"Now I'm sure there's a story—any gal who looks like that is going to attract attention. You can bet there's already something going on. Follow me—let's get out of here, go over to my place where we can talk," Cy said, leading the way.

Following Cy Warman, Grant was thankful he'd run into someone who was wise to the ways and people of Creede. This was a big break, and he knew it.

~

At a poker table in a saloon known as the Orleans Club, owned and operated by Soapy Smith, Billy Rogers sat musing over a poker hand of four jacks with his perpetual little smile, his eyes black and deep and offering no clues as to the cards he held. Dapperly dressed, he was in his environment, cigar smoke and the smell of whiskey heavy in the air.

"Another drink?" a saloon girl asked, flirting with a smile.

"I'm fine, thanks," Billy answered, waiting for his prey to make a move at the table.

"I'll raise you twenty dollars," the gruff miner said, pushing coins out to the pile of money in the middle of the table.

The other players folded as Billy studied the man before him. This was the chance he'd been waiting for. "I'll see your twenty and raise you fifty more."

The miner slammed his fist on the table, his nostrils flaring, anger rising in his dull eyes. "You ain't gonna buy this pot!" he stormed as he shoved more money out. "I call."

Miners were easy pickings when it came to poker or selling a fraudulent claim, Billy realized. His pleasant smile increased as he spread his four jacks on the table, sure the man before him couldn't beat it.

"You always have a good hand!" the miner said furiously. "Makes me wonder if you're on the up-and-up."

As Billy raked in the pot with one hand, his other hand slipped into his coat pocket to clutch a small pistol. His pleasant smile gave no clue to his thoughts. "Sir, if you can't afford to lose, I would suggest you not gamble. I'll kindly disregard any insinuations you made as to my poker playing being questionable."

"It ain't right," the miner said, nevertheless backing away. To accuse a man of cheating meant risking a fight, maybe even a duel. The rough old miner wasn't so sharp at poker, but he did realize that Billy probably had a gun. The pot wasn't worth that.

Knowing his business, Billy had known the man would back down, if for no other reason than to avoid having a bullet dug out of him by some unskilled doctor who may or may not have had medical training. It was considered acceptable to shoot a man if he accused you of cheating and couldn't prove it.

Suddenly Billy felt crowded, as if someone was standing too close. He turned to see a man on each side of him, big tough men who were undoubtedly good with their fists and with their guns. He knew they worked for one of the town bosses.

"May I help you, gentlemen?" Billy asked coolly.

"We need to speak with you—outside!" one of them said.

"Kind sirs, if you'll excuse me," Billy said to the other men at the table, gathering his money and shoving it into his pocket. The three walked outside to the far end of the covered boardwalk where they could talk in private.

One of the toughs was gifted with enough of a brain to communicate coherently; the other stood speechless with a threatening demeanor. "Our boss sent us—he has an offer for you."

Billy couldn't imagine what he might have that would interest a town boss, unless of course it was his silver mine. The mine produced low grade ore, barely worth mining, but few knew this. Billy had bought premium grade ore with which to salt his works, even fooling some of the employees who worked for him, tricking them into believing they had a producing mine so the word would spread. Sooner or later some interested party would approach him with hopes of purchasing the mine and works. This had been his plan all along. But he knew he would have to be careful whom he sold it to, because a town boss might retaliate. "If it's about my silver mine, it ain't for sale, fellows," Billy proudly announced, the same thing he always said when first questioned, a way to drive for a better deal.

"It ain't about no mine," the tough said rudely. "You know a girl goes by the name of Abby?"

Completely caught off guard, Billy for once lost his smile. "Why, of course. Is she in trouble?"

"She ain't in no trouble—she's for sale," the man said, his face close to Billy's, his breath stinking.

"For sale?" Billy laughed weakly. "People aren't for sale."

The tough usually had a hard time expressing himself or his boss's wishes without arguing. Any arguing he did, he did with fists or guns. "Ten thousand dollars," he continued, repeating what he'd been told to say. "If you want to see her, you bring the money and hang around The Exchange; we'll find you."

"Ten thousand!" Billy protested. "I don't have that kind of money. Are you crazy?"

It was too late. The toughs had already turned to leave, having delivered their message.

Standing alone, his thoughts racing, and being a con man himself, Billy realized exactly what had happened. How it had slipped by him he couldn't imagine. Someone had grabbed Abby in a lawless town for exploitation or extortion. He slammed his palm against his forehead in a fit of frustration, angry at being so stupid. The problem now was the money. With the best swindle, the mine might bring 10,000 dollars, but that was doubtful since it was a small claim way back in the mountains, away from good roads. He only had a thousand dollars on hand, not enough of a stake for a real poker game where he would be playing with professionals and stood little chance of winning. Skinning miners was easy, but they didn't have that kind of money to lose.

Another option, Billy figured, was to track down the man who held Abby, try to reason with him. Gunplay or threats were out of the question, for a town boss usually had a variety of employees, each good at some particular action harmful or painful to others. Sitting at a bargaining table with a town boss seemed ridiculous too; Billy had nothing to bargain with.

Strolling down the boardwalk while lost in a confusion of thoughts, Billy realized there was probably little or nothing he could do. He liked Abby very much, but some things were plain and simple, like this. All he could do now was wait and see if something would turn up or if something would happen. He'd been through a variety of difficult situations before, and if it wasn't something he had to skip town over, it was like the weather—it would change.

～

Cy Warman's place was a newspaper office, a bedroom, and a kitchen all rolled into one, and it was messy. With a lantern on a paper-littered desk sitting between them, Grant told his story, his background, his experience, and all about his sister and the man she had chased to Creede. Cy sat silently listening, like any good newspaper man, taking in every detail, his shock of gray hair covering his forehead, the wrinkles around his eyes badges of wisdom.

"If what you say is true, I agree a hundred percent," Cy said, finding a cigar in a cluttered desk drawer. He examined the cigar closely, looking for tiny wormholes, then stuck it in his mouth, and talked around it while he searched for a match. "No doubt she's in some kind of trouble—has to be. Like you said, I could see this one coming before it ever started. But it's an old story, happens all the time. It's how you tell it that's important—got to grab folks' interest." He was trying to determine the best newspaper angle when he finally found a match, dragged it across the side of the desk, and lit his cigar.

"I'm not interested in the story," Grant made clear. "I just want to find Abby."

Warman liked this young man. "How much do you actually know about the newspaper business? Can you set type? Run a press? Write stories? Interview people?"

"All of the above," Grant said modestly. "See that old press over there? I was running one like that when I was nine years old."

Cy leaned back in his swivel chair and enjoyed the cigar for a moment, his thoughts obviously busy. "Where you staying?"

"Nowhere yet," Grant answered.

"You won't find nowhere either," Cy said, pulling the chair forward to bring himself upright. "You can stay here—there's another bunk over there."

This appealed to Grant. "As long as you don't charge me too much."

"You can work it off," Cy said, having already thought it out. "I can't be everywhere and do everything at once. I could use some help. All I can pay you is room and board."

"That's all I need," Grant said, surprised but happy with Cy's generosity. He learned later that Cy only put out an issue every now and then, whenever he managed to get one together and get it run off, and it was usually just a single page. "I may not be around long, if I find my sister. But I'll be glad to do all I can while I'm here."

"You might be around longer than you think," Cy said knowingly. "This is a town of secrets, a maze of information and all of it guarded, and all of it centered around money."

~

Cy Warman was correct in his assumptions, and as the days passed, Grant could find no sign of Abby or Billy Rogers. Working together, Cy and Grant wrote the story of the petrified man, whom they called McGinty, adding their own thoughts and assumptions. Part of the story read:

> From the depths of mud and mire comes a link with the past, a man as hard as stone, his face frozen in time. McGinty, as we have chosen to call him, might have been an early explorer, his face cold and smooth and expressionless in his deep somber, his voice silenced for so many years. Yet he tells a story.
>
> A wayfarer of decades and centuries, McGinty has traveled through time to visit us once again, only to reveal his undecayed body, like a statue carved of stone. We can only assume what thoughts he might have had, what the cold lips once spoke; but he poses as a marvel for all to see, revealing his naked stone body, modestly hiding nothing, yet holding his secrets dear, locked in stone forever and ever.
>
> McGinty might have come from another land far away, traveled the high seas, forged through mountains and streams, climbed to the high country, to finally come to rest in a place where weather and conditions were right to fossilize him in whole so he could journey to this present day and join mankind again. Oh, McGinty, what would you say if you could speak?

Grant found McGinty fascinating, as did Cy, and their printed words revealed the same. Editing out speculations of exact origin, they appealed to the imagination of the reader.

One day the old press was slow but did its job as Grant applied ink and cranked the handle, turning out another hundred newspapers. The office and smell of machine oil, ink, and kerosene reminded Grant of his youth in Virginia City when he worked with

Jason at the press. Though still a young man, he reminisced about how quickly life passes, how things change and yet we go on, and how looking back we can see things so much more clearly and our understanding of past experiences becomes crystal-clear. But the future still holds mysteries, coming forward a moment at a time. Grant wondered about Abby and if he would be able to find her, if he'd be able to rescue her from whatever trouble had ensnared her.

"You're like an old hand around here," Cy complimented, his gray suit matching his gray hair, wrinkled and unkempt. "Looks like you're in another world, the way you're looking off into nothing."

"I was thinking about Abby," Grant confessed as he removed a stack of freshly inked newspapers from the tray. "I know she's here somewhere, and I think she's in trouble."

Cy's mouth drew into a fine line, his brow furrowed. "I tell you what, why don't you take the afternoon off and have a good look around. Keep your eyes and ears open. There are stories, and then there are *stories*. I have a feeling you know what I'm referring to."

"I do," Grant said, removing his ink-stained apron. "I've walked the town, but I didn't take a close look, didn't go inside all the establishments. There are so many businesses here, so many people. It may take a while to see all of it."

"Don't you worry none," Cy said, looking over the newest edition about the petrified man. "There's enough papers here for now, and this story will sell like hotcakes." He grew quiet, his eyes skipping over the single page of small print. "Like this petrified man, everything is a mystery until it's exposed. The answers will come, Grant. They'll come."

"I hope so, Cy. Thanks for giving me the afternoon off." Grant pulled on his leather coat and grabbed his Winchester. "I'll see you later."

∼

Much to his dislike, Grant explored the insides of Creede, mostly the saloons and dance halls and gambling parlors. Moving quietly and unnoticed, he walked past tables of card games, through rowdy bars filled with heavy drinking, through dance halls where the steady drum of banging piano keys never ended.

"Say, mister, how about a dance—only fifty cents," a girl said, tugging at Grant's arm.

Stopping, Grant studied the young girl's face. She had the hard and rough look of wear and abuse, the light of youth practically gone. Her blue eyes had no luster but seemed dull and tired. For a moment, he could see Abby in her.

What Grant saw was very real, and he knew that in Abby's case what he was seeing was a future possibility. He understood that men and women have a choice and can select their future; they have freedom of choice. Grant was determined he would make a difference— he would prevent Abby from becoming what stood before him.

"No thanks," Grant said kindly, watching the girl's face show no emotion, no rejection. She simply moved on to another man and made the same request, like some kind of machine.

Moving on, Grant came to a big saloon on Creede Avenue, called The Exchange. It was another smoky gambling house with bar and tables and a heavy crowd of customers. Stepping sideways to get through, his eyes searched every face, and he listened to nearby conversations. There was so much to see and hear—he had to determine what was worth noting and what wasn't.

"That's him over there," a man was telling an acquaintance. "That's Bob Ford—he owns this place."

"That little feller? He don't look old enough," the acquaintance said.

"He was old enough to pull the trigger! Killed Jesse James right in his own home!" the man said, showing off his knowledge.

Grant had heard enough, and the conversation quickly faded as he stared at the little man known as Bob Ford. There had been dozens of newspaper accounts of the episode, and Grant remembered it well, saddened by the thought that Jesse was dead. Grant remembered the early days of Leadville when he was assaying. Jesse and Frank James had come into the office and later they saved Grant's life in a freezing blizzard.

Somewhere Grant had read Bob Ford's own account of what

happened in a report he'd written to Governor Crittenden. In it, Bob Ford admitted shooting Jesse in the back of the head while he was unarmed and had his back turned.

Ford appeared to be entertaining a few gentlemen he sat with, telling them some story. Watching, unable to control his feelings, Grant had an immediate and extreme dislike for Bob Ford. Nearby a few of Ford's toughs hovered, the kind Grant could spot anywhere. Apparently, like Soapy Smith, Ford was one of the town bosses, his finger in every pie, hoarding more and more money.

Stepping out of the saloon for some fresh air, Grant tried to sort through his emotions. He had temporarily felt he was hot on Abby's trail, or was it simply seeing the murderer of Jesse James that had disturbed him? Either way he felt close to something; but like an image in the fog, he couldn't quite make it out.

He glanced up and down the street. It looked the same, packed with busy men and their busy plans. Buildings, all made of new lumber, were so crowded together, they seemed to be leaning over the street. Creede was a town that didn't believe in paint; with the exception of signs, nothing was painted. Grant noticed a two-story building across the street with the window boarded up from the outside. The town had been thrown together in such haste, they must have forgotten to bring glass. Moving on, Grant had plenty of places left to search, but he would remember Bob Ford.

CHAPTER
~ 20 ~

The Good Samaritan

Another day had passed, and Grant felt desperation tugging at him. Unlike other towns, Grant rarely showed the picture of Abby, for it might reveal him as a threat to the person or persons holding her. It also occurred to him that maybe Abby and Billy were safely together somewhere else, but strong inner feelings told him otherwise. If Billy was around, he was doing a good job of staying out of sight, but that wouldn't be hard in a town like Creede.

Walking heavily down the dirty boardwalk, men stepped aside for the big, rifle-toting young man with a reddish beard and a fierce hunger in his eyes. The fashion of the day was suit and white shirt and tie, topped off with a derby or short-brimmed felt hat. Grant was an outcast as far as fashion was concerned, with his tanned leather coat and pants half-shiny from use, his western-style hat, the high-top riding boots, a Winchester in his hand. Nobody wanted to mess with a man like that. His size alone was intimidating—six feet tall, with 200 pounds of lean muscle.

Mixed smells of garbage, sewage, and smoke hung low to the ground as Grant made his way up Cliff Street, still searching for a sign or a clue. Creede already had all kinds of businesses, proving that even in a rustic and new boomtown, supply and demand ruled. The fabled silver mines of the area—the Holy Moses, Ethel, Amethyst, Champion, Rio Grande, Wandering Jew, Texas Girl, Happy

Thought, Sybil R., Yankee Girl, Bachelor, Kentucky Bell, Phoenix, Ridge, New York, and Solomon—all poured forth high-grade silver ore like water from a river, filling and overflowing Creede with money to spend and money to waste.

A big ten-ton load of ore came thundering down Creede Avenue with the driver pounding his mules and shouting at the top of his voice, people scattering before them. Grant watched the runaway team, spooked by gunshots, as the driver smoked the brakes, screaming against the iron-rimmed wagon wheels. It appeared that somebody would be killed for sure, run over by a team of stampeding mules and cut in half by sharp wheels under 20,000 pounds of weight. With the wagon barreling down the avenue, Grant glanced out to the street as men rushed and scurried out of the way.

In the mud and dirt out in the middle of the avenue, an old man was sprawled out, hopelessly drunk, unaware of the danger coming down on him. The driver was standing now, the reins wrapped around his leather gloves as he pulled on the brakes with all his might. The mules were having none of it, being at a full run and being unable to stop quickly due to the momentum of the load.

Without thinking, Grant dashed out into the street, snatched the old drunk by the nape of his neck, and pulled him out of the way. The ore wagon roared by in a flurry of dust, noise, and debris, leaving a choking cloud in its wake. Some of the onlookers cheered and clapped their hands at Grant's heroics, not because of his courage or bravery, but because it was entertaining to see that kind of daredevil effort.

Shocked out of his delirium, the old drunk realized what had happened and looked up at Grant through glassy, hopeless eyes. A stench reeked about him, his beard was filthy and his silver hair tangled, his suit worn through and full of holes. Grant pulled the old man to his feet with one hand, noticing there wasn't much to him, just skin and bones. Leaning against a post, the old fellow coughed and raised his head, looking at Grant in a sad way. "What'd you save me for?"

"Seemed like the thing to do at the moment," Grant answered, realizing the old fellow was in such a bad way that he probably preferred death. Yet there was something unique about the man. He was not the typical drunk one stepped over in the street; he somehow seemed out of place in his dilemma. Having no idea why he was doing it, Grant led the old man across the street to the Windsor Bath House.

"Wash this one up, and burn the clothes," Grant ordered, handing the old man over like a dirty shirt.

A few of the dandies hanging around were offended but lacked the backbone to make any remarks around the burly young man with a red beard.

"Give him a shave and a haircut while you're at it. I'll be back directly," Grant said as he left.

The eyes of the dandies on the porch followed Grant as he disappeared into the crowd, all shaking their heads in wonder and murmuring their questions to each other.

Grant felt compelled to help because of his supernatural experience high in the mountains on that cold and clear night, though he couldn't have put this into words. He just knew he was going to help a man who preferred dying to living, wanting to show him that men can be decent, even in Creede.

Returning in an hour, Grant held out a brown paper package to one of the proprietors. "I guessed at his size, but they ought to fit," Grant said.

The proprietor gave him a look of disapproval and took the package into the back. Talk had already stirred about the strange-looking young man and his benevolent ways. Nobody could figure it out, but they looked upon Grant as a gracious man.

Sobered and raw from being scraped clean, the dirty old man who had entered soon emerged wearing a stiff new suit that fit loosely on his slight frame, his face red and his silver hair neatly combed. He had a look of astonishment, wonder filling him like a newborn just beginning his life. Stepping forward, Grant said, "C'mon, let's get something to eat."

A few doors away, Grant and the old man sat down at a table with a pile of fried chicken in front of them, steaming yeast rolls on the side, and a dab of butter in the middle. Bones piled up beside them as they had their fill, the old fellow eating like a starved wolf. Finally, well-satisfied, he said, "Why are you doing this for me?"

"I don't know," Grant answered. "I just hate to see a man give up and die. Things could never be as bad as that. All you needed was a little help."

Nodding, the fellow began to blink away tears. "I don't deserve anything like this," he mumbled, his head down. "I've been a wicked man." He glanced up and stared at Grant.

Witnessing the confession, Grant saw a familiar face. It had the look of intelligence, the kind of face that appeared trustworthy. Cleaned up and in his new clothes, he looked as respectable as any, his expression one of wisdom.

"How'd you get so down on your luck?" Grant asked. "You don't look the type."

"It was God's revenge," he answered. "I was once very successful, had a lot of money and respect, but I grew greedy and stole from the ones who trusted me the most. Maybe it was my conscience working on me, but things began to fall apart. I lost it all and wallowed in my guilt, then became a drunk and lost hope."

"Put it behind you," Grant said. "Today God is giving you the chance to start anew. Think of the good things you can do. It's never too late to start over again. All that's required is that you turn to God and are still breathing."

The story of what Grant had done swept through the town like a prairie grass fire. It inspired others to perform acts of kindness as well. The manager of the cafe, a tall, lean man with thinning hair and a white apron, came over and placed his hand on Grant's shoulder, his face lit up with a smile. "It's a fine thing you've done, son, and in a place that needed to see something like that. There's no bill for the dinner—it's on me. I want to be part of this too."

"God bless you, brother," Grant said, pleased. "And thanks."

"Yeah, thanks," the old man said.

The manager smiled and walked away as Grant turned to the old man, now showing a hint of a smile. The man understood there were more far-reaching aspects of this deed than his own survival. "Seems like you've started something."

"Something good, I hope," Grant said, feeling satisfied. "Say, what's your name?"

The old fellow was coming around now. The light had returned to his eyes. "I've gone by many names to avoid being held responsible for my wrongdoings, but my real name is Dick Shaffer. I graduated from a fine college back east and learned how to handle money and investments. But I have failed miserably."

Of course! Grant thought, his face expressionless, not revealing the memories racing through his mind. *Dick Shaffer and his investment firm were in Leadville years ago. He left town with huge amounts of other people's money, a million or so of it belonging to Jason and Mother!* But Grant refused to be angry, realizing there was no way any of the money could be returned—it was gone forever. As he thought about it all further, he realized that if the money had not disappeared, Jason and his mother probably would have never found the peace they now knew, nor the trust they now had in God. As for Dick Shaffer, he had suffered a grueling punishment. "Funny how God works," Grant mumbled.

"What?" Shaffer asked.

"Oh, nothing," Grant said. "Let's get out of here."

Standing, the two left, again thanking the owner for the free meal. "You be sure to pass the good deed on," Grant said, "and then you tell that person to do the same—let's see how far this can carry."

Smiling for the first time, Dick shook Grant's hand, his grip feeble but determined. "I will, young man. You've inspired me. What's your name anyway?"

"Jason Stone."

Holding his chin, Dick seemed lost in thought, then said, "That sure rings a bell, but I can't place it. It'll come to me in time, I'm sure of it."

"I hope it does," Grant said, then took off down the boardwalk.

Dick Shaffer watched him leave, still amazed at how his day—his life—had changed, all because of a few simple actions by a young man named Jason Stone. "Jason Stone," he muttered to himself, still puzzled.

∽

The sun was high and the day bright, the town abounding with smells of cooking and smoke and livestock as Grant proceeded with his search, checking almost every business establishment along the way—mostly saloons, from the small to the big and fancy. Like rambling cattle, people filled the streets.

Stepping up on the boardwalk to the big Watrous Saloon, Grant saw a group of finely-tailored gentlemen standing out front cheering on two boxers fighting in the street. One spectator especially stood out. The way his coat flared at his hips, Grant could tell he was wearing two big pistols. His expensive top hat and sharp suit were impeccable, his dark eyebrows and mustache unmistakable. He had a slight but mischievous smile. Grant knew the familiar figure was none other than Bat Masterson.

The spectators wagered boisterously on the fight as the two men stripped down to their waist, then began darting and jabbing, boxing with the skill of the sport.

Grant tapped Bat on the shoulder. Slowly turning and removing a cigar from his mouth, Bat glanced at Grant with some annoyance. "Can I help you, sir?"

"Bat, don't you remember me?" Grant asked, smiling.

Studying the young man closer, Bat answered, "I don't recall having seen you before, if that's what you're asking."

"Grant DeSpain," Grant said extending his hand. "Leadville. You were the best man at my mother and stepfather's wedding, Jason and Jennifer Stone."

After an expression of consternation, Bat's face lit up. "Grant! How are you? I didn't recognize you behind that red fur on your face."

The men fighting in the street were fighting in earnest, forgetting the skill of the sport of boxing and now just exchanging angry blows. Bat gave them a glance, then turned his attention back to Grant. "So what brings you here, Grant? This isn't the sort of place where I'd expect to see you."

Turning serious, Grant tried to explain over the cheering of spectators rooting for the fighters. "It's Abby. She's missing, and I believe she's here in Creede. I think she's in trouble."

Dividing his attention between Grant and the fight, Bat said,

"Abby? That beautiful sister of yours? What would she be doing in Creede?"

When both boxers were quite bloodied, a referee jumped in and raised the hand of one of the fighters, declaring him winner. The crowd cheered, and money changed hands. The bout was over, and the crowd began to disperse. But the loser of the fight shouted an obscenity at the winner and jumped on him, throwing blows as fast as he could.

"It's a long story," Grant tried to explain, growing annoyed at the confusion in the street.

Bat glanced at the two men bludgeoning each other, then back at Grant. "I'm sorry, what did you say?"

Now clearly irritated, Grant said, "Bat, the fight's over, and now it's just a personal scuffle. Can't you do something about it?"

"I own the Watrous Saloon where I run things inside," Bat said, then pointed his cigar at the fighters. "That, sir, is out of my jurisdiction."

"Well, it's not out of mine!" Grant said, handing his rifle to Bat and stepping into the street in between the fighters. He placed his arms in between them and spread them apart. "This fight is over! It's time to go your own ways!"

One of the fighters threw a roundhouse punch at Grant, but Grant caught his fist in an open hand and began crushing it until the man dropped to his knees in pain. The other boxer jumped on Grant's back, his arms wrapped around Grant's neck, trying to wrestle him down. Reaching over his shoulder, Grant grabbed the man by the hair and pulled him off, gave him a shaking like a dog would a rag doll, then slung him into the dirt next to his competitor. "Unless you want to deal with me, this fight is over! Now, both of you get out of here!"

Like whipped puppies, the two bloodied men staggered to their feet and wandered off with help from others. Grant came back to the boardwalk and his conversation with Bat.

Bat was quite surprised at Grant's display of patience and strength. "Remind me not to mess with you!" Bat complimented. "How'd you get so big anyway? Was it the buffalo steaks?"

Grant shrugged. "I can take care of myself."

"I can believe that," Bat said, placing his hand on Grant's shoulder. "Come inside, tell me this story about Abby being in trouble."

~

In another saloon not far away, Billy Rogers sat at a poker table playing for high stakes with men in suits, men who were good at the game. Things were not going so well as Billy placed his bet. Of all the rules a poker player lives by, Billy was violating one of the primary regulations he preached regularly: "Scared money never wins!" This echoed through his head until he had a headache. With funds dwindling, he cashed out and came to his feet. "Good day, gentlemen," he said and left the table.

Billy was down to 300 dollars and no prospects of selling his mine. Thinking about Abby's dilemma angered him. He'd found her first, and he figured no one else had a right to her. Besides, she liked him, and he liked her; so nobody should be allowed to interfere. Ideas of going into The Exchange Saloon and hanging around there made him nervous; he didn't have the money they wanted, but maybe they'd be willing to take the mine in trade. Before they found out it was a scam, he and Abby could leave town. Not knowing what else to try, this became the plan, and Billy mustered up what little courage he had and ventured on down to The Exchange.

A while later, leaning on the bar, Billy ordered a drink and tossed it down, then ordered another and guarded it, waiting to be approached. It wasn't long before a man came up to him, this one more sophisticated than the toughs who had delivered the message, one of Ford's men who worked the inside. His name was Ed Martin. The man had a skimpy black beard and a head of curly, black hair. His eyes never looked away, as if trying to stare Billy down. "You have the money?"

Going into his best showmanship, Billy smiled and slammed his palm on the bar in an effort to dramatize his offer. "I have something better! Something worth much more!"

Impatient, the man declared, "What's worth more than money?"

"Silver! Lots of silver!" Billy exclaimed with a skilled amount of exaggeration.

The man knew what he was talking about—not silver money but silver from a mine. Now the deal had turned into a different offer, one he was not delegated to handle. He stared at Billy some more to insure intimidation, then said, "Wait here."

Smiling, Billy felt confident. He would sell the deal, and he and Abby would be together again. He finished his drink and ordered another. The saloon was crammed full and noisy all around him. Removing the deed to the mine from his pocket, he gave it a quick looking over and then replaced it inside his coat. Ed Martin soon returned, Bob Ford following him.

Ford wore an expression of impatience, disgusted the deal hadn't gone through as planned. Mines meant little to him—he wasn't in the mining business. Nevertheless, he couldn't neglect looking at the offer, for he knew some mines had made men rich.

"What mine do you have?" Ford questioned, planting an elbow on the bar, his mood all business.

Removing the deed, Billy slapped it down on the bar next to Ford. "It's the Lucky Lady, up the creek a ways."

Ford grabbed the deed and looked it over.

"High-grade ore," Billy added.

Judging by the hastily drawn map, the mine was almost out of the local district. Ford knew a scam a mile away, and he sensed one here. Casually, he opened Billy's lapel and stuffed the deed back into the pocket, then motioned toward the door with his head.

Immediately two toughs lifted Billy by his collar and escorted him to the door, his feet skimming the floor.

"Wait!" Billy cried. "Wait, it's real—it's a real producer!"

When they reached the door, the toughs threw Billy headfirst into the street, where he rolled in the mud, dirt, and manure. A crowd of onlookers roared with laughter, making the experience even more humiliating.

Livid, Billy scrambled to his feet and shook his fist at the saloon. "I'll get you for this! I will!" He stomped away, humiliated and angry, brushing his soiled clothes with his hand.

What made Billy the most angry was that he knew he lacked the guts to do anything about what had happened. He would think about revenge and ramble on with cheap talk about big plans, but the bottom line was always the same—nothing would happen.

~

"That's quite a story," Bat acknowledged after hearing Grant out. "What exactly do you propose to do about it?"

"When I find her, if she wants, I'll take her home," Grant said simply.

"I don't think it's going to be that easy," Bat said thoughtfully. Leaning closer, he added, "If some town boss has her under his employment, you may have to face his toughs to get to him."

"So?" Grant answered as if that weren't a problem.

Bat leaned back and chuckled. "I don't think you understand. These are hired gunmen, and they won't hesitate to kill an opponent—it's their job."

"Well, it's my job to find Abby and get her out of here," Grant persisted. "If that means going against some gunmen, too bad for them!"

Bat gave an expression of surprise. He glanced at the rifle Grant had handy. "Are you that good?"

"Good enough," Grant answered.

Nodding, Bat wasn't so sure. He thought for a moment as he fished a long cigar from his vest and made a business of lighting it, then said over the smoke, "I'll tell you what, let me help. I have a lot of eyes and ears in this town. Let me see what I can find out and what the deal is. Then when I do, we'll decide what proper action to take."

"Too bad there isn't any law in this town," Grant said.

"There's plenty of law in this town," Bat corrected. "But it's the wrong kind of law—the law laid down by money and toughs and guns and bullets. He who dies, loses. A while back some of the business owners formed a town council and decided to collect taxes. The rest of the town wanted to know who was going to collect them. They said they'd get them a marshal. But the council quickly disbanded when they were threatened with hanging if there was any more talk of law."

Grant listened in disbelief. The town actually preferred chaos over order! He was growing fidgety, anxious to get moving, and Bat could see this. "You keep your hat on for a day or so. I'll find out something," he promised.

"I think time is important here," Grant said, revealing his inner thoughts. "I can't tell you why, I just feel that way."

"Maybe," Bat agreed. "But it takes time to get things done."

I guess you're right," Grant said. "Forgive me for being restless. It's just getting harder to think of anything except Abby. I'll appreciate all the help you can give me."

"You have it, friend, any time," Bat said.

⌇

Cy Warman knew from experience that the situation with Abby would sooner or later develop into a news story, whether it ended up good or bad. Still, a story was a story, and he wanted in on it first and had already schemed up a few tantalizing details from what he already knew. A romance gone from bad to worse, slavery, maybe a daring rescue. He knew that the man who carried the Winchester carried it for a reason, more than likely because he was good with it. He knew Grant's type, the kind of man who would pursue his goal until the going got tough, and then pursue some more. Something was bound to happen, and it was drawing closer and closer with each passing day. It was just a matter of time.

"Any luck?" Cy questioned one morning while he made his horrible coffee.

"I may have some help," Grant said. "I talked with Bat Masterson yesterday—he's going to see what he can find out."

"You know Bat Masterson?" Cy squeaked in surprise.

"Yeah. I knew him from a long time ago in Leadville. He was best man at my mother's wedding."

"Well, I declare!" Cy said, thinking the outcome of this story might make an even more glorious newspaper headline than he'd thought.

"You do whatever you think is best. Don't let work around here ruin any of your plans," Cy offered graciously. "If you need to go looking for your sister, you go right ahead."

Grant did exactly that, stalking the town of Creede with the patient hunting skills of a predatory bird. He stood and watched and listened, waiting for the moment when he would spot something that would lead him to his lost sister.

Toughs and Cowards

Reports came to Bob Ford about a big man in leathers who carried a rifle and was searching for Abby. Ford called a meeting of some of his best men, hired men who carried out dubious deeds in the dark of night.

"I don't know who he is," Ford announced, standing in front of his desk in a small back office of his Exchange Saloon. "But I want you to keep an eye on him. Under no circumstances should you let him approach me."

The men all nodded, their faces unshaven and hard.

"Why don't you let me and Tom work him over good?" Charley Sanders said with a crazy look in his eyes. He was a big man with a scar that ran across his cheek and nose, the kind of man who enjoyed bullying and fighting.

Pondering the thought, Ford responded, "I'm afraid if you didn't kill him he might be even more of a problem."

"So we'll kill him," Charley suggested, rubbing his meaty palms together, hungry for violence.

Shaking his head, Ford said, "No, that could be bad for business. I can't kill everyone who gets in my way." He paced in front of the group, thinking aloud. "And yet, if he finds out I have the girl, he could be a problem. I don't want that rifle stuck in my face, you understand? He looks like a hired gun to me." He paced some more. "I wonder who sent him. Maybe she has a rich family."

"Might be her husband," one of the toughs suggested.

"I don't think so," Ford replied. "Besides, she claims that joker Billy Rogers is her husband, though her story doesn't hold water. At any rate I don't have time for all this. The girl is worth a lot of money to me, and this man is jeopardizing my plans."

Sitting on the desk now, Ford placed his hands squarely on the desktop, his arms stiff. "Charley, you take Tom, catch this guy at night if you can. Don't kill him, but be sure to smash the hand that works that rifle. Without his rifle, I doubt he's any threat."

A big grin spread across Charley's scarred face. Half of his teeth were broken or missing. He slapped Tom on the back in a gesture of good faith. "I can't wait to get my hands on that rascal!"

Tom Barton was simple, short, round, and had inhuman strength. His head was small in comparison with his massive shoulders; his long arms dangling, some thought he looked like a gorilla. The rest of the group considered him an oaf. With limited speech and his slow way of thinking, he often stood near the door of The Exchange, ready to toss out sore losers and undesirables. But one characteristic was outstanding—his incredible strength. One man had beat Tom senseless, his face bloody. But once the man wore himself down, Tom reached around his tormentor and bear-hugged him until witnesses could hear ribs cracking. The man's screams of agony gave the toughest among them nightmares.

"Do this job right," Ford said sternly, "and there might be a little something extra in it for you both."

Charley was always especially motivated when there was a bonus. Bob Ford was like a god to him, able to produce special favors or make things happen in ways Charley couldn't understand. Charley liked Ford, and he liked his job, and the last thing he ever intended to do was to let Ford down.

～

Walking and watching, the town abuzz around him, Grant had a feeling he was being watched. He saw quite a number of toughs standing idly, watching him carefully. Grant was leery, glancing into every alley as he passed, watching questionable men from the corner of his eye. It was like watching a storm brew. He thought about seeking shelter but was willing do anything to find Abby, no matter how dangerous.

It had been another day of disappointment, the usual routine, in and out of saloons and businesses, learning nothing new. Creede was full of aggressive businesses, mostly immoral ones that would use any means to get a slice of the pie. Like animals in the wild, the people there were either prey or predators, constantly aware of the dangers that lurked around every corner. A town rich in silver but impoverished in morality, Creede thrived like an infected sore. As he made his rounds, Grant saw that the love of money reigned supreme.

Darkness had fallen, and the night crowd was beginning to gather. Men who worked during the day in the nearby mines came to spend their wages on whiskey, women, and gambling. Grant knew this was an especially dangerous time. The noisiness of the crowd could give his enemies the opportunity to strike against him without anyone knowing it. Taking slow and steady steps, he looked ahead for any place that might serve as a spot for a good ambush. He caught a glimpse of someone peeking around a building just before a head popped back out of sight.

His heart racing, Grant moved ahead cautiously. If they thought they were going to catch him by surprise, they had another thought coming. Coming to an alley, Grant boldly stepped out to face whoever was hiding there, his Winchester ready.

A big man stood there looking foolish, like a child caught in a cookie jar. He had a jagged scar across his face and a silly smile. "What do you want?" Grant demanded, raising the rifle barrel so it pointed at the man's chest.

"Want? I don't want nothin'," the tough said, bemused.

Out of nowhere somebody grabbed the Winchester and stripped it from Grant's hand. At the same time the tough in front of him caught Grant in the temple with a crashing blow, causing him to see bright lights in the darkness. Grant, trying to shake his head clear, realized he was being held in the strong grasp of the man behind him.

The tough in front of Grant said, "I don't want nothin' except to beat the livin' daylights out of ya!"

He threw a heavy punch, but Grant ducked, causing the blow to hit the man behind him square in the nose, making him release his grip and fall to the ground.

Now free, Grant unleashed the seething anger that had been building since his search in Creede began. Grant felt the blood flowing from his temple and into his beard, the throbbing pain driving him into an uncontrollable rage.

Charley Sanders, the man who'd attempted to hit Grant, saw the rage in the livid green eyes and knew that the fight in this man came from his heart, not his size. When his assailant hesitated for a split second, Grant used his leg and shoulder strength to place three well-aimed blows on the man's jaw, sending Charley sprawling unconscious on his back.

Spinning around to meet his other adversary, Grant noticed that the heavy-built man had regained his footing. He was slow and cumbersome. Grant threw two quick blows to the man's head, making him stagger. The man had his arms extended and was charging like a bull. Grant saw that the man wasn't much of a fighter, trying to grab him rather than knock him down. Agile and quick, Grant stepped aside as the beast-like man rushed past him and crashed into a wall. Grant watched the man gather himself for another assault.

Grant realized the man was slow in his thinking but unusually strong, an asset that could easily be exploited by unscrupulous men who were smarter than he. Harming him would be like hurting a dumb animal. With this in mind, Grant let the man charge again, only this time he planted his feet and threw all of his weight into a jab that landed right in the middle of the man's lower chest, stopping him dead in his tracks. Grant heard the wind expel and realized he had found his mark.

Tom Barton's long arms fell limp at his sides, a helpless look on his face. He crumpled like a shot animal, falling first to his knees and then onto his side. After a long moment he began gasping for breath like a man who'd been held underwater too long. Grant knelt beside him and slapped his back, trying to help him resume normal breathing.

"Sorry, partner, but you didn't give me any choice," Grant said, feeling somewhat sorry for the man.

Choking, Tom finally caught his breath, his eyes wet with tears.

"Here, let me help you up," Grant said, lifting the heavy fellow to his feet. "Just take little breaths for a bit."

Doing as he was told, Tom gradually caught his breath. He had never experienced anything like this and felt for a while like he was going to die. He looked at Grant with respect, nodding to indicate that he was all right, happy to be breathing more or less normally again.

"Who sent you to do this?" Grant questioned, still holding Tom by his huge arm.

Tom rolled his simple eyes up to meet Grant's. He seemed ashamed and embarrassed. With great effort, he formed the words with his mouth. "Bob Ford."

"I see," Grant said, angry that a town boss like Ford would take advantage of this simpleminded man. "What's your name?"

"Tom," he groaned.

"Listen to me, Tom," Grant said, throwing his arm around Tom's hunched shoulders. "You shouldn't be doing this kind of job—it's not right. You're a strong man. You could work lifting things and make an honest living, and people would like you for being that kind of man."

Tom generally understood what others said to him; he just found it difficult to verbalize his own thoughts. His mind could understand simple concepts but could handle only one subject at a time. What Grant said made sense, but it conflicted with Tom's loyalty to the man who took care of him, Bob Ford. He couldn't figure this out all at once. Tom turned to see Charley lying out cold and walked over to look down on him. He nudged him with his wide boot toe, and when Charley didn't move, he leaned over and picked him up, then hefted the big man over his shoulder like a sack of potatoes. He glanced at Grant with sad eyes and walked off, carrying his load like it was a bag of feathers.

Grant watched the man leave, feeling sorry for him. But at least now he knew who held the key to Abby's whereabouts. His head throbbing and blood still oozing from the cut, Grant went back to the newspaper office. He was tired and had a thundering headache and knew he needed to call it a day.

Grant entered the office and heard Cy snoring on his bunk. Quietly he found the washbasin, wet a rag, and wiped his head. He removed his coat and sat on his bunk, trying to think sensibly despite the headache. Part of him wanted to go confront Ford right then, while another part declared it would be wiser to wait until tomorrow. Exhausted, Grant fell back on his pillow and soon dropped off into a troubled sleep.

∼

"That's a beaut. Where'd you get it?" Cy asked, making faces at the bruise with a cut in the center near Grant's temple.

"A couple of toughs jumped me last night," Grant said.

"Why'd they do that? Did they rob you?" Cy pressed. He liked to get all the facts, the typical newspaper man.

"No, it wasn't like that. They were sent by Bob Ford, to discourage me, I guess." Grant looked squarely at Cy. "I think Ford has Abby hidden somewhere, or at least knows where she is. Why else would he care?"

Cy studied Grant carefully, pondering all he knew about the situation. "I think you might be on to something. What happened to the toughs who attacked you last night?"

"One carried the other one back," Grant said.

Cy made an expression that showed he was impressed. He had been right—Grant was as rough as they came when it came to a showdown. "There'll be more trouble, you can be sure of that. If you sent Ford's toughs back whipped, he'll do one of two things. Either he'll give up your sister and set her free, or he'll move his aggression up a notch. He can't afford to back down—he'd lose the respect of his men and the rest of the town. If I were you, I'd be ready for just about anything. Keep your eyes wide open all the time. He just might do something more drastic, maybe even have you shot."

"Well, I'll tell you one thing—he won't have to figure out where to find me because I'll be paying him a visit," Grant said.

"You're crazy," Cy said, coming to his feet. "Getting yourself shot isn't going to save your sister. If you go into Ford's place and you don't know who all is working for him, they'll gun you down before you can even face Ford. You need a plan."

Cy was right, Grant realized. He couldn't just bust into the big saloon and make his demands. Thinking it over, Grant decided to go see Bat Masterson; he would know what to do.

◝

"Nice one!" Bat teased, his face jovial as he looked at Grant's wound. "You want me to get a piece of beefsteak for that?"

"No, it's not as bad as it looks."

"How about the other fellow—what's he look like?" Bat questioned, somewhat amused.

"There were two of them—a big man with a scar across the middle of his face and a half-wit named Tom. Tom carried the other one off after it was all over."

Suddenly Bat turned serious. "Let's sit down over here and talk about this." He pointed as he moved toward a table that offered more privacy. Once they were seated, Bat continued, "Those men work for Bob Ford. You're lucky they didn't beat you into oblivion—that's what they do best. What'd you do, get the drop on them with your rifle?"

"No, I just hit them," Grant said.

"Are you serious?" Bat said, baffled. "I didn't think anyone could whip Charley. He's a mean one. And as for Tom, why, you could break a brick over his head and I don't think he'd know it."

"Charley was easy, the half-wit another story. But he found out he doesn't do so well when the wind's knocked out of him. I think that really scared him."

"I see," Bat said, shaking his head in disbelief. "Well, my sources have told me Ford is your man. You could have come here and found that out without getting into the ruckus."

"They jumped me!" Grant said defensively.

"Then Abby must be very important to Ford," Bat mused, relighting his long cigar. "Ford probably thinks he can make a fortune with Abby, demand exorbitant prices, once you're out of the way at least. What are you going to do now?"

"That's what I came to ask you," Grant said. "I can't just go into Ford's saloon and confront him. He'll just deny it, and there'll be a fight, and I'll lose—he has too many men."

"That much is certain," Bat agreed, smoke pouring from his cigar now. "I've been in that situation many times—outnumbered and nobody to count on."

Grant questioned, "So what did you do?"

Bat didn't answer right away. He didn't like the answer, though it was the only one. He drew patiently on his cigar and finally said, "I called them out."

"Called them out?"

"Yeah, I called them out into the street for some face-to-face gunplay." Bat exhaled, relaxed, then continued, "Grant, you might be good with your rifle, but you're not a gunfighter. If you call Ford out, his men will stand in front of him. You'd have to shoot them all before you could get to Ford, and he can shoot well too. He's murdered before, and I doubt he'd be bashful about killing you."

Grant sat in dismay, tossing ideas around in his head. "I don't see that I have much of a choice."

"If we could find out where Abby is, maybe we could break her out in the middle of the night. You and she could be on the next train out of here," Bat recommended.

"But Ford will be watching me like a hawk," Grant said despondently. "Anyway, something could go wrong, and she could get hurt."

"Those are the problems you have to deal with," Bat said, removing his cigar and raking his palm across his worried face. "Don't panic, Grant, whatever you do."

"There has to be a way," Grant persisted, coming to his feet. "Thanks for the advice."

"Anytime," Bat acknowledged. "Don't try anything stupid; be careful."

"I will," Grant said as he walked out of the Watrous Saloon.

Discouraged, Grant made his way through the crowd on the street, trying to figure out what move he should make. He needed to do some serious thinking, and some serious praying.

～

With nowhere particular to go, Grant ambled around as various ideas presented themselves, then disintegrated in the face of logic. Nothing seemed like it would work. He was at the mercy of that little tyrant, Bob Ford.

Passing a busy saloon, Grant glanced inside over the swinging doors. It looked the same as all of the other saloons—busy and crowded, men playing poker, the bar lined shoulder to shoulder with a drinking crowd. He was ready to move on when he saw the profile of a face he knew—Billy Rogers.

Making his way inside, Grant stood next to where Billy sat, holding his hand of cards close to his face. "I want a word with you!" Grant demanded.

Barely glancing at Grant, Billy rudely said, "In a minute, cowboy. Can't you see I'm in the middle of a game?"

With a thrust like a mule's, Grant kicked Billy's chair so hard, a leg snapped off and went sailing across the saloon. Billy fell to the floor, landing flat on his back, his cards flying every which way. An immediate hush fell over the crowd.

Out of reflex, Billy's hand went inside his coat pocket, grabbing the small revolver and cocking the hammer. The small barrel, though hidden in his coat pocket, was aimed at Grant.

Grant knew the gun was there, but the muzzle of his Winchester was inches in front of Billy's face. "Go ahead!" Grant insisted. "I'll spread your brains all over the floor."

Time seemed to stand still as Billy considered his options. The men at the poker table sat with their mouths open, and the entire barroom stood in total silence. Smoke hung still in the air as everyone held their breath.

Billy suddenly recognized the greenish eyes. "Grant?" he uttered sheepishly. He removed his hand slowly from his pocket and held it up in defense. "Grant, what are *you* doing here?"

"You know good and well what I'm doing here!" Grant rumbled, tempted to give Billy the whipping of his life.

Billy scrambled to his feet, the convincing smile returning. "I'm glad you're here—there's a problem."

The muzzle of the rifle remained in Billy's face. "Outside!" Grant ordered.

Billy scooped up his money from the poker table and tried to walk with some dignity, but Grant shoved him with the rifle barrel, causing him to almost trip, increasing his humiliation. Through the swinging doors they went and stopped out front, where Billy turned to confront Grant.

"I ought to teach you a lesson," Grant said, lowering the barrel as if he were going to strike the man with his fist.

Stepping back, Billy pleaded, "Grant, I didn't know! Believe me, I'm as concerned about Abby as you are. Just hear me out!"

Regaining his composure, Grant settled down some but still fought the urge to knock Billy into the next town.

"Abby was kidnapped," Billy said nervously, waving his hands as he talked. "I tried to meet the ransom, but I don't have enough money to do it."

Once the onlookers realized the fight had become mere conversation, people went back to their drinking and gambling.

"You should have never led Abby here!" Grant fumed. "That's the stupidest thing I've ever heard of!"

"I know, I know," Billy confessed. "Ford wants 10,000 dollars. I'm trying to make it at the tables."

"You should be the one to pay it," Grant insisted. "You got her into this mess."

Billy dropped his head and dragged the toe of his shoe back and forth on the dirty boardwalk. His hands hanging limp, he looked up at Grant with a sorrowful expression of defeat. "All I got is 1,200 dollars."

Grant stared, waiting to hear more, his anger still just beneath the surface.

"I tried to give Ford my silver mine, but he wouldn't take it. It's worth a lot more than 10,000," Billy said, his voice almost a whimper.

Grant wasn't fooled any more than Ford had been. He was sure the mine was a fluke. "So what do you propose to do?" Grant interrogated.

"I—I don't know," Billy said weakly.

Grant studied the man before him, a weak coward. All he was good at was talk, and talk wouldn't rescue Abby.

"Then you're going to help me," Grant said firmly.

Billy's face brightened with anticipation. "You have an idea? That's great! What are we going to do?"

"We're going to get you a real gun, and we're going to call Ford and his men out. There's no other way."

Horror came over Billy's face, making it a pale green. "A gun-fight? But, Grant, I can't shoot good enough for that."

"You were willing to shoot me in there a few minutes ago," Grant reminded him.

"Yeah, but I was mad."

"Well, get mad then. We're going to save Abby." Grant took a firm grip on Billy's arm and pulled him along like a little child.

~

"That's a good-looking piece," Grant said, holding the pistol in his hand. He slipped it in and out of the well-used holster that came with it. The gun shop smelled of fine gun oil and leather. The man waiting on them was sharp and alert.

"Here, slip this on," Grant said, handing the gun and holster to Billy.

Nervously, Billy pulled the belt around his waist and tied the holster to his leg. He imitated a quick draw, then did it again and again.

"That gun used to belong to Sid Saline, the gunfighter. The trigger has been filed and the hammer polished so you can fan the shots. It's in good shape. The holster has been modified for a real quick draw too."

"Good," Grant said. "He needs all the help he can get."

"Where's this gunfighter, Saline, now?" Billy asked, his voice shaky.

"Oh, he's buried up on Shotgun Hill."

"How'd he die?" Billy wanted to know.

"Lost a gunfight," the proprietor said, unmoved.

"That's great, Grant," Billy whined. "He lost a gunfight with this gun. I'm carrying a dead man's gun."

"Shut up," Grant said. "Give him three boxes of shells too. Pay for it, Billy."

His hands shaking, Billy paid for the goods and stepped out of the store with Grant.

"We're going to walk a ways up the creek here and find a place where you can get adjusted to that thing." Grant took off, his steps long and fast, and Billy trotted to keep up with him.

"Practicing once isn't going to help," Billy complained.

"Won't hurt either," Grant said.

Up in a clearing away from the main section of town, Grant set up targets in front of a dirt embankment. "Now load the gun, draw it fast, and shoot at those targets."

Dumbfounded by his predicament, Billy fumbled with the car-tridges but managed to get them loaded in the gun. He dropped the pis-tol snugly into the holster and stood with his hand in the air above it.

"Now draw!" Grant shouted.

Billy drew and fired into the ground right in front of his shoe. Out of frustration he cried, "See? I can't do this. I almost blew my toe off."

"Calm down and try it again," Grant ordered. "Point it before you squeeze the trigger."

Trying his best, Billy pulled the gun, pointed it at the targets, cocked the hammer, and pulled the trigger. The bullets were hitting in the general area of the bottles and cans, perhaps close enough to hit a man.

Grant made Billy repeat the procedure four or five times, then said, "That's good. All you have to do is what you just did. Let's go."

"Where are we going now?" Billy asked, tagging along like a pet goat.

Grant stopped and turned to Billy, never more serious in his whole life. "We're going to call out Bob Ford."

❧ 22 ❧

The Desert

Abby's life had become like a desert. As far as she could see, feel, or think, there was nothing but vast emptiness, with no water of life to be found. She had lost count of the days, long and monotonous days that blended together like a mixture of bad and crazy dreams. She saw no hope in any direction. She felt lost, exhausted, defeated.

Her mind was continually overshadowed by the dark cloak of impending death. Before, when she thought of days past, it was as if she was gazing from a cool, safe haven onto broad, brightly lit green meadows. But now she saw only the hard, burned tones of the desert. Distant memories of love and security had disappeared behind a dusty cloud of agony.

During earlier hard times in her life, she had relied on her resiliency, her stubborn will, her strong beliefs, and even her anger at God to keep her going. Her father's death had led her to feel deep resentment and distrust toward the God who had taken away from her the one she'd loved the most. He had let her down in other ways too. At one point in her life she'd known great wealth, and during that time she felt the Creator had redeemed Himself, making up for the hard life she'd suffered earlier. But just as quickly as the riches had come, they disappeared, reaffirming her belief that God was a tyrant.

Abby believed that her hatred and self-will gave her the strength to face trials and cross barriers. In every test and situation, that was what she relied on to keep herself going, to make certain she would survive in spite of God's letting her down again and again.

Abby's life had consisted of living one day at a time, believing that some future day would again bring her into a life of luxury and happiness. One day might be another day of misery, a test of strength and will; but the future held the possibility of a better life, and she would make it happen herself, she'd thought. She'd believed it was only a matter of time before the right man would come along, a man with great wealth, a man who would love her and whom she would love. When that happened with Billy Rogers, she had fallen in love head over heels, determined to make all her hopes come true, to fulfill the ecstasy she'd long dreamed of. But the dream had become a nightmare in an unfamiliar place far from home, a place where evil men far outnumbered the virtuous. And God had let it all happen.

A desert engulfed Abby now, leaving all her plans and thoughts in the hazy distance of yesterday. All she had left was self-pity and bitterness. She couldn't bring herself to feel differently.

Abby wondered why the deal she'd offered Bob Ford didn't pan out. Why hadn't Billy paid Ford off and gotten her out of there? She was tired of asking herself questions for which she had no answers. She was tired of thinking, tired of living, tired of everything.

Adding to Abby's misery, she was filthy and smelly, having no opportunity to wash up, let alone bathe. Although Lulu had been good about picking up her dinner trays and changing her chamber pot, the room had a rank and nauseating odor that grew more offensive each day.

Small cracks in the boards nailed over Abby's window let only slices of daylight in, a reminder of the world outside. Often she stood at the window peeking between the slats, taking in the sights on the busy street below. The town and its people were so close and yet an eternity away, visible but out of her reach.

Sleep had become the only escape, albeit temporary. But now Abby had slept until she couldn't sleep anymore. She wished she could go to sleep and never wake up again. But no matter how much she willed it, it didn't happen, and she was not delivered from her bleak existence.

In her empty desert she saw only two possible futures—she would submit to Ford and become a prostitute, or she would kill herself.

~

Abby felt like a rabbit being kept in a dark box. Every time the box was opened, such an animal would panic. And every time Abby heard footsteps and keys in the door, she panicked, her eyes wide open and dilated, her heart racing with a fear that was inevitable because of her defenseless and weakened condition.

The door squeaked open, and Abby's nemesis stood there, a sly smile on his young face. The little man with crazy eyes stood guard behind him just in case. Coming into the room, Ford eased the door closed behind him, confident he was winning this inhuman game.

"Getting a little rank in here, Abby," he said sniffing.

Abby sat leaning against the headboard, her knees pulled up to her chin, her arms folded around her legs. She stared at Ford, saying nothing, ashamed of her condition.

Ford shoved his hands into his pockets and paced back and forth like a prosecutor in front of a jury. "You are strong—I do admire that in a woman," he said softly, occasionally looking at her in the dim light. "I thought you would have come around by now."

Abby remained silent, staring at Ford with hateful, frightened eyes.

"You know, you don't have to do this to yourself," Ford continued in his easy manner. "It's not like you think. I'm not going to throw you to the wolves. I take care of my people, see to their needs." He waited, but there was no response. "Believe it or not, you'll enjoy yourself and make lots of money. I don't expect you to know the ropes to start out with. You can work yourself in at your own pace."

Abby hadn't moved, her chin stuck between her knees. She watched Ford like a bird watching a snake.

Pacing a little more, Ford stopped and glanced up. "I don't understand you, Abby. What are you holding out for?" He waited, but Abby said nothing. "People are always afraid of the unknown, but once they get there, there's nothing to fear anymore."

The room was too quiet, and Ford's expression became dangerously impatient. "Your thickheaded ways aren't doing anyone any good, especially yourself. Look at you—you're a mess. What a waste for such a beautiful girl."

Abby stubbornly refused to break her silence.

Ford could barely restrain himself, sinister evil coming into his eyes. "I can hold out longer than you can!" he warned, raising his voice. "You're not as smart as I gave you credit for!" He paced back and forth faster and faster, then glared at her. "You can rot in here as far as I'm concerned. Can't you understand the futility of your resistance?"

Abby started to shake, terrified of the evil before her.

"Have it your way!" Ford stormed and turned around to leave.

"What about Billy?" Abby croaked. "Did you find him?"

Ford was reaching for the doorknob but stopped in his tracks and chuckled. "Billy Rogers," he said pitifully as he turned around to address her again, barely keeping a leash on his anger, "Billy Rogers is a two-bit con man, Abby. Yes, I found him, and he doesn't have a thing to offer. He doesn't even have the guts to stand up for you. I could buy a hundred just like him; they're a dime a dozen here in Creede."

Pausing, Ford decided to drive home the point. "How could you ever take an interest in a fellow like that anyway? What is it you see in him? He's just a spineless coward."

Ford hoped he could provoke Abby into talking further, but she withdrew back into her shell, refusing to accept what he was saying. Now thoroughly disgusted, Ford stomped out, slamming the door behind him.

Abby found herself back in the desert, her last hope swept away in a dry and scorching wind. Her head hurt from trying to think, Ford's voice echoing in her thoughts. He was a wicked man, but some of the things he said were starting to make sense. She could forget what she'd been taught about right and wrong and become something she knew nothing about; at least that way she'd be alive. But the sudden realization of what she was thinking repulsed her, making her feel sick and weak. She wasn't ready to give in yet. Not quite.

～

Bob Ford had more important business to tend to—namely, the young cowboy with the red beard.

In another meeting back in his office, Ford lashed out, "You bumbling fool, Charley! I sent you out to do a simple job, and you botched it! What's wrong with you?"

Charley was already in a great deal of pain, his jaw tied shut with a strip of cloth that was wrapped around his head. He was fairly sure his jaw was broken, causing him intense agony. He wanted to speak up, to defend himself; but with his jaw tied shut, he couldn't say anything. He wished he could tell Ford that he wanted to kill the man who did this to him. He wanted to tell Ford that the young man had the fastest and hardest-hitting fists he'd ever run into, that no man could beat him in a fistfight—he'd have to be shot. But unable to express himself, he could only stand there and take his boss's abuse.

"Why didn't you have Tom hold him? Did that even cross your mind? Tom could hold back a team of mules!" Ford glanced at Tom, realizing it was a waste of breath to ridicule him. Because of his state of mind, he just didn't understand. Once Charley was down and out of the way, the young cowboy probably simply outsmarted Tom, an easy thing to do.

"I want all of you men to hang around the saloon here," Ford said, "at least until this thing blows over." He addressed at least a dozen grizzly toughs, all on his payroll. "There's no telling what this fellow might do, but you can bet he'll be coming here. I want him to make his call right here! Is that understood?"

A mumble came from the men, all nodding their heads. Grant had won their respect when he made easy work of Charley. Most of the men didn't expect him to show up, since he would be badly outnumbered and wouldn't stand a chance. Nobody took him to be that stupid.

Tom stood in the back of the group, his simple mind trying to sort out the facts. Bob Ford was talking about the man he'd had a run-in with, and Ford expected that man to come calling, looking for trouble. Ford was ordering the group to defend him. Tom was having trouble understanding why all these men should fight against the one man who had been nice to him. He and Charley had attacked him for no apparent reason, and all the young man did was defend himself, and he did it well too. Why was the young man a threat?

∼

With her hopes of Billy bailing her out now gone, Abby sunk into a deeper depression. She continued to check the street below, and the saloon across the way, wishing she could see something hopeful, anything encouraging. But it was always the same, a never-ending stream of wagons, horses, men, and music, a crowd of meaningless faces passing by below.

The door opened, and Lulu Slain stepped in, performing her daily duties of bringing food to Abby, like an assigned jail keeper.

"Gettin' a mite strong in here, honey," Lulu commented as she set the covered tray on the chair. "Too bad I can't open a window."

Abby was beyond feeling embarrassed. She didn't care about Lulu, though Lulu was the only person she still had a chance to talk to.

"Ford was here this morning," Abby said coldly.

"What'd he want?" Lulu asked, knowing the answer.

Abby turned her face away. "He was telling me what it would be like, you know, working for him."

"Maybe you're considering it now, huh?" Lulu commented wryly. "I don't know why you make it so hard on yourself. It's a livin', honey."

"It's not living," Abby argued.

"This here ain't neither, in case you haven't noticed," Lulu quipped. "This is squalor, and you're bringing it all on yourself!"

"Why can't he just let me go? I don't like him, and I don't want to work for him," Abby said.

"Truth be, I wish he would let you go," Lulu said sincerely. "I don't want you competing with me. You'd get all the good customers with pockets full of money. They'd be sending you gifts instead of me."

Abby turned to look at Lulu. Her way of living had taken its toll; she'd had her share of abuse, as evidenced by the pain in her face. It wouldn't be long before Abby had the same look if she gave in. "I'd rather die than work for Ford," she said evenly.

Lulu had to listen to this kind of talk every time she came to the room, and today she finally lost her temper. "Let me ask you something, honey!" she said angrily. "What makes you so good, huh? What makes you think you're so much better than me, Miss High and Mighty? You ain't nothin', you hear me? You ain't nothin' special, just some girl who thinks she's made of gold or somethin'. Well, before long you'll be comin' down off that high horse, missy!" Lulu quickly did her work, setting the old chamber pot outside the door and bringing in a clean one.

"If you want my opinion," Lulu kept on, "us workin' girls are the smart ones. We're the ones havin' a good time with the men; we're the ones they share their secrets with."

Abby again felt threatened and assaulted, but Lulu was telling her about something that was sure to happen, just as sure as the coming of another day. *What's the use?* Abby thought. *Lulu's right—I am nothing special. Just another girl who Ford will force into a life she doesn't want.* For a second she considered telling Lulu she'd had enough, that she was ready to surrender to Ford's demands. At least that way she'd have some kind of freedom and a hot bath and nice clothes and sweet-smelling perfume. The thought of money and comfort and men fighting over her appeared at this moment infinitely more appealing than the filthy life she was now living.

What am I thinking? she thought sadly. *What's happening to me?*

～

When night came, Abby sat on the edge of the bed ready to give up again. She was dead tired but found it almost impossible to sleep. Nothing seemed important any longer—not Billy, not money, nothing. The desert had overwhelmed her and turned her into someone who's alive but dead. She had no more feelings or emotions.

She was like a fire that had burned out, with only ashes remaining. She had nothing to show for the life she had lived, nothing real or decent to be remembered by. She felt like she was getting her wish and would in one sense be dead soon.

And yet, beneath the pile of ashes remained one tiny ember of life. Abby could feel it burning in her soul. Stripped of all pride and dignity, she turned her face to the God she had hated so intensely.

For a long time Abby sat in silence, still as a statue, searching in her mind's eye for the all-powerful God she knew existed. She feared Him, but she knew He was her last chance. The crucial moment had come. She would approach God, beg Him for help, and see if He would forgive her, if He could save her.

It was humbling for Abby to drop to her knees to approach a God she had disrespected, to pray to a God she had spoken against. What must God think of a person who waits until they are in the worst position of their life before crawling to Him for help?

"Dear Father," Abby prayed, "You don't know me, and I'm not sure I know how to pray, but I'm sorry. I wish You could forgive me, give me another chance. I have lived wrong, thought wrong about everything, and now it's easy to see what's important in this world and what isn't. I have proved I am nothing. Even so, I pray that You will overlook my stubborn pride. I've been so blind and have acted so stupidly, never thinking of anyone but myself. In the name of Jesus, could You please send me some help? I don't want to live a sinful life—I don't want to live any kind of life without You any longer. Dear Lord, please hear my prayers. Amen."

The tiny ember turned into a glowing warmth as Abby stretched out on the old, lumpy bed. The prayer made her feel much better. She had confessed her sins and had become right with God, turning her troubles over to Him. She felt her burden lift and was confident she'd been liberated from her guilt. Now she could sleep, and she would patiently wait for rescue as long as it took, for the strength she now had was from above.

～

Cy sat in his office sucking on a cigar, feeling the intensity of the growing darkness outside. A story was in the making, and since it was his job to report the news and sell newspapers, he would make sure he was there to capture it. Never had he seen a town like Creede. Grabbing a pencil, he began to scratch out a poem that demanded to be set free.

The Illusion of Creede

Here's a land where all are equal,
Of high or lowly birth—
A land where men make millions
Dug from the dreary earth.
Here meek and mild-eyed burros
On mineral mountains feed;
It's day all day in the daytime,
And there is no night in Creede.

The cliffs are solid silver,
With wondrous wealth untold;
The beds of its running rivers
Are lined with purest gold.
While the world is filled with sorrow,
And hearts must break and bleed
It's day all day in the daytime,
And there is no night in Creede.

Feeling rather satisfied with his tongue-in-cheek poem, Cy set it aside. He worried about Grant, who was running unusually late. But Grant would have to take care of his own affairs; Cy wouldn't wait up for him. Crawling into his bunk, he felt an uneasiness deep within him. He rolled over, trying to calm his thoughts, but the noisy disorder outside wouldn't let him.

Showdown

Big, tumbling gray clouds rolled over the gulch town of Creede, darkening the afternoon sky as swirling cold winds of dust and dirt rushed up and down the street. Suddenly it had turned into a gloomy day, the chill an indication of a norther coming in full and strong. Men tightened their hats and pulled up the collars of their coats as the pleasant fall weather lost its hold and fled further south.

Undeterred, Grant took full strides as he made the long walk from deep in the gorge back down to Bob Ford's saloon. Billy scrambled along beside him as men stepped out of the way of the determined red-bearded man in the lead. Grant carried his rifle, his other hand swinging free, his mind made up to tangle with Ford at any cost and resolve the matter. There was no mistaking his look; he was ready to fight.

Billy Rogers plowed along beside Grant, doing his best to convince himself he was doing the right thing, trying to muster up some courage. The truth was, his stomach was in his throat, and his throat was so tight he could barely speak. "What if Ford has all his gunmen waiting for us?" Billy asked, his voice high-pitched with fear.

"Shoot in the middle of the group as fast as you can," Grant ordered, his mind set on getting the job done as he pushed through the forever present crowd. He wasn't going to be persuaded by anyone to change his mind—he was set on freeing Abby from the grasp of Bob Ford. If he got gunned down, so be it, but he was trusting God to grant them victory. At the same time, being human, he figured that if he died in the attempt, he'd take as many of the toughs with him as he could, and maybe Bob Ford too.

"Grant, why don't we get more men, more help?" Billy suggested, afraid this was all happening too fast.

"There is no one," Grant answered, not missing a step.

Billy wished he was as fearless as Grant, but his knees felt weak, and he stumbled along, thinking of all the things that could go wrong. He might even nervously drop his gun and get shot down in front of the bloodthirsty crowd. Anything and everything he envisioned was horrible.

Soon several men were hurrying along behind Grant and Billy, like wolves smelling blood, catching the scent of an imminent showdown.

"Who is that man?" one fellow asked, rushing along in a small group behind Grant.

"I don't know," another said. "But he sure totes that rifle like he means business."

"Who's he going after? He looks mean."

"I don't know, but we're going to find out."

The excitement grew like a wind-driven wildfire as the word spread behind Grant and Billy. Men vacated their poker games, leaving cards on the table. Others forgot their drinks at the bar, and some dropped their dance partners and rushed out of the dance hall doors, fancily dressed women following suit. Piano players slammed their pianos shut and grabbed their coats. Everyone rushed in one direction down the narrow street like a river from a broken dam.

Billy had thoughts of dropping out and running away, but the heavy crowd behind the two men pushed them on, leaving no visible exit. They were beginning to yell and scream, overcome with a lust for blood in the street.

Beneath the Gateway Cliffs Grant pushed on, the flat valley of lower Creede opening to a dull gray sky of heavy clouds. Down Creede Avenue Grant marched, Billy picturing his perfectly good suit and shirt full of bloody bullet holes.

The Exchange Saloon was visible ahead as Grant stepped into the middle of the street and pushed forward. Anything and anyone in his way quickly made room for the two men and the wedge-shaped group behind him. Heads popped out of windows and doors.

"What's going on?"

"Gunfight!"

"Gunfight?" others called back, hurrying out to witness the spectacle.

Coming to The Exchange, Grant stopped and faced the building. He checked his rifle one more time and chambered a round. Billy stood beside him shaking in his boots.

The men lounging on the front walk of The Exchange, some sitting in chairs, stared dumbfounded at the men in the street. Then it dawned on them that the cowboy meant business, and they scrambled away from the building, chairs flying.

"Bob Ford, I'm calling you out!" Grant shouted loud and clear for everyone to hear.

A mumble went over the crowd, and then they fell into a hush. All was silent except for the cold wind whistling through loosely constructed clapboard buildings.

A whiskered face appeared over the swinging doors and took in the sight on the street—the tall form of a big man in leathers with a cowboy hat and a red beard carrying a Winchester. The face quickly disappeared. There was a pause, the piano music came to a halt, and patrons rushed from the saloon in a stampede, emptying the building and taking a stand at a safe distance.

Grant's eyes looked straight ahead, focused on the front door of The Exchange Saloon. Fear never entered his mind. He had a job to do and had every intention of seeing to it that the job got done. Next to him, Billy stood helplessly, turning his head to look around at the eager faces of the crowd. He was wondering how he got to where he stood, ready to face certain death. What seemed like minutes earlier he was sitting comfortably at a poker table, well out of harm's way. Now he stood waiting for Bob Ford and his professional toughs to gun him down. He imagined a photograph of himself propped up on a board, dead and full of bullet holes.

"I'm waiting!" Grant shouted.

In a moment a hand appeared on the swinging doors, and then a man with a black beard stepped through them cautiously. He was Cliff Jenkins, gunfighter. He had his holster strapped to his leg and had the look of a scroungy dog, mean and full of bitterness. Behind him came Charley Sanders, a white cloth tied around his head like he had a toothache. Hatred showed in his eyes, a lustful hunger for vengeance apparent in his quick movements. Then another and another appeared until a dozen or so of Ford's hired men stood in front of the saloon, only six of them shooters and ready for gunplay. The rest had their pistols ready but were unskilled in the art of shooting. Nobody saw a man scurry from the back of the saloon, a rifle in his hand as he moved like a shadow.

Once all of Ford's toughs were lined up in front of the saloon staring down the two challengers, Bob Ford eased through the swinging doors, careful to stay behind his men. His young face had the easy smile of a man holding the trump card, his demeanor friendly, his movements slow and confident. Tom stood beside him, a blank look on his round face.

"You want to see me?" Ford called like it was a social visit.

"Turn my sister loose!" Grant ordered in a firm voice. "Now!"

Ford's expression was dubious, turning to some of his men as if he were insinuating there was some question he didn't understand. "Sir, I have no idea what you're talking about," he replied innocently.

"You know exactly what I'm talking about," Grant said, raising his voice and lifting his rifle a few inches. "You have Abby locked away somewhere, and I'm telling you to let her go."

Grant's movement caused the gunfighters to swing their coats back away from their pistols, their gun hands ready. All of this drew a murmur from the heavy crowd spread in a big circle around the event.

"Ford, show me where she's at and we'll leave. The rest of this isn't necessary," Grant said firmly.

"Like I said, I don't know what you're talking about. Now, if you want to pursue this, that's up to you," Ford said, then smiled deviously.

"Stand aside!" Grant called to the men in front of Ford.

Instead, the gunfighters stepped down from the boardwalk into the street—six men lined up, ready for gunplay. Ford mostly hid behind Tom. His smile gone, he watched eagerly, wanting to see the fools in the street shot dead.

By now Billy was visibly shaken. He could hear his heart pounding, and his knees felt like they were knocking together; his hand was shaking so bad, he was sure he would drop his pistol. His fear had been building like an inner storm. They were outnumbered six to two, and he couldn't shoot worth a lick. His eyes darted around as he thought he might be looking at the last sights he'd ever see. The fear erupted, coming to a whining climax. Billy turned to Grant, although Grant wouldn't look at him, his eyes busy with the gunmen.

"Grant, I can't do this!" he whimpered. He began backing away.

"What about Abby?" Grant said, not looking at Billy.

"She ain't worth dying for!" Billy whined. "Nobody is." Billy broke and ran, pushing his way through the onlookers who roared with laughter, jeering the coward as he made his escape.

If ever a man stood alone, Grant did now, the center of attention in an evil town. Straightening his big shoulders, he took a deep breath. Billy had shown his true colors, and now Grant had to face Bob Ford by himself. He didn't have time to think about Billy or even to be angry at him; the business at hand demanded all of his concentration. Many in the crowd admired him as the bravest man they'd ever seen, standing up to the most powerful town boss and his toughs. However, they were also betting he'd be dead in a matter of minutes.

"Looks like your odds have just changed," Ford taunted.

Grant responded with silence.

"That's a fact!" a voice shouted from the crowd, and Bat Masterson stepped forward to join Grant in the street. A mocking smile on his face, he swept his coat back to reveal the two famous ivory-handled Colts.

The gunmen before Grant and Bat were suddenly worried, glancing at Ford for orders. Aggravated, Ford gave a hushed shout to his men. "Stay put!"

"What took you so long?" Grant whispered to Bat, his eyes locked on Ford's men.

"I was getting a haircut," Bat whispered coolly. "I'll take the ones on the left, you take the ones on the right."

"What's it going to be, Ford?" Grant called, his eyes slits under the big hat brim that dipped over his face.

"Let the cards fall where they may," Ford called back, safely hidden behind the width of simpleminded Tom.

Ford's gunfighters spread out so they had room to maneuver. The odds were well in their favor, and they knew it as evidenced by the lust in their greedy eyes. Everyone was waiting for someone to make the first move.

Dead silence fell over the crowd. The town of Creede seemed to be hanging on the edge of a perilous cliff with death lingering below. It was a moment of confrontation, of finality, a moment when everything a man owned or knew could be taken away from him forever.

Grant's future dangled dangerously before him. He thought of what his life had meant to him. He had tried to honor God in his choices between right and wrong. If living by God's rules meant dying, that was that; he would stand for what's right no matter what. He regretted not having had a chance to enjoy life with Mendy, but he clung to his faith in the Almighty, certain that God was standing with him.

~

Morning had come for Abby, and she woke up feeling rested for the first time in a long time. Because she had opened her heart to God, she no longer suffered grueling anxiety. She had decided to do what was right, and if it meant suffering, she would suffer. Glad to be right with God, she let the day take its course, the hours passing without worry, the former grim thoughts of fear having been replaced by God's assuring presence.

A new wind rushed down the gulch, bringing cold air from the north as the day outside the boarded-up window darkened. Abby wrapped herself in a blanket, trying to stay warm. Peeking through the cracks in the boards covering her window, she saw that things were normal outside as men rushed about, Ford's saloon across the way as rambunctious as usual.

Settling back in the comfort of her bed, she wondered when Lulu would be by, and how she would react now that Abby was in a different frame of mind. A calm fell over her as she slipped into daydreams of more pleasant things, the little things in life she had once overlooked and taken for granted. Her old daily routine back in Leadville, by comparison, seemed like a wonderful life now—running the bakery, joking with the friendly miners who came in, enjoying the love and closeness of her family. It all seemed a lifetime away, a way of life she now dearly longed for.

As for Billy, she had no information to draw from other than the fact that he couldn't buy her freedom. That might not even be his fault as far as she knew. Surely he was doing everything he could.

A sudden strangeness fell over Abby, and she couldn't place the cause of it. Somehow she knew something was wrong. She heard something, the wind swished through the cracks in the window, and she heard the unfamiliar sound again. It was growing louder and louder, like a flood coming from a distance.

Hurrying over to the window, she peered between the cracks. Down below men and wagons rushed to clear the way, as if in a panic. She tried to see down the street, but her view was restricted. She watched and waited, the noise growing louder now. It was the racket caused by a furious crowd.

The street below now empty, Abby saw two men walk rapidly into her view and take a stand right in front of her building, facing The Exchange Saloon, their backs to her. The noisy crowd spread out around them. Excited men made bets, laughing and waving their arms in expectation. She turned her focus back to the two men just below her. The stance of the big man in leathers looked familiar. Then he called out loud and clear, "Bob Ford, I'm calling you out!"

Grant! Abby thought, shocked as she moved closer to the window. "Grant!" she screamed "Grant!"

But he couldn't hear her muffled cries; nobody could over the boisterous racket below. *What's he doing?* Abby wondered. Then she recognized Billy, his face scared as he glanced around at the people surrounding them.

Then it came to Abby as clear as day. Grant and Billy were calling Ford out in order to rescue her. She swallowed hard as her heart began to beat, thinking of what a daring and bold move this was, one that would inevitably bring gunplay. Grant and Billy were putting their lives on the line for her.

The saloon cleared, and Ford's men came out, standing their ground like the professionals they were. Abby bit her lip, scared half to death, afraid to watch, afraid not to. This was all crazy—men would be shooting each other over her. Guilt showed its face momentarily as she wondered if she was worthy of such gallantry after the way she had treated others, thinking only of herself.

Footsteps came banging up the stairs outside Abby's door, and she turned to see who was coming. Whoever it was crashed into the room next door, the one Poker Alice had first stayed in. Then came the sound of furniture being scooted across the floor, and then silence. Somebody was evidently using that room as a vantage point to watch the exhibition below.

Returning to the window, Abby watched nervously, wondering when Grant had come to Creede and how all of this had come about. More words were exchanged between Grant and Ford. Ford denied any wrongdoing, making it appear that Grant had no cause. But Grant stood his ground stubbornly, his back straight and his shoulders wide.

Tears filled Abby's blue eyes. It was silent below, almost tranquil, gripping all who watched. Maybe if she called to Grant and Billy now they'd hear; but if she did, and they turned their attention toward her, that could give Ford's men the opportunity to gun them down. She sat quietly, tears running down her cheeks.

All of a sudden Billy said, "Grant, I can't do this!" and began backing away.

She heard Grant say, "What about Abby?"

"She ain't worth dying for!" Billy squealed, sounding like a spoiled child. "Nobody is!" He began fighting his way through the crowd, everybody laughing at him and calling him a coward.

Whatever feeling of love Abby thought she'd had for Billy left with him. The betrayal revealed what kind of man Billy Rogers really was, and she was glad she understood now.

A man dressed in a fine suit and derby hat suddenly stepped out of the crowd and stood side by side with Grant. He pushed back his coat, and two ivory-handled silver revolvers flashed. Abby recognized Bat Masterson, an old family friend. "Thank You, dear Lord," Abby whispered, scared that any noise or movement she made might interfere with the situation below. She held her breath and watched.

～

All of a sudden the wind stopped, and all stood motionless, silent and watching. Charley Sanders was the first to go for his gun, eager to get the bloodletting on with, anxious to put a bullet through Grant. He gritted his teeth painfully and made his play.

Like a ten-foot bullwhip whizzing through the air, the gunfight was on. Crouched and shooting from his hip, Grant whipped the lever-action Winchester into a frenzy. Hot ejected cartridges sailed past his face in a blur, the rifle muzzle barking fire, flames, and smoke like a runaway locomotive.

Beside Grant, Bat fanned the hammer of one big pistol into a storm of thunder, its aim deadly and accurate, the bullets hissing fast and furious, finding their mark. Smoke shot out of the blazing barrels as hot lead flew wild and recklessly.

Ford's men weren't as fast, except for Jenkins who cleared leather and fired immediately, the rest shooting frantically, careless with their aim. A bullet caught Grant in his left arm, causing searing pain, but Grant didn't let it distract him as the big rifle's slugs sent men spinning in the dirt of fine gray rock and clay.

The smoky street was full of the pungent odor of burned gunpowder as onlookers stood with their mouths gaping. Bat holstered his empty Colt and pulled the other one, ready to use it while Grant grabbed more cartridges from his shirt pocket and fed them into the hot Winchester. The event was quickly over.

All six of Ford's gunmen squirmed in pain in the dirt, their guns lying harmlessly beside them as they clutched their gushing wounds. The rest of Ford's men, the non-gunfighters still on the boardwalk, dropped their pistols and held their hands up. The incredible display of marksmanship had been more than enough to convince them to not keep the fight going. Angry and scared, Ford broke for the swinging doors in hopes of running away, but Tom's quick hand put a vise-like grip on Ford's arm, sending a shock wave of pain strong enough to cause the man to bend over double, screaming in the process.

"Nice shootin'," Bat complimented, glancing at Grant. "You're hit. Looks like it's bleeding bad."

"I'll live," said Grant, proud of the outcome.

Above and behind Grant and Bat, Abby watched in horror from her window. From the window in the room next to Abby a rifle barrel was aimed squarely at Grant, the sharpshooter Ford had sent out of the back of the saloon earlier. The finger tightened on the trigger.

Bam! The shot rang out, surprising everyone.

Grant and Bat raised their weapons not sure where to aim, not sure where the shot came from. Behind them a rifle fell from a window and bounced to the ground; then, following the rifle, a man toppled like a loose sack of flour, dead before he hit the ground. Grant saw the real shooter first, a clean-cut old man with straight silver hair holding a smoking pistol.

"I owe you a drink," Bat said, speaking to Dick Shaffer.

"That was a brave thing to do," Grant said, walking over to Shaffer. "You saved my life."

Shaffer proudly put the pistol away. "No more than you did for me, Grant DeSpain." He smiled. "I remembered who you are, and it's not Jason Stone. You worked for Jason, your stepfather."

Grant nodded. "Looks like things are working out, Dick. Excuse me." Grant turned to see Tom dragging Ford, squirming like a guilty schoolboy.

"Lead the way, Ford, before I order Tom to rip your arm off and beat you to death with it," Grant said, knowing he had gained the confidence of Tom, who looked pleased to be manhandling Ford.

"This I've got to see," Bat said, following as the group moved to the building Abby was locked in.

Across the way the wounded were being tended, none of them hurt bad enough to die. Every man Grant shot was winged in the shoulders or arms, rendering them lame, while three more that Bat shot were all hit in their shooting hands.

Ford led them into the hotel, and soon Abby's door squeaked

open and Grant rushed in. Abby fell sobbing into his arms, happy beyond her wildest imagination, more grateful for answered prayer than at any other time in her entire life. "You were so brave!" Abby bawled, hugging Grant's neck.

"Are you hurt? Are you all right, Abby?"

"I am now," she cried, hanging on him like a frightened little child.

"Then let's get you out of here," Grant said, helping Abby along.

Ford stood next to the doorway, still in Tom's grip, with an impudent smirk on his face. As Grant passed, against his better judgment he couldn't resist throwing an elbow, putting his whole shoulder into it, catching Ford under the chin and slamming his head back against the wall. Ford crumpled, falling limp as a dead fish.

Tom grinned a foolish grin. "What do you want me do with him?"

"Why don't you drop him in a water trough outside," Bat suggested.

Gladly, Tom scooped up Ford and followed.

～

"It's an ugly wound, but the bullet went right on through," Lorraine, one of Ford's girls, said as she dressed Grant's wound and bandaged it. A beautiful redhead in a red dress, she did the doctoring when needed since there was no doctor in town. It was fine with her that the toughs had to wait for her services. With nothing left to fear, all of the girls who had worked for Ford had quit and were enjoying the freedom and hospitality Bat Masterson offered down at The Watrous Saloon.

"He's tough," Bat bragged, referring to Grant as he found one of his cigars and struck a match to it. "Good with that rifle too."

"He's a hero!" Lorraine complimented, a good-natured smile on her face as she worked. "At least Ford will be out of action for a while, so we can breathe easy. I don't think anybody is working for him right now, and nobody wants to."

"Good," Grant said, wincing at the pain. "It's about time some justice came his way."

In the next room Abby was being properly pampered in a huge bubble bath by Lulu Slain.

"Honey, that brother of yours sure has some grit. This town could use a few men like that," Lulu said, talkative as she hurried about, pouring hot water over Abby and heating more on the stove. "Wish I could grab me a man like that."

"He's the greatest," Abby said, lavishing in the hot and soapy perfumed water.

"And I'm sure glad the way things turned out. I'm glad to be getting rid of you," Lulu said happily, joking but serious.

"I'm glad to be getting rid of you too," Abby replied happily.

They both giggled like young girls, the pressure off and the truth flowing freely.

～

Cy Warman got his story, a story almost as good as the old story of the gunfight at the OK Corral. "Shoot-out at The Exchange Saloon," he called it. He made a small fortune on the one edition, distorting some of the facts while still giving the real story.

The position of controlling town boss was swiftly taken over by Soapy Smith. The petrified man, McGinty, was proven to be a fake when the concrete chipped away. Bob Ford was killed a year later by Ed O'Kelly, a Jesse James sympathizer, in his own saloon. In 1892 Creede burned to the ground, destroying almost the entire town. With the introduction of the Silver Act in 1893, Creede never recovered to become the booming settlement it had once been. When the 1893 silver depression came, the gamblers, bunco artists, dance-hall girls, and prostitutes deserted Creede for Cripple Creek and other more prosperous camps. Before Cy Warman also abandoned Creede, he wrote a poem:

The Rise and Fall of Creede

The winter winds blow bleak and chill,
The quaking, quivering aspen waves
About the summit of the hill—
Above the unrecorded graves
Where halt, abandoned burros feed
And coyotes call—this is Creede.

Home Again

Still in a mild state of shock, Abby stayed as close to Grant as possible. Grant had made arrangements for them to leave town on the next morning's train and thus leave Creede behind forever. After the long journey and what he had been through, he wasn't about to leave Mister behind, or Peaches either. At the rear of the train, big snowflakes began to fall from a solid gray sky. Grant rubbed Mister's nose as he walked him up the plank to a stall in a boxcar.

"What made you decide to grow a beard? It looked nice, but I like you better now that you shaved it off," Abby commented.

"It's too much trouble to shave when you're living on the trail, but it does get itchy sometimes. I was ready to get rid of it anyway."

"What kind of horse is that?" Abby asked, noting the short, stout, shaggy animal her brother was petting.

"Mister, this is Abby," Grant said happily. Turning to Abby, he said, "Abby, this is Mister."

"I've never been introduced to a horse before," Abby teased. "This is a horse, isn't it?" She ran her hand through his heavy and long thick fur.

"Not any regular horse, mind you. He's a mustang," Grant said. "Brought me all the way from Leadville, over mountains and through hard times. Even saved my life once." Talking to Mister, Grant said, "This is the gal we rode so far to save, Mister. What do you think?"

As if he could understand, Mister turned his big head and looked Abby over with her big bonnet and fashionable dress and gloves, then snorted on cue.

"I think he approves," Grant said, grinning.

Abby didn't know whether to be offended or complimented, but she liked the friendly, shaggy beast. "I'm glad you understand horse talk. You're bringing the mule too?"

"Peaches? Of course," Grant replied as he finally got the animals settled in for the trip.

Back up near the passenger cars, Grant saw to it that all of his and Abby's belongings were taken care of, Abby staying right beside him everywhere he went. By 10 in the morning the locomotive was belching steam, and all the freight was loaded and ready to leave. The engineer sounded the shrill whistle signaling for all to climb aboard, the sound echoing off the cliffs nearby.

Bat Masterson wished Grant and Abby well, his mannerisms friendly as always. The snow was growing heavier by the minute, a winter front the wind had brought in the day before. "Have a good trip, and don't let this pretty girl get in so much trouble next time." Bat leaned over and gave Abby a peck on the cheek.

Smiling, Abby said, "I'm not sure I know how to thank somebody who risked his life for me, but . . . Bat, thank you."

"Yeah, thanks for your help, Bat," Grant added sincerely. "I could have never done it alone."

Bat waved his hand in front of his face like he'd done nothing at all. "Everyday life here in Creede. You be sure to tell that pretty mother of yours hello for me, and give Jason my regards as well."

"I sure will," Grant said, helping Abby up the steps into the passenger car. "Come see us sometime."

"Never know, I might just do that," Bat said, waving as Grant and Abby went inside and found a seat. Abby waved from the window, happy to be leaving Creede.

∼

The train out of Creed was practically empty of people, for numerous passengers were coming *to* Creede, not leaving it. The only men on board were guards, plenty of them, to look over the precious ore shipments loading down most of the cars in the train.

As the locomotive picked up speed, it turned into the valley, giving them a view of the Gateway Cliffs. Abby stared out the window, through the fog of soft flakes, almost hypnotized as she watched the disappearing town of Creede. Grant watched her, wondering what was going through her mind.

"Glad to see that town behind you, I bet," Grant said.

Abby turned to Grant, her pretty face having a distant look. "Yes, it's good to be out of there. I was beginning to wonder if I'd ever . . ."

Grant was curious. "How long were you locked up in there?"

Abby shrugged. "I don't know. I lost track of time. It felt like forever."

Awkwardly, Grant asked, "Nobody harmed you, did they?"

"No," Abby answered, still somewhat detached.

Exhaling a sigh of relief, Grant thought maybe it would be good for Abby to talk about it, to vent her fears and frustrations. "You can talk to me. I won't give you a hard time about anything that happened or anything you've done."

"I know," Abby mumbled. "I can't believe how blind I was about everything in life, how miserable I was for no good reason." She lowered her eyes and licked her lips. "Grant, I'm so sorry . . . I don't know where to begin. It's embarrassing to think of the grief I must have caused you and Mother—Jason too. I feel like a complete idiot." Sighing, she looked up. "But things are different now."

"Think nothing of it—I understand. But what do you mean, different?" Grant questioned gently.

"Well . . ." Abby batted her eyes, thinking. "The day before the gunfight, I had about given up. I thought it was all over, that I'd no longer be in control of my own life, that my destiny was in the hands of evil men. It was like I was abandoned and alone out in the middle of a desert, completely forgotten and out of hope."

"What happened?" Grant asked.

A little ashamed, Abby confessed, "It took something horrible like that to bring me to my knees—I prayed to God."

Grant smiled.

"And He came to me. He opened my eyes and saved me from certain death, and I don't mean dying in a regular way, but a kind of spiritual death. All of a sudden I was filled with His power, a sort of peace I've never known before. Then you showed up in the street below." Abby stopped and wiped her wet eyes with a small hand-kerchief. "It was like He was right there with me, Grant," she said, looking up. "I guess I never really knew God before. Now I'm really alive." She waited, noting Grant's response, then said, "I don't expect you to understand. I was all the way . . . well, as far as a person can go into the darkness. When things were at the very worst, He was my light. He was the living water in my desert."

"I knew something had changed you," Grant smiled, "and not just taking away the fear. You're not the same Abby. You've grown somehow, spiritually, and you seem at peace. I don't see the old anxiety in you anymore, that restlessness you always had."

"No," Abby admitted, "I don't feel that way at all any longer." She wiped her eyes again, and Grant moved over to sit beside her, holding her hand.

"The whole thing was terrible, but meeting God and having Him in my life—well, if that's what it took for me to understand, then it was worth it." Abby glanced over at Grant. "I don't expect you to understand."

"I understand all right," Grant said, eager to tell Abby his story. "The journey helped me grow up too, helped me understand many things I never could figure out before. I met God on top of a tall mountain one night, far away from everything, just me and Him. Nothing like that has ever happened to me before. It brought me to new heights, gave me the strength and confidence I needed. I know what you mean about the light. I saw it too."

Abby squeezed Grant's hand, so proud of her brother. "Mother will be happy to see us. Did you wire her?"

"No," Grant said. "We'll be there soon enough, so we'll just surprise her."

The train wheels clickety-clacked as the countryside turned a bright white under the winter storm.

"What about Billy, Abby? I hope his desertion isn't something that will haunt you."

Abby shook her head. "Another part of my stupid blindness. What I was in love with was some far-fetched ideal. It became so obvious how foolish I'd been when Billy told you I wasn't worth dying for, that nobody was. That hit me like running into a wall. I don't blame *him*— I blame myself. I'm glad things didn't go any further than they did with Billy. Being with him would have caused me nothing but grief."

"At least you didn't have to marry him to find that out," Grant said thankfully.

"Yeah," Abby agreed, grinning.

They sat watching the snowflakes fly in white streaks past the window, thinking, putting the last pieces of the puzzle together.

"It must have been a hard trip for you, following me," Abby said, thinking out loud. "I didn't tell you I was leaving Leadville because I knew you'd try to stop me. I thought I knew what I was doing."

"I realized that," Grant said. "It was a long trip but a good one. I knew I'd find you, and I knew you'd need me when I got there. It was fairly obvious being on the outside looking in. But there was more to it than that. I had to prove something to myself—a manhood sort of thing. I knew this would be the biggest challenge of my life, but I also had an idea I'd find some answers to questions that have haunted me forever."

"Did you find them?" Abby asked softly.

"Yeah, I guess I did," Grant said, smiling. "People and their ways have always baffled me. The Bible says one thing, but many do just the opposite. They know better, and yet they do it anyway. For example, why do men give up everything they have, all the ways they know, any security they might have, to risk their lives, and maybe their families too, to come out here to get rich quick by doing something they know nothing about, risking losing everything in the process? It's foolish, and I've never understood it."

Interested and curious, Abby had wondered the same thing. "So you found the answer?"

"That was part of the problem—it's not just one answer, but many," Grant said, lifting his hand to indicate a vastness. "An old

Indian chief told me I was looking in the wrong place, to look within. I don't know when it came to me exactly, it was just there. My perception was all distorted. I was looking from a biased point of view, and that's why I never could see what I was looking for. I had to set myself straight first, which meant opening my heart to others, seeing their problems, their needs. I was kind of like you, Abby, blind in ways that are hard to explain. I think God wanted men to come to this country and make something of it. Most with any common sense would never take risks to venture into hostile country and try to set up a home. But the precious metals, the gold and silver, attracted men by the thousands, dream chasers. God knew they'd come because of greed, and they did. But if you'll notice, what follows them are women and families and government and most of all the church! God's house and God's Word have spread across what was once wild country.

"The real heroes aren't those who hit it big and get rich from the mines—they usually end up broke or dying unhappy. The real heroes are the ones who tough it out, the men who make it to work every day no matter how rough it gets, the men and women with stamina and fortitude, the fathers and mothers who take care of their families and help others, men who build the towns and give everything they can to make life here work out. These are the people who are the backbone of this country, the responsible and diligent. And these good folk, just like the ones who established this country in the beginning, are well-rooted in the church and in the Word of God. So you see, it starts off as something crazy in order to become something good. At least, that's how I see it."

Abby seemed taken by Grant's words, and especially at the magnitude of such a grand design, how everything, including all men, are part of God's plan. "It's almost more than I can comprehend," Abby murmured, trying to put the whole picture together. "But it makes sense. I can kind of see where I fell into all of that. The lust for something silly brought me around."

"And I gained from it as well," Grant put in.

"So now it's back to Leadville and a life I was bored with. But that looks pretty good after all I've been through," Abby said, thinking ahead. "I guess you'll go back to doing your regular routine too."

This caught Grant off guard, and he quickly cast a curious glance at Abby. "I doubt my life will ever fall back into a regular routine."

"What do you mean?" Abby asked, searching Grant's face for an answer.

"When I started looking for you in Leadville, trying to figure out which way you went, I met someone."

It took Abby a second to put this together, but then her face lit up. "Who is she, someone I know?"

Grant grinned. Just thinking of Mendy always made him smile. "She does your hair—Mendy."

Abby sat straight up, excited. "That's wonderful! Mendy is a dear friend. I never would have thought . . . I should have introduced you to her a long time ago. I didn't know . . . I mean . . . It never dawned on me . . . Is this possibility real?"

"Very real," Grant said. "I can't wait to see her."

Abby sat back, delighted with this information. "I wish somebody would love me," she said, half kidding but half serious.

"Oh, there is somebody," Grant said, remembering. "Butch Cassidy told me to tell you that he loves you."

Again surprised, Abby said, "You saw Butch? I did too!"

"I know," Grant said. "He's as crazy as ever."

"I do love him in a way," Abby said dreamily, "but not the marrying kind of way. More like a brotherly love. In some ways I admire him and appreciate him, but the outlaw life he lives . . . I hope he doesn't get himself killed."

"Me too," Grant said. "I like Butch."

Relaxing, Abby sat back, enjoying her conversation with Grant. The staccato clatter of the wheels and the rocking of the car soon put her to sleep.

The snow outside continued to fall, typical of late fall in the Rocky Mountains, as the train barreled on through the valleys and canyons and around carved mountainsides, all covered in a white wonder.

～

In Leadville, escorting Abby, Grant saw to it that their things would be delivered from the station and that Mister and Peaches would be taken care of as well. The snow was still with them after the two-day ride, having covered Leadville like a white paint job.

Catching a carriage, Grant ordered the driver to take them to the office of *Western Magazine*.

"You ready to see Mother?" Grant asked.

"Yes," Abby said, cuddling up beside Grant in the cold winter air, "I most definitely am."

In front of the magazine office, Grant paid the driver and helped Abby up the boardwalk and into the warmth of the building. Rising from her chair, Jennifer saw who it was and burst from behind her desk, running to take Abby in her arms.

"Thank God you're all right!" Jennifer cried, hugging Abby. "I've been worried out of my mind—and praying fervently every day."

"Mother!" Abby said, squeezing Jennifer with all her might. "I have so missed you."

Pulling away, Jennifer stared at Abby, making sure she was all right, then hugged Grant. "You found her!"

Grant patted his mother on the back as she hugged him. "Yeah, I found her, with God's help."

Jason came up front and joined in on the hugging, a huge smile covering his face. "Must have been quite a trip," he said. "Why don't we all go in the back and have some hot chocolate. You can tell us all about it."

"Sounds good to me," Grant said, shaking Jason's hand.

In the back, sitting around a small table and warm gas stove with their mugs of steaming hot chocolate, the talk began. There were two stories to tell and a thousand questions to answer, Jennifer and Jason shaking their heads in disbelief again and again.

"I don't know, but this adventure sounds like something I ought to write up in a story," Jason said. "Sounds like it would make a good one."

"If you do, I'd like to help," Grant said.

"Absolutely."

"Oh, and Bat sends his regards," Grant added.

"Bat Masterson—that old rascal," Jason said smiling. "How's he doing?"

"Much the same," Grant said, recalling a story. "I was sitting with him in his saloon when a drunk came over and slapped him in the face. The whole place went quiet, thinking Bat was going to kill him."

"What happened?" Jennifer asked.

"Bat smiled and told him he would like for him to try that sober."

"He hasn't changed a bit." Jason laughed.

Saving the best for last, Abby told the story of the gunfight, how Grant had stood up for her against the greatest of odds, how Grant and Bat outshot Ford's hired men and rescued her. Abby told it in a way that brought tears to Jennifer's eyes.

"I have the most wonderful son and daughter," Jennifer said with great emotion, happy as only a mother could be to see them safely home.

Hours later Grant stood up. "It's good to be home and good to see you again, but there's someone I have to find."

A look of surprise on her face, Jennifer questioned, "Who might that be?"

Grant winked at his mother and slid the chair back under the little table, then left.

Abby said, "You didn't know? I think Grant met a woman before he left. He's very interested in her."

Jason slapped his leg with the palm of his hand and laughed at something Jennifer had done. "I told you," he said, talking to Jennifer. "You shouldn't try and be a matchmaker."

"What's he talking about, Mother?" Abby asked.

Jennifer looked peeved. "Well, while you were gone we needed to hire someone to help out in the bakery, so I hired this attractive young woman. She's so nice, and I dearly wanted Grant to meet her. I've told her all about Grant, but she just smiles at me."

Abby rolled her eyes. "Those kind of things hardly ever work, Mother."

Jennifer felt like laughing at herself but changed the subject instead. "Speaking of attractive young women, Abby, you've never looked so good. Your cheeks are fuller, something about your eyes is different, and you look more settled or more relaxed or something. That old aggression isn't there."

Abby smiled and patted her mother's slim hand. "It's called peace, Mother. I've found God."

~

Outside, Grant rushed through the accumulating snowbanks, hurrying across the downtown area to Isabella's. It was early enough in the day for Mendy to still be there. Rushing through streets busy with horses and carriages, the lamplights already lit to counteract the dimness of the day, he finally arrived at the front door of the small business. Hurrying inside, he caught the arid scent of perfumes, making him think of Mendy. Stomping over to the counter, tracking in ice and snow, he pounded impatiently with his fist.

The sharp-nosed, red-haired Isabella, with red dots on her cheeks, impatiently stomped in, demanding to know what the disturbance was about. She glared at Grant, spying the mess he'd tracked in, and said snootily, "What do you want?"

"Mendy! Where's Mendy?"

"She doesn't work here anymore," Isabella gladly informed the rude young gentleman.

His heart sinking, feeling like he'd been knocked down, Grant asked, disheartened, "Do you know where she went?"

"I have no idea," Isabella said snootily.

Realizing he wasn't going to get any information out of the contrary woman, Grant turned and moped on out. Somewhat panicked, he broke into a run for the boarding house where Mendy lived. There he received the same news—Mendy had packed and left.

Dismal, Grant kicked through the soft snow as he headed on back to the office. There he found Jason, working alone. Jason immediately noticed Grant was despondent.

"Something wrong, Grant?"

"No, it's nothing," Grant lied, not wanting to discuss it right then. "Where'd the women go?"

"Over to the bakery. Abby wanted to go there—they just left. Why don't we go get something to eat? You look like you could use some good food to lift your spirits," Jason offered, trying to cheer Grant up. He was afraid to pry at the moment, deciding he would find out soon enough what ailed Grant.

"Sure, why not?" Grant mumbled.

Without saying much, Jason and Grant made their way to the bakery, Jason speaking to friends on the street while Grant walked with his head down, his hands shoved deep into his pockets.

The bell over the door jingled as Grant and Jason entered and shook the snow from their coats, quickly spotting Abby and Jennifer sitting and enjoying a plate of pastries.

"There you are," Jason said cheerfully. "Thought we'd join you for some sweets."

"I forgot how good they were," Abby said around a full mouth.

"Did you find who you were looking for?" Jennifer asked Grant politely.

"No," he uttered, standing by the table.

From the back Mendy stepped forward carrying a tray of muffins, her eyes landing on Grant.

Grant saw Mendy at the same time, and for a second they both just stood there and stared, shocked and disbelieving. Mendy's tray fell, sending muffins rolling across the floor. Grant rushed over to her and took her in his arms and gave her a big kiss. Both were oblivious to the shocked customers and family looking on.

Most stunned was Jennifer, who stared with disapproving disbelief. "I didn't even introduce them!" she stated.

Abby got a charge out of her mother's frustration and confusion, and she laughed herself silly until she could catch her breath and say, "Maybe that's what they mean when they say love at first sight."

Unable to comprehend what was going on, Jennifer kept staring at Grant and Mendy, wondering what in the world had gotten into them to make them behave so boldly in public.

"I have a feeling your matchmaking is going to work out after all," Jason teased, tickled by the scene.

"Apparently so," Jennifer agreed, turning away from the lovebirds.

∽

And so came the end of an era and what was thought a virtually inexhaustible supply of minerals in the form of silver and gold. The boomtowns had always stayed one jump ahead of civilization, offering riches for those brave enough and strong enough to stake their claims and work them. The passing of the Old West was marked notably by the coming of technology, the vast wild spaces now covered with railroad tracks, making even the most remote towns less isolated. The coming of electricity and telephones linked distant spaces, taming areas where only Indians had once lived. By the 1890s the door began to close on some of the wildest days of American history, the fifty-year span of the gold and silver rush days, some towns surviving and thriving to this day, while others were reduced to ashes or were simply forgotten and left to rot away. But the faith of those who truly came to know Christ and began to serve Him will last forever.

Follow the Chronicles of the Golden Frontier

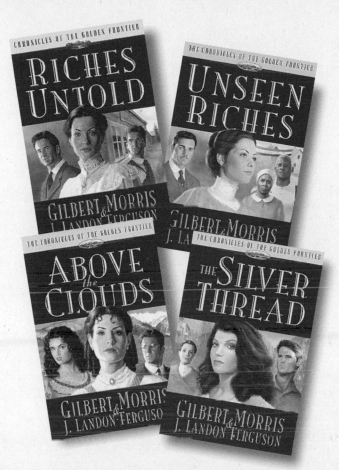

J ennifer DeSpain's life used to be quiet and dull, but that was before a whirlwind romance and marriage—and a tragedy that leaves her with only a defunct newspaper to her name. With hopes of a fresh start, Jennifer and her two children boldly move to Nevada, where she will have to resolve the challenges of poverty, newspaper publishing, a reversal of fortune—and matters of the heart—all with the help of some colorful friends and the Lord above.

Book 1: *Riches Untold*   Book 3: *Above the Clouds*
Book 2: *Unseen Riches*   Book 4: *The Silver Thread*